A Noteworthy Man

This novel is a work of fiction. Any references to historical events, to real people, living or dead, or to real locales are intended only to give the fiction a setting in historical reality and authenticity. Other names, characters, places and incidents portrayed herein are either the product of the author's imagination or are used fictitiously, and their resemblance, if any, to real-life counterparts is entirely coincidental.

A NOTEWORTHY MAN. Copyright © 2024 by Thomas Shields

All Rights Reserved

ISBN 979-8-9919810-0-2 (Hardcover)

ISBN 979-8-9919810-1-9 (Paperback)

ISBN 979-8-9919810-2-6 (Digital Online)

For Shirl, Always

Acknowledgements

I must acknowledge the anonymous woman I observed from my car, whose circumstance sent my thoughts adrift for a year and a half, imagining a backstory, and inspiring me to write this novel. Without her, this story would never have been written.

Mostly, I wish to thank my editor, Shirley Shields, who supported me in this daunting project from the very beginning, who sat with me for hundreds of hours, pouring through page after page of first and second drafts, reading aloud second and third drafts, and always, always demanding better from me. Able to see what I could not, Shirley's astute observations elevated my writing. Let's share another fifty year trial period together, my love.

A Noteworthy Man

a novel

THOMAS SHIELDS

PART I

Allegro

CHAPTER 1

THE SUFFOCATING AIR in the windowless practice room engulfed Ned as he sat, perspiring, staring at the eighty-eight keys before him. How had he let this happen? How would he ever have the piece ready for next Saturday's fall program? Five hours had passed since he had entered practice room E in the high school auditorium that day, and the angst he felt knowing he still needed several more hours to get it right added to the pressure.

He stood and shuffled with fatigue to a faded blue stacking chair that sat sentient in the corner, as if delivering a guilty verdict. Collapsing into the seat, he leaned back with eyes shut, stretched out his legs, and cracked his knuckles, clasping his hands behind his head.

"I can't even think, I'm so tired," he said to the room. He needed fresh air, a shower, some food, and a temporary distraction. The glint of the fluorescent light hovering overhead irritated his eyes. He opened them and stared at the acoustic ceiling tiles peppered in seemingly random, yet beyond doubt, methodically engineered BB holes. Each of the 38 tiles held 266 holes.

Ned took a moment and recalled the afternoon that Hag, always the smartest among his group of friends, had counted the holes, doing the math in his head, announcing the total in an instant. Ned had first met Humberto Abel Glasby when seventh grade homeroom assignments had seated the boys next to one another in Mrs. Marley's classroom. Hag had wasted no time in dispensing with Humberto, insisting to Ned that he should be called Hag. In a matter of days, even the teachers had adopted the self imposed moniker. The lives of Ned Godwin and Hag Glasby would remain intertwined for the next six years and beyond because of alphabetical kismet.

Ned let out a sigh, slapped his thighs, and dragged himself back to his post on the bench. Willing himself to spend twenty minutes more on the E-flat major scales and arpeggios before heading home, his fingers resumed their dance. Even after hours in this cramped chamber, Ned found a reassuring contentment of purpose in his shoulders and arms once the strings of the piano, answering his fingertips, resounded Chopin's notes. He had been here before.

Ned had discovered early in his piano career that, while the performance was the ultimate goal, learning and perfecting the piece of music brought him the greatest joy. When he studied a new score, he didn't see just the notes on the page. He heard them. His hours upon hours alone in the practice room fed his soul. This language of music was a second tongue that opened to him a world that none of his friends understood. It had always been his alone.

Chopin's *Nocturne No. 2 in E-flat major* was a favorite of Phoebe's, and he had selected the piece to surprise her. The tranquility of a nocturne might not inspire a high school audience, but Ned was indifferent to that contention. Wooing the affections of his girlfriend was more important to the seventeen-year-old. The piece still demanded his concentration, and he needed to buckle down and get on with it. Ned intended to give her a wink from the stage before he performed it on Saturday. Phoebe would love that.

Abruptly, there was a whisper of something above the wash of sound from the arpeggios. He stopped for a second or two and listened, but heard nothing, and resumed playing. However, a moment later, the tentative knock at the door was obvious. "Sorry, but I have this room reserved until six o'clock," Ned shouted through the closed door. "You'll have to come back then."

No sooner had he begun to play again than a louder knock sounded.

"It's Phoebe! Let me in, Ned!"

◈

Phoebe and Ned had met in fourth grade when their orchestral lives began, hers with a violin and his with a clarinet. Ned had unabashedly adopted the instrument, in addition to the piano, just to be around her and all the other budding musicians. She was the girl everyone liked and who liked everyone. He had started a conversation with her that first day of practice. "Can I sit next to you? I have no idea what I'm doing here!"

"Me either," she'd exclaimed. "But this is sort of exciting, don't you think? By the way, I'm Phoebe."

"Yeah, I know. I'm Ned." Pointing to the boy sitting next to him, Ned had added, "This is my friend, Simon."

"I go by Si."

"Hi, Si. You have a neat accent. Are you from England?"

And that was that, until by the end of the orientation, the three had received two reprimands for talking and laughing, and now had become the three amigos.

In sixth grade, the trio had been at Phoebe's house, sitting on the floor in a circle with seven other friends, playing spin the bottle at their first boy-girl birthday party. The bottle had stopped spinning, pointing at the birthday girl, and before Ned knew it, Phoebe had lunged at him, planting a big kiss on his lips. Embarrassed, Ned had escaped to the bathroom.

By eighth grade, Ned was no longer a shy twelve-year-old. His growing accomplishments at the piano had breathed a healthy dose of bravado in him. He was feeling all of it when he had spotted

Phoebe across the gym at the spring eighth grade dance. Drinking punch and carousing with friends, Ned had stared in wonder when she'd casually made her way toward him. Phoebe had always been a pretty girl, but that night Ned studied every feature, as if for the first time. His bluster disappeared, captivated as he was by the allure and beauty that radiated from Phoebe's face as she approached. There had been no doubt: he was smitten. And Phoebe was perfect.

⚘

Ned opened the door and swept his girlfriend in with his left hand, bringing his right hand around her slender waist as he leaned in to kiss her cheek.

"Hey, babe, what's up? I am dead."

"Just a sec," she panted. Phoebe must have been running for quite awhile and was out of breath. Pulling her long auburn hair back, Phoebe revealed her flushed and freckled cheeks. Ned handed her his nearly empty cup of water, which she gulped down. He waited for her to catch her breath.

"Look, I know you're working on a deadline but it's about Si. He's finished up a swim practice and the team bus will leave for the sectionals in Peoria in," she glanced at her watch, "15 minutes."

"Yeah, I know, it's all weekend. He doesn't get back to town until late Sunday."

"But he's got that calculus midterm on Monday morning and he's forgotten his math book, and he doesn't have time to go home and get it before the bus leaves," she blurted out in a single breath. "Do you have yours with you?" She looked left and right around the room in search of his book bag.

Ned let out an exhausted 'pfft' and motioned to the floor by the piano. "Yup. Right there."

"Do you think you could run it over to him now, before the bus leaves?"

"Where is he, at the pool?"

Phoebe shook her head. "No, the bus is leaving from the other side of campus by the cafeteria, so he's already heading there. He'd waited behind at the pool for a bit after the rest of the guys started walking, hoping he'd see you 'cause he knew you were around. I saw him pacing there, looking at his watch after my mom dropped me off for practice."

Of course Ned would do this. Si would do the same for him. They'd been best friends since third grade. The arpeggios would have to wait.

Reaching for his sheet music, Ned paused for a moment, then said, "Let me think. All right. I'll see what I can do." He looked at his watch. "Jeez, I've got to hurry!"

"I told him he could count on you, Ned. Thanks. Now get going."

A quick smooch, then Ned raced out of the practice room, bookbag in hand. As he turned his head to get a last look at Phoebe waving two sets of crossed fingers at him, Ned heard the rumblings of thunder in the distance.

Tribute, Illinois, was a small town thirty miles west of Springfield. Surprisingly, for a town of just 28,000 inhabitants in 1967, the campus of Tribute High School showcased a sprawling, diverse menagerie of buildings, some just a single story, others reaching skyward like hands raised in a classroom. Sidewalks and pathways abounded between these structures, but the routes most often taken by students left their own trampled, dusty signatures.

Between Friday night football games complete with marching band, orchestra concerts, drama club stagings, booster club bake sales, and a host of community events, the high school campus was the center of activity in the town. Ned, as familiar with these pathways as with his reflection, knew there was no beeline option to the cafeteria from where he stood on the steps of the auditorium. The rain was just beginning to spit, but he couldn't be bothered with that now. He would have to run to the other side of the auditorium, beyond the academic buildings and gym, then hoof it across the practice fields and come up behind the cafeteria. Simon would most certainly have left the pool that was next to the gym, and run across these same fields instead of taking the sidewalks.

Ned set off at a brisk clip, unable to ignore his annoyance with his best friend. Simon was perpetually forgetful, which mostly just resulted in jabs from his friends. Occasionally, however, it would get him in trouble.

There was a sudden flash of lightning in the distance as Ned approached B Building in the academic quad. Almost immediately the sky opened up, and the rain sheeted down upon him. It would be too dangerous to run across the fields in this lightning storm. He would have to detour, which would add time. "Shoot!" he shouted to the wind.

He rounded a corner, nearly slipping in some wet grass before finding momentary dry shelter under the awning of the grounds shed. As he looked up, he was startled to see Dwight Kato directly in his path. "Hey, Dwight," Ned said breathlessly, puzzled by his presence.

Hearing Ned's voice, Dwight turned to him and said, "What do you want, Ned? Go on, get out of here. This doesn't concern you."

Ned was confused. He turned and surveyed the area behind him, but saw nothing. Then, as he turned back to face Dwight, he spotted Si just beyond, peeking around a bush just past the awning, totally drenched and glum.

"Hey Ned, just leave me the book and go," Si said, stoically, worn out. "You don't need to be a part of this." He paused for a few seconds, glancing at Dwight. "We're fine," Simon affirmed above the roar of the rain.

Another bolt of lightning landed in the distance, silhouetting in the waning light of the afternoon the slight, skinny shape that was Ned's friend, who, at the moment, looked to be about twelve. Simon Sissell stood five foot three and weighed a mere 112 pounds, or, as Si had phrased it, eight Stone. As if that wasn't enough, Si was bald. The blue and gold team sweats which Si wore with so much pride, did little to bolster his appearance as they hung off his shoulders like a wet rag, the hood over his bald head dripping water onto his face. His posture of defeat screamed louder than the words he had just spoken, so Ned quickly grasped what was happening yet again. Si had to be mortified to have his closest friend witness his embarrassment.

"Yeah, Ned. We're fine. Me and Pencilhead were just discussing how lucky you are to have someone as amazing as Phoebe. Si here thinks you and her are probably, uh, well, let me see, how should I put this, doin' the dirty? Ain't that right, Simon?"

"One of us thinks that, Dwight," Si muttered, speaking so softly Ned could barely make out his friend's words.

Ned had been subtly inching forward as Dwight was talking, trying to formulate a plan to defuse the situation. Si looked down, kicking one wet sneaker against the heel of the other, only looking up to wipe his wet face once. This was bad. Ned couldn't understand why Dwight had singled out Si as his target for harassment. The whole thing seemed too cliche to be true. If he left as Si wanted him to do, he was dooming his friend to yet another beating. Dwight Kato would not stop until he'd had his fun.

When his mother couldn't handle him anymore, Dwight had moved from Utah to Tribute about a year ago to live with his father, Kenichi. Glenda had grown tired of losing boyfriend after boyfriend once they met her feckless son. At first, Dwight would be polite and agreeable. "Hello, sir, nice to meet you, sir," he would offer to each new romance that his mother brought home after her third or fourth date. But given the opportunity, in private he would say hateful things to the boyfriends, hoping to drive them away.

Dwight's confrontational, threatening presence would ultimately have its intended effect. At 6'1" and 195 pounds of solid muscle that he'd gained over two years of lifting weights in the garage, purchased for him, ironically, by his mother, every potential Mr. Right would soon beg off with some fiction that typically put Glenda in tears and drink for days.

Now, on this rainy afternoon, the situation dictated one of them needed to leave—that much was clear. Ned fixed his gaze on Dwight. He knew full well Dwight was a formidable threat and therefore he needed to deflect Dwight's attention from Si.

"Dwight, I think it's me you want to talk with about Phoebe. Remember, we didn't finish our talk from the other day," Ned said, eyeing Dwight with a barely discernible wink. Dwight had tried to pry from him intimacies concerning Phoebe and Ned, but Ned had feigned needing to use the bathroom and left the scene.

Dwight looked perplexed for a moment before it dawned on him what Ned meant. "Yeah, you're right! Let's get back into that."

Ned reached into his bag and pulled out his math book, casually positioning himself between Dwight and Simon.

"Here you go, Si. Sorry, I didn't get this back to you after borrowing it. This Fall Program has me snowed under." He glanced at his watch. "Run, man! Before you miss the bus! Go, go!"

Si accepted the book and hesitantly began stepping backwards out into the rain, his stunned look morphing into a smile. As he turned to run, Ned shouted, "Swim like a fish tomorrow!"

Scowling, Ned didn't hold back his ire at the imposing figure standing in front of him. "Really, Dwight, what the hell is wrong with you? I thought you and I had reached an understanding last time."

"Christ, Ned. I'm just having some fun with him. What do you care? He's such a little dweeb, and those stupid British words and accent really annoy me. Why isn't he in England where he belongs with all the other boarding school fags?" Dwight was practically shaking as the words exploded from his lips, spittle flying.

"Jesus, Dwight, calm down. Simon is here because his parents are here. And for the record, Si is an American citizen. He was born in London but his parents moved to the US when he was ten. They're all three Americans, Dwight."

"Whatever, he's still a Pencilhead." Dwight had lowered his head and was looking down at his feet as he said this. Then, looking up at Ned, Dwight added, "You and Phoebe goin' out this weekend?"

Ned hesitated. "I'm not sure. Look, Dwight, I don't need any enemies just now and I sure don't want to talk about Phoebe with you. But, I'm going to say this, man. If you do this again with Si or talk trash about Phoebe again, you'll have to answer to me. I swear I'll come looking for you. Dammit, Dwight! Find something better to do with your time."

Ned pivoted and, with more bluster than conviction, walked away. The hair on his neck stood up, and he asked himself, "Did I just say that?" His hollow stomach churned and his skin prickled as he kept walking. Ned clenched his fists and gritted his teeth to prepare for what might come. After several yards, he courageously looked back and saw Dwight, standing akimbo, in the same place, head straight forward, watching him. Ned suspected this wasn't over.

CHAPTER 2

THE EBBING STORM continued its trek easterly from the school grounds as Ned set out for home on his bike. The mournful rumblings were fading now, as westward, the sun struggled to make one last bow. The fiery mound at the horizon was blinding and Ned shaded his eyes with one hand as he rounded the last curve to 8 Odiorne Drive.

The house was the only home he had ever known. In the years before Ned was born, Dennis and his wife, Isabelle, had longed for a turn of the century house in need of some love in the old neighborhood of Parkland. After saving enough money for a down payment on the house, his parents had left the dingy one-bedroom apartment above Leonardo's Barber Shop on Main Street that they had occupied since marrying in 1947. Isabelle was two months pregnant when they made the move to Parkland.

In 1894, the designer crafted an assortment of dwellings that framed a three-acre park. At the time the idea was met with skepticism by the town planning board because the developer, Oscar DeVries, a bellicose German immigrant who could, nonetheless, present an ebullient, persuasive charm when necessary, expected the city to give him the land outright.

In return, he promised to landscape it, put in a duck pond, install gentle rolling sidewalks with benches and spring bulbs, a children's play area, and even build a gazebo to stage neighborhood musical events on lazy, midwest summer evenings.

DeVries' idea was to construct twelve homes in an arc around the pond, each one different from the others. "Uniformity is to be avoided at all costs!" he had proclaimed, verbally accosting the planning board with a wave of his fist.

Eclectic in style, diverse, using local quarried stone, brick and dissimilar wooden sidings, Mr. DeVries cited esoteric critiques of American architecture chapter and verse, as if a lawyer to a jury. There ensued innumerable meetings between developer and planning board filled with thunder, posturing and pleadings from both sides. In the end, the Board waived its concerns and approved his ideas, but with two admonitions: they would limit the park to only two acres, and they would demand approval of each house design before a single shovel of soil could be turned.

Sadly, the construction of Parkland was never completed. Just four houses were built, including number 8, and Mr. DeVries' dream died with him. Just two years into the project he was shot to death in a bar altercation on Chicago's south side while visiting his only sibling, a troubled younger brother, Helmut.

Ned could see Karina's sun-bleached 1962 green Ford Falcon with the telltale dented hood in the driveway. She had damaged it when she slammed the hood closed after checking the oil, discovering too late that the hood prop wasn't down. The light glowed from his father's workshop as Ned coasted his bike to a stop. Today his father was listening to Sinatra, but it could just as easily be Peggy Lee, Elvis or the latest Beatles release.

"There you are, Neddy." His father smiled as Ned carefully inched his bike past the table saw inside the shop. Dennis Godwin's grin evaporated when he saw his son's face. He reached over to the volume knob on the radio and Frank's voice faded. "I was getting worried about you out there on that bike in this storm."

Removing his safety glasses and wiping his brow in one swift motion, Dennis brushed the sawdust from his apron with the other hand. "Are you hungry?" He looked his son up and down, perhaps sensing something was off. Dennis continued to probe, "You okay? Did something happen?"

Ned stashed the bike and turned back to his father. "No. I mean yes. I mean, no, nothing happened to me. Si forgot his math book and I had to race over to his bus in the rain, without my bike, which I'd left at the racks, and give him my book to take with him to study this weekend for the midterm on Monday."

"Oh, right, Si has an away swim meet this weekend. How did you know he didn't have the book?"

"Phoebe found me in the practice room and told me."

"Oh."

Ned's shoulders were sagging and he stared at the saw. Abruptly inhaling deeply through his nose, Ned exploded with a sawdust sneeze and wiped his nose on the sleeve of his jacket. Fidgeting, he flicked his eyes up for just an instant, then back at the saw again, sliding his finger along the edge, plowing a pile of powdered oak. Ned could sense his father's gaze. "He knows there's more to this," Ned thought.

"But why did you say yes?" his father asked.

"What?'

"A second ago when I asked you if something was wrong, you started to say yes."

"Oh, no. I meant yes to being hungry. It smells like Karina has cooked macaroni and cheese and hotdogs." Then, remembering, "Oh yeah, we always have that on Friday night." He was so tired.

"Well, why don't you get inside. You look like something the cat dragged in. Go take a shower and put on some dry clothes before we eat." Dennis stopped short, not yet finished. Ned could tell he was hesitant to ask the question. "How's the sonata?" he finally asked.

Ned knew that was coming. "Let it go," he thought. Ignoring the question, and pretending not to hear, Ned flung his bookbag over his shoulder and dragged himself up the three steps into the fragrant kitchen. As he was closing the door, his father tossed out to him, "That's okay. We'll talk later. And wash your hair tonight! It's ripe."

⁂

"Hi Karina," Ned volunteered flatly.

Dropping her fork, Karina jumped, startled, as she turned from the stove where hotdogs sizzled in a frying pan. "Oh lord, you scared me to death, young man! Thank God you're home safe and sound." She stooped to pick up the fork and wiped it on her apron. "What a storm that was!"

Karina continued a monologue on the weather report, how the electricity had flickered off just as the dinner was cooking on the electric range, and then, oh, what a relief when it came back on in just ten minutes or so.

"Do you know how to reset this clock on the stove, Benedict?"

Karina Gardeen was just 26, but seemed older than her years. Ned had no knowledge of her background, except that her father and mother came from Finland, nor of how she had come to know and care for his afflicted mother, but she had been a presence in their house for the past eight years. Straight blonde hair hung lifelessly to her shoulders. Hers was a face that told a story, a long one with tears, Ned supposed. Her cheeks and forehead, lined with premature wrinkles from years of cigarettes and too much sun, framed two clear blue eyes and a lovely, feminine nose that in her teens had likely caught the eye of more than one young man. But her deportment in more recent times hinted that life since then had been a challenge.

She had been married once upon a time, but never spoke of her ex-husband. Ned had gleaned from his father that the man was the troubling sort. When Karina first came into the family, she had occasionally brought her daughter with her. The youngster, who, at the time, was three or four, would play in the yard while his father gardened. Karina periodically shouted harshly at her to keep out of his way, but Dennis would always say something like, "That's okay, Karina. Elizabeth and I are having a fine time." It had been a long time since Ned had seen the little girl.

"This supper will keep a good while, Benedict, so you can go upstairs and clean up. Today was laundry day and all those towels in the bathroom are clean. You'll have to get your own washcloth, though, I swear someone is stealing those things out of the dryer." Stirring the hot dogs, she chuckled and suggested, "It's most likely the same person who steals the socks!"

"Okay. It won't take me long; I'm starving."

"Well, then, wait a minute." Karina looked toward the garage door window, then speared a hotdog out of the pan with her fork. "Here you go, growing boy with the golden hands," she whispered with a loving smile, offering it to Ned's outstretched hand. He stuffed the whole thing into his mouth and bounded out of the kitchen and up the stairs. Ned barely heard Karina as he was closing his bedroom door, "You got time to stop in and say hello to your mom?"

The steamy bathroom was comforting as Ned emerged, refreshed from the shower. He toweled his hair, all the while singing "Mirage" along with Tommy James and the Shondells on his transistor radio. The tribulations of the day's events blurred as the aroma of dinner wafted in beneath the bathroom door. He stood at the sink, facing the mirror, wiping the fog away with a squeak of his towel. Bending forward for a closer examination, he took a slow, deep breath and assessed his reflection.

His teeth were just average looking. They were white enough and big enough, but they overlapped a bit on the top and even more on the bottom, although they weren't as crowded as his dad's. "Why didn't the gene genie give me straight teeth like my mother's?" Ned grumbled.

His father's forehead and jawline stared back at him. These, Ned felt, were his best features. The rantings and ravings of acne would eventually taper off but at least he would always have "good bones".

Running a brush through his hair made him think of his friend, Mitch. The goof was forever coming up behind Ned in the halls, tussling his long hair, or trapping him in a bear hug. Ned had known his brawny friend, who was a second string linebacker on the football team, since Cub Scouts. Their desks in eighth grade English had been next to each other, and they had joked back and forth all the time. Mr. Logan, their teacher, was famous for using his favorite phrase, "Give me three paragraphs", be it when calling on students and drilling them on the current unit of study, "Shingler, give me three paragraphs on *A Tale of Two Cities*", or on a test, "Answer in three paragraphs or more, one of the following two questions". One day in class, Ned had whispered to his friend, "Psst, Mitch, give me three paragraphs on why you hate English." Poor Mitch had roared with laughter, which earned him a hall pass to the vice principal's office.

His friends had no inkling that Ned kept his hair long in order to hide his ears. As he pulled his hair back to examine them, his broad hands came into view. His hands. They still retained some of their summer tan, except for his right ring finger, on which he had been wearing his class ring since May.

"These are my hands." Ned said it out loud, and his voice echoed back at him off the tiled surfaces, surprising him. Fanning the ten large digits that filled the mirror, he studied each one, then rotated his wrists to reveal the palms. Each one displayed its own unique pattern of folds and creases formed in the womb, a signature of sorts. Ned wondered what secrets these fateful lines of life held. He continued to stare as, oddly, his fingers quivered. With mock solemnity he announced to the mirror, "With these hands, on October 11, I will fill the high school auditorium with beautiful, undulating tones of Chopin. I will play the notes with perfection, I will make love to every stanza and it will be awe-inspiring to the audience. I will be remarkable and Phoebe will love it." Then he laughed.

Leaning in close to the mirror, Ned scrutinized his ears. "Ugh," he mumbled. They weren't especially large, but they protruded and splayed from his head near the top. In his mind's eye, he entertained the idea of his reflection in the bathroom mirror taking on the role of a witty and amusing sidekick in a television cartoon. Ned smirked back at himself, "Thanks for these, too, Dad."

❧

"I'm sorry, Sweetie, but I can't go out tonight. I'm just too wasted." As he lay on the couch after dinner with the telephone propped by his ear, Ned waited for Phoebe to reply. He sensed the disappointment in her silence. "I'm feeling pretty squeezed with this sonata, which isn't all there yet. And, in the morning, I need to deliver 110 papers, then the fat Sunday editions that Si can't help with because he won't be home until the evening. I've gotta get some sleep, babe. Please understand."

"I understand Ned. I'm just disappointed. Did you get your math book to Si this afternoon before the bus left?"

"Yeah, I did. That is, I got the book to him over by B Building and then he dashed off to get the bus. Look, I'll make this up to you next weekend, I promise. The concert will be over on Friday night; we'll go out afterwards, maybe meet up with the crew somewhere or maybe just the two of us for a late movie?"

"Okay, Ned. It'll be nice once this concert is over. We'll get to see more of each other."

"Right. Well, I gotta go. Dad is trying to mouth something to me. Love you."

"Love you, too."

Ned hung up the phone, then looked over at his father. "What is it, Dad?" Ned asked as his father stopped on the stairs.

"Oh, I just wanted you to know that I told Mom you'd speak to her in the morning after the papers. I said you're bushed tonight and that you had a tough day. She's concerned about you, but I told her everything is okay. That's true, right?"

"Yup, I'm all right. How is Mom tonight?"

"She's had a pretty good day. Her head seemed clearer than usual and she was more alert. I think the new medicine she started last week is helping. We'll see how it goes."

Isabelle Godwin had always been a mysterious presence in Ned's life. He had no memory of his mother ever being like other mothers. He couldn't recall if she had ever kissed, cuddled or even hugged him. She had never read stories to him or packed his school lunch. Even way back when she wasn't living out of her bedroom, it felt as though she was a visiting relative. He could recall moments at the piano when he would spot her watching him from the kitchen, or looking up from the book in her lap. But she never spoke to him like a mother to a son. Ned found it hard to think of her as his mother. His dad was always his go-to person for questions, while Karina took charge of running the house, handling the cooking and cleaning. Years ago Ned had asked his father if his mother would ever get better. Dennis had answered, "That's a tough question to answer, Neddy. But, I'll tell you this, the girl I fell in love with 21 years ago was bright and smart as a whip. Her life before I met her was difficult and to this day I don't understand everything about those early years. But what she wanted most in life was to be a wife and mother. I think we sort of chose each other since we both wanted the same things. There was nothing about her then that hinted at how she would change so soon after you were born. We've made a commitment to one another, vows, you understand.

"The doctors have been vague about the diagnosis, but it seems to be some kind of depression or possibly dementia. I'm not sure we'll ever know for sure what caused it or what to name it, and I suppose that doesn't much matter. I believe your mom is in there and trying to get out. We just need to be steady and do all we can to help her do that."

Ned had thought about what his dad said, then replied, simply, "Okay."

Dennis stood and stretched.

"Dad, who is Lucy?"

Dennis whipped his head around, his face flushed. "Where did you hear that name?"

"From Mom, a few days ago, when we were talking. Or, I should say when I was talking to her. She wasn't quite with me at the moment."

Dennis narrowed his eyes, looking straight into his son's. "What exactly did she say?"

"Um, I don't remember exactly, something like 'Where are you going, Lucy?' or 'What are you doing, Lucy?' It was something like that. And then she just closed her eyes. I asked her who she meant, but she didn't answer me."

Dennis exhaled. "I think maybe there was a Lucy that she used to work with years ago at the Lincoln House. Maybe it was her. I'm not sure."

"Hmm," Ned shrugged.

"Anything else, buddy?"

Ned hesitated. "My hands were shaking just a while ago when I got out of the shower. Well, my fingers were. I've never seen them do that."

"Mine do that sometimes, usually after I've been working with a chisel or holding them in one position for too long. Did you do anything like that today?"

"You know, I was chiseling on the white keys on the school piano this afternoon." Ned winked, laughing. "Do you think it was from that?"

"Go to bed, Goofy."

CHAPTER 3

It was the second Sunday in November. "Look at that," Si said to Ned, pointing to the corner house, as they hauled the bloated newspapers in his red, beat up Radio Flyer wagon onto Bugbee Street. "Halloween is barely over and they've got Santa on the porch! Crikey, can we at least get through Thanksgiving first?"

"What do you care?" Ned grinned at his friend as he tossed the bagged Sunday edition onto the steps.

The Latmores lived here. A nice couple, they were old when Ned first noticed them, when he was about five, and since he started the paper route in ninth grade, he had watched them age even more. Mrs. Latmore, when she wasn't busy sweeping the front porch, or washing the windows, or weeding her flower beds, enjoyed sitting in the three-seat glider upholstered in giant orange poppies, sewing or knitting with head down and bifocals tipped just so, all the while maintaining a watchful eye on the happenings on her street. She wanted Ned to call her Betty, but he just couldn't bring himself to do that. If she spotted him coming around, she would offer him cookies if she'd been baking. The baked goodies were a welcome treat, if not quite award-worthy. Ned wondered how a just-baked cookie could be so hard.

She never failed to ask him how his piano "hobby" was going. "Are you still taking piano lessons, Benedict? You must play "Für Elise" for me some time!" she would holler from the front door. He would nod and shout back, "Yes, Mrs. Latmore. I'm still taking lessons." She didn't understand that his "hobby" was so much more than that. Mrs. Latmore had never seen the articles, year after year, that appeared in the Arts section of the Tribute Courier, tracking the remarkable achievements of the piano prodigy, her paper boy, living nearby. Cataracts impaired her vision, so she refrained from reading the newspaper.

According to Mrs. Latmore, her Earl, who did read the paper, paid attention to only sports and national news, and didn't have many other interests. He was a grandfatherly figure with strong opinions. He always wore the same pair of Levis and a red plaid shirt. When it was summertime, he would roll his shirt sleeves up, but he never opted for shorts. Earl was the talkative sort and Ned frequently received a nod and wave from him as Earl engaged in conversation with a passerby, Bugbee Street being a popular pedestrian pathway to the IGA supermarket two blocks north. Though never himself a participant in these chats, Ned imagined them to be more of a lecture given by Earl, his stature and demeanor hinting at an avuncular life lesson to those in his grasp. Ned surmised his turn would come soon enough.

Somehow it felt all right to call Mr. Latmore, Earl, probably because he had heard his dad refer to him that way, his father having experienced his own personal turn with the man in the past. Ned could picture it, his dad marching off to the IGA, minding his own business, yet aware of Earl in the yard with a rake. Earl stops, leans on the rake, removes his hat and wipes his forehead and says, "Dennis, my friend, step on over here and give me a minute of your time." And his dad, Ned thought, does so because he is that kind of a man.

"I just want to have time to savor Thanksgiving first, whilst I consume vast quantities of turkey and pumpkin pie," Si declared. "It is the best holiday, you know. We don't have it back in England."

Si took his turn with the next paper. The boys were in no hurry. Si enjoyed helping his best friend with the Sunday papers and had been doing so for about a year. Ned hadn't asked for his help, and truth be told, Ned probably didn't need it. Si just enjoyed spending time with him.

"So, are you going to apply to Cornell Architecture School?" Ned asked.

"Of course. It's a great program and that's where Dad got his degree, but still," Si wavered, "I just don't know. Dad doesn't want me to study in England, which is fine with me, because I want to stay here in the States. I suppose I should apply to the U of I, too, but I'd like to at least go out of state. It's a big country, after all."

The two of them trudged forward with their cargo, lightening their load house by house. The morning was clear, the cold air clean except for a whiff of smoke from burning leaves in someone's backyard.

Ned broke the silence. "Gretchen wants to talk to me about something at my lesson this week."

"What do you mean, 'something'?"

"I don't know. She said that now that I've finished the Chopin sonata and that I played it so well at the Fall Concert, it's time to talk. Those were her exact words. 'It's time to talk.'"

Ned loved Gretchen Polk. He had become her pupil when he was in first grade, and they had clicked immediately. She was kind but ran a tight ship. He was a determined student, even back then, and didn't mind her serious nature with him. Now that he was older, they communicated more as friends than teacher and pupil.

"Maybe she just wants to talk about your music school applications. Have you done anything more with them?"

"No. I'm feeling kind of anxious about stuff lately and I don't know why. She's been encouraging me to apply to Berklee in Boston and even Julliard but the idea freaks me out. I don't know if I'm good enough. Well, I suppose I know I'm good. All right, I'm very good. But, really, I don't want to move that far away from home. I'm thinking more like Chicago, or Cleveland or even the U of I."

"Ned. No. You need to go where you can grow your talent the best. Concert pianists come from Berklee and Julliard, not the U of I." Si put the tip of his finger to his lips. " Still, that would be pretty cool. We could be roommates in Urbana," Si said.

"Yeah, that would be great. But, we both know that U of I is not the best place, for either of us, given our career choices."

"No, I suppose not."

They had neared the end of their delivery loop. Ned squinted at the sun-drenched sky as they meandered back, each of them deep in thought. That was one of the things he liked about Simon—the guy was so easy to be around. He was smart, like Hag, but Si was emotionally astute, unlike their friend Hag, who, if one was truthful, seemed stunted in that department. Si possessed a serenity of mind as Ned imagined an old soul might. It astonished their group of friends when they were hanging out and Si would chime in with some factoid or observation of the family of man, as though he mused about philosophy and anthropology all day long. Here was this short kid with no hair, wire-rim glasses, cheeks as pure as a baby's, and the sweetest smile one could imagine. How was it possible this diminutive teenager possessed the tools to deliver such elegant words of wisdom at just seventeen, they wondered. The guy never failed to be illuminating. Ned strongly believed that he could not have thrived in the same way Si did had he shouldered the weight of Si's burdens. The duo shared an unspoken regard for one another that developed soon after they met. Whether walking, riding bikes or eating candy bars at the pool, Si and Ned could go for minutes at a time without speaking, so at ease with each other were they, it never felt awkward.

"What kind of bird is that, circling around up there?" Ned asked, pointing. He was looking beyond a dense copse of white birches that had dropped their leaves. He recognized it was some kind of bird of prey by the way it hovered.

"That's a falcon, a kestrel, I believe" Si announced with assurance.

Ned shot a challenging glance at Si. "How do you know that?"

With an impish grin, Si replied, "Well, this is going to sound weird. Dwight Kato told me."

"Get out! What are you saying?"

"I'm telling you, I learned it from Dwight."

"But why would he be talking to you about birds? He hates you!"

"I don't know, Ned. He came up to me in the hall about three days ago. At the moment I was talking to Hag about this party that Phoebe's having." Si waited for a nod from Ned. "So, I thought, 'Oh crap, here we go again'. As he came closer, I could see that he was all knackered like. He was just shuffling along, but he wasn't all puffed up in the shoulders like he usually is, if you know what I mean." Once again, Ned nodded, picturing the scene.

"Okay, so now is when the story gets bent. Dwight looks at Hag and says, 'How're they hangin', Hag?' or something like that, not even looking at me, like I'm not even there. Then Hag goes, 'Very well, my fine fellow. And have I told you about the urologist that decided to dissect his own testicle? He said he was going to halve a ball!'"

Ned rolled his eyes. "Go on."

"Anyway, by now I'm noticing there's what looks like a bruise on Dwight's temple, faded like, and a Band-Aid on the back of his hand. I'm wondering what that's all about. Well, I'm just the bystander here, which is a genuine relief to me, 'cause Dwight and Hag talk on about this falconry club they've joined and how cool these birds are. Then, Dwight pulls out of his notebook this pamphlet with birds on it, big ones, you know, birds of prey, all in color and he opens it up to a photo and says to me, 'You ever seen one of these, Pencilhead?'"

Ned is hanging on every word at this point. He can't believe

Si has waited until now to tell this story. "Well? Don't stop now, Sissell!"

Si continues on, "Righto. Well, so now I'm scared again, thinking all this so far has been some kind of set up between him and Hag, but I can't figure out the angle with Hag. I didn't even know they knew each other, did you?"

"Si! No, I did not know they knew each other! Would you just get on with it already?"

"Righto. Where was I? Oh yeah, so Dwight asks me if I know what the bird is and I say 'No', because I don't. And that's when he tells me it's a falcon."

Ned is waiting. "And? And?"

"Then he just looks at me like he's waiting for me to say something. Hag is still standing there too, waiting for me as well, I suppose. So, I decide I better say something before Dwight punches me, so I say, 'Oh, what a beauty!' And then we're all just standing there looking at this bird picture. Finally, the warning bell rings and Hag says 'Later' and tears off and now I'm left alone with Dwight. But all he does is close the pamphlet and say, 'You should check out the club. Then he just traipses off down the hall with a limp I hadn't noticed earlier."

Ned was speechless. "Why are you only telling me this now? Talk about burying the lead."

"I wasn't going to say anything until I understood better what's going on with Dwight. I hope I don't have to worry about him anymore, but I think it's too early to tell. He could be on some drug for all I know. And why's he all beat up and bedraggled?"

"Yeah, pretty strange. What does Hag say about all this?"

"I don't know. I haven't spoken to him about it."

The two had reached Ned's driveway. "Wait here. I'll ask my dad if I can drive you home. Are your folks okay with you riding with me driving?"

"I guess we'll find out when you drop me off," he laughed.

❧

"What's that you're working on?"

Ned jumped, his hands pulling back from the piano keys as he pivoted on the bench to see his dad looking at him.

"Jeez, Dad, don't sneak up on me like that!"

"Sorry."

"This is nothing, just drills and exercises."

"Oh. Do you have much homework to do today?"

"Not now, no. I'm done for the weekend. I just need another hour here. Why?"

"I thought we could take a drive over to the Elks Club and shoot some pool and catch the football game together. What d'ya say?"

"Yes! Definitely! Can we leave around," Ned tipped backward to look at the clock in the kitchen, "three? I still have some things to do here before my lesson with Gretchen on Tuesday."

"That's fine. I'm going out to the shop for a bit. Holler when you're ready."

❧

Dennis exited the house and flipped on the lights in the shop. He had a good bit of planing left to ready the boards for his next commission piece, a Mission Style coffee table. Dennis needed to thickness plane the lumber down to 3/4 inches and allow it enough time to acclimate to the shop environment before he could begin any final joinery work on the wood. But he didn't want to start up the roar of the thickness planer and dust collector just now. He wanted to listen to his son play the piano.

Lately, Neddy had gotten funny about his father being in the room when he was practicing. The old upright sat in the parlor below the window with stained glass wildflowers. No one had moved it in the twelve years since Dennis first acquired it from an estate sale in Decatur. It wasn't much of a piano, but he kept it in tune with yearly visits from Tom, the tuner, who would always lament, "Dennis, you can't expect this piano to stay in tune when you have it against this outside wall. Why don't you move it over there on the other side of the room?" It was a game they played every year, with each knowing his role. Dennis would shrug and say that he liked the piano where it was, although he secretly agreed with Tom. The truth was, Neddy liked the piano beneath the window. When he practiced in the afternoon, he enjoyed the stained glass wildflowers coming to life as the sun spotlighted this west wall of the house.

Dennis brushed off the workbench and pulled out the tools to hone his chisels. They needed it before he began this next project and he could listen to Neddy play while he sharpened.

He found it hard to believe so many years had passed since his son first sat at that piano. It seemed such a short while ago that his five-year-old had banged on the keys, figuring out melodies on his own. Dennis listened now, stopping what he was doing and closing his eyes. What a wonder, this child of his. He could never have imagined how blessed he would feel with the birth of his son.

It had been a challenging pregnancy for Isabelle, especially during the first trimester when she and Dennis lived each day with the anxiety of wondering if this pregnancy would end in miscarriage as had the first two. The doctors warned them that Isabelle had to be mindful to avoid unnecessary worries or responsibilities. There could be no lifting of any kind, no housework, no cooking. She wasn't told to stay in bed, but it may as well have been the case, as she became reluctant to venture beyond the bedroom door. Dennis bought a secondhand sofa and ottoman, a small table, and a television to outfit a sitting area in Isabelle's bedroom.

She passed the hours reading historical biographies and Civil War accounts mingled with crossword and jigsaw puzzles. Dennis cooked and delivered her meals to the bedroom, but soon hired a cook/housekeeper for these chores since his woodworking business was flourishing. The first woman he hired stayed just a week, claiming she couldn't stand the sound of the machines in the shop. But when he found Karina Gardeen, he knew he had a winner. Isabelle loved her and the two formed a strong bond that comforted Dennis.

Isabelle's labor was long, lasting two exhausting days, with Dennis unable to offer any comfort to his wife because of hospital rules. Finally, they brought Benedict Dean Godwin, his beautiful boy, red and swaddled, to him in the father's room. Dennis was so overcome with joy, he just cried as he held the boy in his quivering arms. It was the happiest day of his life.

❧

As they walked to the car, Ned asked his father, "Can I take the wheel?" He'd had his driver's license for two months and he wanted to drive everywhere.

"Yes, of course, of course," Dennis replied. "Be careful with the four-way stops, Neddy. You can't assume the other guy's going to follow the signs. Always be defensive and look twice."

Ned rolled his eyes. "I know. I always do."

The Elks Club was on the other side of town. Ned hadn't been there since he was eleven.

"Has the Elks Club changed much since the last time you took me there?" Ned asked as he negotiated a traffic circle.

"Well, let me see. The main part of the first floor is the same with the bar and tables and pool table and TV. There's a banquet room and kitchen that was added on two years ago for events and such, but that'll be closed off today unless someone's using it for something. We'll just hang around the barroom."

Ned drove on, monitoring the speedometer and making sure he was at his best behind the wheel, to impress his dad with his driving skills. He relaxed a bit. The Beatles sang "She's Leaving Home" on the radio.

"Dad, I have a problem I'm dealing with and it's making me anxious."

"What's that, son?"

"Did you ever get into any fights when you were my age?"

The question surprised Dennis. "What, you mean like a fistfight?"

"Yeah, like a fistfight, with another guy."

"Did you get into a fight, Neddy?"

"No, not yet, but I'm afraid it may come to that soon. And I'm kind of shaky about it because the guy is really strong, and big. He's been picking on Si and I just need to, um, protect him, I guess."

Ned's eyes stayed focused straight ahead as he started braking, approaching the Mattis Avenue intersection. The Mattis Avenue hill was the only true hill in town, climbing steeply to the east from the intersection with Main Street. It was a busy intersection, even with the traffic light. As they sat, stopped with the other vehicles, waiting for the green light, Ned knew to be on his toes.

"Who is this bully? Do I know him?"

"No, he's new this year at school. His name is Dwight. He was threatening Si a few weeks ago, and I happened by. I was able to intervene before any punches were thrown, but it was a scary moment for me, and for Si too, of course."

The light changed and the cars moved forward through the intersection. Ned looked left and right as he eased ahead. He turned down the radio.

"Well, to answer your question, no, I never had a fist fight when I was your age. I had some minor scuffles on the playground when I was little but nothing when I was older. I was always bigger than most kids my age so troublemakers tended to leave me alone."

"Can you show me some defensive moves? Like boxing and that kind of stuff?" Ned asked. He signaled a right turn on to East Buffalo Street, approaching their destination.

"Just pull in behind that Chevy up there and we can walk across to the Elks. Yeah, Neddy, I can show you a couple of things. We can practice while the game is on in the bar."

The letters "ELKS CLUB" had been chiseled in a stone header over the weathered oak doors many decades ago. The smells of the bar engulfed the two as they entered the high-ceilinged hallway through a pair of glass-paned doors. Now Ned remembered the smell of alcohol and cigar smoke from his last visit. As they walked deeper into the space, the smell of hops and whiskey sharpened the air further. Ned loved it.

A few men conversed while others enjoyed the game, nursing their drinks. Two of them gave a shout out to Dennis, who tipped his hat and returned, "Hey Steve, Dave. This is my son, Neddy."

Dave nodded hello as he swallowed a gulp of his beer and Steve shouted with a wave, "Nice to meet you, Neddy."

"Hello, sir, nice to meet you, too. It's just Ned."

"Let's get you a Coke and we can go over to the pool table and shoot some while we have a drink," his father said.

Dennis turned to the bartender, who, to Ned, looked to be about eighty years old. A line ran across the lenses of his glasses that sat at the tip of his mottled nose, the frames performing a balancing act that was certain to fail any minute. His shoulders seemed to be in a perpetual hunch, perhaps from some spinal ailment, and his gnarled hands shook as he wiped the counter with a wet towel. Ned imagined he had been doing this since they built the place.

The man stared directly into Ned's eyes and said, "The usual, Ned?"

Confused, Ned said, "What?"

"Oh, I'm just funnin' ya, son. Chester Mains, at your service." Chester turned to look at Dennis who had a big smile on his face. "How 'bout you, Dennis, same as usual?"

"Yeah, make it a draft this time, Chet. My son'll have a Coke."

"I'll have those up in a jiffy. I gotta change the CO_2 tank for the Coke. I'll be right back. Go on over and start your game and I'll bring 'em over to you."

"Thanks, Chet."

Dennis gave a subtle nod to Ned and Ned added, "Yes, thank you, sir."

As Chester walked away, he turned his head and gave Dennis a half nod and wink of approval.

⁂

"Eight ball in the side pocket," Ned announced as he lined up the shot.

"That's a tough angle, Neddy. You're liable to scratch in the corner and lose the game with that shot." Dennis grinned at his son.

"Oh, Dad, come on! You're not lookin' at some amateur. I know that. Just watch and learn, old man." Dennis chuckled at the remark along with the onlookers. Ned had cleared the table of all his solid balls in just two turns, including the break, leaving the cue ball half an inch from the rail. Only the eight ball remained. His dad's three remaining striped balls told the story to several other men who had ambled over to the table for a closer look.

Dave chimed in, "Yeah, old man, I think he's got you in a pickle, Denny. Yessiree."

"My money's on the boy from the looks of things," Steve added.

Murmurs of agreement behind Ned made him smile, but also made him a little nervous.

The chatter stopped and except for Tony Bennet in the background, the room was quiet as Ned lined up the shot with the confidence that years of play in Hag's basement had brought him. He meticulously counter spun the cue ball with the right amount of English and connected with the eight ball, watching it gracefully glide by the sharp rail corners of the side pocket. The cue ball continued down the side of the table, angling away from the corner pocket as Ned showed off by turning his back to the table and walking away, even as the balls continued their leisurely rolls.

"Hot damn, kid!" someone in the crowd shouted, slapping his hip. Applause erupted and beer mugs clinked while Ned leaned with his back to the wall, cue stick in hand, and grinned ear to ear at the table. The biggest grin in the room, however, was on his dad's face.

"I think you're out of my league, Neddy," his dad said, as he put his arm around the boy's shoulder and gave it a squeeze. "Grab your drink and follow me out to the hall and I'll show you some of those moves we talked about."

∽

"So, here's your take away from this, Neddy. Head up, show no fear, protect your face and watch his legs and feet from the corner of your eye. If he comes at you, try to trip him, get him down, and always aim for the nose, not the cheek."

The two had been working this out at the back of the front hall for about 15 minutes. Ned was feeling better now that he had a technique to draw on if he ever needed it. He heard the front doors behind him open.

"But, always, always try to avoid the fight if you can," his dad said, looking past Ned toward the door.

"No, no, no Dennis, don't tell him that! Hell, man, he's gonna get creamed every time with that approach!"

Ned swiveled around. It was Rick Shingler, Mitch's dad. And, behind him were Mitch and his brother John. They were quite the imposing trio. Except for the three-inch difference in height, the brothers could have been twins, they were so much alike. Mitch was two years ahead of John and had more muscle from lifting weights for football, but one could see that John would eventually catch up. All three wore their dark brown hair in buzz cuts. Rick Shingler was six foot four or five, with a chiseled jaw, and was clean shaven.

There was something unsettling in his lopsided sneer that passed for a smile. He smelled of cigarette smoke.

Dennis said, "Hi, Rick. Boys."

"Hey, Ned!" Mitch waved with a smile. His eyes were bright and cheerful as he walked around his father and delivered a big hug to his friend, lifting him off the ground.

"Mitch! Put me down for cripes sake!" Ned bellowed.

"Knock it off, Mitchell," his father admonished with a stern face. Mitch frowned and returned his friend to a standing position. Facing Ned, Rick said, "Son, let me give you the same advice I've always given to these boys. They taught us this in boot camp when I was in the Marines. If you are ever in a head to head face off, never, ever withdraw. In fact, assuming the other guy started the confrontation, always strike first. He won't be expecting that, and you gotta do what you gotta do to take the advantage. He started it, so put the frickin' manners in your back pocket. Don't hesitate. Deliver a quick, hard punch to the nose, not his cheek. It'll hurt like hell and he'll grab his nose then and start bleeding all over the place. That's when you bring your leg around and trip him."

Ned interrupted, "Mr. Shingler, that's exactly what my dad told me before you walked in."

Rick looked at Dennis, stunned. "Oh really, yeah? Well, all right, then." Shingler seemed disappointed and grunted something or other under his breath, apparently surprised by Ned's remark. Then, as if to have the last word, "Just make sure you strike first, is all I'm saying." Mitch looked uncomfortable as he stared out the window at the traffic going by.

※

Ned and Mitch had started their second game of Eight Ball. Mitch asked, "So, what's going on with you these days? I only see you in the halls this year, since we don't have any classes together. You have Mrs. Bowman for English?"

"No. I'm in Comp. Lit. with Mr. Chu. He's got us reading *Paradise Lost*. Ned rolled his eyes. "I don't think I like it. I've been swimming at the Y on the weekends, sometimes, Si gives me pointers. Phoebe and I are dating, of course, but we don't get out too often. Frankly, I don't know why she still wants to be with me because I'm just not that available to her these days. I spend a lot of time at the piano."

"Do you just play classical stuff, or can you play songs?"

"I don't play pop music much. Oh, I can bang out some songs at a party for fun if I have the sheet music, but I spend most of my time playing classical, like the Chopin sonata I played at the Fall Program. Were you there? Did you hear it?"

"No, Ned. I wanted to go, literally just to hear you play, but my dad nixed it. He made John and me help him move some stone in the backyard. He wants to build a patio. I don't know why we had to do it on that night. I was so bummed."

"Oh. Well, maybe next time. There'll probably be something in the spring."

Mitch said, "Maybe you and me could do something together sometime? Go swimming or hike or take a bike ride?"

"Yeah, sure, Mitch, that would be great. Maybe we could get Si and Hag to join us. A little cold now for the bike ride, but a hike could be fun. I know Si loves those trails at Lake of the Woods."

"Sure, Ned."

Ned cocked his ear toward his pal, sensing displeasure in Mitch's voice. The two dads and John, along with several other boisterous men with drinks in their hands, were sitting in threadbare upholstered chairs, engrossed in the Bears game against New York. Rick Shingler's voice rose above the crowd as his lit cigarette dropped ash on the floor. John looked bored. Ned was surprised that Mitch wanted to play a second game of pool rather than watch the game.

"You know, Ned. There's more to me than football," Mitch volunteered. "Once you know me better, you'll appreciate my finer qualities," he proclaimed with a toothy grin as he finished his drink.

Chet came over to them with two more Cokes. "Here you go boys."

"Thanks, Chet," they chimed back.

Studying Mitch, Chester said, "Watch that one, Mitch," pointing to Ned. "I wouldn't place any wagers on the game or you're likely to leave without your shirt. He had a hot hand earlier today."

"Is that so?" Mitch said with raised eyebrows. "We'll have to see about that."

CHAPTER 4

GRETCHEN POLK STARTED the tea kettle in preparation for her lesson with Benedict Godwin at five o'clock. To still refer to their time together as a lesson seemed wrong. From time to time she felt guilty for not encouraging her pupil to study under one of the master teachers in Chicago, or even someone in Urbana. Still, Benedict would soon move on after high school graduation in the spring, and she wanted to keep him as hers until then. It wasn't as if she was holding him back. He had a considerable talent, no question, but he didn't fully grasp the enormity of what he possessed. Not really, not yet.

She had never had a piano student like him. Even back in Germany, before the War, where she had taught many talented and motivated children until the horror began, none of them could compare to Benedict. He had been a self starter from the very beginning, even at age five, as if he'd been born to accomplish this mission, always looking forward to the next challenge, always wanting to forge ahead and learn more. Once his hands were large enough to span the eight key octaves, his skills surged, mastering progressively difficult sonatas one by one.

Gretchen sat at the kitchen table and watched the birds through the window above the sink. They were delightful, and insatiable this time of year. William, her husband, had just filled the feeder three days ago and he would need to do so again tomorrow. She continued her gaze, lost in thought. Maybe it was wrong for her to keep Benedict here, but he made it easy for her to do so. He didn't want any other teacher. He had told her so last year when she broached the topic. "Don't you want me as a student anymore?" he'd inquired, perplexed. She had to keep in mind that he was still just a boy. Children always think it's their fault when adults aren't happy. Even at seventeen, Benedict still sought her approval.

She recalled an afternoon when he was eight or nine years old. Mother's Day had arrived, spring recital day for her twelve students. When it was Ned's turn to perform, he took the stage, scanning the audience that included his father, who sat alone. Dennis gave Benedict a thumbs up and an encouraging smile, however Isabella was not present and Gretchen could almost sense the boy's dismay.

Gretchen couldn't recall just now what the piece was, probably Bach at that stage, and she couldn't recall if he had played well, or even if the audience had applauded. No, she couldn't recollect the performance at all. "How strange," she thought.

Her primary memory of that day was the moment after the recital when parents and friends of the pupils were milling around, drinking punch and eating cookies. She remembered being exhausted by this time and stumbled her way to a chair. Grasping the braided fabric of the chair arms, she had collapsed into the seat cushion.

As she had collected herself, Gretchen stared out the window at a cloudy drizzle of rain that cast a melancholic haze over the afternoon. The sight of a group of daffodils reminded Gretchen of a rainy Mother's Day in 1941. Closing her eyes, she could see William and Conrad as the three of them huddled together in the underground shelter, listening to the familiar muffled explosions of Allied bombing overhead. Conrad had hidden a daffodil under his jacket and presented it to her in the dank dungeon. Though waste and acrid clouds of death and desolation would greet them when they finally received the all clear to ascend to the street, Gretchen had been, for that brief moment, happy.

She had been resting in the chair a few minutes, holding back tears, when Benedict had charged up to her, startling her out of her woeful recollection. With an ear to ear grin on his face, he had looked into her eyes and said nothing. She'd returned the smile, clasping his hands in hers, and asked, "Benedict, dear, what is it?"

"I love you, Mrs. Polk!"

Then, just like that, he pivoted, and was gone, as quickly as he had arrived, thundering across the room and shouting something about dinner.

And then she cried.

∽

Gretchen Polk's music studio had all the furnishings one would expect. In the center of the room stood a well tuned fifty-year-old baby grand piano with matching bench, both bearing scars inflicted by dozens of children. There was a tall oak bookcase stuffed haphazardly with books and sheet music. White plaster busts of Haydn and Mozart and Bach dotted the shelves in an effort to maintain order, but with little success. However, Gretchen had no trouble locating whatever piece of music she sought.

On the sofa, a green damask slipcover hid scratches and tears that her departed cat Felix (Mendelsohn, of course) had made when he was not languishing on a mother's lap as the child sat at the piano. Two floor lamps and a pair of brown leather Chesterfields book-ended the hearth, where a fire never burned. The andirons stood abandoned, their only companions a handful of white birch logs artfully arranged, reclaimed years before from a tree felled to accommodate the garage. Beneath everything, a giant Persian rug held all the secrets of the room but, alas, no longer held its fringe. Upon closer examination, however, there was more to discover. Another piano was tucked into a corner, almost as an afterthought. This one, an upright, was so worn that the maker's brand was no longer visible.

On the top of this second piano sat framed black and white family portraits, most of them featuring a boy. In one, he appears to be about eight years old, kneeling on a woven rug with his arms around a long-haired dog that is staring into the boy's eyes as the child smiles at the photographer. In another, the same boy several years older sits on the porch steps, hands clenched, flanked by a man and a woman, all three subjects looking over the photographer's head. No one is smiling.

On the north wall hung a gilded mirror with a bronze plate at the bottom bearing an inscription in German, dated August 4, 1939. A lavishly framed photograph of an orchestra sat atop the mantel, the musicians posed in their formal attire, holding their instruments, while the conductor, holding a baton across his chest, faces the photographer. On a side table, a porcelain dish, the lid adorned with an enameled ballerina en pointe, was positioned next to Gretchen's lesson book and calendar.

※

Ned entered the studio and flopped down on the sofa. Gretchen handed him a glass of water and she sat down in the Chesterfield nearest the baby grand. Lifting the teacup to her lips, she said, "So, Benedict, let's talk. First, tell me, how is your mother?"

"Oh, she's about the same. There are some days when we can talk a little, but most of the time she seems distracted when I visit her in her room. I hear her talking with Karina often; they seem to have a connection, but not so much with Dad and me."

"I'm sorry. That must be pretty hard for you."

"Well, yes and no. I'm used to it being this way; it's been like this for a long time. I've never actually known her any other way.

It's not like we shared something and now it's gone. I feel bad for my dad, mostly. I can tell he's lonely." Ned took a drink of water. "What did you want to talk about?"

Gretchen set her cup of tea on the table and leaned forward. "Benedict, what kind of music would you like to work on between now and graduation?"

"Hmm. I haven't given that a lot of thought." Ned leaned back, lacing his fingers together. Gretchen relaxed and didn't rush him. "I want to work on something new, of course. I would like to play at the graduation ceremony, if the school would let me do that." Ned shifted in his seat, thinking. "Perhaps something a little different, not another sonata, maybe even a more popular piece, really upbeat, that the class can really get into."

Gretchen smiled. "That sounds terrific. Perhaps you could even do a medley of pieces. I can do some research, as can you, and we could get more specific when we talk in two weeks."

"Yeah, that sounds good."

"Let me share with you another possibility you may want to consider." Gretchen picked up her cup and looked about the room before taking a sip and returning the cup to the table. Ned gazed at her, his curiosity piqued.

"As you know, William plays oboe in the Springfield Symphony Orchestra. He informed me that the orchestra occasionally in the past has held a concert in the spring featuring a young artist, usually a high school senior. They would like to do so again this spring, on a Sunday in June. William has shared with me that you will shortly receive an invitation in the mail from Jonathan Rimble, the conductor in residence, to audition for this honor. Apparently, there will be five students from five different high schools in central Illinois that will receive such an invitation."

Ned interrupted, "These are all piano students?"

"No. In fact, you are the only pianist. I don't know names but the other four invitees play the violin or cello. The plan is for each student to prepare a significant portion of a concerto, presumably a challenging section, with which to audition by the middle of January. Then, the orchestra will select a winner and have a discussion about the details of the piece, usually a single movement. Then they'll acquire the sheet music and start rehearsing. The last rehearsals with the full orchestra will begin no later than May first."

Ned didn't know what to say. He felt his heart beating faster. Gretchen drank her tea, then offered Ned a plate of cookies.

"Why was I invited to audition?"

"Well, I hope you'll forgive me, but I submitted your name, along with a recording of the Chopin from the Fall Program."

"Oh," Ned replied. "What concerto would I play?"

"That would be your choice."

"Really? I would get to choose?"

"Yes, Benedict, it would be your choice."

Ned's head was whirling as he absorbed this. Could he actually do something like this? He'd get to play with a full orchestra. "I would play with the full orchestra behind me, a true concerto performance?"

"Yes, Benedict. It will be fully orchestrated, as the piece dictates. The concert organizers will publicize the event and sell tickets, and your family and friends can attend."

"Oh, yes! I most definitely want to do this. And I want to do one of the Beethovens. I've listened to all five piano concertos."

Gretchen smiled. "Then you understand what you're getting into. I'm so pleased to hear you choose those. Do you have a favorite?"

"I love the third but the fifth concerto, the one they call *The Emperor Concerto*, is my favorite. It's tremendous! I'll need to start right away, Gretchen. The arpeggios and cadenzas are ridiculous. Do you think I can play them?"

Without responding, Gretchen rose from her chair and retrieved a huge binder from the bookcase. She brought it over to the piano bench and laid it open.

Beethoven had composed his fifth and final piano concerto in 1809, as his hearing was failing. The composition consisted of three sections, or movements. With a moderately fast tempo, the longest part was the first movement, the "Allegro", which followed the familiar form of a sonata, including an exposition, a development, and a recapitulation. The second movement, the "Adagio un poco mosso", meaning slow, but not too slow, was musically romantic and intensely emotional. A nocturne, it was darker than the Allegro, yet undulating in its melody. The final movement, the "Rondo: Allegro ma non tropo", lively, but not too fast, revisited the motifs of the first movement, in a manner, expressing Beethoven's desire to go on despite his impending malady.

"Here you go, Benedict. I think I even have the orchestral reductions for piano, so we can rehearse together, making sure you'll be prepared and familiar with the orchestra's part going into the audition." She removed the necessary pages and handed them to her student. "Here, look through them and decide as soon as possible which movement you want to tackle."

"Oh, boy," Ned breathed out. He smiled nervously at his teacher. "I don't know what to say."

"This is very exciting, Benedict. I'm so happy and proud you've been given this tremendous opportunity. The recording of the concert will go a long way in your application to Julliard and the other schools. Perhaps you might even receive a scholarship."

Ned nodded briefly. He was overwhelmed. "If I win. Are we doing anything at the piano today? I'm so bushed, I don't think I could play chopsticks just now."

"No, dear," she chuckled. "Let's call it a day before your brain explodes. We'll meet next week and get the piece settled. You'll have just two months to prepare for the audition. There is no time to waste!"

"There is no time to waste." Gretchen's words resounded in his ears as he donned his coat, a wave of anxiety coming over him.

"Am I reaching too far?" he thought. To master such a monumental piece of music and then perform it in front of an audience suddenly seemed like a mountain before him. Ned's hands were shaky, and he had a prickly feeling in his armpits as he reached for the doorknob to leave, longing to get home and go to bed.

A turbulent wave jounces Ned from side to side as he sits on the floor of a ramshackle rowboat, one oar in hand. He looks down at the oar and mutters, "Where did this come from?" There is water in the bottom of the boat and he's alarmed that the boat will sink and he'll drown.

He raises his head and is momentarily relieved to see that the boat is floating in the Parkland duck pond, just a few hundred feet from his front door. He knows this is where he lives, but it doesn't look like his house. This house is ancient and the roof shingles are failing. Behind a wooden porch swing a broken shutter dangles by a rusted hinge, obscuring a wedge of the window. Blue paint is peeling from the clapboard siding and there are posts missing from the porch railing. "Why hasn't Dad fixed these things?" Something is wrong.

Ned sits on a wooden bench on the far side of the pond now, his back to his house. The boat has disappeared. "Where is everybody?" He turns around, searching, but there is no one. He is alone. "Where are you, Dad?!" he shouts to the wind. No answer. Again, louder this time, "Dad! Where are you?"

"I'm right here, Neddy!" He hears his father's voice.

"Where?" Ned stands up and franticly looks all around, but cannot see his father. "Where?" he repeats. He listens as the word echoes in his ears even as the sound of it drifts away over the roof of his house.

"Can't you find your dad, Ned?"

Ned whips his body around to face the pond again. But the pond is gone now. Dwight is standing in front of him with a big glove on his hand.

"These ducks are really mean, man," Dwight tells Ned as he motions to a nearby group of five. "Don't get too close; they'll tear you apart, I tell you."

Ned stares at the birds incredulously.

"What are you talking about, Dwight? They're just ducks. They can't hurt you."

"Better take a closer look, you idiot." Dwight points his gloved hand toward the ducks and motions with his head for Ned to look.

Now the ducks all have hideous white fangs dripping with blood. Ned jumps back in horror.

"Jesus, Dwight, can't you get them out of here!" Ned continues to step backward, cringing with trepidation, begging Dwight, but keeping his eyes focused on the monstrous birds.

Dwight seems delighted to see the fright in Ned's eyes and titters, "I don't think they'll bother you right now, man. As you can see, they've just finished eating."

Ned looks at Dwight's face. The smile is gone now, a morose mask of defeat in its place as he points to his left, beyond the bench. "They've butchered my falcon. Don't you see?"

Ned's anxiety and fear overwhelm him once again, leading him to search for the boat. If he can get in the boat, he can get away. He spies it once more, this time sitting on the far shore of the pond, which has reappeared but is now empty except for some cattail reeds and mud. "Oh no!" he cries out. "What am I going to do?"

The next thing he knows, his fear vanishes. Except now he is in the sky, hovering over the community of houses, gazing down like some omniscient observer. Below, as if watching a scene in a stage play, he sees his father speaking tenderly to a wee slip of a girl who can't be more than four years old.

"Oh goodness, sweetheart," his father says, "this poor thing needs some attention." He reaches behind and pulls a pair of garden gloves from the rear pocket of his pants, dons them and reaches forward to handle the pathetic creature. "Let's see what's wrong with him." The deep timbre of the man's voice is soft, each word a feathery caress of kindness, like a lullaby.

"But what happened to her?" the little girl cries out. She is beside herself with fear and sadness, her cheeks smeared where she has used the back of her soiled hand to wipe at her tears. Even through the disheveled blonde hair hanging over her face, Ned can see the panic in her eyes.

"Oh, Mr. Godwin, she must be hurting so bad! Can't you do something? Please!" By now, the child is so worked up she is dancing from foot to foot, unable to control her tiny, hysterical screams.

Dennis Godwin stoops in front of the little girl, resting on his haunches. In his right hand he holds a slight rust colored bird. The bird's head hangs off the side of his palm at a right angle. There is blood on the bird's black wing and one nearly detached talon is all that remains of the left foot. With his left hand, the man gently pats the devastated wing, then raises the bird's head and supports it as the girl reaches for it. Dennis reaches out to stop her before her hand can touch the lifeless raptor.

"There, there, honey. The poor thing isn't suffering anymore. Do you see how peaceful she looks? It's because she's gone to heaven."

The girl sniffs back her running nose, choking on her words. "R-really? H-how do you know? What if she wakes up and starts hurting again?" She cries anew.

Dennis sets the bird gently on the grass, removing his gardening gloves one at a time, returning them to his pocket. He opens his arms and extends them to the child as she wraps her small arms around his neck and rests her wet cheek on the shoulder of his flannel shirt.

"She won't wake up, sweetheart. Her soul has left her injured body and is at peace now. She's a kestrel falcon, the King of Birds. And when her time here on earth is over, her spirit rises high in the sky above the clouds. And that's where her spirit is now, living on, even though her body does not."

The child's shoulders and arms relax a bit around Dennis' neck. He continues holding her lightly, rocking side to side for several moments as she settles down.

"Now then," he begins, holding her shoulder as he draws her hair behind her ears and dabs her tears away with his handkerchief, "Will you help me gather some soft grass to nest this little kestral's body? I have a shoe box and we can bury her in the backyard and we'll always remember how special she is."

Ned continues watching as the pair walks away, hand in hand.

CHAPTER 5

THE REID HOME sits on a private cul-de-sac nestled next to the fourteenth fairway of the Tribute Country Club. The estate is expansive with a front lawn of half an acre enclosed by white picket fencing. Fresh snow has dusted the swags of pine and Christmas lights, which were draped along the fence the day after Thanksgiving. A winding driveway bordered by flagstone planters disappears behind the house, passing the white pillars of the front portico. On this Saturday evening in December, snow muffles not just the aforementioned lights, quieting their glow, but also the sounds of the street traffic beyond the cul-de-sac. Nearing the house, pop music and chattering laughter tumble outside.

Earlier, on the other side of town, the kidnapper had stealthily entered an unlocked front door, crept from behind, and blindfolded the victim as he slouched in a wing chair, engrossed in *The Grapes of Wrath*, before taking him from his home despite protests. The victim had been advised to be quiet, that no harm would come to him if he cooperated. At least that's what had been said, although he couldn't say by whom, as some sort of device had contorted the speaker's voice, similar to the robot on the television show "Lost In Space".

All the while, the victim's guardian, conspiring with the

perpetrator, had helped to usher the poor bloke out the door and into the running get-away car before returning to the house. The perpetrator, now behind the wheel of the car, did not speak to the victim during the serpentine journey, which was designed to disorient and confuse the prisoner.

By the time the vehicle stopped and the engine shut down, Ned, still blindfolded, hadn't a clue where he was. The driver helped him out of the car, leading him by the elbow across the driveway, onto the front porch, and banged the knocker three times, then twice more, as though it were a secret code. Soon, Ned could hear footsteps approaching. There was a delicious aroma of cinnamon and pine wafting across the threshold as Ned heard the door open. The sound of The Beatles filled the air as Phoebe abruptly ripped off his blindfold and said matter-of-factly, "It's so nice to see you! Ned, isn't it? I'm so glad you could join us! Please, come in and warm your weary bones."

"All right, all right, that's enough," Ned chuckled, shedding his coat as a roar of laughter erupted from across the living room. He reached out and gave Phoebe a proper kiss on the lips.

"Honestly, Ned, I didn't know what else to do. I just couldn't bear it when you told me you couldn't take time away from practicing that concerto to come to my party. I finally called your dad and cried to him, begging him to force you to come."

"Well, he didn't. I could have told you that wouldn't work," Ned smirked. Phoebe wore a red and white peasant top that revealed a hint of cleavage below a modest pendant of a Christmas wreath. She had on bright red bell bottom dress pants, belted at the hips and sandals. Light rouge gave her cheeks a glow, highlighting her beautiful green eyes. Still holding Ned at arm's length, Phoebe smiled with a sparkle in her eye.

"But it *did* work, don't you see? It was your father's idea to kidnap you!"

"What?" Ned responded, not understanding.

"He's been concerned about you, too, Ned. You've been working non-stop. So we concocted this scheme to get you away from it and have fun with us, with the aid of you know who," Phoebe said as she turned and smiled fondly at Si, the mysterious abductor.

"I'll get you for this, Mr. Sissell," Ned replied, pointing his finger like a gun at his best friend.

Phoebe took hold of Ned's hand and threaded her way past the raucous throng of classmates in the living room as he trailed behind her, laughing. Ned's friends jostled and teased him as Phoebe led him into the dining room, where a selection of drinks was artfully displayed on the mirrored oak sideboard, accompanied by petit fours and candles. She handed him a snowflake-etched glass of eggnog and picked up another for herself.

Then, still not letting go of his hand, Phoebe continued leading him, this time up the back stairway toward a cushioned window seat on the mezzanine that overlooked the backyard. It was the same window seat on which they had first made out last summer while her parents lay below on their chaise lounges poolside, backs to the window, ignorant of the goings on above. It had been wickedly exciting then, both of them practically naked in their swimsuits and smelling of suntan lotion, their lips on fire, erotic sparks building with every caress. Ned felt the excitement returning even now as they sat next to one another.

"Oh, Phoebe," Ned whispered.

꼭

Downstairs in the living room, Hag was holding court with his classmates. By the time he was on his fourth joke, it was evident to all of them that he was high on something.

"You look legless, man. What've you been smoking?" Si whispered in his friend's ear.

Hag just smiled. "Who me? Nothin', man. I'm as clear-headed

as you are." Facing the others now, Hag changed the subject. "So you guys, what's everyone writing about for this damn senior paper we have to do?"

The English class or Comparative Literature class at Tribute High School requires each senior to write a term paper in the spring semester. Mrs. Bowman, the English teacher, and Mr. Chu, the Comp. Lit. teacher, set the parameters and requirements for the students. Regardless of the details, extensive research and a formal structure is required and the paper counts for 50% of the final grade. Each student must submit their subject and preliminary outline for approval by Christmas break.

"Oh, Bert, stop! This is supposed to be a party. Nobody wants to talk about school tonight," said Josy, Hag's date for the evening.

Hag's friends didn't know Josy Steib well, but she was bubbly and eager to be part of the group that night. Josy was a junior Hag had been dating off and on since last spring. Her face was rather plain—fleshy, round cheeks and a straight forward nose that seemed too large, a troubled pale complexion she was managing with makeup. But, her eyes were bright and when Hag spoke, she stared at him as if he were the only person in the room. When her braces finally came off, her smile would be dazzling.

Josy never called him Hag. She hated the nickname, always referring to him as Bert, which is what his mother called him, rather than his given name, Humberto. By now, even students who weren't friends with the boy knew him as Hag. As far back as seventh grade, upon noticing his graffitied "HAG WAS HERE" inked in the pencil trays of scores of desktops, it had become an unwritten rule of the student body to write it on any virgin desk encountered. The class joke continued after moving to the high school, much to Hag's delight, and by now, it was unlikely there was a single desk in the Tribute secondary school system without the tattoo.

Hag said, "Speak for yourself, sweetie. Personally, I'm pretty psyched about my topic."

"Oh really," Mitch chimed in. "This should be good." Mitch gave the group a wink. "Okay, let's hear it."

"I'm writing about Lenny Bruce."

Hag's announcement landed with a thud and everyone stared back at him in silence. At that moment, the just released "I Am The Walrus", by The Beatles played on Phoebe's stereo.

"Who is Lenny Bruce?" Si asked. The others looked at Hag, apparently equally ignorant.

"Oh, come on, you guys. Am I really the only cool person here?" Hag surveyed the group as they continued to look at him with vacant stares. "He's only the coolest, funniest, most innovative, biting, profane and profound comedian who ever lived, that's all. I can't believe none of you have ever heard of him. You lead such sheltered lives. Clearly, I'm hanging out with children. I guess you'll just have to wait for my award-winning senior paper to discover what you've been missing."

"Where can we hear this guy, Hag?" asked Si.

"You can't. At least not live. He died last year from a drug overdose. There are some recordings, but they're not commonly available, sort of bootleg stuff from recorded performances in The Village and such. He swears a lot, you see, so the record companies won't record him. I can't believe Mrs. Bowman is letting me write about him."

Si jumped in. "I'm writing about my mom. She had an amazing life when she was young, over in England. She lived in London during World War II and survived all the German bombings during the Blitz."

"What about your dad? Where was he during the war?" asked Josy.

"He was at Oxford whilst the bombings were occurring. Hitler didn't bomb Oxford because he'd visited there before the war and really liked the place, thought it would be this twee, idyllic town to settle in after he'd defeated Britain. That didn't work out, as we all know."

"This song is so weird!" Mitch tossed out after taking a gulp of his punch. "These guys are amazing, you never know what they're going to do next. You know, there are The Beatles and then there's everybody else. They're in a class by themselves; nobody can touch them. Well, maybe The Stones, but they aren't really the same type of musicians."

"I still think The Rolling Stones' "Paint It Black" is the best thing that's come out of the British Invasion," said Hag.

At that moment, Mrs. Reid strolled confidently toward them, carrying a glass of champagne. Connie Reid was dressed to the nines in a black cocktail dress with tiny sequins at the dropped neckline that flattered her svelte figure. The dress flared at the waist and the hem stopped just short of her knees. She had her hair up in the latest fashion and around her neck were pearls that matched her earrings. She wore a diamond tennis bracelet on her left wrist and an emerald cut ruby ring on her right hand.

"Oh, God," Mitch nudged Si. Cupping his hand, he whispered, "I think this must be Mrs. Robinson," referring to the newly released movie, "The Graduate".

"It's so wonderful to see all of you tonight! You all look so grown up! Hello, Simon, Mitch. I'm sorry, Bert, I don't believe I know your lovely companion."

"Mrs. Reid, this is Josy. Josy, Mrs. Reid," Hag said without any embellishment.

Connie reached her hand forward, palm down, as if she expected Josy to kiss it. Josy awkwardly took it in her right hand and said, "How do you do, Mrs. Reid? You have a lovely home."

"Ah, but you must call me Connie, all of you. You're not children anymore." She raised her glass, swallowing the rest of her champagne as she eyed the guests. This was not her first drink of the evening. "So, what are you all discussing over here, so seriously? I may have to put a stop to it if it interferes with the festivity." Resting her hand on Mitch's shoulder, she added, "This is a Christmas party, after all.

Mitch, dear, be a gentleman and get me a fresh glass of champagne. I seem to have finished this one."

She handed the glass to Mitch, who replied with a bow, "Certainly, Mrs. Reid, I mean Connie."

"Now that's better!" Connie remarked, beaming. Mitch marched toward the dining room, pleased with the opportunity to see where Ned and Phoebe had stashed themselves.

Si said, "We were just discussing our senior papers. We have to submit the outlines for approval before Christmas break. Do you know what Phoebe is writing about?"

"You know, Si, I don't. The girl tells me nothing about school. I wasn't even aware that you're required to write a senior paper. Sometimes I think Phoebe must have been switched at birth, as they say. She's always been so stubbornly hard-headed, so unlike me. We were constantly butting heads when she was younger. I finally gave up. She's going to be whoever she's going to be and there's nothing I can do about it. Why, I couldn't even persuade her to put on a dress tonight for her own party! I mean, her legs are lovely. Instead, what does she wear but bell bottoms and a top like some sort of hippie."

Connie opened a leaded glass container on the end table next to her and extracted a long, filtered cigarette. Handing a heavy, golden lighter to Hag, she placed the cigarette between her lips and leaned toward him. Hag didn't miss a beat, calmly lighting it and returning the lighter to the table as Connie inhaled. Nobody knew what to say. Things were getting uncomfortable.

"And now she's with your friend, Ned. He's a pleasant fellow, yes?" She looked at the three of them, as if requesting confirmation. She didn't wait for an answer, but kept on. "Yes, he's really a decent boy. I mean, I like him just fine. Why, his father, Dennis, made that cherry coffee table over there." She pointed to the back of the sofa, the coffee table just visible on the other side. Their heads all turned in unison toward the table, and back again, as she resumed her narrative.

"He's such a talented craftsman, that Dennis. We first met, let's see, it must have been around 1955. We wanted an Arts and Crafts bedroom set made and a friend had mentioned his name. So he did that for us. Of course, we have since redecorated our bedroom after moving in here three years ago, but we still have the set Dennis built. In fact, it's in Phoebe's room now." She paused and looked toward the dining room.

Hag interjected, "Will Mr. Reid be joining the party tonight, Connie?"

Si smiled, knowing full well that Hag asked just so he could call her "Connie".

"That's hard to say, Bert. Or is it Hag? My husband has been in his office for the past hour doing God knows what. I suppose he'll come out and mingle if Phoebe asks him. Where is Mitch with my drink?" She turned back, smiling at them with a twinkle in her eye. "He's such a handsome boy, don't you think? And a star football player, no less."

Si didn't want to burst her bubble. It was true, Mitch was handsome, and strong, and charming, but he wasn't exactly a star on the gridiron. Si knew that Mitch only played the game because his father told him he must. He could recall hearing Mr. Shingler's voice at many games chastising the coach for not putting his boy in, only to berate Mitch's performance once he was on the field, to the embarrassment of his classmates in the bleachers, not to mention poor Mitch. It had always puzzled Si how demeaning Mitch's father was toward his son. It was so in contrast to his own mother and father, who were always his biggest cheerleaders at swim meets, even when everyone knew Si would never achieve greatness in the water.

"My daughter could do worse than go out with that young man. I think it's important at your age to not focus yourself on just one person. This is the time to play the field, as they say—date lots of people, try them on, for heaven's sake." At that, Mrs. Reid seemed to stumble. She fell silent, perhaps realizing that she had said too much.

Mitch returned with a fresh drink for the hostess. "Here you go, Connie. I don't know where Ned and Phoebe are."

"Well, here comes Phoebe, anyway," Hag remarked, motioning toward the other side of the room, searching for, but not seeing Ned.

Phoebe nonchalantly approached the tight circle, somewhat flushed. Her friends stared and Josy suppressed a smile.

"Hi, guys. Mother. Ned'll be along in a minute. He said he needed to use the bathroom." She stumbled with her words. "Too much eggnog, I guess," she giggled, covering her lips with the back of her hand..

Setting off, Hag said, "Well, excuse me, too. I think I need the same thing." Looking over his shoulder, he added, "Oh, where is it, that bathroom?"

∽

"There's another one just at the top of these back stairs, young man," said Frank Reid. "I assume you're looking for the bathroom?"

Startled, Hag jumped, turning around to see just the right hand of a man sitting at a desk, smoking a cigarette. Hag leaned forward through a cracked door, beyond which was an office of some sort. He tentatively opened the door further and looked at the man.

"It's okay, come on in. Hag, isn't it?" the man said.

Hag nodded. "Sorry, Sir, didn't mean to disturb you."

"The bathroom you're looking for is currently occupied by my youngest daughter, Rachel, and her best friend, Cindy. Apparently, there's been a hair crisis. They could be in there for quite awhile. I suggest you use the bathroom at the top of the stairs."

The man rested his cigarette in an ashtray and raised a glass of amber liquid on ice. Bourbon, Hag guessed. Clearly, he was the man of the house, Phoebe's father. Hag had never met him before, but somehow the man knew who he was. Interesting. Perhaps from a class picture.

"Oh, thanks Mr. Reid. I'll do that," Hag chuckled.

He had just started backing up when Frank Reid added, "And by the way, let's make that your last cocktail."

"Wha-what do you mean?" Hag said with a mock look of puzzlement.

"I saw you spike your egg nog a moment ago with that flask inside your jacket," Frank said. He stared fixedly at Hag as he took a sip of his bourbon.

"Oh, uh, hmm. All right. I guess you caught me, Mr. Reid. Sorry about that. But it seems hypocritical, don't you think, that at eighteen the government can send me off to Viet Nam to die but I can't have a little cocktail?"

"But you're not eighteen. Moot, I'll give you that. Still, I'm legally responsible for you drinking alcohol in my home. Yes, it's a party, and yes, I agree with the hypocrisy you cite, but the reality is something different at this moment. So, go ahead, finish your drink and we'll keep this just between the two of us."

Hag grinned conspiratorially. "Thank you, Mr. Reid."

"Enjoy your evening, young man."

After exiting the room and climbing the stairs, Hag encountered Ned emerging from the bathroom.

"Phoebe's dad sent me up here because the one downstairs is occupied." Hag fingered the joint rolled up in his pocket, wondering if Ned had ever gotten high. "Wait out here a sec, Ned. I want to ask you something after I take a leak."

Ned sat back down on the window seat. The view had changed from last summer. Hibernation regalia covered the chaises and tables, even the pool. Fresh snow softened everything, frozen in time, like a life on pause. He started ruminating about the concerto. He had so much still to do. It was a seemingly endless, all-consuming path he had chosen, and he wasn't sure he could handle it. Gretchen had never answered him when he had asked her if she thought he was capable. He started sweating. And then there was the nightmare.

Where had that come from? He couldn't remember having nightmares since he was a kid when he dreamed of falling. Scanning the backyard through the window, Ned suddenly realized he hadn't mingled with his friends yet. He needed to get downstairs. The bathroom door opened and Hag walked into the hall, still zipping up.

Ned caught a whiff of alcohol on his friend. "Jeez, Hag, here? Really?" Ned shook his head. "So, what did you want to ask me?"

Hag pulled out the joint and waved it in front of him. "I was going to ask if you wanted to share this with me."

"No, Hag, I don't. It's not my bag."

~

Dennis stood at the curb and watched as Si drove away with Neddy blindfolded in the back seat. "Drive carefully, Simon. Precious cargo aboard," he thought. Taking a moment to look at the neighborhood, Dennis saw the aging park and neglected pond looking remarkably fresh in the fallen snow. Beyond the gazebo, the house lights from Number 2 twinkled through the frozen mist.

He recalled the day he and Isabelle had moved in twenty years ago, and it brought a smile to his face. What a happy and exciting time of their lives it had been. Everything that happened to them, everything they did, was new. Two months pregnant, Izzy hadn't struggled with morning sickness yet and never really did as the weeks unfolded. The two of them could hardly believe they were about to become parents. He was so eager to be a father and didn't care whether it was a girl or a boy.

Dennis still wondered if he had been more observant back then, might he have prevented Isabelle's dive into depression. The doctors had assured him he couldn't have, that there were triggers and chemical changes he was powerless to affect. Still, he felt as if he had failed her.

He walked back to the house, the snowy prints of the two boys already obscured beneath the unwavering fall of snow. He would have to hang the Christmas lights on the porch by himself this year. Neddy was so occupied with the concerto he was working on that he hadn't yet acknowledged that the season was even here. The two of them had always put up the lights together and driven to Russell's Farm to cut a tree. They would stop for breakfast at LouAnne's Diner on the way home and have pancakes and bacon. But not this year. The boy had no time for anything but the piano on top of school work and the paper route.

"I hope he's having a little fun tonight," Dennis thought. His son's commitment to excel and master the concerto was so single-minded that Dennis feared he was neglecting his friends. He felt certain the recurring nightmare his son had described was due to the stress he had imposed upon himself. A kid that age needs friends, he knew too well, remembering with sadness his own teenage years. Dennis didn't want his son to isolate himself from the frivolities of being a teenager. He heard the disappointment in Phoebe's voice, and Si's also, when his boy would turn down yet another social opportunity. The last time Neddy had gone out with any of his friends was the Friday night football game over a month ago, when they had all cheered on their friend Mitch.

Dennis closed the front door and hung up his coat on the rack by the telephone table at the foot of the stairs. Karina had gone home for the evening, so he and Isabelle were alone in the house. He listened for a moment on the steps. Not a sound. "Perhaps she's nodded off," he thought. "I'll take her a cup of tea in a minute."

Surveying the living room, he closed his eyes and imagined the room six months from now. The old, beat up piano that never stayed in tune, that Neddy hated to play but would never admit, always finding reasons to practice at school, would be gone.

Dennis sat down on the bench, his back to the piano, and looked around the room. The ticking of the mantel clock atop the bookcase was the only sound. He gazed beyond the sofa, studying his reflection in the mirror, and saw a man he didn't recognize. This isn't what he thought his life would be. Where are all the children they had planned to have? Where are the slamming doors and high pitched gleeful shouts? Why are there no raucous conversations at the dinner table? He closed his eyes, his mind drifting to the bittersweet scene he was helpless to avoid.

There they are. He sees them all now, as they jump on the couch and squeal with the unbridled glee that only young children can experience. Dennis leans his head back from the piano bench. There is his Isabelle, standing just behind him, her warm arms draped over his shoulders as he relaxes, the two of them watching their brood, just as the young couple had planned from the very beginning. He knows without looking over his shoulder that Izzy is smiling as triumphantly as he. Together. "We did it, babe. Aren't they all just splendid?" he asks matter-of-factly of his bride. They had decided four would be the right number. And there they are.

Dennis opened his eyes. "But where did you go, Izzy?" he lamented out loud. "Why won't you come back to me? Please, I'm so lonely."

Isabelle called from her bedroom, "Dean? Is that you? Where are you? Could you bring me a cup of tea with two sugars, like you always do?"

Dennis shouted back up to her, "I'll be right up, Izzy. I just have to put the kettle on." He wiped his eyes and walked into the kitchen. The gas burner clicked as he turned it on beneath the teakettle. Lifting two worn mugs from the dish drain, he set them on saucers, then took a box of Lorna Doone cookies from the pantry. Sometimes she could grasp that he wasn't her brother when she saw him, but not always. Neddy, Dean, Dennis, the names were all interchangeable in her mind. Dennis wondered if she had any memory at all of who he is, of who her son is. Doctors had told Dennis her earlier memories were easier to recall than the later ones, so her memories of Dean were most likely the clearest. Sometimes, Dennis wished his own early memories weren't so vivid. But the images, the smells, and the sounds never seemed to fade.

The kettle whistled that the water was ready. He poured the steaming liquid into the cups with the Earl Grey tea bags, placed the teaspoons in the cups so as not to slosh the tea as he walked, set them on a tray with the Lorna Doones and two napkins, then climbed the stairs. "Here I come, Izzy. I've got two cups, so we can sit and have a nice long chat, my love."

CHAPTER 6

Icy January winds whistled past his ears as Ned rounded the corner and headed up Crescent Drive to deliver the last twelve newspapers in his bag. The wind chill factor stood at 15 degrees, however his hands were warm. In his pockets, fueled by cigarette lighter fluid, were Aladdin Jon-E hand warmers his dad had gotten him for Christmas.

The transistor radio played The Monkees' "I'm a Believer" and Ned sang along even though he thought The Monkees were lame. It had been a great day, and he was looking forward to his meeting tonight with Gretchen.

Since choosing to audition with the first movement of Beethoven's fifth piano concerto, *The Emperor Concerto*, Ned's preoccupation had become a passion. He was, in fact, in love with the piece. The technical challenges all occur in the first and third movements, yet Ned recognized that the second movement carried the entire piece. It was the Adagio that spoke to him, beyond the notes. Nevertheless, he remained focused on the first movement, as the second movement could not stand on its own.

During relentless hours, days and weeks leading up to Christmas vacation, he had painstakingly mastered the composition, escalating the tempos of the credenzas and trills through judicious use of the metronome.

"Start small," Gretchen had reminded him. "Then build out, return, expand, repeat."

Ned had remained steadfast in his practice discipline, even honing basic techniques that Gretchen had instilled in him years before when she had introduced smaller pieces. Ned felt in command of the Allegro now. He was ready.

The Bachman's schnauzer, Rascal, began barking at Ned as he made his way to 1027 in the late afternoon darkness. "Hey, Rascal, it's just me," Ned said calmly, quieting the dog as he pulled a newspaper from the bag and rubber-banded it before tossing it on the porch. He gave Rascal a quick scratch behind the ears and turned to continue on as the dog wagged his tail.

Gretchen and Ned had met every day during the break to tear apart every section, build up each one, start and stop, over and over, until he knew it backwards and forwards. As she played the orchestral reductions on the upright, together they developed a well executed rhythm. Ned seized upon this dance between pianist and orchestra to personalize the phrasing, making the piece his own.

"I'm just astonished at the maturity with which you perform this, Benedict," Gretchen had remarked.

This concerto, this transcendent masterpiece for piano and orchestra, became a part of Ned in ways he could never have imagined. Whether playing it or listening to it, Ned found a serenity of spirit that was comforting. The music belonged to him now.

He dedicated additional hours to rehearse on his own in the practice rooms at school, developing the muscle memory in his hands, and training his fingers to play parts with his eyes closed for a significant portion of the time. He considered subtleties and nuances that might make his performance stand out when the time arrived. Of course, it would be yet another leap when it came time to play with the orchestra, if that time ever came. He still had to audition and win. It was both nerve-wracking and exhilarating. He listened to the entire concerto, all three movements, every day.

He had read that Beethoven composed the concerto for a friend, a pupil, even as the composer's hearing was declining. And yet, the maestro hadn't given up. He had kept composing, kept celebrating life even as his aural acuity failed him. The message was inspirational to Ned. He understood Beethoven's emotions as the concerto progressed. The prayer that was the Adagio had become his own leitmotif. It would be amazing if he could play the entire concerto. Ned had worked on the impossible final credenza of the third movement in secret, and had it down now. The audition was three days from now. He would be ready.

Ned shoved his hands deep into his warmed pockets and headed home, the route complete. He'd have a shower, eat dinner, then drive to Gretchen's house.

Ned bounded into the kitchen and hung his bag, then his coat on the hook. He removed the Jon-E warmers and set them to cool on the tile floor below.

"Where's Karina?" he thought, "And why isn't there any dinner cooking?" He walked into the living room and saw Karina sitting on the piano bench, clutching a handkerchief to her face, eyes red.

She motioned her head across the room to Dennis who had his ear to the telephone, looking solemn. He was listening to whomever was at the other end of the line, occasionally muttering "I see" and "Okay".

Then Dennis asked, "Are you certain, William, that there is nothing I can do to help just now? When can we see her?" Dennis continued listening as he motioned for Ned to sit down. "All right, William. Thank you for calling and I'm so sorry. Ned just walked in, so I'll explain to him what's going on. Yes. Yes. Okay. Promise me you'll call if you need anything at all. Very well. Okay, take care,

William, and send Gretchen our love when you're able to speak with her. Goodbye."

Ned sat frozen, his hands clenched beneath his thighs, afraid to ask.

"Gretchen has had a heart attack," his father said.

At that, Karina broke out with loud sobs, alarming Ned even further.

"She's at the hospital and the doctors are doing everything they can for her. She's alive."

"We need to go to the hospital!" Ned blurted out, standing up.

"Just hold on now. We wouldn't be able to see her, Neddy. Even William is not permitted to be with her now; she's being medicated and the ICU team is working on her. We probably won't know anything more until tomorrow. William will stay at the hospital tonight and he'll be in touch with us in the morning as soon as he knows something."

"What happened, Dad?"

"I don't know, son. I didn't ask. There will be time for that later on."

The three of them sat still, staring blankly at one another. Finally, Karina blew her nose and wiped her face. "I'm going to rustle up some dinner for you. Why don't you go upstairs and get a hot shower and warm up, Benedict, while I cook."

"Good idea, Karina," Dennis said as he put his hand on Ned's shoulder. Ned obediently climbed the stairs. He was no longer cold, but was numb with sadness. "She can't die. She just can't," he thought. "I was just there, two days ago, and she was fine."

Ten minutes later, Ned was in the bathtub, all his energy gone. He had turned on the exhaust fan before sitting in the hot water, drowning out all noise except for the running faucet. He tried to imagine how frightening and painful this must be for Gretchen. Does she know what's going on? Is she conscious? There were so many unknowns, this was just horrible.

Then it hit him. "Oh, no! Gretchen can't go to the audition with me. I can't go to the audition, not without her! Oh, damn. What will I do now?" he moaned.

From the hallway he heard his dad ask, "You okay, Neddy?"

"I'll be out soon, Dad. I'm just sitting in the tub," Ned choked.

"All right, then. Don't lose hope, son; she's in good hands and she's a strong woman. Hopefully, we can go see her tomorrow."

Ned said nothing. He sensed his dad still standing motionless on the other side of the door, then heard his footsteps falling away toward his mother's room. Ned listened as his father entered the bedroom, the door closing gently behind him.

At that, Ned held the hot washcloth over his face as the exhaust fan silenced his sobs.

❦

"Are you sure you don't want me to go with you?" his father asked.

Ned had gone back and forth about this in his head. In the end, he decided he should do this alone. Once they had determined that Gretchen was going to survive, he had come to his senses about the audition. Of course he would still go. It wasn't as though Gretchen could have been present in the auditorium, anyway. Her recovery was going to take weeks and he needed to get used to preparing on his own.

"Dad, we talked about this. I don't want you to hear me play this until I perform it, if I actually do. Si will take me there and he promised not to talk to me on the drive over so I can stay focused. He can sit at the back of the auditorium while I audition. The house lights will be off, so nobody's going to know he's even there. I can do this."

"Of course you can."

"The weather report is clear, the roads are dry, no snow, and Si's an excellent driver. We're leaving early so we have plenty of time to get to Springfield well before my audition."

Dennis waved his hand. "All right, it's a plan, then. You'll drive straight home, though, no stops anywhere. I'll be waiting right here for the good news!"

"I won't know whether I passed the audition until Monday, Dad."

"Oh, right, I forgot. Well, you can tell me how great you played, anyway."

"Okay, I'm off to pick up Si now."

"All right. Here, take this," his dad said, handing Ned a paper bag. "There's Fritos and candy bars inside. Not exactly health food, but at least you won't be hungry when you have your audition. Do you have some water in the car?"

"Yeah, I've got the thermos and a couple of cups. We're good. I've got the sheet music in the car. I'm all set, Dad."

"Well, come here, then."

Ned could see his father's eyes glisten.

" Whatever happens, win or lose, you know I'm so proud of you and all the effort you've put into this."

Dennis reached forward and enveloped his boy in a full hug. And to his surprise, Neddy, didn't pull away this time.

⁌

Simon Sissell stood at the curb in front of his house, waiting for his friend to arrive. His diminutive shape cast a long shadow in the late afternoon, like some sort of doppelgänger, revealing the true stature of the slight boy. The still air was frigid as he kept warm by playing fetch and keep away with Bobo, his four-year-old golden retriever, whom his parents had given him as a present for his thirteenth birthday.

The dog was in heaven, one moment frolicking, the next moment chasing and comically nipping at Simon's heels, then darting madly off to retrieve his chewed up tennis ball when Simon tossed it. More often than not, though, Bobo would get to the ball and look at it, then back at Simon. Striking a downward dog pose, he'd then bury his nose in the snow and freeze, as if to say, "Look what I can do! I bet you can't do this!"

"Bring me the ball, you foolish animal!" Simon hollered. Bobo stuffed it into his mouth and pranced back to his master, who tackled him. They wrestled for just a few seconds, when Simon had to pause with a smile. Another déjà vu! The scene rewound like a movie inside his brain.

When he was little and had the experience of something happening before, Si had told himself it was magic. Magic was real and delightful. He tried telling his friends what it was, but nobody his age knew what he was talking about. He thought he was the only one who had this magic, so he stopped sharing the moments. Then, in third grade, he was on the playground at school spinning on a swing when a boy nearby muttered to nobody in particular, "That was a déjà vu! I've been here before." And that's when he suspected that the magic wasn't his alone, and that it had a name. And that this boy, Ned, knew about it, too.

And so their friendship began. By the end of the week, they had discovered their fathers knew each other. Si's dad was an architect and had collaborated with Ned's dad on several house projects requiring custom oak detailing on the interiors, true to the Prairie style genre, in which Mr. Sissell had established himself as an expert.

Si didn't have any siblings, but in his new friend he'd found a brother. From then on the two boys did everything together, often sleeping at one another's houses for days at a time in the summer. They could ride their bikes for miles, starting after breakfast and not return until dusk, investigating construction sites along the way, playing miniature golf, swimming.

They were an odd couple. Even though the same age, Ned towered over Si a full eleven inches the day they had met. And while Ned sported a thick crop of curly hair, Simon was bald. He'd been born with alopecia areata, which prevented his hair from growing. Ned couldn't imagine what that must be like, but Si never mentioned it or complained, despite all the teasing from classmates. Si's dad had always told his son that everyone has something they wish they could change about themselves. The key was to not be sad about what you don't have. Rather, be glad about what you do have.

And that's how Si lived his life. He found it easy to be a carefree kid and possessed a bon vivant of spirit. Until braces in ninth grade closed the gap between his two front teeth, Si spoke with a lisp ("My name ith Thimon Thithell") that doomed him to never ending abuse and mockery from classmates. But Simon, ever the sagacious child, refusing to be stung by these jibes, could simply laugh with his tormenters, for he knew his affliction was temporary and he understood that sometimes kids just can't resist being mean.

"Don't expect empathy from a ten-year-old, Simon," his father had implored.

Simon's dreams pulsed with vitality. Over the years, he had been a young shepherd in the days of Jesus, a thief driving a get-away car from a bank robbery (he'd had a fever that night), even a horse, in a barn, swatting flies with his tail. Each episode seemed as real to him as any other. He supposed his dreams might sound bizarre to his friends and he was reluctant to share them, so they remained in his long-term memory as beloved adventures, the details never fading with time. Despite his misfortunes, Simon charged forward in life, eager to try everything, fearless, but not without respect for the vicissitudes he would encounter, always ready for the next new and exciting day. Si spotted Ned approaching and coaxed Bobo back inside the house. "I'm off now! I'll grab supper with Ned. Later!" he yelled to his parents, not waiting for a reply.

∽

All five soloist auditions were scheduled in the main auditorium on the same day. Ned's audition, at 7:00 pm, was the last of the five. The trip to Springfield was uneventful, and Si kept his vow of silence during the drive.

Ned tried to remain calm and focused as they neared their destination, relying on imagined mental images of him attacking *The Emperor Concerto* with finesse. Gretchen had taught him many years ago how best to prepare for a performance, and it had little to do with practicing. He visualized himself alone in a practice room, serene in his confidence, playing the piece yet again for the umpteenth time, with nobody listening. This had always worked well for him. Then, after settling himself on the piano bench, he would look at Gretchen and watch her smile as she gave him a subtle thumbs up.

There was no Gretchen to pad his confidence this time. Even Si would be absent, as he had been told he could not be in the auditorium during the audition.

"Not to worry, Ned, you'll be fine. Just let your fingers do their thing. I'll work on my English paper out here." Si gave his friend a quick pat on the back and walked away. Ned wasn't as confidant as Si. He found his way to a practice room and warmed up, waiting to be called.

It was 8:30 by the time the audition was over and he burst through the double doors to the lobby.

"Holy cow, Ned. I thought you'd never come out. What took you so long?" Si asked.

Walking briskly toward the exit, Ned replied, "I'll explain in the car, Si. Let's get out of here and get some food. I'm starving." But, once outside, Ned couldn't contain himself any longer. He grabbed Si by the shoulders. "I did it, man! I did it, I did it!".

"You won the audition?"

"No, I mean, I don't know. They didn't tell me. They can't announce the winner until Monday."

"Then, what do you mean?"

"Well, I'll tell you. It started out awful, Si. I came out and the conductor, Jonathan Rimble, shook my hand and introduced me to three other orchestra members and two board members. And there was a pianist there to play orchestral reductions. Gosh, I can't even remember her name now. We chatted about things in general. Jonathan asked me how long I'd been playing, and how long I'd been working on the Allegro, the tempo, stuff like that. Then he said let's start at the beginning whenever I was ready, no rush. So I said okay and sat down and got myself ready. The orchestra starts first, so I just gulped and took a breath and nodded to the pianist and moments later, I started playing.

"Almost immediately, my right hand got tangled, and I broke down. I had to stop. It was a nightmare. I told him I was sorry, I don't know why I did that. But, Si, he was so nice. He said that sort of thing happens all the time, even to established performers, and that I needn't worry about it at all. He said he knows how nerve-wracking auditions can be, with so many strangers present and that once we know one another better, it would be a lot easier for me. So, he told me to take a drink of water and we'd have another go at it whenever I was ready."

"Well, you know he's right about that, Ned."

"Of course. So, I drank some water, shook out my hands and took some deep breaths, and I felt better, focused. Then, we did take two, and I played really well. We stopped and started many times, moving through the music, discussing phrasing and how to lead the orchestra when I'm about to play. And as we did all this, I could feel myself totally settle in. I was in my element, Si. I wasn't nervous at all. It was incredible!"

"So, did you play the entire movement? Is that why it took you so long?"

"No, I didn't play the entire thing. In fact, I was done with the audition after just twenty minutes."

"What?"

"Listen to this. Here's the amazing thing. Mr. Rimble asked me if I had any questions or concerns. And that's when I told him I'd been faithfully practicing the entire concerto and would like the chance to display my ability to perform the entire piece.

"I suspect he didn't believe me and he reminded me that there had never been a student performance of an entire concerto before. I said okay, and that I understood. Then I just asked if it would be okay if I showed him what I could do, and he said sure. We agreed I would just play solo with no accompaniment and so I picked it back up with the final few measures of the Adagio, it's very slow, and seamlessly transitioned to the third movement, which jumps right into the main melody. And then, Si, I finished it with the incredible coda arpeggio at the end, which is so, so challenging."

"What did he say?"

"That's just it, Si. Nobody said anything, at least not right away. They all just stared at me and then at each other. Eventually, Mr. Rimble told me I play very well and that I would hear from them on Monday. So, we shook hands, and I walked out."

"I bet you got it, Ned. I bet you did."

"I don't know if I did or not, but I know I played and performed as well as I could have hoped. If that's not good enough, then so be it. Let's grab a burger and fries and eat while we drive home. I promised Dad we'd drive straight back and he's eager to hear how it went."

CHAPTER 7

NED STRODE THROUGH his front door after school that pivotal Monday afternoon in January, encountering his father in the hallway, extending an envelope toward his son.

"Open it, Neddy. It came this morning, special delivery. I signed for it."

Anticipating the letter, Ned hadn't been able to concentrate in his classes all day. He couldn't remember a single word from the vocabulary quiz in Comp Lit, nor the relationship between sine and cosine in trigonometry. He may have failed the chemistry quiz. As he caught his breath from running home, he stared at the envelope from the Springfield Symphony Orchestra. This was it. Their eyes met as father and son stood frozen in place.

"What if I didn't win?"

"Then you didn't win and you'll move on, Neddy. It won't be the end of the world."

"It feels like it will be."

"I know."

Ned kept his eyes focused on the envelope, rubbing it between his thumb and index finger. He felt a tingling sensation in his arms again and his hands shook.

"Go ahead, Neddy. It'll be all right."

And it was. Ned would never forget the pride and joy on his father's face when he read the letter out loud. He had won the competition. "This will be the first time," the letter read, "since the competition began in 1959, that we are inviting a student to perform an entire concerto. I am honored to grant you this opportunity." Jonathan Rimble had signed the letter.

"Wait. You're going to perform the entire concerto? Not just the first movement?"

"Yes, Dad. I get to play the whole thing!"

※

The snow had been gone for weeks. Green shards snaked up from beneath the brown fields of winter detritus, licking the landscape into new life. The migratory birds were returning, each flock vying for dominance, nesters choosing the prime locations. Spring bulbs of yellow daffodils and grape hyacinths dotted yards throughout the town and whispered scents of nature's perfume filled the air. Spring fever was in full bloom and nowhere was it more evident than among the senior class of Tribute High School.

Between the escalation of the war in Vietnam and the assassination of Martin Luther King, Jr., just a few weeks before, 1968 was proving to be a tumultuous year for the country. Conversations about the draft and the presidential candidates abounded in the halls and the social studies classrooms. The graduates would soon face the reality of adulthood.

Mother's Day was upon them, with each family honoring the day in the traditions of the past. The Reids were at the country club for an afternoon luncheon, Phoebe dressed in a lilac shift and with flowers threaded through her hair. Hag washed his hair for the occasion, cleaned his room, and gave his mom a card while Mitch and his brother had taken their mother out for breakfast. Si and his dad drove Mrs. Sissell to Chicago to visit her widowed sister.

For Ned, Mother's Days always seemed like a scene from a play. He and Dennis would fuss over Isabelle, taking her for a walk around the neighborhood, and gifting her little treasures to open. It had been Chanel No. 5 one year, a set of earrings the next. This year Ned had wrapped his senior portrait and presented it to his mom. Isabelle had smiled when she opened it.

"Oh, how lovely. My, what a handsome young man. He reminds me so of Dean. I must put this on my bedside table. Karina! Where are you, dear? Come help me with this."

Dennis put his arm on Ned's shoulder as the two of them smiled at Isabelle. "Now then, let's all have that beautiful lunch that Karina made for us. I think it's warm enough to eat on the patio. What do you think, Neddy?"

"Sure, I think that would be fine."

Isabelle shook her head. "You two go ahead. I'm a bit tired. I think I'll just have my lunch upstairs."

"Okay, Mom. I'll walk you up. Dad will get your lunch and bring it up in a little while," Ned said, acknowledging his father's nod of agreement. He took his mother's arm, and the two ascended the stairs.

In recent months, Ned had calmed his emotions concerning his mother. He no longer fought the gloomy feeling that his mother did not love him. He knew now that the truth was deeper than that explanation. As a child he had felt abandoned by her, resentful even, especially when he saw Si with his mother. Through the years, his father attempted to assuage the hurt with words of love, encouragement, and forgiveness, but they fell deaf on his young ears. As he matured through his teens, and came into his own through school and friends, musical passions and accomplishments, Ned better understood that his mother was not the way she was by choice. He saw how his father treated her with a devotion that comes only from love of the deepest kind. As his father would remind him, "It's not that your mother doesn't love you, Neddy. Your mother's understanding of love has been shattered, and she's lost everything that it meant to her. She can't find it. She can't find us. You and I are the lucky ones, though, don't you see? We have each other. And we have your mother to love, even if she can't love us back. Sometimes life denies you things you feel you deserve. It's true for everybody, son. Everybody."

⁂

In the ensuing weeks that had followed the audition, Ned's existence became that of isolation, spearheaded by a determination and focus that worried his father and bewildered his friends. Immersed in perfecting *The Emperor*, Ned had eliminated any socialization with classmates. Even at school, during lunch and study hall, he ventured off to a practice room, using every available minute at the piano. The effort was yielding results. By June, Ned was comfortable with the piece, his anxiety easing with each passing day. During rehearsals at the auditorium, Ned had become an integral part of the orchestra, Jonathan and the musicians joking with him and treating him as an equal. Many times in the last days before the performance, he had thought, "This is what I've always wanted. This is where I belong."

Ned drove to Gretchen's studio for one last tête-à-tête with his piano teacher before the last dress rehearsal with the orchestra. William had broken the news to her as soon as the orchestra had been told that Ned was the winner of the competition. Her pride and joy upon hearing the news spoke of a new found liveliness in her spirit that physical rehabilitation couldn't command. And while her days of teaching piano were waning because of her health, she had insisted on meeting with Ned through that spring to help with his biggest challenge yet.

Ned turned into the driveway and shut off the engine, singing with Friend and Lover on the radio as they belted out "Reach out of the Darkness". With a spring in his step, he approached a waiting Gretchen, just inside the door.

"Well, hello young man. It's so good to see you today", Gretchen said as she reached out and embraced Ned with a prolonged hug.

"Hi Gretchen. How are you feeling these days? You look great."

"Oh, I'm returning to peachy," she laughed. "Following your antics these days certainly helps. Just look at you. I swear you're taller than your father! Graduation is just around the corner, too. Are you going to the prom?"

"Of course," Ned replied with an ear to ear grin. "Phoebe can't stop talking about the dress she's going to wear. I only know that it's pink."

"Well, sit down and tell me about things before we get down to business. What's that you've got there?" Gretchen was pointing to a manila envelope that Ned was holding.

Handing it over to her, he sat in silence as she opened it and perused the contents. It took a couple of minutes and Ned knew she was about finished reading when he watched her dab at her eyes with a tissue. He had brought along acceptance letters he had received from the Cleveland Institute of Music, Berklee, Julliard, and the New England Conservatory of Music. They had all arrived within the past two weeks. He was still waiting to hear from the Curtis Institute in Philadelphia.

Gretchen finished reading and looked at the boy she had known for thirteen years. He wasn't a boy anymore. This young man was going to be famous. She couldn't hide her pride, her love.

"Outstanding, Benedict. Isn't this just wonderful? I am not at all surprised. So, where are you going to go?" she asked, leaning forward in her chair.

"I'm not sure yet. I think it will depend on the financial aid offers. I haven't heard from Curtis, but that's a long shot. They only take about 100 students and it's a free ride for all. Cleveland is close to home, which I like, but I suppose I need to think outside my comfort zone and consider Boston and New York—and Philly. I've never been to any of those cities."

"Well, talk to your dad, see what he has to say. Those are all wonderful music schools. He'll probably want you to stay close, don't you think?"

"Actually, no. Dad insists I need to think about this as an opportunity to grow beyond the music. He tells me to think big. He wants what's best for me and my potential career at the piano. It's all scary, but exciting, too.

"Gretchen, I want to send a recording of my Concerto performance to all the schools to see if I can get more scholarship dollars. Dad isn't rich and I hope I don't have to borrow a lot for college since it will take a while after graduation before I earn much as a professional musician. They'll be tape recording the dress rehearsal and I've arranged with Mr. Rimble for copies that I can send out before the actual concert.

"And Gretchen," Ned choked, stumbling on his words, "I don't know how I can ever thank you for everything you've done for me my whole life. Those incredible letters you sent to all these schools, and speaking to the Dean at Cleveland about me, well, I know they played a big part in me being admitted. I wouldn't be here now if it hadn't been for you." Ned stood and reached forward to embrace his teacher once more.

"Trust me, Benedict, you've given me much more than I've given you. Watching you take your talent to the highest level, seeing your dedication and love of the piano, the performances, it has all been my privilege. You can't know how special—"

A muted knock on the door interrupted her as William stepped inside, hesitantly.

"Sorry to disturb you, but I wanted to make sure I talked to you before you dashed out of here Benedict. I spoke with Jonathan about your request."

After the newspaper had printed the announcement for the June 18th Father's Day concert, there had been considerable buzz at school about it. The Springfield Orchestra offered 100 reduced price tickets for students and once they announced it at school, the tickets sold out on the first day.

That afternoon, a bereft Mitch had flagged down his friend in the hall.

"Ned, good buddy! I've been looking for you all day! You've got to help me!"

"What's up, Mitch?" Ned had chuckled even as Mitch squeezed his shoulders with his powerful hands.

"I really want to see you play at your big concert, but I'm going to be held hostage on Father's Day with a family thing that my parents won't let me out of. I tried to tell them how important it is to me to see you perform, how it'll be my last chance, but no luck. Phoebe told me you have a final dress rehearsal on the Friday before. Do you think maybe me and Phoebe could sit in on that? We'd be real quiet."

Ned had told Mitch that the request had little chance of being approved due to the dress rehearsal's no spectator policy. Ned would ask Mr. Polk to speak to the conductor about it, but to not get his hopes up.

William continued, "At first, his answer was no."

Ned hung his head down. "Shoot."

"At first. But I got him to come around and he finally agreed. But, and this is, as I'm sure you understand, imperative, I had to promise him your friends would be silent and invisible. They'll need to sit in the mezzanine where there will be no house lights. No clapping, no voices. It must appear nobody is there. Got it?"

"Yes, of course, William. I can't thank you enough for doing this for me. Mitch will be so glad. I'll read him the riot act on behavior. He's never been to a classical concert and knows nothing about how they go. Phoebe will be with him, though, and she'll keep him in line." Ned laughed as he said this.

"Excellent. And Benedict, I have to say, this is so thrilling for we orchestra members, too. *The Emperor* is such a gorgeous work and so exhilarating to perform. It's rare for our little orchestra to attract premiere artists, let alone a pianist who has mastered this entire concerto. I knew someone during the War who told me he had performed it, but I never heard him play, but that's another story. We're downright giddy that Tribute's very own 17-year-old Benedict Godwin is to be the star! It's a first for most of us. We're all confident that you're going to wow the audience completely. You know it's sold out, right?"

"No. I didn't know that."

"Well, it is. Okay, then. I'll see you at the dress rehearsal."

"Okay, William. And thanks again."

⚜

Dennis Godwin did not own a sport coat, let alone a suit, but he wasn't concerned. He was sure Ned would not want his father chaperoning his senior prom. So, when asked by the senior class advisors, Henry Chu and Donna Bowman, if he would do just that, he was confident that it wouldn't happen. "I'd be glad to, but only if Neddy says it's okay. I don't think high school boys want their fathers chaperoning their prom."

Dennis was shocked days later when Ned said he was fine with the idea. "Si's parents are also chaperoning, Dad, so you can schmooze with them all night and ignore me, ha ha." He had added that as long as Dennis would ride with the Sissells and let Ned drive their car for Si and his date and Phoebe and him, then he was good with the plan.

Dennis considered asking Ed Sissell if he had a sport coat he could borrow to wear for the evening as they seemed to be about the same size. But in the end, it seemed tacky and might embarrass his son. Dennis went to JCPenneys and bought himself a navy blue sport coat and some black dress pants. Once he tried them on, he realized he needed some new shoes as well. At least the outfit was neutral enough to be versatile for any future dress needs.

All four kids had left over an hour ago for their elegant pre-prom dinner at Mario's, where prom couples had reserved nearly the entire restaurant. Dennis took care to snap a few photos of Neddy's foursome before they left. He finished dressing and looked in the mirror, declaring himself passable. Splashing some English Leather cologne on his neck, he remembered when Neddy had gotten it for him several Christmases back. He would never use it up. Karina walked past his open bedroom door carrying a tray, then did a double take and stepped back.

"My, my, look at you! Who is that handsome man?"

"Do I look all right, Karina?"

"You look perfect, just like a father should. But don't worry, nobody's going to be looking at you tonight with all those beautiful young ladies in the room."

"You're right about that. You sure you don't mind staying over tonight? These things seem to go on well into the morning, as I recall."

"I'm fine, Mr. G., don't worry. I'm going to sit with Isabelle a bit and we'll drink some sun tea I made this afternoon and have scones. There's more in the kitchen if you get hungry when you get home."

"All right, then. Thanks, Karina."

Dennis combed his hair and put on his better watch he brought out for special occasions. He opened his top dresser drawer and retrieved a clean handkerchief, but paused before closing it. Staring for a few seconds, then lifting the drawer liner, he pulled out the piece of paper he had been keeping there. His eyes traveled to the bottom of the page where the ledger read, "Balance Due: $0.00." He had waited a long time to see this last entry. It was for Neddy's graduation gift, yet it had a deeper meaning for him. He thought back to that rainy day, ten years before, when he had wandered into Feldman's Music Store in Chicago, killing time before his train left for Springfield. He wandered around the store, admiring the gleaming brass trumpets, the scores of sheet music categorized by composer and instrument, the dozens of guitars that hung on the wall. And the pianos.

At the front of the store, displayed for passersby, sat a black, baby grand piano with the top open, exposing the inner workings. Dennis had never seen the inside of a grand piano, only the upright piano at home. This piano was beautiful. He ran his hand along the keys and played a few random notes, just to hear it. The sound was so different from the one at home, richer, fuller. A salesman came forward and said, "Go ahead. Sit down and play something. The sound is remarkable."

Dennis replied, "Oh, no thank you. I don't play, but my son does." The moment had always stayed with him, hearing himself say, "but my son does." Neddy, still just a boy of seven, could play Mozart sonatas. At the recitals Gretchen held each spring, the youngest students would play first, except for Neddy. He always played later in the program with the high school students because his repertoire was so advanced. Dennis recalled the previous July when he had taken Neddy to a piano institute that Gretchen had urged he attend at Queens University in Kingston, Ontario. Over 200 students of all ages assembled on the campus for a week of lessons and recitals, eating in the dining hall and sleeping in the dormitories. They had a marvelous time, and Neddy had performed so well on the massive Kawai concert grand piano. Dennis realized right there in Feldman's that his son was a prodigy, a personal gift from a God who had never been kind to him before.

He had stepped inside the store to get out of the rain, finally exiting two hours later to find he had missed his train. But it didn't matter. He was in high spirits and filled with resolve. It might take him ten years to pay for it, but on graduation day, his boy would have a piano worthy of his talent.

❧

"What was your high school prom like, Dennis?"

Edward Sissell and his petite wife, Portia, twenty years his junior, surveyed the gymnasium of Tribute High School, which the students had transformed into a lovely, elegant night club, circa 1950. The prom committee devised the unique idea of transporting the venue back to the year when most of the senior class had been born, blending a mid-century atmosphere with the latest 1968 fashion and music. Everyone seemed to have fun with the little cocktail tables, tiny lamps, and pastel drapings camouflaging the accordioned bleachers, while the band played "(Sittin' On) The Dock of the Bay".

Edward studied the face of his friend, awaiting his reply. They had been friends for fifteen years, yet their conversations always seemed to revolve around their sons, seldom delving into their younger years.

"Who, me? I never went to my high school prom. In fact, I never went to any high school dances. I couldn't dance. Didn't have a girlfriend, either, so what was the point?" Dennis sampled the punch, which surprisingly turned out to be quite tasty. "What about you two? I know you didn't go to any school dances together," he chuckled, "but did you have proms and such back in England?"

"We most certainly did," Portia spoke up. "But the War was still on when I finished secondary school. A good many of the boys in my class had already left to begin basic training, so the turnout was very lopsided, too many girls and not enough boys. Still, we all cherished the time to let loose and have a go at something to laugh and smile about whilst the rest of the world was exploding."

The band had begun their best imitation of Sly and the Family Stone's "Dance to the Music" as the three watched. Dennis wondered if Edward and Portia were thinking the same thing he was, that in just a couple of months, their sons would leave home for college. Dennis didn't know what he was going to do when that day arrived.

"Oops, something's gone wrong with Hag's date over there. What's her name again, Dennis?" Portia was pointing a finger across the dance floor where they could see some sort of drama unfolding with Josy. The distress on her face was drawing some of the other girls off the dance floor to come to her aid.

"Her name is Josy. Josy Steib. She's not a senior. She's a year behind Hag, a sweet girl." Dennis said.

Portia said, "I'm going over there and see what's going on. Maybe I can help. Here, Ed, take care of my drink."

Josy was clearly distressed as Portia escorted her out of the gym, presumably to the ladies' room where she could repair Josy's failing shoulder strap. Phoebe and Hag followed a few paces behind.

Surmising that the disaster had been averted, Dennis asked Edward, "Has Simon figured out where he's going to college?"

"Yes, only just this week. He's going to study architecture at Rice University in Houston, of all places. All along he'd been leaning toward Cornell or Penn, but when he got accepted to all three, he decided Rice would be the best fit. I think he's eager to experience the south and broaden his world. I'm really proud of him. It's almost as if he wants to defy the problems he will no doubt face in that niche environment. Being so short and bald, not to mention the accent, always makes him stand out."

"I think your son is a giant, Ed. Neddy couldn't ask for a better friend. Did Si tell you he's taking over his paper route from now until the concert so he can focus on preparing? Neddy didn't even ask him. Simon just sort of told Neddy the other day that he would be doing it, like, of course, it's a done deal. Those boys are going to miss each other as much as we're going to miss them," Dennis concluded.

"You must be incredibly proud of Ned, Dennis. The three of us are really looking forward to his performance—we have season tickets with the Symphony. How is he doing with it all?"

Dennis pursed his lips. "I suppose he's doing well. I say that because he doesn't talk to me about it and I never get to hear him practice. Our piano just isn't up to the task for the demands of that piece. The middle register is always off and the action of the keys is terrible. It just can't support the tempos for the trills and arpeggios. So, he'd been practicing at Gretchen's a lot, until her heart attack, and since then the music department at school allows him to use their grand piano. I think he rather enjoys that I can't hear him play. He told me it's to be his Father's Day gift for me."

"Where is Ned heading after graduation?"

"He doesn't know yet. Some biggies have accepted him, but I believe he has a strong preference for the Curtis Institute in Philadelphia. They only take 100 students and they don't send out letters until late June, but it's all tuition free. He hopes the tape recording of his concerto will tip the scales in his favor. He'll be eighteen on June 29, that would be some birthday present! He's really just a small town kid, Ed. He's torn. Excited about going to a big city like New York or Boston, but scared at the same time. With so few students, I think Curtis could make the big city of Philadelphia feel a little smaller for him."

*

Portia turned her head as she and Josy made their way down the hall to the ladies room.

"Phoebe, I have a sewing kit in my purse and I think I can mend Josy's strap. Why don't you and Hag wait here. We'll have this girl back on the dance floor in a jiffy."

Phoebe and Hag stopped walking.

Hag said, "I guess that's what mothers are for, Phoebe."

"Thank goodness Mrs. Sissell was here with her needle and thread. How unlikely is that?" Phoebe blurted out. "Say, Hag, I'm feeling adventurous tonight. Did you maybe bring something to mix with this punch?"

Hag reached inside his sport coat and removed the flask of gin he had stowed.

"At your service, mademoiselle." Hag poured some in Phoebe's cup and added a bit more to his own. They smiled at each other, tapped cups mischievously, and said, "Cheers!"

※

The next morning came early for Si as he set out to deliver Ned's Sunday morning papers. Still groggy from the previous night and with just five hours of sleep, he nevertheless set to bundling the extra thick Sunday editions in the Godwin driveway. There didn't seem to be any activity inside, so he assumed they were all still sleeping. It was just 6:30. As he retrieved the wagon for hauling the cargo, he noticed a note taped to the handle: "Thanks a bunch for doing this for me, Si. I owe you big time. I'll be at school practicing most of the day. Ned" He loaded up the papers in the wagon and was reviewing the map Ned had made for him when the garage door opened and Dennis Godwin walked out, coffee cup in hand.

"Morning, Si. I see you got Neddy's note. I don't know how he did it, but he was up at the crack of dawn and out the door lickety split this morning. How are you doing?"

"Oh, I'm good, Mr. Godwin. I'll likely grab a nap this afternoon to catch up. But I'll be fine."

"Good, good," Dennis replied. "Let me ask you a quick question before you head out. Did anything happen with the four of you after you left the dance last night?"

Si grimaced. "Happen? What do you mean?"

"I'm not sure. It's just that Neddy was oddly quiet when he got back home. I had waited up. He really didn't want to talk, said he was tired and just headed up to bed. It seemed a little weird after seeing how happy you all were at the dance."

"Well, Mr. Godwin, I feel kind of funny telling you this, but

I guess maybe you can know, what with his concert coming up in two weeks and all."

"What is it, Si? What happened?"

"The short story is that Phoebe and Ned had a big fight in the car on the way home."

"Oh. I guess that would explain things. Why were they fighting? They seemed to have a fine time at the dance."

Si hesitated before answering, not because secrecy about the incident was important, but because it felt like a betrayal of his friend to be talking about him when he wasn't there. This is something his father should ask Ned himself.

"Mr. Godwin, I have to decline telling you anymore out of respect for my friend. I will say it isn't anything awful and that they've had troubles in this area in the past. You should ask Ned yourself. My guess is they'll make up soon and get back to normal."

Dennis let his shoulders relax. He was pretty sure he understood what had happened. It must have been about the lack of time they spend together. Still, it seemed strange that this happened on such a festive night.

"I'm sure you're right, Si. All right, I won't push you any further. Thanks for being such a friend to Neddy. You want some help with those papers this morning? I'd be happy to lend a hand."

"Naw, that's okay. I've got this. Tell Ned when he gets home I'll see him in school tomorrow." And with that, Si headed toward the curb, wagon handle in hand.

*

Dennis had been at work in the shop for several hours that same afternoon when the telephone extension rang. He shut off the saw, removing his ear plugs as he picked up the phone from its cradle on the wall.

"Hello."

"Hello Mr. Godwin, this is Phoebe."

"Oh, hi Phoebe, how are you today? You really looked lovely last night. Did you have a good time?"

"Oh, Mr. Godwin!" Dennis heard her crying.

"Phoebe, what's wrong? Why so sad?"

"Oh, I'm so embarrassed. I promised myself I wouldn't cry like this. Forgive me. Is Ned there by any chance, or is he at school practicing?"

Dennis heard her sniffling. "He's at school, practicing the concerto, Phoebe."

"Of course he is, as he should be. Mr. Godwin, I must speak with him as soon as possible. I did something really stupid last night. I'm afraid I may have ruined things between us." Phoebe's sobs became louder. "I don't know if he'll ever talk to me again. I feel so ashamed."

"Phoebe, don't beat yourself up so. It can't be as bad as all that. Listen to me for just a moment. You know, believe it or not, I was your age once. I remember how intense the good times can be and how awful arguments can seem. I promise you, this isn't the end of the world. Look, Neddy's been completely focused on this upcoming performance, and I'm sure he hasn't been the most attentive boyfriend to you these past few months. But I know he loves you. Whatever happened between you two, just give it some time. Let things be and I'll bet once the concert is over in two weeks, you two can pick up where you left off and have a beautiful summer together before you all head off to college."

"Oh, Mr. Godwin. Do you really think so?"

"Yes, Phoebe, I do. Why don't you give each other some space for the next couple of weeks until this crazy, special thing in his life is finished? Can you do that, dear?"

"Yes. I think so. You know that I'm taking Mitch to Ned's dress rehearsal the Friday before Father's Day?"

"Yes, Neddy told me."

"Will you tell Ned when he gets home that I'm sorry? Tell him I love him and I'll talk to him whenever he wants, even if it isn't until after the concert. Would you do that for me?"

"Of course, Phoebe, I'll tell him. Don't worry now. Enjoy your last couple of weeks of high school. Have you decided where you are going to college?"

"I'm going to the U of I to major in business. It scarcely feels like I'm going away at all since Urbana is just up the road. Dad wants me to join his investment company at the bank when I graduate."

Dennis could hear her voice relaxing a bit. "Excellent! Are you feeling any better now?"

"I think so. I'm still not sure I can fix this, but I'll do as you say and let time do its thing." She sighed once more. "Thank you, Mr. Godwin."

"You take care now, Phoebe. Bye bye."

CHAPTER 8

Jonathan Rimble had advised Ned to wear his tuxedo to the dress rehearsal. Ned hadn't thought he would, in order to avoid wrinkling it before the concert, but Jonathan set him straight when he related a story about a pianist, years ago, who had to perform an entire concerto before an audience of thousands with a dry cleaning tag gnawing at his waist the entire time. He had dressed without realizing it was there.

"You never know, Ned. Keep the surprises to a minimum, or even better, zero," Jonathan had remarked.

Standing before the mirror, decked out in his rented tuxedo, Ned felt relieved that he had been cautioned. No tags were digging into him, but the shirt was too snug in his armpits, restricting his movements. He took it off and reached for the white dress shirt that hung at the rear of his closet. "Well, that's that, I suppose. It's not ruffled, but will have to do. It fits, and it's comfortable. Maybe the audience won't notice," he hoped. He removed the outfit, folded it with care and packaged it into the rental box, bowtie and all.

The dress rehearsal would follow the same procedure as the actual performance scheduled two days from now. When Ned arrived at the auditorium, he entered through the stage door entrance that was monitored by Phil, the security guard.

"Break a leg, Ned," he said as Ned passed through the door.

"Thanks, Phil."

Ned and Jonathan spent some time together on stage discussing minor details and ensuring that the piano and conductor's podium were perfectly positioned relative to each other. Ned then sat down at the piano and spent a few minutes checking out the action of the keys and pedals, being certain that the height of the bench felt correct.

After making his way to his dressing room, he changed into his tuxedo and walked down the corridor to the soundproof green room. He wondered why it was called that, since the walls were beige. Here he would remain, warming up, until the bell signaled it was time to take the stage. He was ready.

∽

Phoebe pulled into the driveway at Mitch's house and watched him as his eyes bulged upon seeing her car. He was so intent on checking it out from all angles that she finally had to give him a toot on the horn, causing him to jump as she motioned him to get in.

"Oh my God, Phoebe! Is this yours?" Mitch stammered. She was beaming back at him. Then he realized, "Of course it is. Is this your graduation present?"

The two were sitting on gleaming white leather bucket seats in a brand new 1968 powder blue Ford Mustang. Every kid dreamed of owning the car, except for the rare Pontiac Firebird fan such as Hag.

"Will you be able to take this with you to Urbana in September?"

Phoebe frowned. "No, freshmen aren't permitted to have cars on campus. It'll have to stay here until sophomore year."

"Would you like me to take care of it for you?" Mitch laughed.

"Wait! You're going to still be in Tribute next year?" Phoebe couldn't believe it. That's all her friends had been talking about the whole semester, who was going where and how everybody was looking forward to getting out of Dodge.

Mitch took a moment to answer. "Well, not exactly. I mean I don't know when I'll be going, or where, actually, but I won't be staying in Tribute."

"What in the world are you talking about?" Phoebe shifted her body sideways to look at her friend. Mitch chose that moment to examine his shoes.

"Look, we should get moving or we'll be late. I'll tell you about it on the drive to Springfield."

Phoebe pulled away and soon found herself engrossed in his disturbing tale. Mitch reminded her to keep her eyes on the road at one point when she turned her head toward him in disbelief. He swore Phoebe to secrecy, even from Ned. This was his own private story, and he was visibly anxious about what he was telling her, yet there was relief on his face and in his voice as he shared his predicament with Phoebe's compassionate ear.

Rick Shingler had been a combat Marine during the Korean War. Mitch was just a baby when his father left for duty, so for the next two years, it was just Mitch and his mother. His brother John was born soon after his father returned from overseas. Rick charged himself with raising the boys. Mitch's mother cooked and cleaned, but his dad was the boss. He ruled with an iron fist and came down hard on his wife if he caught her babying the boys. Rick believed it was his duty to mold his sons into resilient, disciplined, and loyal soldiers, regardless of their young ages.

Rick decided his first born would become a football player. The father had a specific plan for his eldest son, aspiring for him to excel as both a model citizen and a talented football player, ultimately taking on a prestigious role among the country's military elite. But, as Mitch explained, his heart was never in the game. He had never been a standout on the gridiron, nor did he possess the academic or leadership skills needed for a high ranking position in the military.

"But why didn't you just tell your dad you didn't want to play football?" Phoebe interrupted.

"Phoebe, you're not listening to me. Nobody says no to Rick Shingler. Well, not then anyway. Let me finish so I can get to the point."

And so Mitch continued. His father worked as a supervisor at the landfill operation on the north side of the county. The job suited him because he could be in charge without getting his hands dirty. One of the other supervisors was Kenichi Kato, Dwight's dad. The two of them, ironically, became friendly.

Ken started bragging to Rick that his son, Dwight, was going to enlist in the Army after high school. Ken boasted to Rick that his son would start taking responsibility for himself, once he reached eighteen. Dwight, knowing he didn't have other prospects, would join up when school ended. That's all Rick needed to know. He decided if that loser Dwight with his birds and such could join the Army, then Rick's son sure as hell could become a Marine.

"So now you're going to be a Marine because your dad says so?" Phoebe spat at him.

"Hell, no, I hate the Marines. But I don't have any prospects either, and I can't stand being at home anymore. Phoebe, I'm never going to be who my father wants me to be. If I'm ever going to live my life and make my own decisions, I have to get out of Tribute and away from him."

"Oh Mitch. I'm so sorry. I had no idea. Does Ned know any of this?"

"No!" he shouted abruptly back at her. "And you can't tell him any of this, at least not yet. I don't want him to know this about me! You can't tell anyone, Phoebe."

"All right, all right." Phoebe reached across and put her hand on top of Mitch's. "I promise."

They were quiet after that, both staring straight ahead at the highway, while Linda Ronstadt and the Stone Poneys belted out "Different Drum" in the background. When the song was over, Mitch turned off the radio.

"I enlisted in the Navy last week. I'll find out where I'm going sometime after graduation. Dwight and his dad say I can stay with them until I leave because I can't go home once I tell my dad what I've done."

Phoebe was speechless. All she could do was continue driving and try to remain composed.

Mitch patted her shoulder as she drove on. "Don't be sad for me. I'm not. It's taken me a long time to figure out some things, but now I know it's up to me to have my own life, and that's what I'm doing. I may be scared, Phoebe, but I'm happy."

܀

The sun was setting by the time Mitch and Phoebe parked the car and spotted the light at the stage door where Ned had told them to enter. Phil was expecting Ned's guests and cautioned them to be quiet. He accompanied them to the front lobby and guided them to the mezzanine area where they had been instructed to sit. Every step they took echoed in the silence of the huge auditorium before they found their seats and sat down. Gazing past the brass rail in front of them, they marveled at the Steinway concert grand piano spotlighted front and center on the stage.

Mitch turned to Phoebe and murmured, "My God. This place is enormous. And you say it's all sold out for Ned's performance on Sunday?" He was astonished. He didn't appreciate until now the magnitude of the event.

"Yes, Mitch." They watched as musicians populated the stage, entering from both sides, each one strolling with his instrument to the assigned position and settling into his seat. Phoebe became all business as she turned to face her pupil, speaking in whispers. "Mitch. I need you to listen to me now. Seriously, I want you to hear me without interrupting. I'll explain everything. All right? This is what's going to happen."

And so Phoebe explained the protocols of orchestral music and the specifics of the three parts of this concerto, Beethoven's *Piano Concerto No. 5 in E-flat major*, commonly referred to as *The Emperor Concerto*. Mitch didn't interrupt her, but instead sat immobile, fixated on her every word. She described how the first movement, the Allegro, would begin with the orchestra sounding the first of three chords that Ned would answer with arpeggios, trills and chords before diving into the first of three musical themes of the first movement. Phoebe explained that while the second movement, the Adagio, is much slower, shorter, and may seem simpler, he mustn't be fooled. While she had never heard the second movement, or the third, Ned had shared with her a few key elements that were inspirational to him. Despite its gentle nature, the Adagio was the pivotal component that made *The Emperor* so breathtaking for Ned. He had entreated Phoebe to relax, even close her eyes, and take in every note of the second movement to the very end. If she could do that, he promised her eight unforgettable minutes.

As she continued to share information, Phoebe watched as Mitch took it all in. She knew he had never seen or heard anything like what he was about to witness. "Mitch, you're going to see a very special person do something amazing. Sit back, get comfortable, watch his fingers and take in something sublime. You'll never forget this night. Oh, and one last thing, Mitch. Look at me because this is really important. Do not applaud at any time for any reason. Do you understand?" Mitch nodded.

As they gazed down from their darkened perch in the mezzanine, personnel moved about the stage with clipboards and watches, shifting chairs, arranging sheet music, and all the while, each musician practiced bits and pieces of his part. Mitch was enthralled, his face constantly adorned with a grin. As if on cue, the players quieted their voices and sat motionless as auxiliary personnel vacated the stage. Phoebe crept forward to the edge of her seat and placed her hands on the brass rail for support, Mitch mimicked her actions, anticipating the start of the performance.

And then the orchestra began tuning their instruments. William Polk's lone oboe broke the silence as he played a crystal clear A note that resounded throughout the conclave of woodwinds, brass, and strings, yet somehow seemed to fade away to nothing as it reached the edge of the stage. The first violinist, the concertmaster, stood and took over as the orchestra smoothly completed the process in just a few seconds, followed by utter silence. Jonathan Rimble entered from stage right, baton in hand, and made his way to the front of the stage. He and the concertmaster shook hands and Rimble mounted the podium. "It's all happening just as Phoebe said it would," thought Mitch.

Now, after the briefest silence, Ned emerged, also from stage right. Could this elegantly dressed man who sauntered onto the stage with an unassuming confidence, head held high, be the same seventeen-year-old Ned they knew and loved? This man seemed much older as he shook hands with the conductor. Ned sat down on the piano bench, adjusted his position and folded his hands in his lap. With an almost imperceptible glance toward the mezzanine, Ned couldn't disguise his grin.

The conductor tilted his head left to catch Ned's eye and held it there, patiently waiting for the young star to signal his readiness to begin. Ned tenderly touched the keys with his fingertips, breathed in, then slowly exhaled, returning his hands to his lap. With the barest hint of a nod, his eyes caught Jonathan's, at which point the conductor turned to face the orchestra and raised his baton. The musicians, in perfect unison, lifted and readied their instruments in one singular motion, eyes glued to the conductor's baton in anticipation. There was a hush in the auditorium.

The giant orchestral E-flat major chord resounded and with it, the magic began.

※

Beethoven's *Emperor Concerto* is regarded by many as the most beautiful concerto ever written for piano, and orchestras perform it more frequently than any other piano concerto. However, both Mitch and Phoebe were unfamiliar with the music. Mitch had never heard his buddy play the piano, ever. And, while Phoebe had listened to Ned practice bits and pieces of various sonatas, and had attended two of his recitals in the past, she had not heard him perform anything since the Chopin sonata last fall. Therefore, the twosome, sitting in the dark and hollow vastness of the empty auditorium, unobserved by the musicians, watched with awe the prowess, facility, and heartfelt emotion that Ned showcased over the next 39 minutes.

Mitch never imagined that his friend could play the piano like this. "How in the world had Ned trained his fingers to do this? When did he do this? How did he find the time?" he thought. Mitch was spellbound watching Ned's hands glide effortlessly across the keyboard, incredulous when he trilled scales of music so incredibly fast, bringing the piano to life. This was not what he had imagined. This was something altogether different, altogether unexpected, altogether amazing. Mitch pried his eyes away from his friend's hands and studied Ned's face now. He had never seen him look this way before. There seemed to be a piercing, almost mystical connection between Ned and the keyboard. Unbelievably, Ned closed his eyes as he trilled yet another scale! "How could he possibly do that?" Mitch wondered. He was overcome with emotion as Ned brought the Adagio to a close. "He plays magnificently," he thought, as his hands clutched the arms of his seat. Each note, just as Ned had suggested to Phoebe, was wrenching, pleading for the listener to hang on for just one—more—moment.

Ned seemed to be immersed in an experience apart from that of his select audience. It was as though the notes were emanating from his fingers, from his brain, and the piano was merely the amplifier. Mitch understood now how this music so motivated Ned. "Just look at his face," he thought, "this is his life's passion." There was no doubt the piano would always be, unapologetically, Ned's first love. And at that singular moment, Mitch knew he wanted to feel that way, too.

Peering over the railing now, for the first time taking in the intimacy between the musicians and the soloist, Mitch understood that each required the other to bring the notes to life. As he heard every deliberate, agonizing sound draw the movement to its inevitable close, Mitch regarded his own smile as it grew with each note. Even so, there could be no denying the tear that wended its way down his face.

"Thank you, Ned," he whispered to himself.

※

Phoebe bolted upright, startled by the sudden intensity of Ned's fingers on the keys as he began the last movement, the Rondo. She had been in a private stupor for most of the performance, up to when she spotted Mitch white knuckling his chair arms. In that moment, witnessing the tear on his cheek, she had placed her hand over his.

Ned's captivating command of the dynamic third movement left her enthralled, her mind racing with excitement. "Oh, Ned, how could I not have known? Where have I been these past two years?" She knew he played well, for they had grown up together in the school band. The two recitals of Ned's she had attended were very nice, and he had played the Chopin sonata so flawlessly months before, but what he was doing now was astonishing. Phoebe realized in that moment she had lost Ned. His future was so out of her league. What must he have thought of her needy whining all this time? First thing on Monday, she would apologize to him for her lack of understanding about his calling. From now on, she would have to settle for reading about him in the newspapers.

It occurred to her that everybody but her was moving forward. Simon was going to be an architect and was going to Texas. Hag achieved a perfect score of 36 on the ACT Exam and was awarded a full scholarship to NYU. And now Mitch would leave for the Navy. Even Hag's friend Dwight was now an accomplished falconer. That everyone else had been growing while she'd been coasting along was a sobering thought. Was she, in truth, just a shallow little rich girl? She didn't even know what she wanted to major in at college.

Phoebe drew her attention back to the stage. Ned was magnificent. She plunged back into the present and joined Mitch in soaking up the last minutes of the Rondo. The two sat captive as they listened now to the synchronous coda of the performance, punctuated brilliantly by Ned's incredible final cadenza and the orchestra's finish.

She and Mitch stood up promptly, but it was Mitch who foiled Phoebe's applause, restraining her arms as the orchestra praised Ned. He was beaming as he turned to look at them. All he would have seen was darkness, but he knew they were there and sent an inconspicuous wave their way.

※

Saturday dawned with clear blue skies and Ned hummed to himself as he descended the stairs to the kitchen for breakfast. The buzz of the table saw could be heard in the background as his dad worked in the shop.

"Yum, Karina. That smells so good!"

"Well, you timed it perfectly. Do you want juice with these pancakes? Oh, what am I saying? Of course not. Milk, yes?" Karina asked, recalling the incident many years ago when pancakes and orange juice had made him wretch on the school bus. "So, your dad says your dress rehearsal last night went well."

"Yeah, Karina, it did. I'll play it one more time tomorrow at the concert and then I think I'll throw away the music. After six months of it, I think I'm ready for something else."

"I can't wait to hear you play, Benedict. Your father was so nice to buy me a ticket—two, actually. I'm bringing my friend Bonnie with me."

"Great. I hope you like it.

Ned started gobbling just as his father came in from the shop, swatting dust off his trousers.

"Stop, Mr. G! I've told you before. Please do that before you step inside," Karina admonished.

"Oops." Dennis stepped back out to finish the task, if a bit too late. "I'm going up to shower real quick, then I'll be ready to eat. Neddy, you still want to shoot some pool at the Elks Club later, right?"

"Yep, you don't have a chance today, old man. I'm in the zone after last night!"

"We'll see about that. We can go for pizza at Monicals after," Dennis shouted as he climbed the stairs.

Dennis had been on pins and needles for days, anticipating his son's performance, and it would be on Father's Day, like a gift for him. Gretchen would sit with him front and center, like old times when Ned was just a boy.

Still, he had to admit he was looking forward to having more time with his son after the concert. There would be graduation, Ned's birthday, his last summer at home before heading off to college. He couldn't wait to see the surprised look on Neddy's face when he saw the new piano, all sparkling in ebony, tuned and ready for him to play. The delivery arrangements were set in place for next Saturday, down to the scheme to keep Neddy away from the house all morning. It had been necessary to let Simon in on the secret as he needed him to steal his son away and ensure he showed up back at the house at just the right time for the surprise.

∼

"Did you speak with Phoebe last night?" Dennis asked. Ned had just backed out of the driveway when Dennis asked the question. He waited, hoping Ned would volunteer something.

"No, I haven't spoken to her or Mitch."

Dennis let the issue drop as Ned drove along Odiorne Drive, past the gazebo, and headed out of Parkland.

"Look, Dad, Phoebe and I are, well, I don't know what we are at the moment. I was pretty upset with her after the prom and I had so much on my mind with the concert coming up that I just didn't want to talk to her about any of it. I guess she feels bad about what happened and maybe I wasn't very forgiving. Anyway, we haven't talked but we will after tomorrow. We'll have to wait and see what's left of us, if there is an 'us'. She'll be off to Urbana and I'll be off somewhere else, and we're both going to meet other people, so I'm not sure our relationship will last going forward."

Dennis briefly rested his hand on Ned's shoulder. "I think that's a sensible way to look at it, Neddy. I hope you two can patch things up and have fun together this last summer before college."

"Build Me Up Buttercup", by The Foundations, started playing on the car radio, and Ned, never tiring of this song, turned up the volume and hummed along. Hearing it would always remind him of the first time he had heard it. It had been playing on WLS radio out of Chicago over the loudspeaker at the bowling alley when he and the crew were having a Friday night blast.

Dennis shouted, "What group is this, Neddy?"

"The Foundations!" he shouted back. Then he turned the volume down a bit and asked, "What kind of music were you listening to when you were eighteen, Dad?"

"Well, let's see." Dennis paused as he pondered how to answer the question. He couldn't even remember music at that point in his life. His life was so unhappy then, he'd struggled to get through the basics of day to day living. So, it would have been 1936. Wow. He recalled much from 1936, but not the music. "We didn't have a radio, Neddy, but I think the jazz bands and the big bands were starting around that time. You know, Benny Goodman, Guy Lombardo, stuff like that."

"Oh yeah, I know that music. It's pretty good. Of course, not as good as rock and roll."

"I suppose it always depends on your generation. When you have children, you'll probably look back on your rock and roll as the best music and you probably won't be much of a fan of your kids' music."

Ned laughed, "That's probably true."

Ned changed radio stations to skip the commercials and landed on The Supremes. "Si can't get enough of The Supremes. He thinks they're the best group out there. I think it's because he loves to dance and Motown puts out terrific songs for that." Ned slowed down as the traffic toward downtown thickened. It would be stop and go now as they approached Mattis Avenue. It looked like a wedding was just finishing up as guests poured out of the Presbyterian Church on the other side of the intersection.

"Ed Sissell tells me Si has decided on Rice University in Houston for architecture school," Dennis said.

"Yup, he's locked in there now. I still don't know what Mitch plans to do. Hag is heading to NYU, and Phoebe, of course, is going to the U of I. It's kind of sad that we're all going to split up and go separate ways, but we're excited about it just the same. I guess the time is right to move on." Ned held onto the thought for a moment. It dawned on him that maybe his dad would be sad about him leaving.

"You're absolutely right, Neddy. It's time for the next page for all of you. This may be the most exciting time of life, you know, when you're young with so much ahead of you. You need to grab it and go find out where you belong."

The light at Mattis Avenue turned green and Ned inched forward into the intersection, but had to jolt to a stop when a parked car pulled out into the lane three cars ahead of him. Ned kept nosing forward when he could, uncomfortable being trapped in the intersection like this.

Dennis continued, "I've been meaning to talk to you about some things, so maybe we can do that after your concert. There are some things you need to know. Forgive—" Dennis stopped abruptly, his attention drawn to the clogged intersection, and on instinct, glanced left at the setting sun, then quickly glanced right. "Neddy, move! Now!"

He heard the panic in his father's voice and turned his head toward the passenger seat. In less than a second, Ned captured every detail. He realized he was trapped, with nowhere to go. Cars at the front and rear had him boxed in. Ned glanced at the rear-view mirror, but only for a flash when he saw that the biggest problem was the semi-tractor-trailer truck heading into the intersection from the Mattis Avenue hill on the right. Eyes bulging, panic-stricken, Ned couldn't understand why the truck wasn't slowing down. "The guy's brakes must be failing!" Ned thought.

"Dad, he's not stopping! Dad! What do I do? What do I do?" he screamed.

The truck was barreling down on them with ferocity now. It would slam into the right side of the car in seconds.

"Dad! Dad!"

And then, as if in slow motion, Ned watched as his father unbuckled his seat belt and threw his body on top of him, wrapping his arms around his son and cradling the boy's head to his chest. Ned smelled the faint scent of English Leather on his father's neck as he heard him murmur, "Oh, Neddy."

PART II

Adagio un poco mosso

CHAPTER 9

Mitch

THE SUMMER OF 1968 had been a confusing and treacherous fog for Mitch. Like all of Ned's friends, the automobile accident that had killed Dennis Godwin and critically injured Ned had devastated Mitch. Graduation rehearsals came and went, each of them drifting through the motions, unsure of what was real. How could Ned not be with them? Would he recover and pick up where he left off? All of them felt the joy of prom and graduation tainted by these worrisome emotions.

Mitch had visited several times in Ned's early weeks in the hospital. The two of them had awkward conversations that neither of them recalled hours later. Mitch tried not to stare at the horror that was the traction apparatus for Ned's left leg. The pins and cables were like something out of a Frankenstein movie. Bandages, casts, wraps, IVs, it was all so overwhelming, yet he still came to see his friend.

Mitch soon learned that each visit felt as if it was the first time. The cocktail of medications Ned consumed around the clock prevented him from processing events in any meaningful way. Often, his mutterings made no sense. Yet, the doctor encouraged all the friends to continue visiting and to talk to him, even if he didn't respond.

"You see," Dr. Mayfield had said, "Ned has experienced a severe trauma, not only physically but mentally. His mind is being bombarded with memories of past and current events that are just plain confusing to him. I'm not sure he remembers what has happened, or even if he knows his father has passed, despite having been told. He asks about his left hand every day, but it's the same question each time. It's clear he remembers he plays the piano and that he wants to know when his arm will heal enough to play again, but doesn't remember that we're unable to give him answers. So, Mitch, tell your friends to keep coming. Give him some time and know that your voices alone are therapeutic."

And that's what he did. Mitch was in limbo, awaiting his next and last interview before receiving orders for his basic training assignment. He had passed his physical months ago, filled out forms, got measured and weighed. He continued living at Dwight's house, and once school ended, insisted on paying Mr. Kato weekly rent of $50, which he had finally agreed to accept.

He and Dwight had found work at the Double Tree Lumber Yard. The physical labor was uninspiring, yet his exhaustion at the end of each day was gratifying. He returned to the Kato house to shower before venturing out each night for an evening meal.

But, as he lay in bed at night, the depressing thought of who he was would return to strangle him. Who the hell was he, anyway? He didn't know anyone like him. Was this a phase that would pass as he matured? He earnestly hoped so, but in his heart he knew that wouldn't happen. The loneliness of his secret was paralyzing. He thought back to that evening when he and Phoebe had watched Ned perform his concerto. Marveling at his friend's performance, Mitch could see that Ned had figured out who he was and what his life would be. Focusing on it with total commitment, disallowing the trivialities of high school to interfere with his life plan, Ned had remained true to his talent. Phoebe undeniably came in second. Mitch had sat there in the mezzanine, misty eyed, yearning desperately for the courage to follow his own destiny.

Now he was joining the Navy. If he was honest with himself, he would have to admit that in truth, he was just running away from a father that didn't understand him, a town that didn't know him, and from himself. Mitch stared at the ceiling. He kept the bedside radio set low as the walls were thin and he didn't want to disturb Mr. Kato, whose bedroom was just on the other side. Aretha was belting out "RESPECT".

He kept yawning, but couldn't fall asleep. One a.m. passed, then two a.m. "What am I going to do? Am I going to be honest with myself or am I going to join up? What will I do if I don't join up?" he ruminated. He couldn't stay in Tribute; there was nothing here for him. He couldn't face everyone. The thoughts kept circling in his head until at last he dozed off.

※

President Teddy Roosevelt founded Naval Station Great Lakes in 1911. By 1968, it had grown to be the largest naval installation in the United States, churning out thousands of sailors every six weeks.

Mitch was assigned to Division 11, along with 800 other recruits. Recruit Training Command was the fancy name given to boot camp. RTC dictated every aspect of Mitch's existence each day, from the moment he arose at 0500 until lights out at 2100. He had few problems adapting to Navy life in the three weeks since arriving. He had made some friends, performing well in the classroom and excelling in the field. But during orientation, he had lied on his induction questionnaire and again under verbal questioning on Day 2 at RTC, and was filled with worry now, certain he'd made a terrible mistake by enlisting..

By October 20, he found himself, duffel bag in hand, marching through Chicago Union Station, searching for the Track 5 train that would transport him to San Francisco. Tucked away in the bottom of his duffel was his discharge from RTC. Titled "Entry Level Separation (Uncharacterized)", it officially dismissed him from service "without any prejudice". By law, no one but the Navy and Mitch knew the reason for his departure. He took a deep breath and walked briskly, disregarding the exhaust fumes and the crowds. He had not expected to be freed from duty without tremendous repercussions. And yet it had all been so straightforward. Yes, he had to report up the ladder three different levels before his Division Commander finally approved the MILPERSMAN 1910-134 (separation by reason of defective enlistment) clause. He had signed dozens of papers, relinquished all of his RTC standard issue: uniforms, shoes, hat, notebook, etc., then was assigned to Ship 17, where all dismissed recruits were housed while the paperwork for separation was being processed. These included those servicemen with medical issues, mental illness, training failures, and homosexuals like himself. Everyone kept to himself and nobody questioned reasons for separating. Mitch was there for nineteen days.

After finding Track 5, he sat on a bench and waited for the boarding call. Mitch didn't know what he would do when he got to San Francisco. He had the $800 he had earned at the lumberyard in his pocket, which he knew wouldn't last long, and though his future out west was uncertain, he couldn't help but smile.

⁂

In San Francisco, in 1968, the only place to be for an eighteen-year-old seeking independence and adventure was Haight-Ashbury. He'd heard of no place else in the gossip. The Haight was all about hippies, free love, sharing, caring, and peace. Naturally, drugs were also present, but his knowledge was limited to one joint he had smoked with Hag on Phoebe's patio during her Christmas party. Hag had offered the opportunity to Ned but he had declined. To be truthful, at the time he was so cold and nervous he scarcely felt anything and only pretended to inhale most of the few minutes it took them to reach the last toke.

So, after climbing down from the train at Caltrain Station, he located Buena Vista Park on a giant map on the wall. It looked to be just a couple of blocks from the Haight-Ashbury intersection and a walkable distance. He set off, pulling down the brim of his cap to shield his eyes from the setting sun, nervous but eager.

It was dark by the time he spotted a giant red rooster on the sign for the Chanticleer Bar on Ashbury Street. The door was propped open with a brick, and the sound of Country Joe and the Fish lured him through the threshold and up to the first stool at the bar. Despite the darkness outside, it was still too early for the joint to be bustling. Nevertheless, there were a considerable number of people inside. Mitch scanned the room, thinking he must have stood out like an alien. While he was no longer in uniform, it appeared the rest of the patrons were. Long hair, beards, bellbottom jeans, and sandals filled his line of sight in every direction. He ordered a Budweiser draft and, after a couple of deep gulps felt his nerves settle down enough to quell his self-conscious flutters.

He couldn't believe he was in San Francisco, at Haight-Ashbury, drinking a beer with nobody telling him what to do. The bartender had been busy at the other end of the bar but now settled in just opposite him at the underbar sink, washing glasses. Just like everyone else in the place, he appeared to be in his twenties. He wore a stud earring in his left ear and possessed a meticulously trimmed mustache that matched the deep brown color of his closely cropped hair. Dimples materialized when he smiled, causing Mitch to deduce that he smiled often.

"Where you from, buddy?" the bartender asked.

During the long train ride, knowing people were bound to ask,

Mitch had thought long and hard about what to say to this question. He had finally decided to just tell the simple truth since most of the time people don't want to know the deep details.

Mitch answered, "Well, most recently I—"

"Wait. Stop. Let me guess. I know that accent. It's definitely Midwest, am I right?"

"Yep," Mitch replied, surprised by how swiftly the bartender had pegged him.

"Okay, let's see if I can get it down to the state. Let me look at you."

Mitch was smiling now, enjoying the attention. Standing aside the barstool, he backed up a step. Still grinning, he took off his ball cap and did a 360, arms away from his torso as if he was about to be frisked, then sat back down. "Well, what do you think?"

"Man, I may not get the state just right, but I'm pretty sure I know where you just came from. Your hair is the biggest tell, then the way you stand, all erect like at attention. You're strong as hell, no facial hair. I'm pretty sure I've got your number. I'll bet you another round that I get it right. You game?"

Mitch was loving this. This guy was a riot. "Sure, I'll take the bet. But what happens if you're right? What do I owe you, uh..."

"Bill, my name is Bill."

"All right, Bill. What do I owe you if you're right?"

Bill scrutinized Mitch's eyes, a hint of a squint as he assessed the new arrival. "I'll tell you what..."

"Mitch."

"I'll tell you what, Mitch. If you lose, you have to go with me to the club tonight after my shift ends at ten."

"What club?"

"The Eight Ball Club. It's a music, dance, pool hall place about four blocks from here on Haight. Do you play pool?"

"A little," Mitch answered. This was more than he had planned.

He didn't know this guy from Adam. What if 'Bill' just wanted to lead him down some alley and beat him up and rob him?

"Look, I get you might be a bit leary, being new here and not knowing anything about me or the city, but you'll be okay, I promise. We'll walk over with some other friends." Bill motioned with his head and Mitch swiveled around to take a look. Three women and a man occupied a round, high-top table next to the mirrored wall at the back. They were all looking his way with smiles. One woman was raising her glass as if to toast him.

"Those are my friends and they like to dance, so we can all walk together. Hey, but I'm getting ahead of myself. I haven't even won the bet!"

"No, you haven't," Mitch replied, but suspecting, and hoping he was about to lose the bet. "All right, bartender, where am I from?"

Bill clapped his hands together once. "Yes! Okay, listen up. I'm originally from Chicago. I grew up in Iowa before moving to Chicago when I was nine. So I know a thing or two about the Windy City." Bill was enjoying this. But, just then, looking down the bar, he said, "Whoops, you'll have to wait while I take care of business," and off he went to the other end of the bar where four guys had just angled up.

"What the…? Seriously, Bill?" Mitch belted out.

Bill didn't answer, just laughed and waggled a finger back at Mitch.

When Mitch turned back around, he discovered that the woman who had toasted him from across the room had taken the seat next to him. "Oh, hello," Mitch stuttered in surprise.

"Sorry, I didn't mean to startle you. I'm Sandra."

"Hi Sandra, I'm Mitch."

"So, are you and Bill buddies now?"

Sandra was all smiles as she took a sip of her drink. It wasn't beer but some kind of yellow cocktail. Her eyes were a brilliant blue, evident even through the granny glasses pitched on the bridge of her nose. She had long, straight blonde hair with a pink flowery vine woven through it. A faint scent of incense hung in the surrounding air.

"Hmm, that's a good question. I'm not sure yet." Mitch still couldn't believe all of this was happening. His mug was empty by now, but his heart was feeling full. So this is what it's like to be free, to feel relaxed. He felt completely engrossed in the moment, eager to continue, wanting to know what came next. "You see, Sandra, Bill and I have this bet going about whether he can guess where I'm from."

Sandra scooted closer and now was sitting at the edge of the stool with her sandaled feet on the floor. She leaned forward with just her drink separating the few inches between their faces and said, "Oh, really? And what happens when you lose the bet?"

"What makes you think I'm going to lose?"

"It's just a feeling. I've known Bill now for, let's see, three years? Yeah, a little over three years. He's not a gambling sort of guy. So, if he's wagering a bet with you, he must feel pretty sure he's going to win. So tell me, what will you lose?"

The mixture of alcohol and fruit on her breath was not unpleasant. Her teeth were even and white and she was as beautiful as Bill was handsome. Just then, Mitch jolted in surprise as Bill slammed down another mug of beer. The sloshy foam spilled over the edge of the bar, wetting Mitch's pants.

"Oh, sorry, mate. Those'll dry in no time. I see you've met Sandra."

"Yeah, Bill," Sandra said. "Mitch was just about to tell me what happens if he loses your bet. But what happens if he wins?"

"If he wins? If he wins, this beer is on the house. If he loses, aww, I'll let Mitch tell you. Okay, Mitch, you ready for my guess?"

Both sets of eyes were on Mitch now. "Go for it, man. Where am I from?"

"Why you're ex-military, Mitch! You may as well be wearing a sign, man! What's more, you've come from the Great Lakes Navy Station."

Mitch couldn't say he was surprised. Well, not about the ex-military part. But Bill had a bit of luck with the rest of it. "You got me," he said.

At that, Sandra chimed in, "Haha! Are you serious? Oh, Mitch, you've just been taken, dear boy! Tell him, Bill."

Bill gave them both a puzzled look as if he had no idea what Sandra was talking about, but then slammed his palm on the bar, laughing and shouting, "I'm ex-Navy, too, Mitch! I came through there eight years ago myself!"

⁂

Mitch was lying in bed, half awake, his brain afloat. His eyelids felt heavy as he tried to open them, but couldn't. "Never mind," he thought, "I'll just stay here awhile longer." He fell back asleep, but someone or something awakened him soon after. It could have been hours later, he couldn't be sure. Sensing daylight in the room even with his eyes still closed, he remembered where he was, but something was going on. He was aware of a puzzling, albeit pleasant, sensation between his legs. Peaking through his eyelids, then bounding awake, wide eyed, he saw Sandra straddling him and smiling. He continued to lie there, not quite grasping the situation.

Unexpectedly, from behind Sandra, Bill peaked over her shoulder, grinning as he brought his arms around her, caressing her breasts and kissing her neck. Sandra ran her hands across Mitch's chest and only then did he realize they were all naked. "I guess this is what they mean when they talk about free love," Mitch chuckled, then immediately regretted saying something so stupid.

Bill leaned back, then bounded out of bed and stood next to Mitch. Bending forward, he planted a kiss on Mitch's mouth. "Oh, wow," Mitch exclaimed, dumbfounded. He delicately lifted Sandra away from his body. "This is far out. Way far out." He looked around the bedroom, trying to get his bearings, and shook his head back and forth, which only served to ignite a splitting headache. "Oh, God. Not good," he thought as his hands went to his temples and Sandra and Bill casually put on their underwear. "I think I need to pee," Mitch realized. "Uh, where is the bathroom?"

"It's just down the hall on the left. You can't miss it," Bill answered.

Mitch jumped out of bed, trying to cover himself while searching for his clothes. They were nowhere in sight and since his bladder was in command, he just scooted down the hall. When he came out of the bathroom, Bill was standing nearby, waiting his turn. "Have you seen my clothes?"

"You must have left them in Joel's room. At least that's where you started last night, rather this morning. Don't you remember anything about last night?"

"I'm not sure. Some of it, I guess. I don't know. I remember being at the club and feeling more drunk than I've ever felt." Mitch was rubbing his hands over his face as he spoke.

Bill laughed. "That's from when the speed you took wore off. Then we all smoked some hash when we got back here. Remember? Downstairs? We all sat on the floor around the coffee table and got high."

"Oh, yeah, I guess I remember that. That's when we started playing strip poker. Oh, God! It just came back to me. I couldn't stop laughing. I threw off all my clothes in the living room, didn't I?"

"That would be correct, stud," Bill said with a straight face. "But don't fret, old friend, nobody minded. We were all just as stoned as you." He embraced Mitch in a bear hug, then slapped his backside with both hands.

"Jeez. I gotta get it together, man. So where again is Joel's room? Somewhere downstairs, right?"

"Yeah, just off the kitchen."

Mitch grabbed a towel from the bathroom, wrapping it around his waist as he headed toward the stairs. It was already 1:20 in the afternoon, yet nobody seemed to be downstairs, to his relief. Making his way to Joel's room, he was remembering more and more now. A jumble of his clothes rested by the bed. He dressed quickly, but panic set in almost immediately when he discovered his wallet was not in his pants pocket. "Oh, damn! This can't be happening! My God! All my money was in there!" He started tearing through blankets and pillows and clothes. He crawled on the floor, looking under the bed and the dresser. Nothing. Mitch lay on the floor, groaning. "I can't believe this. I am so stupid."

"How stupid are you?" a voice asked from the doorway.

Without moving his head to see who it was, Mitch said, "I don't even know when I lost it, my wallet, or when it got stolen." He pulled himself up to a sitting position and saw that the person standing behind him was Joel.

"Sorry, man. I have your wallet. Everything's cool," Joel reassured him.

"Oh, God! I was ready to jump off the Golden Gate Bridge."

"Aw, don't go and do that, man. You'll make me feel like a one-night stand," Joel winked.

Mitch laughed, but quickly added, "Where is it, and why do you have it?"

"There are so many people that come in and out of this place every day. And last night when you were stripping down in the front room, I saw your wallet fall out of your pants pocket. So I retrieved it and stashed it in my personal vault."

"You have a vault? Here? In the house?"

"Of course not. I have a hiding place where I put stuff I don't want stolen. Now, if you'll get out of here for a minute, I'll get it for you."

✌

And that's how it all began. Mitch's thoughts frequently returned to that first incredible night in San Francisco. Even though it had been six years ago, it sometimes seemed like yesterday. He often wondered where might he be now if he'd picked a different bar and hadn't walked in to The Chanticleer that night. If he hadn't met Bill, he wouldn't have met Joel, who let him share his room on Ashbury for months. Joel wouldn't have introduced Mitch to his uncle Richard, who owned a construction company in Oakland and hired Mitch on as a general hand. Richard wouldn't have invited Mitch and Joel to dinner where Mitch wouldn't have met Richard's wife, Nadine, who, as a senior photographer for the world famous Zoli Modeling Agency wouldn't have done a photo shoot of Mitch, who would not have then moved to New York City to begin a modeling career. In 1970, they chose Mitch to be the new Winston man in their cigarette advertisement campaign that showcased his stubbled jaw, cigarette dangling from his lips, on the back cover of Time, Newsweek, and People magazines.

Mitch moved to Los Angeles in 1971, where he secured his first acting role in a Budweiser television commercial. The head of the agency, Zoli Rendessy, recommended Mitch to his friend, Bill Backer, who had just produced the iconic "I'd Like to Buy the World a Coke" commercial. Within a year, Mitch bought a bungalow in Laurel Canyon in celebration of filming his first season of "Guiding Light" in the role of Jason Fane, the landscaper and May/December love interest of Linell Conway, played by Christina Pickles.

CHAPTER 10

Hag

THE TRIBUTE PENTECOSTAL Church sits just inside the city limits on an abrupt, riverine elevation, constituting four acres on the east side of the Tribute River. Erected in 1892, the building served as The First Methodist Church of Tribute. But, within twenty years of its founding, the disinterested, crumbling congregation could no longer tithe sufficient support to maintain the structure or the minister, and the church fell into disrepair, decaying both physically and spiritually. The decline compounded during the depression of the 1930s, aided in no small part by young, unemployed men with nothing more to do than toss rocks through its windows, loiter in its sanctuary and express their misfortune with scrawls of despair on its walls.

Enter the Reverend James Glasby, a Pentecostal would-be minister from Omaha in search of a following. Having embraced the teachings of evangelist Charles Fox Parham, and upon attesting to having borne witness to The Holy Spirit hovering above the water and speaking to him in tongues as he fished from the banks of the Tribute River, 13 miles southwest of the town, the Rev. Glasby took that as a sign of his calling. God wanted him to establish a church on the banks of the river in the town of Tribute.

A group of God-fearing settlers had named the river "Tribute" in 1788. They crossed a nameless tributary of the Mississippi and, in accordance with their Puritanical ways, honored the Lord by giving it the name. Glasby interpreted this as further evidence that his mission was preordained. And so the Reverend, like a shepherd gathering his sheep, found himself with a growing crop of disillusioned citizens in search of a leader as he began preaching each Sunday his "Full Gospel" on the oak-shaded grounds of the fading Methodist Church building. By the end of World War II, the building had undergone restoration, if not fully reinstating its former glory, at least satisfying the mayor and the Tribute Building Department. An occupancy permit was issued and the Tribute Pentecostal Church congregation began worshiping and volunteering their labor to transform the tired building into a welcoming edifice as one entered the city.

Bonnie Abel and her first husband, Bert, had married the day before he shipped out as an infantryman to fight in France. Shockingly, the soldier became a casualty of war on only his second day of battle. The widow continued her assembly line work for the remainder of the war, heartbroken at the loss of her husband, whom she had adored, and sought consolation in the Pentecostal Church. Here, she received the support of a congregation that knew all too well the devastation and loss that the War brought to so many of them. The kindness and kinship of other young widows helped ease the loneliness after the loss of her soul mate, Bert. The Reverend, though devout, found himself drawn to Bonnie and pursued her as a potential wife. Bonnie finally gave in, acknowledging that while she may not have loved James, he seemed to love her in his own way, she supposed, and she held onto the possibility that one day her feelings might change. The Reverend Glasby married war widowed Bonnie in 1945. In James, Bonnie found a reliable, moral man, capable of giving her the children she yearned for, despite being ten years her senior.

Children did not come as Bonnie had fervently hoped, and she resigned herself to her loveless, childless marriage. James, constantly busy with his church, had little time or inclination for activities that his wife enjoyed, such as walks in the park or road trips to visit her family in Springfield. With each year that passed, the fire and brimstone the reverend preached on Sunday followed him home as he tyrannically subordinated his wife to that of a classless domestic servant.

Then, as the waning years of that war decade came to a close, God finally looked down upon Bonnie with love. On December 19, 1949, she gave birth to a 7 pound, 5 ounce son, Humberto Abel Glasby. James, surprisingly, did not argue when she insisted on naming the boy in honor of her lost husband and he left the care of the child to her. However, he insisted, the boy's religious education and discipline would be his, and only his, domain, which proved to be unrelenting in its mental cruelty to the boy.

❦

At 10:20 on a chilly Friday morning in October, Hag clambered into his roommate's Volkswagen, suitcase in the back seat, to begin the three-hour drive northwest to Delhi, 160 miles from his New York University dormitory. It had taken several days of pleading and haggling back and forth with Eric before his roommate eventually gave in and handed over the keys. Only after Eric relented did Hag confess he didn't know how to drive a stick shift.

Eric had driven Hag to a deserted parking lot in the garment district and given him a one-hour lesson. "I guess you'll be okay; you don't seem to be having much trouble. But those hills you'll be driving through, man, they won't be this easy. You sure you want to do this?" Eric later implored, even as he watched Hag pack. "You put one scratch on that baby and I'll kill you, understand?" Eric had threatened. "And it better be back in its assigned spot in the garage by noon on Sunday, washed and clean as a whistle."

Hag had been confident Eric would loan him the car. He and Eric had become friends within minutes of their meeting one another in Room 223 of their dorm the previous month. Hag kept Eric in stitches with his stand-up routines, and Eric kept their room neat and organized. Eric, being a clean freak, felt embarrassed by it, so he made it clear from the beginning that he didn't expect Hag to be as neat as himself, as long as Hag didn't mind Eric picking up, cleaning up, and tidying up to maintain his personal sanity. Truth be told, Eric couldn't believe his luck in getting a roommate who not only tolerated his obsessive-compulsive affliction but wholeheartedly embraced it, but not without occasional biting jokes that would roll off his back. As for Hag, he saw it as free maid service. It was an arrangement in which they both came out ahead.

Hag had been especially grateful for the loan of the car when he had discovered that the Trailways Bus ride to this God forsaken little town in the middle of the Catskill Mountains would first take him to Albany, then over to Syracuse. Only then would the transfer bus take him on to Delhi. Overall, it would be a 17 hour ordeal. Now, on the road, Hag realized that the 160 miles were going to take much longer than three hours to complete. It had taken over an hour just to clear the first 30 miles out of the city. Then, despite the roadmap he brought along, he missed three turns along the way, one which took him seven miles off track before a sweet old lady selling pumpkins at the roadside set him straight.

Behind the wheel of the shiny orange Beetle, Hag rounded a long, gentle bend in the two-lane road before encountering a narrow gap that workers had blasted to make way for the road. The steep granite walls of the cliffs soared skyward on both sides as Hag slowed down to take it all in. He had seen nothing like this back home in Illinois. With no one behind him, he continued creeping along, peering up into the sun. Leaning over the steering column, he observed a few scraggly pines fighting to survive within the soilless crevasse of granite near the top. The bright sun in his eyes made him sneeze, and he pitched back into the driver's seat, wiping his nose as the car finally cleared the monolithic pair. "It's a stone cathedral," he said out loud to nobody. But in that instant, the captivating spell was shattered as he remembered his father's stone cathedral in Tribute and the countless episodes of misery from his childhood.

But now he was on the last leg with no other turns to make. In the middle of a Hendrix riff, he turned off the radio, trying to recapture the sanctitude of the passing mountains. Hag had many reasons to feel morose. His father had rejected him when Hag refused to enroll at the religious college in Omaha that the man wanted his son to attend. Hag was going to NYU, in the sinful city. There would be no spending money coming from his father, no phone calls on the weekends asking how he was doing, wondering if college was hard, looking forward to his first break, sending him his love. Even his mother, while supporting Hag's decision, was not a beacon of support, the bottle being more important in her hierarchy of needs.

Hag was majoring in economics and conquering his classes with ease. He ventured into the comedy clubs of Manhattan on Friday and Saturday nights to check out the comedians, Eric sometimes tagging along, wiping his chair seat with a handkerchief he brought along for just that purpose. The two of them would laugh and groan at whomever was onstage. Eric would lean toward Hag, feeling no pain due to his new friend, Jack Daniels, to whom Hag had introduced him, and in a barroom slur, whisper, "Jeez, Hag, you're funnier than that. When're you gonna get up there?"

⁂

The main entrance to The State University of New York at Delhi was easy to find. Hag had never heard of the school when Simon Sissell's mom told him that was where Ned was attending college. After the horrific accident in June, he heard through the grapevine that Portia Sissell was taking it upon herself to be the clearinghouse for all matters related to Ned. After the hospital released Ned to her care, Portia Sissell amassed names and addresses and telephone numbers of all Ned's friends and notified everyone where he was staying. They could reach him by sending mail to Simon's house once he left for college. She withheld the phone number for contacting Ned, sensing he wasn't ready to talk.

Now that he had arrived at the college, Hag could see the folly in his escapade. Ned's whereabouts this weekend were unknown to him, and even if Ned was on campus, his friend might not want Hag's company. He followed the signs to Farrell Student Union and parked in the visitor's lot. There were only three spaces, all of them vacant. The campus was charming in its bucolic isolation, with the fall rainbow of foliage speckling acres of trees across rolling lawns. A modest circular fountain bisected the stone walkway leading to the student union entrance, offering an inviting sound. Hag couldn't imagine himself living here and was more than a little curious to find out what had brought his chum to such a remote school. "What the hell do you do here for fun?" he wondered, as he climbed the steps and entered the central foyer.

"Excuse me, but can you tell me where I could find a friend of mine? He's a freshman here." Hag put on his most charming smile as he made eye contact with a short girl who was seated on a stool behind the front desk, engrossed in an open book filled with mathematical equations. He recognized it as Calculus I.

"I'll see what I can do," she smiled back. She rotated the stool to face a wall of drawers and asked, "What's your friend's name?"

"Ned Godwin," Hag replied, thinking maybe this would not be so hard after all.

She flitted her fingers through the drawer. "Hmm, no Ned Godwin here. Are you sure that's his name?"

Hag had to swallow his laugh. This was not the time to alienate her. "Why, yes, uh," Hag glanced at her name tag, "Cindy. I'm pretty sure. I've known him my whole life."

Now Cindy laughed. "Stupid question. I'm sorry. It's just that we can't give out any student names if you don't ask about someone in particular, privacy and all that. There's a student with that last name, but the first name is different." Cindy turned from the student catalog and playfully eyed Hag, twirling her hair with her index finger, lips parted.

"Is she flirting with me?" Hag thought. The nightclub scene in Manhattan had been an eye opener for him. There were so many college coeds! He had felt pretty sophisticated and savvy with girls back in Tribute, but city girls were something else. The flirting game was constant, with guys and girls all vying to attract someone for an evening of fun and games. Hag couldn't be sure if Cindy was game, but decided he would play this out and have a little innocent fun. She continued staring him down, as if daring him to play. He stifled a grin when she tossed her hair. Two could play this game. "Well, Cindy, let's see. How many guesses do I get before my chances are timed out?"

"What?"

"Never mind. Now I'm the one being stupid. How about Benedict Godwin?"

Her grin blossomed into a warm smile. "There you go, uh...?"

"Just call me Hag."

"There you go, Hag. I can't tell you where he lives, but I'll ring up his dorm floor and maybe the R.A. can put him on if he's in his room."

"Thanks, Cindy. That would be great!"

Jeff, the R.A., told Hag that Ben, not Ned, was not in his room. Jeff couldn't provide information on Ben's whereabouts since the class schedule posted on his door showed no classes on Friday afternoon. Before hanging up, Jeff added, "You night try the natatorium. He likes to swim laps."

After another fifteen minutes chatting up Cindy, with both of them understanding that this spontaneous flirtation would go no further, yet enjoying the sport all the same, he set out on foot across campus with a map showing the way to the pool.

※

Hag stared down at the six-lane swimming pool through a spectator's window on the floor above. He never understood the appeal of swimming laps, going back and forth, back and forth, endlessly, it seemed. What in the world did swimmers think about as they glided up and back? There was no game to be won doing that. At least Si raced, that he got. As evidence of his assessment, he observed that only two lanes were occupied on this Friday afternoon. There was a girl in one lane and a guy in the other, but it wasn't Ned. He should have asked Jeff to leave a note on Ned's door to meet him somewhere later, but he had wanted his visit to be a surprise. He looked about, surveying the swimmers and checking out the lifeguards, who looked bored. Some benches offered a view of the pool, and he sauntered over to one after locating vending machines. With a Coke and candy bar in hand, he thought about his next move.

Up and back, the two swimmers went. The girl was fast, with very little splash, all lithe and flip turns. The guy wouldn't put his head under water, which made Hag's neck hurt just watching the contortions the kid put his upper body through as he crawled toward the opposite wall. Hag stood and carried his trash to the garbage can, examining along the way swim team plaques and trophies on the SUNY Delhi Wall of Fame. "Big fish in a little pond," he surmised.

When he returned to his seat, another swimmer had entered the deck area. He was sitting on a bench, shedding his warm-ups and fidgeting with his goggles. The presence of a full beard and hair flowing down to his shoulders made it clear the guy was not someone who seriously pursued swimming, yet, the guy spent a long time donning his swim cap, and adjusting his goggles just so, before rising to walk toward the pool. Observing his gait, Hag recognized his friend.

༄

Ned stood up from the bench and navigated his way along the wet tile toward unoccupied Lane 4. He left his cane with his coat and warm-ups, being careful to take small steps. His left leg was like a ball and chain. He didn't see how it was ever going to heal completely. He supposed it was a miracle that the doctors had saved it, for all the good it did him. Nevertheless, he conceded that today was an improvement from a month ago. Ned continued to work the muscles in the college gym and walking to class was improving his stamina.

Sitting at the edge of the pool with his feet in the water, Ned thought about how much he missed Si. His best friend always came to mind each time he found himself about to enter the pool. He felt fortunate that Si had taught him the more sophisticated aspects of swimming: dual side breathing, keeping a straight line, head position, proper kick sequences, flip turns, even how to keep count of the lap numbers. Slipping in and savoring the cold water, Ned pushed off with just the right foot, and began his journey to the opposite wall.

༄

Hag scarcely recognized Ned. If they had passed on the street, he wouldn't have given him a second glance. Perhaps if they were face to face, he might recognize Ned's eyes and mouth, but from the neck up he looked like any other generic college student. But Hag winced when he saw the contortions Ned put himself through to lower his body to the pool deck, his left leg behaving like a useless appendage. If he were closer, there would be some tells that it was his high school friend, but, from this angle, Ned could have been a stranger.

Hag couldn't imagine what it must be like for Ned to lose

everything he had. He chastised himself when he thought back to the envy and jealousy he had sometimes hurled at his friend behind his back. Hag always felt that Ned had everything going for him — intelligence, looks, girlfriend, a caring father, and his prodigious gift at the piano. His talent would launch an amazing life, a famous life.

The Tribute Courier had gone to great lengths following the accident to extoll accolades upon Ned's prowess and promise at the piano, praise equally intertwined with lamentations of a career now lost because of the young man's hand injury. There had been quote after quote from the conductor and orchestra members about his incredible performance at the dress rehearsal. Mitch couldn't stop talking about it at Dennis' funeral. Phoebe had been such a mess, she couldn't talk about it at all. Hag felt ashamed, now, for the things he thought back then.

He watched Ned settle into a rhythm after a few laps. Simon had no doubt coached him. His strokes were smooth and even, although they did not propel him forward with much speed. Hag sat still, watching his high school friend swim laps, wondering why he'd thought it was a good idea to come here. His mind drifted back to the question he had posed earlier: "What is Ned thinking about as he moves back and forth in that silent underwater world?"

꽃

Ned flipped the turn and began lap four, what he envisioned as the "four square" lap, recalling Si's lesson years ago.

"The trick to keeping track of your laps," Si had expounded, "is to assign a visual image to each number. When your mind wanders, and it always does when you're not racing, you'll forget if you just finished number seven or are just starting number seven, or is it eight? But if you plant a picture in your head every time you turn, it won't matter where your mind goes after that. You'll still remember the image as you approach the wall to begin your next lap."

Si had been right. So now lap five's image was his hand with five fingers, lap four had been a four square court and lap six was the six pip side of a game die, and so on. Ned had created an image for every number up through 18, then he would start over again, since 18 laps of a 25 yard pool equaled a half mile.

Thanks to his buoyancy in the water, Ned hardly noticed his leg when he swam. The stiffness in his left hand didn't have any impact, either. The water was the most comfortable place for his body to be, so he gravitated toward the pool in his free time. But despite counting laps and planning his classwork, he couldn't escape the tragedy that plagued him.

Ned thought about the day he left the hospital after being discharged and how Portia Sissell had taken him under her wing. "You're not going home to live by yourself, Ned," she had simply stated when he announced he thought he could take care of himself. "Your mom is at Gentle Breezes Nursing Home now and even though Karina lives at your house, she works all day. You can't recover by yourself, that's all there is to it."

Portia had supported him in creating a list of tasks to be completed before college began. The most challenging part had been the mountains of legal paperwork, it being nearly impossible for Ned to think clearly. On top of the crushing pain of losing his dad, Ned felt lost without his piano career. He didn't know who he was anymore. He'd had no choice but to rely on Joe Mains, his father's lawyer, for help.

Joe Mains had been a fixture in the Godwin house for as long as Ned could remember. He was a giant of a man and must have weighed 300 pounds, yet moved with a grace that defied his frame. He came to dinner every couple of months and in the summer held backyard barbecues and pool parties that Dennis and Ned attended. Ned thought of him as an uncle, and Joe was kind to him. He had never married, which Ned always felt was too bad because Joe would have made a great dad.

"It's hard to feel depressed when you physically exert yourself," Joe had said to Ned, that day at his office when he'd called Ned in to discuss his father's estate. "When you're feeling low, get up and move! It works every time, I promise you. You might not know it to look at me, but I start each day with a brisk walk around the block, rain or shine. Get's my heart pumping, you know what I mean?" Ned had started to say something but didn't get the chance. Joe had motioned for him to sit, then settled into his own chair behind an enormous desk. Ned would never forget what came next. "Now, before we get down to business, Ned, do you mind if I say something about your dad?"

Ned sat in a leather chair with his head down, fumbling with his broken fingers as he faced the gentleman behind the desk. "No sir, I don't mind. I don't mind at all."

"You've been through something awful and I know you're feeling like it's all your fault, but it isn't so. It was a terrible accident that you couldn't have prevented. The police know that. Heck, the whole town knows that. You need to understand the truth about that, too. You and your dad had a special relationship, Ned, what with the unfortunate circumstances with your mother. Son, look at me, please. I've known your father since the day he and your mom moved to Tribute. I've known him longer than you, in ways that a son can't know his father. And I want you to understand this, if nothing else. Dennis loved you more than life itself. Why, I can't tell you how many times he made an appointment to see me about some trivial little thing that he could have just told my secretary about over the phone. That was fine. I didn't mind. I knew he just wanted to brag on you. But in all those times he came in, over all those years, even here in 1968, he never bragged about your piano playing."

Ned straightened up in his chair and focused on Joe, his lawyer now.

"I can see that surprises you. The thing is, the piano is yours,

Ned, not his. His pride and his joy came from just being your dad and watching you grow. He was proud of how you were turning out, as a human being, I mean. Raising his child in the way he had always wished he had been raised was something he cherished. Knowing that as we both do, Ned, you have to know and believe that your father would not want you to stop living your best life. Don't you agree that's so?"

Joe folded his hands on the desk and stared forward as Ned realized Joe's question was not rhetorical. Yet he couldn't respond. The words "best life" echoed in his head. He hadn't considered any life, let alone some kind of best life, since the accident. He couldn't even imagine what that might look like. "If I'm not a pianist anymore, what am I?" he thought.

"Ned?" Joe asked, waiting for an answer.

Jolting back to reality, Ned mechanically replied, "Yes, Joe, I think that's true."

"All right then," Joe said. "Let's get down to business and let me tell you how things are. I can't bring back your dad, but I think maybe you'll feel a little bit better when we're done here."

After Joe explained Dennis had left him financially secure, Ned was, indeed, less despondent that afternoon. Yet when the sun rose the next day, it had been a struggle to get out of bed, the anguish in his heart still tearing him apart.

Ned flipped a turn, completing lap eighteen, the "voting booth". Lost in thought, he started over. Uno.

∽

Hag left the natatorium before Ned finished swimming. He walked back to the VW, climbed inside, and set off for the city. Ultimately, he recognized he had no right to intrude on Ned's life like this, especially considering what Ned had endured since his world crumbled. The plan had been foolhardy. Maybe Ned left Tribute so he could figure things out without running into his past every time he looked up. After all, wasn't he doing the same thing in New York? Weren't they all doing that? Phoebe, Mitch, Si, even Dwight, were all trying to figure out who they were and what their lives were about.

He stopped for gas and a car wash in Fort Lee before continuing into Manhattan and had Eric's cherished Beetle back in its home a whole day early. Eric was relieved. Hag was tired, but he wasn't ready to go to bed. He needed to shake the sadness that had come over him since watching Ned swim. He showered and changed, tucked his flask inside his coat, and headed for the subway without inviting Eric along.

CHAPTER 11

Phoebe

It had been an awkward match for the rich girl from Tribute when Phoebe first met her freshman roommate at the University of Illinois in Urbana. Regina Kimani was the first black person Phoebe had ever known. There had been a scattering of black students at Tribute High, but she had known none of them. Despite integrated schools, the mingling of blacks and whites had been infrequent.

Politics, the war in Viet Nam and civil rights had been the topics on everyone's mind during the spring of their senior year at Tribute High. Hag staged war protests in front of the school each morning, just off school grounds, before classes, combining forces with his friend, Alan Marks, from the political science club who would promote Eugene McCarthy for President. And in the weeks following the assassination of Martin Luther King, Jr., there had been several scuffles in and out of the high school buildings during which some black students erupted in their fever of anger and mourning by turning over desks and throwing chairs, one episode occurring in Phoebe's English class. It had been frightening for her to witness that kind of rage.

Regina was a "townie". Her family had lived in Urbana's twin sister town of Champaign for the past six years. Regina's mother, Darla, received her degree in library science from Spelman College and worked at University Library. Omari, her father, was born in Kenya and educated at Spelman, where he met Darla, then received a PhD in history from the University of Chicago. His first academic position was at Knox College in Galesburg, Illinois, where Regina and her two brothers were born. He was now a tenured full professor at the U of I, focusing on twentieth century history.

The two freshman girls could not have been more different when they met in the fall of 1968, yet each had been looking for new experiences, something exciting and free of parental controls. By 1969, their skin color had become just about the only difference between them.

Phoebe was majoring in business, but wasn't sure it was the right path for her. Her father had thought it could be a successful field for women, given the new political scene. Opportunities were opening everywhere for the "new" American woman, liberated from the traditional, confining and demeaning roles of the past. Phoebe was certain her father saw it as the first step to drawing her into his banking and investment business in Tribute. Football games, Friday night Greek parties, Rush, and dating held Phoebe's attention more than classwork. Her freshman courses weren't demanding and since she no longer was playing violin in an orchestra, she had ample free time.

Most fraternity boys, in her observation, had a predictable fixation on one thing, and while she didn't always decline, when she accepted, she often felt regret and disappointment afterward. Ned was her first love, and nobody could quite measure up to the passionate feelings she'd had for him. Their relationship had been so amazing until it soured just before Ned's life unraveled. Phoebe tried to distract herself when her thoughts returned to those woeful days after the accident, when the sadness she felt about how she had hurt Ned was overwhelming. Remorseful that her selfish attitude had so hurt someone she loved, she regretted she hadn't insisted on speaking with him to set things right. But Ned, she believed, was moving on, studying Construction Management, of all things, somewhere in New York. Si's mother had written her a very kind letter just after college started. Ned must have told her something about their breakup because Portia had comforted her with heartfelt words of understanding. Still, the unsettled way things had been left continued to bother her for weeks.

⁂

What a difference freshman year made. The Kimanis took Phoebe in as if she was one of their own. She became a regular at their Sunday dinners in Champaign and embraced the opportunity to discover a family dynamic so different from her own. Mealtime was a boisterous affair during which eating almost seemed an afterthought.

Darla and Omari bombarded their children with questions about their days at school and challenged them with questions about the state of the nation. The current events of the times were at a boiling point after the assassinations, what with the war in Viet Nam, the racial and political tensions, the music, the hair, the rebellion. Regina's parents didn't lecture or scold, rather, they sought the opinions of their children and expected intelligent commentary from them. Phoebe joined in the loud, exuberant debates. Shouts across the table from one sibling to another, arguments about facts, fists pounding the table at one another amid disagreements with the all-knowing opinion of 15-year-old James, and refereeing, when necessary, by the adults, were typical at the Kimani dinner table. Listening earnestly, week after week, as she empathized with their struggles, Phoebe gained a better understanding of what it means to be Afro-American. What intrigued Phoebe the most about these moments, in which she, too, was a participant, was the tremendous love and respect the Kimanis held for one another, when all was said and done. They didn't use demeaning or hateful words, even in the throes of heated exchanges. The hugs and kisses at the end of the evening were as much of the ritual as the cacophony of conversation moments before.

After Phoebe mentioned to her mother in a phone call home that her roommate was Black, Connie's first words were, "How exotic!" For a long time after, Phoebe refrained from suggesting Regina accompany her home for a weekend, dreading the gaffs and insensitivity that her mother would inevitably display. Eventually, however, as Phoebe and Regina grew to know and understand each other better, Regina joined Phoebe for an overnight trip up the road to Tribute.

Phoebe, by this time, was not the obedient daughter of her youth anymore. She had made it clear to her parents that she had a brain and an opinion and that the playing field would be more even from now on. Regina spoke candidly and offered her viewpoint on national issues without reservation. It took just a short while that weekend for Connie to understand that, if she was wise, she would smile and limit her comments to more benign topics rather than embarrass herself and her daughter with ignorant, bigoted opinions. After dinner, Phoebe was pleased to see her father sitting back, apparently enjoying the show, and giving his daughter a covert wink as he sipped his brandy.

✢

Amid required freshman courses of sociology, economics, French, philosophy, and British monarchs, during encounters with new students from Albuquerque, Bombay, New York City, and Rio, and while at the bars on Saturday nights, chatterboxing with other intoxicated freshman without last names, Phoebe felt herself changing in welcome, unexpected ways. She no longer saw her future as some pre-charted course to her parents' upper middle class existence. Phoebe felt embarrassed to be seen driving her Mustang. She attended war protest rallies, initially because everybody else was going, but in due course because she believed in the cause. Her desire for new experiences entrenched in her a new appreciation for the world beyond Tribute, Illinois. The yearning to make her life count and accomplish something worthwhile now defined the young woman.

Over the dinner table on Easter Sunday of her sophomore year, Phoebe announced to her parents her plans to join the Peace Corps. While she had decided months ago to pursue this choice, she had held back sharing her wish with her parents until now. The past year had been difficult for them since her sister, Rachel, had gotten pregnant the previous summer. Despite Phoebe's new persona as a modern woman, she still loved her parents and didn't want to upset them. Rachel had just returned from Virginia, alone, her child having been given up for adoption, and seemed eager to start fresh, and, hopefully, wiser. Phoebe and Rachel had always gotten along pretty well, despite their different interests. However, hearing her mother's sobs at night, in spite of her father's attempts to console her leading up to Rachel's departure, had dampened any empathy Phoebe might have felt for her sister and her plight. But now Phoebe sensed a change in Rachel that registered remorse for her foolish and impulsive behavior of the past. The sisters engaged now in thoughtful, even playful conversations that their parents found encouraging. Perhaps the grievous chapter in the Reid family story was at an end.

Maybe Connie saw her older daughter now with a bit more pride, less discontent. Whatever the case, Phoebe had been correct in her timing, as her mother maintained a civilized tone in her reaction to Phoebe's announcement. It was Mr. Reid who had fearlessly asked the troublesome questions.

"Dad, nothing is going to happen to me! Thousands of college students have done this. It's the Peace Corps, for God's sake. I'm not heading to Viet Nam to fight guerrillas in the jungles of Southeast Asia!" Phoebe had exclaimed. She ended each retort by pursing her lips and shaking her head back-and-forth.

Her father let her have her say, sitting back staidly, calmly waiting his turn. "I hear you, Phoebe, but just grant me a smidgen of respect for my concerns about sending my first born into any jungle. First of all, I fully support your plan." At this, Phoebe relaxed her shoulders, emitting a sigh as she leaned back in her chair at the table. "But I must share with you a true Peace Corps story. In 1966, a young man serving in the Peace Corps in Ethiopia was eaten by a crocodile while swimming in a river. I tell you this not to frighten you—well, maybe a little to frighten you—but mainly to remind you to always be on guard when you're in the wild, especially if you're unfamiliar with the area. Because women washed their clothes in that river, this young man and other Peace Corps volunteers assumed it to be safe. Assume nothing, Phoebe. Think for yourself. Be alert and be smart. That's all I'm saying."

⚜

How long ago it all seemed now. Phoebe wasn't at all certain she could go back to school and pick up where she'd left off. She was part of a different world now. She had seen it with her eyes, felt it with her hands, and had absorbed it into her heart. It was the collective efforts and interactions with the other Peace Corps volunteers, as well as the families from the Cameroon villages where they had been stationed, that had played a crucial role in shaping her and bringing about a noticeable change in her character.

Phoebe felt a buzz of excitement as she boarded the plane that would take her to Chicago. True enough, she assumed it was in anticipation of seeing her family again, but as she reflected on her year abroad, she realized the suspense for what it truly was. It wasn't her family that was drawing her back. And it wasn't Urbana or Tribute. It was the fervent knowledge that she knew now, for the first time, what she wanted to do with her life.

Hours later, Phoebe wrestled the airline blanket from beneath her and used it to block the cold air blowing on her from the ceiling above the passenger next to her. The man was sleeping peacefully now, so she carefully redirected his fan away from her seat, twisting the knob to a gentler setting. He must have moved it while she was sleeping. She had grown used to accepting whatever sleeping conditions she was afforded. After building bridges, clinics and schools in Cameroon, catching naps on dirt floors or against a wall, or zipping up mosquito netting over a cot on 100 degree nights, her sleeping skills were among the most valuable she had gained in Africa. She could sleep anywhere, anytime. Phoebe stretched back and closed her eyes once again, remembering that girl she used to be.

The captain's voice over the speakers, advising the crew to prepare the cabin for arrival, startled her awake. The man next to her sat up simultaneously. He turned sheepishly toward Phoebe and said, "I'm so sorry. I hope I wasn't snoring."

"No, not at all," Phoebe graciously fibbed. "I was sleeping most of the flight myself." Now she focused her mind toward the future, reflecting on how fortunate she was. "Life is good," she whispered to herself as she negotiated the narrow aisle toward the plane's exit. Anyone looking her way would have been entertained by the sight of the young woman sporting a grin ear to ear, slinging a threadbare duffel bag over her shoulder as she made her way off the plane in her worn out, wrinkled attire.

*

"Tribute seems small now," Phoebe realized as she walked down the sidewalk from the library. She would return to Urbana in just a few days to resume her studies in business with a renewed focus, but this afternoon Rachel had asked her to pick up a Robert Browning book of poems, *Men and Women*, from the library. Phoebe found it surprising that her sister would have any interest in poetry, having hated it in high school. Approaching her Mustang, Phoebe was relieved to see she hadn't gotten a parking ticket since she hadn't bothered to feed the meter. It had taken longer to find the book than she had expected. As she turned the key in the driver's door, she glanced across the street and said out loud, "Could that really be him?"

She froze with the key still in the lock. The beard and mustache made him seem older than twenty-one, but his hair was still curly, although longer than she remembered. It had been nearly three years since she had seen him. Observing his gait, her heart sank. Still, he walked erect, head up and intentional in his stride. She called out, "Ned! Ned Godwin! Is that you?" Stopping in his tracks, Ned squinted in the bright sun to see who had called his name. Now Phoebe was certain. It *was* him.

She moved around the car and approached the oncoming traffic. Cupping her mouth with her hand, she shouted, "It's Phoebe, Ned!" In starts and stops, she weaved her way across the four lanes of the busy city street, then ran to him, throwing her arms around his shoulders, enveloping him in a hug. "Oh, Ned, it's so good to see you," she gushed.

Ned willingly returned the embrace, then replied, "Phoebe!" What are you doing in Tribute? I thought you were in Africa somewhere."

"I was. In Cameroon. I just got back a few days ago, but I'll be off to Urbana soon to get back to school." After three years, Phoebe didn't know if they had nothing, or everything, to say to each other. It was clear Ned didn't seem to know what to do or say either, so she continued, "Are you home for summer break? You're somewhere in New York, right?"

Ned finally smiled slightly. "I'll be a senior this fall at The State University of New York. I'm at the Delhi campus majoring in Construction Management. Are you still majoring in Business?"

"Well, technically yes. Oh, but that's a story. And you must have one or two yourself."

"Yes, I suppose I have. Nothing as exciting as Africa, though, I'm afraid."

Phoebe couldn't help herself. She reached forward and gave Ned another quick hug, then stepped back and said, "Oh, Ned, I can't believe it's you. But hey, you looked like you were on your way to an appointment or something when I spotted you. Hope I'm not keeping you."

"Actually, you're right. I'm on my way to my lawyer's office. I'm sorry."

"Oh, no. No problem." Phoebe's heart melted just then at the sound of Ned's voice. She had thought often about him while they had been apart, but had not suspected the timbre of his voice would strike such a longing for what they had been together. His eyes remained locked on hers even as they retreated from one another. She couldn't leave things like this. "Would you want to meet for some pizza and beer tonight, Ned? We could catch up…" she trailed off, fearing she'd gone too far. "Oh, why does this have to be so weird?" she thought, "We're both grownups."

Ned's genuine smile gave her the answer she wanted.

"Sure," he said. "That would be nice."

"Are you still a fan of Monical's Pizza?"

"Does the sun rise in the East?"

They both laughed, at last shedding some of the awkwardness the encounter had occasioned.

"Okay. Why don't we meet there at 9? Is that good for you?"

"That would be fine." He glanced at his watch. "I've really got to run now. Glad you spotted me. I walk with blinders on, sometimes," he trailed off.

Ned headed down the sidewalk as Phoebe darted her way through the traffic back to her car. He was still hobbling along when she glanced back his way before easing into the Mustang.

⚜

"So, Construction Management? What is that?"

Ned sat opposite Phoebe in the back booth of Monical's where they had sat so often before. The decor in these well worn, busy little family restaurants never seemed to change, even when it should, she supposed, eyeing the tear in the vinyl seat that she recalled seeing five years ago.

Ned grinned back at her. "It has to do with building and construction. I'm actually focusing on the residential end of things. We learn how to manage projects, directing the construction, deal with contractors and architects and such. It's a promising career; SUNY Delhi places 98% of their grads with companies after graduation, and the starting pay is quite good, usually."

As Phoebe scrutinized his face to see beyond the beard, she gazed into Ned's eyes as her ears took in the voice that she had loved so long ago. "Oh Ned," she silently lamented, as all those times in senior year came flooding back to her. "What made you pick that major? And why in New York?" she asked.

"I don't know. That time after graduation is just a fog. I couldn't even think about college for most of the summer. I was kind of a mess."

"Do you remember your days in the hospital? I must have visited you a dozen or more times. We all did."

"Yeah, I know that, now. I just don't remember much about the visits. I should have written to everybody to thank them. It's just, I have little bits and pieces up here," he tapped the side of his head, "of seeing some of you then, but I don't really recall conversations." He stopped for a moment, breathing in Phoebe's scent, then fixed his eyes on hers. Caressing her hand and bringing it to his face, he said softly, "I remember your perfume, Phoebe."

Phoebe let her arm linger across the table, feeling the heat from Ned's breath on her hand. It was titillating. For what felt like an eternity, but in reality was only a moment, they locked eyes as if they were back in high school before composing themselves as they sat back and drank from their mugs. Phoebe tried to remember where they had left off in the conversation, but her mind was a blank. She had asked Ned a question but couldn't remember what it was.

Ned said, "Mrs. Peat, the guidance counselor, actually helped me find a major, or at least an area of study. She had me fill out a questionnaire where I answered a gazillion questions about things that I like to do, don't like to do, you know, picking me apart to see what my natural talents are."

"Oh, that's intriguing. So, what did the test show?"

"It said that I was good at math, had a talent for figuring out how things can get done, and I was artistic. I don't know about that one. Anyway, it suggested I would have a high potential for success in engineering, teaching, drafting and management."

"Did you answer questions about having a musical background?"

"It asked about manual dexterity, but no, not about music in particular. I don't think it was that type of survey."

The server came by and they ordered a pizza with pepperoni and peppers and a couple more drafts. Phoebe changed the subject. "Are you happy in Delhi?"

"That's a good question. I suppose so. I'm happy enough with the course of study. Didn't quite know what to expect when I got there, of course. I had two roommates for the first year. They were both artsy, one a ceramist and one a painter, so they were constantly working on projects when they weren't in class. And I ended up in a similar situation where I had to work together with other students on practical assignments that demanded regular meetings outside of class. To tell the truth, I was fine being so busy. My roommate skills weren't that great. I wasn't very open or friendly with them, if you know what I mean. To be honest, Phoebe, I was in a blue funk and still am, I guess. They wanted me to go to Woodstock with them, but I declined. Can you believe that?" Ned took a long chug of beer and looked across the restaurant, coming back around to face Phoebe once more. "But what about you? What made you join the Peace Corps? I want to hear all about it."

Phoebe told him about her adventures. The beer had relaxed her and the nervous tension of the meeting had disappeared. To his credit, Ned never seemed to lose interest. He wanted to know what the villagers' lives were like, what they ate, what she learned while she was building bridges and homes. With each new question, he lead her on to another story, which she was so eager to share. Eventually, she realized he was deflecting the conversation away from himself. Phoebe felt certain Ned wasn't going to share anything personal over pizza. She thought, "He's still so damaged, even after three years." She wanted to change the subject and talk about what had happened between them, but just didn't dare go there yet.

"I have an externship in Texas next semester," Ned volunteered abruptly.

"Really? Texas. Oh, wow! Si's down there. Will you be able to see him?"

"I'm sure I will at some point; I haven't been very good at keeping in touch. Portia told me he keeps asking about me."

Phoebe could see that Ned was a little buzzed from the beer as he hung his head forward over the table..

"Oh, God, Phoebe. I've been just terrible… not keeping in touch with any of you, especially after you visited me and wrote me letters and everything."

"Don't do that to yourself, Ned. We all get it. I think you're doing great. Look, nobody can know what it's been like for you." Ned turned his head, his eyes searching the room for nothing in particular. Phoebe was dying to ask him the question that had been on her mind since she saw him on the street earlier.

"Have you been playing?" she asked, then instantly regretted it.

Ned seemed unfazed by the question as he stared vacantly across the table at her, as if defeated. He didn't respond right away, but soon enough took a deep breath and let it out. "Have I been playing? I wondered when you were going to ask." Ned drained what remained of his beer.

"Phoebe, I play every day. Every hour of every day. I play when I read, when I swim. I play when I'm walking to the dining hall to eat. I play while I'm in a lecture. I hear it all, *The Emperor*, that is. All the time. I can't get it out of my head. Each note, every inverted scale, every arpeggio, every trill. I hear the orchestral parts, too. Can you believe it? And when I'm particularly low, I let the Adagio consume me. I finger those incredible, slow melodies I adore, as they play in my head until I can hardly stand it. It brings me to tears, sometimes, Phoebe, so help me. When I think I can't stand it one more time, that I can't bear to hear those final beautiful, pleading notes as the Adagio fades, do you know what I do? I play it again. Isn't that sick?"

"Oh, Ned," she whispered, choking on the words.

"I loved it *so much,* you see. Not only the music itself, I loved the process. How I could read notes on a page and turn them into something sublime. How my fingers were so agile, so capable, as if there was nothing I couldn't play. Even now, I close my eyes and pretend I'm on stage, playing for you and Mitch that night. Do you remember it, Phoebe, that amazing night? I do, every minute. I imagine seeing my dad in the front row watching me perform for him on Father's Day. Ah, my dad." He wiped his eyes with a napkin, neither of them saying a word. Phoebe drew his hands to hers, kissing the scarred digits of his left hand.

"When I'm feeling good, I play the parts that are joyful for me. I sit at my desk and finger it," he said, all the while his fingers joggling in the air between them. "They haven't forgotten the notes,

Phoebe." Ned paused, lifting his mug for another swig, then finding it empty, returning it absentmindedly to the table. "I'm sorry. The proper answer to your question is no, I haven't played a note."

"But why?" was all she could say.

Ned pulled back his hands, resting his elbows on the table, while he spread his fingers apart, palms facing him, staring at them, as if examining them for the first time. "The right hand is fine. It wasn't injured at all." Ned stopped himself, debating if he wanted to share more with Phoebe. They had been soul mates once upon a time, so at ease in the company of the other that they told each other things they would never have told another living soul. "I've kept this part to myself, Phoebe, but the day they took the bandage off my hand, I wanted to die. It had hurt very little while bandaged because of the pain medicine they gave me for the leg, so I figured my hand would heal and I'd return to playing in a few weeks. But it was so much worse than I'd imagined." He traced the scars with his fingertip, adding, "These wounds were so ugly, the skin all torn up, dozens and dozens of stitches. I nearly vomited at the sight, didn't see any point in being alive anymore." Ned raised his head and looked into Phoebe's eyes, so grateful she was here with him now. "Just before the truck hit us, Dad unbuckled his seat belt and wrapped his arms around me and covered my body with his. That's why my right side wasn't injured. The left side took the damage. My face." He traced his fingers along the four-inch scar, running from the side of his nose down to his jawline. The scar, barely noticeable beneath his beard, was a continual reminder of the day. "My leg was fractured in five places. They probably told you all this at the hospital."

"No, Ned, they didn't. I mean, maybe they said some things, but nothing specific. The hospital was very protective of your privacy. I didn't know the part about your dad. Please go on, I want to hear anything you want to tell me. It's just so good to be sitting here with you after all these years." She squeezed his hands, forgetting his injury, but softened her grip as she remembered.

Ned said, "The leg has mended as much as it ever will, I suppose. You've seen the way I walk. I've come to grips with that. I get along with the cane, but in this hand, you see where the surgeons did all the stitching and repair work on the three middle fingers? They look pretty straight and really, they're quite functional." Ned made a fist, opening and closing it. He wriggled the fingers all around to prove his point.

Phoebe looked at his hands, then up at Ned's face. "And so?"

"The problem is that the hand isn't supple. The fingers can bend, but only together as a unit, see?" He showed her how, even when he would try to press an imaginary key on the table with his index finger, the second and third fingers would follow with it.

"And physical therapy hasn't helped?"

"This *is* what physical therapy did. Before PT I couldn't use them at all. I have some exercises I do to keep them as flexible as I can, and there's a warm wax bath I sometimes put them in when it's freezing because they ache in the winter. I suppose they're better now than they were a year ago, but I don't expect a full recovery. That's why I don't play, Phoebe. I can't stand the thought of it not sounding like it used to sound. Or of it not sounding like it does in my head."

"So what? Ned, you still have this enormous talent. It's not gone, it hasn't disappeared. Different, maybe. Look, I'm not one to give advice. What do I know about playing the piano? But I have to tell you something I've learned this past year. I watched the people in those African villages. They genuinely have nothing. They live in what you and I would call poverty. The children run around without clothing or shoes. All of those homes and bridges that we taught them to build? Half of them will be gone in five years, from the rains. Half. They all know it. Their crops may grow well, or they may not.

"You might presume their lives are filled with despair. But you'd be mistaken because they're inherently content. Don't get me wrong. In many areas of Africa, and elsewhere in the world, poverty is so extreme that people perish every day from disease and malnutrition. But, in the villages that I worked in, the families have some resources, the UN helps, and so they're able to sustain their communities. And they are communities, Ned. They all rely on one another every day, offering each other a helping hand. I'm taking a long time to get to what I want to say. This is what the native people of Cameroon taught me, Ned: The future is uncertain, you don't know what tomorrow holds and you can't relive yesterday. To make your life count, you *have to* own each new day for what it is." Phoebe paused for only a second or two before adding, "and it's okay to rely on your friends, that's why we're here."

In the quiet that followed, Ned and Phoebe leaned back in the booth, both exhausted from their intense conversation. Ned's head was swimming from too many beers, but he didn't regret having been so open with Phoebe earlier. It was just the two of them tonight, and an otherwise empty restaurant. Still, he could hear the voices of all their friends echo in his mind as if it was a Saturday night, and he'd be up at dawn the next morning to deliver newspapers. He smiled at the lovely woman across from him even while registering a note of lingering nostalgia for days gone by.

Phoebe's eyes wandered over to the piano that sat where the bands played on Saturday nights. She smiled at Ned with a mischievous look in her eyes. "Why don't you go over there and play me something, with just your right hand, if you like. Would you do that for me, Ned?"

With a diffident smile, Ned ran his fingers through his hair, pulling it behind his ears. Massaging the back of his neck, he studied the ancient upright piano in the corner. Finally, he stood, but didn't walk to the piano. Phoebe's shoulders dropped.

"It's late, Phoebe. Are you all right to drive or should I get you a taxi?" he asked, offering his hand as she stood.

"I'm okay, Ned. This was lovely."

They walked hand in hand outside to her Mustang.

"It's still a beauty," Ned remarked.

"Yes, I suppose so. G'night, Ned. Best of luck with your externship." She gave him a hurried peck on the cheek, then climbed into the driver's seat and revved the engine. Without looking back, Phoebe journeyed home, sobbing inconsolably.

CHAPTER 12

Simon

NED KNEW THIS house, this kitchen, as well as his own. He had helped paint it the current shade of yellow when Si's dad had promised to take the boys to Cedar Point Amusement Park in Sandusky, Ohio, for an overnight back in the summer of 1967 if the two boys would do the job. It was their first experience painting, and Edward had to instruct and supervise so much that he surely could have completed the task more expeditiously by himself. But he seemed to enjoy teaching the boys a useful life lesson that would come in handy.

Ned thought Si's mother and father were about the nicest, most wonderful parents a kid could have, not that Ned didn't love his parents, because he most certainly did. At Si's house, Ned saw the couple act as a team, and witnessed how, together, they parented and interacted with their only child, their twenty-year age difference not causing any apparent issues. Ned's own life lacked this family dynamic because of his mother's illness.

Ned would forever be indebted to them, particularly Portia, for taking care of him after his release from the hospital that summer of 1968. He hadn't wanted to impose, but Portia had just taken over and insisted that he stay with them, occupying Si's bedroom since Si had begun early summer studies at Rice before the freshman fall semester began. The plethora of doctors, nurses, and therapists involved in his post-operative care had done a good enough job, as far as Ned could tell. He hadn't been in any condition to make such an assessment with any authority, or interest, for that matter. They had performed well, taken meticulous notes, measured, assessed, poked and prodded, until his chart was inches thick. But Portia seldom was interested in rehashing the minutiae that was his physical recovery. Ned surmised she was aware of others taking charge in that endeavor. Portia was more concerned with what was going on inside Ned's head. He wanted to reassure her and told her he was feeling more clear-headed day by day. It wasn't exactly true, but Ned thought he could make it true if he kept saying it. And even though he had been withdrawn, morose, and depressed, Portia had a knack for knowing what to say, what to ask, and perhaps most appreciated, when to remain silent. Still, he struggled to move on from the day that changed everything in his life.

The May air outside was hot and sticky as Ned sat across from Portia Sissell at her kitchen table. Although the sun had just risen, both individuals were wide awake and holding onto their cups of Earl Grey, fingers laced around their cups as if afraid they might slip away. "I've packed a few more of these scones in a box for you to take along in the car, Ned," Portia remarked as she watched him take a bite out of his second one. "You're sure you don't mind taking this kit bag to Simon? I realize it's not that big, but I know you must have limited space in your Jeep." Portia stood and reached for the bag on the floor behind her.

"Oh, gosh, no problem at all, Portia. It can sit up front with me in the passenger seat." He stood and looked at her with a heavy heart. She approached Ned and wrapped her arms around him.

"I can hardly bear to let you go." She stepped back and pulled a tissue from her apron to wipe her eyes. "You're all grown up now, all of you, off to see the world and find your place." She motioned to the bag with her head. "I don't think Simon will ever live here, at home, again. Those are all of his keepsakes, Ned. He asked me to gather them up, when he called last week. I could hardly see through my tears as I put them together, so many memories. It makes me sad, but Edward and I are proud of him, you know. I do feel better knowing you'll be seeing him these next few months during your externship. You two are good for each other. When he called, I could tell that something was going on with him, you know? I wouldn't say he sounded troubled, per se—and Edward says he doesn't know what I'm talking about, that Si sounds just fine to him—but a mother knows these things."

"I spoke to him just the day before yesterday, Portia, and he sounded great, thrilled that I'm coming down. I'm sure everything is all right."

She eyed him with doubt and a loving smile. "Righto. Now, you best be moving along. Miles to go and all. Pull over and take a nap if you need to, those mid afternoon drowsies can sneak up on you, Ned."

"Okay. I'll watch out for that. And I promise to drive carefully and not speed." He picked up the kit bag and stepped outside the front door, walked down the drive, and drove off with a wave to the misty-eyed Portia.

⁂

Ned snacked on the scones, but just outside Memphis he was craving some proper food. Spotting a sign for Billy Bob's BBQ, he decided to give it a try. He'd never had any true southern barbecue, so he was eager for a taste. After consuming half of his pulled pork sandwich and all of his Coleslaw and fries, he decided he was unimpressed. "Maybe it's better in Texas," he thought.

The scenery along the route was new to Ned, and he enjoyed

anticipating what lay around the next bend. Spring turned into summer the further south he traveled, the trees filled out and the temperature climbed. Even though it had been nearly three years since the accident, his thoughts were forever on that terrible day each time he passed an eighteen-wheeler. If one came around to pass him on the left, he'd perspire and his entire body tensed. He wondered if he'd ever get used to seeing one without being stressed.

Despite the cup of coffee he brought along from lunch, Ned got drowsy within an hour, just as Portia had predicted. He pulled over at the next rest stop, deciding to take a half hour nap. Finding a shaded parking spot, Ned settled in. He reached back to retrieve the pillow he'd packed and propped it against Si's bag, but it didn't feel quite right. Something hard and unforgiving was in the way. He didn't think Si would mind if he unzipped the bag and adjusted whatever was pressing against the side. It was a tin of cookies that Portia had packed for her son. Ned didn't touch them, but lifted the tin out of the bag. Staring back at him were Si's junior year swimming trophy, a stack of rubber-banded letters, a small souvenir baseball bat from the Louisville Slugger Museum, and an assortment of items that likely held sentimental value only for Si. He was about to zip the bag closed when he noticed a sheaf of papers tucked in an extra compartment along the inside. He pulled them out and quickly recognized them. They were Si's prize winning senior paper about his parents. Si had titled the thirty-page document "An Unlikely Union" and there, on the cover page, after "by Simon Sissell", was the big, red A+ that Mr. Chu had awarded it. Si had also been the recipient of the senior award for best writing at the graduation ceremonies, but, of course, Ned had not been there to congratulate his friend. There, also in the pocket, was the certificate. He recalled seeing the paper in Si's bedroom during his convalescence, and Portia had encouraged Ned to read it if he chose, but somehow he never got around to it. Ned was, he would have to admit, too consumed with self pity and anger at the time to venture beyond his own misery.

Now, though, he began reading it. Ned hadn't read anything Si had written for school and was unprepared for the beauty of his prose. Si told a story that utterly reshaped the impression Ned had of Portia and Edward. He had only known the couple as Simon's parents, never considering their lives before Si was born, lives he assumed to have been as boring and uneventful as his father's. Despite being engrossed in their personal history, Ned fell asleep in the afternoon heat and didn't get back to the tale until that night in his motel room just south of Little Rock, where he'd kicked off his shoes and jeans, laid back in bed, manuscript in hand, and didn't stop reading until the end.

❧

Born in 1905 to working-class parents, Edward Sissell was the youngest of four children. The boy was undeniably a surprise, his nearest sibling, Anna, being ten years old when Edward was born.

At age thirteen, Edward narrowly escaped perishing in the great influenza pandemic of 1918. Because he was the youngest and their only son, Edward's parents interpreted his recovery as a sign from God that the boy was destined for glory. His older sisters were all married, with husbands and children of their own by this time.

During secondary school, Edward excelled in mathematics and physics, leaving behind his cricket bat and soccer ball for a slide rule and graph paper. So it did not surprise his mother and father when he gained admission to Oxford University on a scholarship. Edward's award supported his tuition, but as a resident in the nearby village of Wolvercote, just a short bicycle ride from Oxford, he lived at home while pursuing his undergraduate degree in Materials Science. His father was particularly proud, as Edward would be the first college educated member of an extensive Sissell family tree. The young man's field of study could offer an ambitious graduate a solid footing upon which to find employment and establish himself in order to provide for a wife and family.

But as sometimes happens, the young graduate found he was not happy or fulfilled in his chosen career. He developed a probing curiosity about the design and architectural details of the buildings he often had to evaluate to ensure compliance with the building codes of the time. To the dismay of his parents, the now resolute Edward sailed abroad to the United States to study at Cornell University School of Architecture.

The class assignments were not without challenges, but he found that with his expertise in materials science from Oxford, he could be the firebrand that propelled his study group forward, often completing projects with time to spare. Edward's group engaged in late night debates regarding the successful architects of the era, from Mies Van Der Rohe to Frank Lloyd Wright. Edward's style matured, his self-confidence solidified, and his admiration for the Arts and Crafts genre intensified during his years in Ithaca, NY.

Not long after receiving his architecture degree in 1930, Edward traveled west to Wisconsin. He was among the first of Frank Lloyd Wright's architectural apprentices at Taliesin, Wright's innovative campus for architectural creativity, and followed the master to Arizona when Taliesin West was established. Edward's background in materials again asserted itself when Mr. Wright plucked Edward from the pool of apprentices to join his team in the development of a residential project in Mill Run, Pennsylvania. Wright envisioned a house that could blend into the land and river around it, naming it "Fallingwater." Edgar Kaufmann, the owner of Pittsburgh's Kaufmann's Department Store, had acquired the property, and according to Wright, it was to be a completely unprecedented construction. Though the novel, untested design placed extreme demands upon the materials chosen by the architect, Wright had confidence in his radical plan. Edward's team would be tasked with producing the preliminary calculations, as well as the final drawings for obtaining the permits. But just a year into the project, Edward had had enough of the renowned architect. Wright had become increasingly demanding, yet absent. It might have been a case of figurative disagreement, but Edward was eager to establish his own practice, and he missed England and his family. So, in 1937, he returned to Oxford and set out to become the town's finest architect. He was 32 years old.

Portia Coulbeck was born on November 14, 1925, in the maternity ward of London General Hospital. She was the second of three children born to Simon and Marian Coulbeck. Simon's oldest brother, Cedrick, was a Member of Parliament, and his twin brother, Nigel, was an oral surgeon. Though not as glamorous as the careers of his twin brothers, Simon's real estate business was successful, employing twelve agents.

The responsibilities of business ownership required that Simon work six days a week, which meant he saw little of his wife and children. When Hitler invaded Poland on September 1, 1939, Simon, at 44, was too old for national service, but he volunteered to prepare his neighborhood for any eventuality of war. And while he was altruistic in his deeds, he also wanted to keep his own family in the best possible position of safety. The inevitable declaration of war with Germany came from Churchill just two days after Germany's invasion. Little did anyone know it would last nearly six years, or that the Blitz would take the lives of Portia's parents, brother and sister.

At age 35, Edward Sissell had been called to service in 1940, enlisting in the Royal Air Force. After six months of training, he was flying missions. He survived his tour of duty and returned to Oxford in 1943. The war had put a stop to new construction, so Edward had little architectural business and earned a living teaching mechanical drawing and materials classes at Oxford. Hitler had visited the town years before the War, deciding it could be a proper place to live in the future, so had ordered its preservation. The town would remain untouched by German bombs.

It was there, at Oxford, that the teacher met the pupil. Their paths crossed quite by accident in the cafeteria. She was a student of art history, which fascinated him. He had attended college in the United States, which intrigued her. They would both later describe their meeting as "magic". In spite of their age difference, the two married in 1944. After the War, Portia gave up her university studies to follow her new husband back to the US, where he could establish his own style of architecture. While employed by Frank Lloyd Wright, Edward had visited Springfield, Illinois, to consult on one of Wright's private home projects. It was here the young couple settled and where another previous FLW apprentice, Jackson Wood, was kind enough to offer Edward an associate position until he could get his name established.

Portia was delighted to be living in "The Land of Lincoln." The war years and deaths of her family had taken a toll on her, and she was looking forward to a new and better life. She began working at the local library and volunteering at the art museum, but before long found her calling as a docent at The Lincoln House on 8th Street.

After trying to get pregnant for five years, Edward and Portia resigned themselves to being childless, despite the doctors finding nothing wrong with either of them that would prevent Portia from conceiving. In the end, a doctor suggested that the stress of trying to conceive for five years could be a factor. He suggested they stop "trying" to have a baby and "just have fun". Four months later, Portia was pregnant. They named the baby Simon, in honor of her father.

❧

The sweeping plains of Nebraska and Oklahoma, with their sprouting crops of spring grains contrasting with imposing oil rigs, intrigued Ned as he passed by them. It was as though he had entered another country, so foreign to him was the landscape. One could spot a farmhouse on a knoll, yet not see another one for miles. He wondered what it must be like to grow up in such isolation. Nonetheless, a child brought up in this geography would see these surroundings as normal. He could imagine a large family with everyone playing a role in the family enterprise: feeding the chickens, milking the cows, stacking the hay. He supposed even the littlest ones could gather eggs, and by his age, the boys would be operating tractors and combines.

Some homesteads Ned saw were dilapidated and abandoned. Even with peeling paint and rusted fences, Ned saw beyond the decay and imagined these places in their prime, when they had sustained a family, even before the Depression. "These are like those dust bowl homes Steinbeck described," he thought, remembering *The Grapes of Wrath* from twelfth grade English. Another tractor-trailer passed him with a diesel driven "whoosh" and he once again thought of his father, who had grown up on a farm, then served in the Army during World War II doing desk duty stateside. He had shared little more than that with Ned and rarely spoke about his life before he and his mother married. How could Ned not have pressed him for more about life on the farm? Could his father's life actually have been as plain as the man had led him to believe? Surely there had been school chums and picnics with other farm neighbors. Or was it something else? Maybe he had been among those dust bowl victims. Ned didn't even know in what state his father had grown up. His eyes clouded as he regretted this unexplored part of his relationship with his father.

He shook his head and reminded himself to stay alert, for he would soon be in Texas and would need to follow Si's directions to their rendezvous point. Si had told him the map would prove useless once immersed in the dense traffic of the suburbs and the city of Houston. In fact, Si had arranged to be dropped off at a Big Boy restaurant on the city's edge where he would meet Ned and finish the drive to Si's apartment near the Rice University campus.

Ned felt his excitement mounting in anticipation of seeing his friend again after so long a separation. Being with Si back in Tribute had always felt like wearing your favorite tee shirt, but he didn't know if it would feel the same now, because people can change. Ned wasn't the same as he had been the last time he and Si had seen each other. Si had left for Texas before any visitors could visit him in the hospital and though Portia had kept Si informed about his progress, the question remained: how did Si feel about his oldest best friend now?

※

The sofa in Si's living room was lumpy, too short for Ned's lanky limbs, and was upholstered in a fabric marginally softer than burlap, but Ned didn't mind. By the time he and Si had arrived the night before, it had been after midnight. They had talked little in the car, Ned being dead tired from the day's 460 mile drive and Si exhausted from an all nighter the previous day, under deadline to complete a project. Si promised Ned a spectacular Texas welcome the next day and ordered him to get some sleep but be awake and ready to go by nine in the morning. Any doubts Ned had entertained the night before about reuniting with his friend had flown away like a canary out the window.

As Ned lay in the sheets on the sofa, he realized he hadn't felt so at ease in a long time. Si wouldn't look at him with examining eyes or conspiratorial glances that belied some hidden agenda to dissect Ned's state of mind. They would just talk, like they used to do. Ned hadn't been able to do that with anyone since the accident.

"Okay, cowboy," Si shouted as he and Ned climbed into Si's VW Microbus, "first things first. I can't be seen around these parts with anyone as green as you are right now." Si looked Ned up and down. "The jeans will do, but they aren't gonna fit over the boots, so we'll get you a pair of boot cuts at the salvage store. They'll have all manner of worn-in boots for you to choose from. Next, the hat. Now the hat is gonna be my gift to you, pardner. I'll show you a few that you're allowed to wear and you can pick the one you want. How's that sound?"

"Jesus, Si. Do they really let you get away with that down here?"

"What're you talkin' about? Course they do! You're lookin' at the star of The Golden Spur Bar on Southmore Boulevard. Why, I can line dance with the best of them and the locals here cannot get enough of my good ol' boy speak. I'm telling' ya, Ned, I never would have believed someone like me could have so much fun around cowboys and oilmen."

Mouth agape, Ned couldn't help but stare back at Si. Seeing his buddy like this filled him with joy. People do change, that is for sure, and Simon Sissell was exhibit A, or so it would seem. Maybe it was more a case of just another version of the same guy, for this had always been Si's persona: bloom where you're planted, find the good in people, search out the next adventure and go with the flow. Ned admired these qualities, and they were a major reason he loved being with Si. "Portia was right," Ned thought, "this will be good for both of us."

By noon, Si had turned Ned into an acceptable, if not yet believable, Texan. The boots and jeans felt right, but he wasn't at all sure about the ten-gallon hat. As they were making their way across town to a BBQ joint Si boasted couldn't be challenged, Ned decided not wear it. The brisket at Calhoun's had won the Houston BBQ Showdown for the past two years. It turned out to be true that BBQ was better in Texas and the brisket was heaven on a plate.

After lunch, Si drove over to the house where Ned would live during his externship. SUNY Delhi had a relationship with the couple who lived there, Walter and Phyllis Gainer. The couple was in their sixties and rented out their guest wing to the students that came down from Delhi. It was a pretty sweet deal for both parties. The couple did not have to advertise the space each semester, and the students got a bedroom, kitchenette, and bath with a private entrance for a below market rent. Si helped Ned unload the car, then they just dumped things inside his room. He hadn't brought much, just necessities. He could get organized tomorrow, for, as Si said, "We're goin' out tonight, my friend. I've got folks you need to meet, and you've gotta learn some dancin'."

They drove around Houston for the remainder of the afternoon. Ned located the address, just east of Houston in Deer Park, where his externship with Proteus Builders was located. Proteus specialized in building near the Gulf, around the water, and Ned was looking forward to practicing the management skills he had been taught. "I read your senior paper that your mom packed for you in the duffel bag, Si," Ned volunteered as they waited at a red light. "Hope you don't mind."

"Course not. What did you think of it?"

Ned hesitated for a moment. He wanted to give Si a thoughtful reply. "I think you write really well and your parents' story blew me away. It's like something out of a movie."

Si gave a laugh. "Isn't it?"

"Does your mom talk about her family much?"

"Not so much anymore. Not because it's painful to do that. It's just that she told me all the family anecdotes when I was growing up and now she has this life here in America. I only found out about the deaths when I was thirteen. I'd asked her about the War, specifically the Blitz, after I'd seen a show on the telly about it. That was the only time she ever talked about that part."

The light changed and six lanes of traffic inched forward, three against three.

⁂

"But you've gotta wear the hat!"

Ned had been trying, to no avail, to talk his way out of wearing the cowboy hat. It wasn't that he didn't like it or that he felt foolish in it, it just made him feel like a fake, like he was trying to pass himself off as an authentic cowboy, and it felt as though it would fall off if he moved. "All right, already!" Ned gave in, after Si fussed with the adjustments like an eighth grader pinning on his date's corsage for the big dance. "Now get away from me. I'll wear it!"

As Si drove his VW to the Golden Spur, he briefed Ned on the plan for the evening. "When we get there, we can get a couple of longnecks and play a game of pool. You good with that?"

"I'm good with the game of pool, but what's a longneck?" Ned asked innocently.

Si's eyes bugged and he stole a disbelieving glance across the seat at Ned. "Are you serious?" When he looked back a second time, he saw the smallest hint of a grin as Ned stared straight ahead. Si punched him in the shoulder and their conversation went on like that as they drove.

The Golden Spur looked as if it belonged in Las Vegas. In fact, the neon cowboy on the enormous sign reminded Ned of the movie *Ocean's Eleven* from the fifties that starred the Rat Pack. The place could easily hold three or four hundred people. It wasn't just a bar. The venue boasted a giant dance floor, sixteen pool tables, and an entire room dedicated to pinball machines. Even at the early hour of 8:40, couples were already round dancing to country songs. Si knew the words to all the tunes and started singing along and stepping to the beat when it wasn't his turn to take a shot.

"Si," Ned explained, "You're not thinking I'm going to get out there and dance, are you? You've seen the way I walk." Ned took another swig of beer and said, "three ball in the corner." He meticulously lined up the shot, then executed it with a deliberate ease that sent the red ball gently down to the corner pocket, leaving the cue ball inches away from the eight ball for the winning shot. Si, who was no pool player, and knew it, had likely started the evening with the game in an effort to make Ned feel comfortable and, perhaps, let his guard down.

"Nice shot, Fats. Drop that black ball and let's go sit." Si motioned with his beer bottle toward seating near the vacant band podium at the edge of the dance floor. A half wall separated the dancing area from the bar, with plastic cushioned benches lined up, like in a roller rink. "Nobody's gonna make you dance, Ned. At least, probably not." Then, without waiting for Ned to respond, Si grabbed Ned's empty bottle and added, "Go find a seat and I'll get us two more."

Ned felt alone and clown-like, sitting by himself on the bench in his good ol' boy outfit. He hoped Si would make it fast. Gazing about the club, he listened to the twang of the vocalist and the guitars in the song. "Tammy Wynette, maybe," he thought. He didn't expect to hear The Doors over the speakers here tonight. Si was still at the bar waiting for drinks, so Ned went to the men's room. After coming out of the bathroom, Ned saw Si sitting on the bench with two girls, the three of them engaged in an enthusiastic and simultaneous exchange of words. "Must be a couple of Si's friends," he thought. The girl on the end was blond and seemed tallish from the way she perched herself upright on the bench. The girl next to Si was shorter, but still taller than Si, with jet black curly hair and bronze skin. While the blonde girl was pretty, the girl next to Si was a knockout. She was resting her hand on Si's knee as Ned approached, and the girls looked up at him in unison. Then, seeing the girls look up, Si also turned his way.

"There he is, ladies! See, I wasn't lying, was I?" As Ned grimaced, Si stood and put his palms out, as if presenting the evening's starring attraction. "Now, tell me truthfully, have you ever seen anyone as good lookin' as this bloke, present company excepted, of course?" he continued, now with his fingers on his chest.

The blond girl held out her hand. "Hi Ned, I'm Judy. It's nice to finally meet you. I swear, I half expected you to float over here, what with Simon speaking so reverentially about you. I have to say I'm relieved to see you walk just like the rest of us."

"Hi, Judy," Ned said with a laugh. "Si is obviously prone to exaggeration. Nice to meet you."

Si cut in. "And this," Si tenderly placed his palm on her forearm, "is my Eva."

Ned couldn't stop himself from raising his eyebrows. "Hello, Eva."

The audio system started up a new song and Si and Eva swiftly rose as Si said, "Ah! Eva loves this one. Judy, come give my best friend a sweet little dance lesson. This is an easy one, Ned, not so fiddly as some." Then, to Judy, "Be kind to him, now, 'cause he may look like a cowboy, but he's just a Yankee who's never owned a pair of boots, let alone danced the Texas Two Step."

After a quick wink at his friend, Si escorted Eva to the dance floor while Ned and Judy watched for a few moments. "They've danced together before, haven't they, Judy."

"Yes, that's one way to put it, they have danced together before. We don't have to, Ned, if you don't want to, although I'd be happy to show you some basic moves. It's not so crowded tonight and you can see there are a number of guys out there learning."

"Well, okay. I'll try not to embarrass you."

⁂

By eleven o'clock, the foursome had dwindled down to a twosome, just two guys working on their fourth beers and feeling no pain. Judy and Eva had to work in the morning teaching nursery school at the Baptist Church on Katy Freeway. The girls had become close friends, even though they had met just a few months earlier.

"You had enough of this, Ned?" Si shouted. "We can go someplace else that's not so loud so we can talk."

"Nah, this is fine." Ned was completely buzzed and felt great. This was the most drinking he'd ever done. He looked around the place as he took another swig of beer.

"So, what do you think of Judy?" Si asked with a puckish grin. Ned could swear he saw his eye twinkle.

"All right, what are you up to, Si? Do not try to fix me up with Judy, I'm not interested in diving into anything just now. I've got this new job in a new town and I'm just not ready. What's the story with Eva? Is she your girlfriend or something?" Ned studied Si's face for a clue, but Si was in no hurry to answer the question.

"Hang on a sec," Si replied. He walked over to the bar and started talking to the bartender. Si gestured towards where Ned was seated and the two exchanged nods. The place was quieting down, not surprising, Ned supposed, for a Thursday night. Si returned and took his sweet time before settling back in his seat. Ned sat there, trying to determine what was going on. Si was acting all weird. Ned had never seen him like this. Si fidgeted in his chair, fighting back a smile as if he intended to speak, but no words escaped his lips. "Si! Say something! What's with you? What was that all about?"

"Oh, nothing. That's Griff, a friend of mine. He actually plays guitar with the band when they play here on the weekends." Si pointed at the stage and the empty mics, amps, and piano. "I was just telling him who you are, that's all."

Ned nodded and finished the rest of his beer.

"Griff says it's okay if you want to play something, since the place is so empty now," Si said nonchalantly, then turned away from Ned, sipping at his beer and scanning the room. The loudspeaker had gone quiet and there was no country music to be heard.

Ned didn't reply as he looked around the room, too. He saw the staff was cleaning up, carrying trays of dirty dishes past Griff and into the kitchen, back and forth. Several minutes passed as Ned and Si watched as if the cleanup were a stage show.

"Last call, y'all," Griff finally hollered out.

Ned stood up and took a moment to steady himself before walking the few steps to the band podium. He stopped and just looked at it for a while as Si watched him from his seat. Ned stepped up and walked over to the piano and sat down on the stool. He hadn't sat at a piano since the night of *The Emperor* dress rehearsal. He studied the keys, up and down, eventually spreading his fingers and hovering over a few before returning his hands to his lap.

Si watched his friend, and after what seemed a long time, he decided Ned would not play after all. Si glanced over at Griff, who was observing the scene, along with four servers and the dishwasher, and shook his head. They understood his message and started to disperse just as Ned struck a single key. This stopped them. He played the same note again, delicately. He kept doing it, the same white key, seven or eight times before he hit another, then another, and another. After the sixth or seventh note Si realized Ned was playing what he had heard Ned hum so often: the right hand melody of the second movement of the *Emperor Concerto*. The sound took him back to an afternoon he hadn't thought about in a long time.

It was a Saturday in April and he had just finished a home swim meet. He'd arranged to meet Ned at a practice room at the high school where Ned was working on *The Emperor Concerto*. Si listened outside the practice room door for ten minutes, astounded at the music coming from within, before finally knocking on the door. It was then that Ned shared with him the scope of the piece. Having only played clarinet for a year in the fourth grade, Si had not realized how monumental a work *The Emperor Concerto* was, and, more importantly, he learned what the piece meant to his friend. Over the course of the next ninety minutes, in that tiny practice room, Ned rewarded Si with a narrative and a demonstration of why the composition moved him so. Then and there Si discovered a part of Ned he had never known.

By now, even the dishwasher and manager had emerged from the kitchen, eyes glued on Ned. Si listened as Ned continued with the single notes of the right hand. But then he stopped and stared at the piano as before, with his hands in his lap. After about a minute Ned wiped his hands dry on his pants, brought them up to the keyboard, and began to play the left-hand reduction of the orchestral introduction that begins the Adagio. He was simply blocking the chords, but the gorgeous B major key signature left no doubt what was being played. Si waited for it, that moment when Ned would again play those right hand notes he'd just heard a while ago, and the Adagio would return. And then there they were. So haunting in their lament, yet Si knew this was Ned's most beloved part. He was executing every note of the right hand flawlessly, with a phrasing that spoke to his emotional bond with the music. Si closed his eyes and listened as Ned continued the nocturne, savoring its climb, anticipating what came next. His trills went on and on as he climbed the scale. He hesitated only twice and his left hand missed some notes, but he played superbly. Si glanced over at the bar where Griff and the staff were listening.

Ned began the pivotal descent that would bring the second movement to its close. It was just the right hand now, so simple, yet so impassioned. Note by note, slower and slower until his fingers stopped, and he played the last few whispered notes before the key change back to E-flat major for the third movement. Ned fiercely attacked the keys, signaling the start of the Rondo, slamming into the *Concerto*'s major theme, but abruptly stopped and dropped his hands. He immediately stood and walked back to the bench even as the audience at the bar clapped and hooted. Ned didn't acknowledge their appreciation. Instead, he sat down next to Si and asked, "Now, do you see why I don't play?"

"What? No, I don't see!" Si exclaimed, incredulous.

"It's crap, Si. Total crap. Didn't you hear it?"

"It definitely is not crap, you idiot. Is that the first time you've played since '68?"

"Yeah."

Si was stunned by his friend's demeanor. He couldn't understand it. Certainly, there were complications with the left hand. It was far from being performance ready, but Ned still had everything going with the right hand, even the swift tempo. He didn't understand why Ned was so negative about the way he played. Si wanted to pin him down for a better explanation, but watching Ned slouch on the bench with his arms crossed and lips pursed signaled to Si that his buddy was done. Ned's resignation gave off an air of defeat, so Si changed the subject. Reaching into his jeans pocket, he pulled out a plain gold band and slipped it on his left ring finger. "What do you think, Ned? How's it look on me?"

He scrutinized Si. "What's that?"

"It's a wedding band, you dope. Yes, my friend, I'm married! Eva has one just like it." Si continued showing off the ring to Ned, waving it in front of him.

"What! When did this happen? Why didn't you tell me?"

"I just did!" Si kept grinning back at Ned, wide eyed and silly.

"Did you have a wedding and everything? Do your parents know?" Now Ned was rattling questions at him like a Tommy gun.

Si laughed. "The answers to your questions are, in order: March 15, it was a secret, no and no."

"But why didn't you tell me when I got here? And why isn't Eva with you at the apartment? Si, are you all right? Is everything okay?" Ned felt worried now.

"Everything is fine, more than fine. I didn't want to throw all this at you when you got here. I wasn't sure how we'd be with each other after so long. It was actually Eva's idea to ease into this with you. Now that I'm saying it out loud, it sounds lame, but Ned, this is all so new for me, and for her. We're just feeling our way."

Shaking his head and at last coming to his senses, Ned stood up so fast he listed sideways. Steadying himself, he grabbed his friend's arm and pulled him up, embracing him in a bear hug. "Well, congratulations. Damn! I can't believe this, Si. You're married! Oh man, and what a beautiful girl you've got. She's just stunning. Those eyes. You've got to tell me all the details, man."

"I will, I will. But, there's more, Ned."

"More?"

"Eva is pregnant. With twins."

Si was beaming. Ned had never seen an expression of such pride on his friend's face, ever. The guy was in heaven and Ned didn't know what to say. He stood up, yet again, and gave Si another hug. "You better stop talking now, Si, 'cause if you drop any more bombshells, I'll just fall over. But tell me this, seriously, do you two love each other?"

"Oh, God yes."

"Okay, buddy, here's the biggest question. Are you two happy you're pregnant?"

Si wiped at his eyes and smiled ear to ear. "We really are, Ned. But, help!" he chuckled, "I've just jumped off the deep end and I don't know how to swim!"

※

Ned spent all day Friday and Saturday getting himself organized. He sorted all his belongings and stowed them away, trying to make his little apartment feel like home. On Saturday night after finishing a delivery pizza, he studied the information about Proteus that the school had given him and tried to calm his nerves about his first day on Monday. He wasn't sure what to expect. Would they mentor him by having him shadow one of their job foremen, or were they going to just give him something to do alone and watch him sink or swim? Was he ready for this? How much did he genuinely know about the real world of building? Nothing, he feared. Despite a lingering knot in his stomach, he drifted off to sleep on the sofa, not waking until a knock at the door jarred him awake the next day.

"I'm sorry to disturb you, Benedict, but I just wanted to invite you to supper tomorrow."

Phyllis Gainer stood at his door at 11:00 a.m. "It's sort of a welcome, if you will. In the meantime, here are some cinnamon rolls I baked this morning. I reckon you might be a tad hungry?"

"Oh, thank you, Mrs. Gainer."

"Just call me Phyllis, and my husband is Gerald."

"Okay, Phyllis. These look amazing."

"So, Benedict, you can be here for dinner tomorrow at 5:00, then?"

"Oh, gosh. I start my externship tomorrow. I don't think I can get back here by five."

"Right. Of course not. Tell you what. I'll just make a casserole and salad and it will be ready whenever you get home. How's that?"

"Thanks, yes, that sounds perfect. I'll come straight home from work, I promise."

"Oh heavens, Benedict, stop it, I'm not your mother." And with that, she turned and walked back to the front of the house.

The rest of the day was a whirlwind. Si and Ned swam laps together at the Rice Natatorium, then they drove to the house of Pamela Gomez, Eva's mother, where Eva had been staying. As Pamela bustled about in the kitchen preparing dinner, she rambled on about her daughter and Si, obviously taken with Simon Sissell. Pamela seemed to relish sharing with Ned the story of how her daughter found Si.

The two had met at a BBQ picnic held at his classmate Rick's house last summer. Si had been telling a hilarious story in his best Brit speak to an audience that was in stitches over his exaggerated accent. The laughter had caught Eva's attention, so she had drifted over in time to hear the punch line, but nothing more. As the group broke apart, she had sauntered up to the 5'2", bald orator and charmed him into repeating the whole thing to her. His humorous manner held her captive, and he stumbled over himself, so enthralled was he that someone like her found him diverting. Eva, never at a loss for words herself, had finally asked Si, "When are you planning to ask me out?" The rest, as they say, was history. Their connection deepened after that, to the point where they were inseparable. Eva delighted in being engaged to the future architect and became Si's biggest cheerleader, always prioritizing his studies over frivolities. She would read quietly as he studied, or, when he needed to be at school for classes or project work, Eva would stay with her mother.

Pamela Gomez was a native Texan who married Julio, a Mexican from Valle Hermoso. She called him Jules, perhaps as an homage to her French mother. The couple wasted no time in starting a family, first with the arrival of Carlos, then with Eva, two years later. When Pamela was seven years old, her father died in an oil mining accident. Jules was part of a crew constructing a new rig. The family received a substantial insurance settlement, which allowed Pamela the opportunity to be a stay-at-home mom and focus on raising her children. However, Eva and Pamela were now alone, since Carlos had left Texas to work in Detroit building automobiles. Pamela made no secret of her delight with her daughter's pregnancy as she adored Si. Nevertheless, a clear sense of relief appeared on her face as soon as the young couple tied the knot. Her intention was to lend a helping hand when the babies arrived, ensuring that Si could focus on finishing his degree.

After a huge dinner of authentic Mexican burritos and plantains, Ned was eager to return to his apartment and ready himself for Monday morning.

"I'll drive you back now, Ned," Si said. "I want to make a quick stop on the way. There's something I want to show you." Crosstown traffic had lessened at this hour, but there were still many miles of traffic lights to negotiate before they reached the east side of Houston. "So, Ned, I had a letter from Phoebe."

"Oh, recently, you mean?"

"Yeah, about a week ago. She's sounding so focused, eager to get back to school and all. I guess Africa was a pretty amazing experience for her. She said she ran into you."

"Yeah, she seems to know what she wants. Did she say anything about me?"

"Of course. Look, Ned, don't get mad, but Phoebe told me about the conversation the two of you had. She told me about you and the piano."

"Did she now?" Ned replied, peeved. "You know, Si, I was feeling so impressed with you since I've been here. You didn't ask me a single question about it after I got drunk and played at the Golden

Spur Thursday night. It was such a relief that I wasn't gonna have to get into that with you."

"Well, sorry to disappoint bloke…"

Si pulled away from the traffic light and eased up along the curb, hovering. "Here we are."

"What's this?"

"It's a building, of course. A medical building, to be precise. Look at the sign, Ned."

Ned turned his head and squinted his eyes. Dusk approached, making it difficult to read the unlit sign. "I can't read it, Si, it's too dark. Something "Clinic"?"

"It says Houston Hand Clinic. Then it lists the names of the doctors."

"What's this all about?" Ned was feeling anxious. Anger wasn't far away.

Si reached into his shirt pocket and pulled out an appointment card. He handed it over to Ned.

"What's this?" Ned looked down at the card. It read:

BENEDICT GODWIN
has an appointment with
HERSCHEL ELWOOD, M.D.
on
Friday, June 13, 1971,
at
9:00 a.m.

Before Ned could speak, Si held up his arm to cut him off. "Just listen to me before you say anything. Will you do that? Just let me say what I need to say?"

Ned glared back at him with pursed lips and returned the faintest of nods.

"Okay. First of all, Phoebe had nothing to do with this. In fact, she doesn't even know about it. I've heard about this clinic ever since I got down here because my freshman roommate lost a finger. I mean, he completely cut it off in a table saw accident when he was sixteen, and they reattached it. Anyway, Dr. Elwood is renowned all over Texas as the top hand surgeon. In fact, there's a six month waiting list to get in to see him. I set this up for you six months ago, pretending to be you on the phone. And now that I understand about your left hand, it's like kismet, man. Look, when they repaired your hand in '68, they did it in Tribute. Maybe they had the best plastic surgeon available, and maybe he did an excellent job—maybe. Well, perhaps someone who concentrates only on hands can do a better job now.

"Look, Ned, I'm not saying he can do anything different. Maybe he can't. All I'm saying is you don't know what you don't know. Jeez, man! You're a goddam pianist. That's who you are, buddy! C'mon, it's time, man." Si stopped talking and waited for Ned to respond, but his friend just sat there, fuming. "You know, I can't imagine what this has been like for you. I get that. If you ever want to tell me, I'll listen. But think of this. You've been lost in your past now for three and a half years, hiding yourself away from all of us. It's time to get on with things, Ned. It's time to live your best life." Si stopped himself for an instant before landing the last punch. "He'd want that for you."

"Don't you dare go there, Si! How do you know what he'd want for me? The answer is you don't! Maybe I was a pianist once, but I'm sure as hell not one now."

"That's where you're mistaken, Ned. See, you have it all twisted in your head that it's over, you and the piano. You should go see Gretchen back in Tribute. Play for her, talk to her. She'll tell you what's what, for sure. I don't think you're seeing this clearly."

"Shut up, Si. You have no idea what "I'm seeing", as you put it. You want to know what I'm seeing, really? I'll tell you what I'm seeing. Every day I get up and look in the mirror at the man who killed his father. That's what I see, Si. I see the scar under my beard that always reminds me of that day. Did Phoebe tell you that my dad literally unbuckled his seatbelt and covered me with his body, to save me from that truck driver who walked away without a scratch, that got to go home to his family? Why does he get to have a life?" Ned shouted. "Did she tell you all that?"

"Yes, Ned, she told me."

"How do I live with that, Si? Huh? Tell me. If I'd been a better driver, if I'd watched out better, I wouldn't have gotten us stuck in that intersection! I killed him, Si! I killed my father!"

Si had opened a wound that refused to heal and could see Ned's self reproach stabbing at him, even now. His best friend was drowning and Si was helpless to save him. Ned wiped at his eyes and stared out the window.

"He was only fifty years old, Si. My dad taught me everything. He was always there, every day of my life, and I expected he always would be." Ned took in a deep breath and let out a long sigh. Speaking calmly now, he said, "I realize now that I hardly knew him, not really. I don't know what he thought about, or what his dreams were. Hell, I don't even know where he was born." Ned turned to face Si. "I don't know who I am. But I know I'm not the guy I used to be. Maybe someday I won't be so angry. Maybe one day…. oh, I don't know. Just take me home, Si."

"Ned, you don't have to-"

Ned lashed back at his friend. "Cut it out, Si, and stop trying to fix me. It's not your job. Just mind your own business."

CHAPTER 13

Dwight

"Tell me about your week, Dwight."

Doctor Mary Broadmore sat across from Dwight Kato in her clinical psychology office on the third floor of the Tribute Health Systems building. At 72 years old, Dr. Broadmore was a slight woman with arms still firm from regular weight resistance exercise, but her hair was white and thinning. However, she saw Judy twice weekly at her salon on Chestnut Street to get fluffed and coifed, bought fine clothes in Chicago, and took her time each morning to apply makeup and lipstick. Mary did these things, not out of vanity, but because she believed that presenting a professional image to her clients was a way of demonstrating respect for them. Mary wanted her war veterans to see her as the successful clinical psychologist that she was, in full command of her field, able to understand their trauma and, most importantly, gain their trust. She was proud of her seven-year record of success in helping Viet Nam war veterans recover from their psychological wounds.

There was no cookie cutter approach to use with these men, even though every one of them was alike in the general sense—they were all young men who had battled an enemy in a foreign country and were suffering. The similarities stopped there, however, for each man had his own unique story of pain, loss, terror or horror.

Dwight had come to her three months after his honorable discharge from the Army. He had joined up even before graduating from high school, zealously declaring to his recruiting officer that he wanted to "go kill some commies in Nam, man!"

Finding an eighteen-year-old who wanted to enlist, let alone one who asked for deployment to Viet Nam, was rare in 1968. After completing eight weeks of basic training at Parris Island, Dwight's commanders assigned him to the infantry, and he underwent an additional eight weeks of advanced infantry training at Fort Polk in Louisiana. By the time a helicopter dropped him to join his platoon for day one of his one-year tour of duty, Dwight, while raw, was a credit to his M-16 rifle.

By all accounts, both official and anecdotal, Dwight thrived as a soldier in Viet Nam. He avoided any major injuries, and his fellow soldiers held him in high regard, Dwight often volunteering for dangerous assignments. In 1970, Dwight requested and received a second tour of duty, during which things took a turn for him. As Dwight told it, he went through definable stages of consciousness during that second year. It began with a sensation of mental numbness. Nothing bothered him. Likewise, along with his flat mood, he lost any thirst for amusement. As he explained to Dr. Broadmore, "It wasn't really a bad time for me, Doc. In some ways, I felt pretty comfortable. I'd been in the jungle so long that it felt much like home. I remember clear as day when I started feeling that way.

"My platoon was on patrol, like we'd done a hundred times. We're all of us creeping along, single file, and we all knew Charlie could be anywhere. So I started thinking back to my first patrol, you know, when I was just a grunt, and how scared and pumped up I was, all at the same time, my heart beating a thousand times a minute, sweat pouring down my filthy face. Anyway, I realized that everything had gotten all quiet like. I couldn't even hear my footsteps in the mucky crap we were tramping through, almost as if I'd gone deaf, you know what I mean? Like all the insects stopped buzzing, and the bushes didn't rustle when I pushed past them. Stuff like that. It got so quiet I could hear my heart beat, like that's all I could hear, Doc, as if I'm in some kind of vacuum where there's nobody but me and my beating heart. But here's the important part, Doc, my heart wasn't beating fast. It wasn't racing at all. I could feel it, too, just a calm and unhurried tempo, as if nothing remarkable was happening."

Over the next few months, Dr. Broadmore listened as Dwight continued to tell his story. She learned how, when he came out of his numbness, he experienced the exact opposite feeling. Every sound he heard assaulted his ears, to where he could hardly bear it. Then the death sounds began piercing his once impenetrable armor. Those horrific sounds, whether the enemy's or his platoon mate's, crippled him inside. Days after a battle, he would still hear the wailing that's the same in any language. Dwight would replay over and over in his mind a shattered mate's dying words to the medic as the morphine kicked in, "I want to go home now" or "I need my mother."

By the end of his second tour, Dwight was no longer a teen, no longer an innocent. He completed the third year of his enlistment in Germany at a desk, embarking on his search for peace during this time, finding that order and routine calmed him. The work was monotonous, yet demanded his full concentration. He began keeping to-do lists and found joy in maintaining his living space in perfect order. While stationed in Grafenwohr, Dwight befriended a soldier from Minnesota that worked across the hall from him. The two would eat lunch together, sharing experiences from back home. Dwight would talk to Carl about his falconry hobby in Tribute, and Carl would tell Dwight about hunting elk at Mille Lacs Lake. Carl had a tendency to stutter slightly, but it was only noticeable when he got passionate about the subject he was discussing. It mortified

Dwight that in his younger days he would have used the stutter against the guy for amusement.

After finishing his enlistment, Dwight returned to Tribute and his old job at the lumber company, but only for a short time. His pal, Walt, at the falconry club, had talked Dwight up to his friend who owned a contracting business building houses. The friend hired Dwight on as a carpenter's apprentice, and after ten months, Dwight had learned a plethora of skills, now seeing carpentry as his chosen profession.

He earned enough to support himself, living frugally in a one-bedroom apartment and making payments on a slightly used Ford pickup truck. He continued to rely on an ordered life to help him maintain his balance, and, to his credit, sought mental health support as part of his personal journey.

Looking back at Dr. Broadmore, Dwight gave thought to what she had said, "tell me about your week". The doctor routinely started each session this way, so the request wasn't unexpected, on the contrary. As he'd made his way up the stairs to her office that afternoon, he made a point of reflecting on the events of the past week. But, sitting here now, his mind was blank. He couldn't remember what his week had been like, and he understood why.

Minutes before, he had climbed the stairwell to the third floor and opened the door to the long hallway that led to Dr. Broadmore's office. As he'd headed up the corridor, he spotted a young woman approaching him from the direction of the doctor's door. Her blond hair was striking, pulled back in a ponytail to reveal a face bright with resolve. Though she appeared to be no more than eighteen or nineteen, her stride suggested a savvy determination beyond her years, and Dwight thought, "She's checked off another item on her to-do list for today." As they neared one another, their eyes locked and she greeted him with a warm smile. His face flushed and his heart beat faster as he caught her fragrance. He couldn't help himself and took just four more steps before turning his head to take another look, just in time to see her open the stairwell door and look back his way.

~~~

Ned awoke from the nightmare sweating and winded. He hadn't dreamed about Dwight and the vicious ducks, the little girl and the dead falcon in his father's hands, since before the accident four years ago. "What the hell?" He sat on the edge of the bed and rubbed his face. Where had that come from? There had been dreams during his recovery, all of them variations on the theme of the crash, but those had eventually ended, though not suddenly. They just faded and became less frequent until one day he realized he had not had one for weeks.

In a way, it bothered him to have the dreams end. He thought of them as penance for his role in the death of his father. If the dreams disappeared, then he somehow believed it dampened his guilt, but that couldn't be. He still carried that albatross of culpability around his neck.

Ned pulled back the curtain and looked out the window. The sun was bright, but the weather forecast predicted rain for later in the afternoon. This bedroom held so many treasures for him—the window curtains his mother had made before he could even remember, the bedpost where his Micky Mouse pajamas had hung when he was five. This morning, the mirror on his half opened closet door framed a view down the hallway. He felt bound to this bedroom, and to this upstairs retreat of sleepy spaces, home to years of whispered goodnights, muffled footsteps in the hallway, and the faint clicks of closing bedroom doors. Every little nuance of wear in the floors and walls, in the sink grout in the bathroom, in the scratches on the wooden floors, told a tale of his life, a life he couldn't relinquish. "Will it always feel like this, to be in this house, the only house I've ever known?" Ned thought.

He shuffled along the hallway, his hand on the stair banister, then paused in front of his father's bedroom. Ned took notice of the closed door each time he passed it on his way to the bathroom. He hadn't entered the bedroom since his dad died, and it terrified him to think of what might happen if he went in. He dreaded the possibility of smelling his father's scent, for though he yearned for it, pretending it might bring his dad back for just a moment, he couldn't bring himself to chance it. The mix of perspiration, English Leather and wood had engulfed him in those last seconds before the crash. He didn't know what effect it might have on him were he to confront them again.

Descending the stairs, he walked past the untouched baby grand, hearing the opening chords of *The Emperor* in his head, as always. Today, he would drive to the nursing home and visit his mother. She wouldn't know he was there, but he would, and that counted for something. Then he would stop by the cemetery and visit the gravesite and have a chat with his dad. Today was the fourth anniversary.

He brought some flowers along and tidied up the grass around the headstone. The grave had been without any marker at all in the beginning, as he'd been unable to tend to it at first. Until the stone, bearing the names Dennis Godwin, 1915-1968, and Isabelle Godwin, 1920-, was ready, Joe Mains took care of the site. How much longer it would be until his mother's death date was chiseled onto the stone, Ned didn't know. Karina was not optimistic, for there were days when Isabelle just wouldn't eat.

Rain had started falling by the time Ned resolved to track down Dwight at his falconry club. Portia Sissell had heard through the grapevine that Dwight was out of the service and living once again in Tribute, and Ned wanted to talk to someone from the old days. Dwight was the only one around and even if he hadn't been a close friend, maybe he knew about Hag. Ned had never visited the falconry club. Hag had pointed it out once when they'd driven by, just a scattering of forsaken trees bordering a broken-down barn on the edge of a soybean field. As he parked in a graveled area, he could see seven or eight birds in wooden cages. Greeting Ned at the gate of the fenced property was a sign that warned: NO TRESPASSING — PRIVATE PROPERTY. He drew nearer and called out, "Anybody here?" Walking past the cages, he poked his head around the corner of the barn, where he saw a man approaching carrying a bucket.

"Hey there, what's up, young man?"

"Oh, hi. I'm looking for Dwight Kato and thought I might find him here."

"Well, you might have, but he's not here just now. He keeps his bird here, but doesn't stop in 'til after work. Who are you?"

"Oh, sorry. My name is Benedict. I used to know Dwight in high school, but I've been away at college. I heard he got out of the Army and came back here to Tribute. Just wanted to talk to him."

"Well, I can tell him you stopped by when he gets here. But it won't be before 3:30 or 4:00. What's your last name?"

"Godwin, Benedict Godwin."

"You related to Ned Godwin?"

"I am Ned Godwin."

"You the fella that lost his dad in a car crash some years back?"

Ned hesitated. It seemed like that's all anybody would ever remember about him. "Yeah, that's me."

"Dwight's told me about you. You're quite the piano player," the man said with a smile.

"Well, I used to be," Ned replied, eager to stop this line of conversation. He looked back at the cages of birds he had seen earlier. "Say, do you think you could show me Dwight's bird? I know nothing about falcons or hunting, but I remember he really got into it during senior year."

"Sure, I can do that. Follow me. My name's Walt, by the way." He stepped forward, they shook hands, then Walt led the way to the birds. "Here you go. This one belongs to Dwight. He's an American kestrel, the smallest kind, and Dwight's named him Cheeky, if you can believe it. He started out working his apprenticeship with a North American Falcon. I actually got him and his friend—oh, what's his name?"

"Hag?"

"Hag. Right. I mentored both of them, but Hag didn't stay with it. That boy was just too scattered. But Dwight was all in. Course back then, the boy was troubled, thought he was a real badass. To tell the truth, most of the other guys here didn't want him around, but I wanted to give the kid a chance, ya know? He seemed so taken with the birds."

"What happened to his falcon after he left for the Army?"

"Nothing. He's right over there, semi-retired I call him. He's one of my birds, now. Yeah, Dwight started right back up when he got home last summer. Said he was ready to resume training and trapped Cheeky." The two men watched the kestrel for a few moments.

"How old is he?"

"Well, we can't be sure, but Dwight figures he's about a year old, give or take."

"What's Dwight like now?" Ned asked hesitantly. He knew Viet Nam could change men, but he also knew that personalities generally remain constant.

"He's grown up, I guess you'd say. The service does that to a young man. Were you in the service, Ned?"

"Nah, 4F." He pointed to his leg.

"Ah, well, Dwight is what I would describe as… mellow. He's calmed down quite a bit. Anyhoo, I gotta feed these guys. I'll tell Dwight you stopped by."

"Tell him I live in the same house I used to live in. He'll know where it is. He's welcome to stop by anytime because I'm not working anywhere yet."

"All righty. Pleasure meeting you, Ned."

"Same here, Walt. Thanks."

❧

Ned was in the shop pushing things around, trying to decide what to do. Dennis had been a stickler for neatness, and the place was tidy and organized. He had kept the power tools well serviced and covered when not in use, and every hand tool had a home, but an even coat of dust had settled over the entire shop during the past four years of disuse. The shop appeared to have been buried along with Dennis. He heard a knock at the living room door. Karina was inside, watching soap operas. She would get it.

Ned's eyes wandered to the stacks of wood. His father regularly used cherry, oak, mahogany and maple, even select strands of ebony for stringing and inlays. He reminisced about the days in junior high when he would hang out after supper sometimes and watch his dad work. Still sitting in the corner was the table they had built together when Ned was doing woodworking in Industrial Arts class at school. He hadn't thought too much about it. It was just something to do. In fact, toward the end, he lost interest and his dad ended up finishing the legs and gluing everything together.

Karina interrupted his thoughts, leaning out the kitchen door and announcing, "There's someone here to see you, Benedict." Dwight Kato stepped into view, ambled down the three steps, and grabbed Ned's hand.

"Well, look who the cat dragged in," Ned laughed, suddenly finding himself back in high school again.

"Hi, Ned. It's good to see you."

It only took those few words for Ned to sense that the man before him was no longer the boy he remembered. Dwight was thinner, much thinner, and sinewy. He wasn't all beefed up like he was in high school. His facial muscles seemed relaxed, and he wore a softer edge in his smile. When Dwight spoke, his words flowed with a measured calm, sincere.

"You, also, Dwight. Glad you're here. Walt told you I had asked about you?"

"Yeah, he said you wanted to see my falcon. What did you think?" he asked with the slightest smile.

"I was surprised by how small he is."

"Yeah, most people are. He's my best buddy at the moment. We're still getting to know each other. He's pretty young, but smart. You'll have to come with me sometime and I'll show you what he can do."

"I'd like that. Let's go in the house and sit. Want a beer?"

"Sounds good."

Karina had turned down the volume on the television and began busying herself in the kitchen. She brought out a bag of potato chips. "I'm sorry, this is all I've got in the house for you boys. But, I suspect it'll do. Go ahead and visit. Don't mind me." She wiped her hands on her apron and smiled at Ned and Dwight without moving away. "I'm sorry for staring. It's just that it's been so long since there's been any company here. Benedict only just graduated from college and I've missed the ruckus when you all were in high school."

"That's okay, Karina. Thanks for the chips," Ned said.

Surveying the shop, Dwight noticed the neglected machines and tools. He didn't think Ned ever used them, but was curious just the same. "Have you ever built anything with this stuff?"

"Not really." Ned, with a sudden wave of embarrassment, told him about the table, feeling like he'd somehow failed his father.

"Wish I'd had these kinds of tools when I was in school. I loved industrial arts. I took two shop courses senior year, one in drafting and another in woodworking, but I could never do anything outside of school 'cause I didn't have any tools."

"What did you build in wood shop?"

"I made an oak bookcase first and since that was pretty easy, the teacher let me tackle a desk with drawers. That was a lot harder, I couldn't get the drawers to fit right. They kept sticking. Then the school year ended, and I ran out of time. I don't know what happened to it after that." Dwight caught himself, realizing he may have touched a nerve with Ned, bringing up the end of senior year. He stuffed a bunch of chips in his mouth, then washed them down with a swig of beer, changing the subject. "Why'd you want to see me?"

Ned told Dwight about his nightmare and how he had struggled with it time and time again in high school. He didn't mince his words when he told Dwight that he always felt Dwight was the reason for them. He spoke about the torment the bullying caused Simon, as well.

"Yeah, I was a bastard back then, no lie. And I don't make any excuses for it. But I have a better understanding now of why I was like that."

"And what's that?"

"Oh, I don't think you want to hear about that just now. Why don't you tell me about this work you plan to get into? What was college like?"

"That's funny, Dwight. 'Cause that's something I don't want to discuss now."

The awkward gap in conversation had them both fidgeting, eyes scouring the room, trying to find some common ground. When Dwight arrived, Karina had turned down the volume of the television so they couldn't hear "The Price is Right" contestants at the moment. Nevertheless, their eyes were fixed on the screen, captivated by the suspense of who would come closest to guessing the price of the dishwasher.

Out of the blue, Dwight said, "Right. So, Ned, it's like this. And I'm not telling you this as an excuse, because I'm my own person and I'm responsible for how I behave and all. But the reason I was such a shit is that I hated myself back then."

"What are you talking about?"

"You sure you want to hear this?"

"Why not. I'll get us another beer."

When Ned returned from the kitchen, Dwight took a long swallow and started back in. "I hated myself because I thought I was worthless and unlovable. Unlovable. That's the word my therapist introduced me to. She told me—no, wait, she didn't tell me, she helped me discover that I thought I was unlovable because my parents didn't want me. My dad's family is Japanese. He's an American citizen, born right here in the United States, grew up in Oregon, a big family. Then Pearl Harbor happened and all the Japanese-Americans got herded up and re-settled into these concentration camps because the *real* Americans didn't trust them. Long story short, he turned into this bitter, angry man. After the War, he moved to Chicago, but nobody wanted to hire him. He had it rough for a long time, working lousy jobs like cleaning horse stalls, washing dishes, picking up garbage.

"He got a prostitute pregnant and when she wanted him to take care of her and the baby, he just blew up. Told her she should have taken better care of herself, that he wouldn't be responsible for some white whore and her bastard half-breed kid. Claimed it wasn't his, anyway. So she had to take care of the baby by herself. She was a Catholic girl and didn't believe in abortion. And the baby, with straight black hair and Monolid eyes, reminded her too much of the father." Dwight ran his hand through his straight, black hair. "So, neither one wanted me and they made sure I knew it."

"Jesus, Dwight. I don't know what to say. Do you still see either of them?"

"Course not. Not anymore. I've got too much work to do on me these days, and I don't have room up here for that," he added, tapping his head with his finger. "So, anyway, I want to apologize to you."

Ned interrupted, "Apologize to me? Dwight, you don't owe me—"

"Ned, just let me do this. Please. My therapist told me this is how it's done. As I was saying…"

Dwight pulled out a worn piece of paper from his back pocket, and unfolded the five by seven-inch page, and read, "I am seeking forgiveness for the wrongs I inflicted upon you in the past. In doing so, I attest to you that I embrace the four necessities for the same: one, responsibility for my wrong and hurtful actions; two, remorse and regret for my past behavior; three, restoration, to be of help to you in your recovery from my sins toward you; and four, renewal, that I will overcome these sins of my past and find a meaningful life that benefits my fellow man. Knowing this as you do now, Ned, will you forgive me?" Dwight raised his head and looked squarely into Ned's eyes.

Ned couldn't help but stare back at Dwight as he thought about what his friend had said. Was Dwight even his friend? The guy had done a total one eighty from the person he was in high school. Despite the worn out page, it was clear to Ned that it had just been a prop while Dwight spoke the memorized words, seeking a pardon for his perceived crimes against Ned.

"Okay, yeah, I forgive you, Dwight. But we both know who you should really be talking to."

Dwight nodded his head knowingly. "Simon."

"Yeah, Simon."

"It's done, Ned."

"What do you mean, 'it's done'?"

"I mean I've spoken to Si and he and I are good now. I went to see him last month. Did you know he's a daddy?"

"Yes, I know. You went to Houston?"

"Yes. I had to. It's part of the process, man. It's not enough for me to decide to change. There's restitution, righting the wrongs. Didn't you hear me just now?"

Ned tried to absorb this while peering at the muted television. Ned was happy about Dwight's efforts to make things right with Si and impressed by his determination to create a better life for himself. There was a soap opera on now. Squinting at the screen, he leaned in closer, then turned up the sound. It couldn't be. "Dwight!" he said, pointing to an actor on the screen. "Who does that look like to you?"

"Hmm, not sure. Maybe someone from high school?"

"I can't believe what I'm seeing," Ned gasped. "I'll tell you who that is. That's Mitch Shingler."

They glued their eyes to the TV and listened as Mitch berated a gorgeous brown-haired woman twice his age. A tight, sweaty tee shirt clung to his torso as he wiped his face with a towel. Evidently, she was not happy with him because of his failure to show up for a date they had planned.

"I never said I'd be there, Linell. I do have a life beyond the walls of this estate, you know. Besides, I doubt that you truly missed me. Anders took you home, didn't he?"

Ned shouted out, "Karina, what show is this?"

Karina came into the living room wiping her hands on a dish towel. "Oh, this is *Guiding Light*. I don't watch it very often. That's Jason Gane, there. He's a looker, all right, but he's just nasty. Poor Linell can't help herself, though."

Ned pointed to Mitch on the screen. "That's Mitch. He's a friend of ours from high school. Last I heard, he joined the Navy after graduation. I can't believe he's an actor now."

Dwight recognized him now after the prompt. "He played football, didn't he?"

"Yeah, he didn't want to, though. He wasn't very good, but his dad made him play anyway. They didn't get along. Wow, I can't believe this." Ned was entranced, mesmerized by Mitch on the television screen. The reality of it all confounded him. He recalled his angst-ridden friend in high school, so unsettled and unsure of himself. Ned could never understand why such a commanding figure wasn't more confident. Now Mitch was laughing with another character who'd joined the scene, delivering the final jaw dropping lines to end the episode. The closing credits ran with organ music in the background as Dwight joined Ned in front of the TV. They studied the actors' names as they scrolled down the screen.

"There!" Dwight shouted out, pointing. "Jason Gane played by

Mitch Shingler. Hot damn! He even kept his name. What do you know?"

Ned blurted out, "I'll write him a letter in care of the station. I think you can do that, right? What station is this?" He checked the channel dial. "Channel 3, that's CBS. This is amazing!"

Dwight helped himself to another handful of chips. "What do you see of Phoebe now?"

"I don't. She's back in Urbana, working on her business degree. You know she went to Africa for a year with the Peace Corps."

"Whoa, no, I didn't know that. I wouldn't have guessed she'd be into something like that, with all her money and stuff."

"I saw her on the street last year. She's changed, Dwight. She looked great and seemed like she has her life figured out. We didn't talk for long." Ned didn't care to tell Dwight about the evening Phoebe and he had shared at Monical's.

"She's going to be a banker like her dad, I suppose."

"I don't know, maybe."

"Hag told me he went to see you at… what was that school you went to?"

"It was in New York, a little town downstate in the Catskills. State University at Delhi. And that would be a no, Hag did not come to see me. I haven't seen or spoken to him since high school."

"Oh, then let me update you. He wrote me a letter in care of Portia Sissell, of all people. I was surprised she even attempted to deliver it to me after all the trouble I caused her son. This was before I went to see Simon to straighten things out. Anyway, Hag said he drove up to see you early during freshman year. He was at NYU. You knew that, right?"

"Yeah, I can't remember how I knew."

"When he got to the campus, they told him you might be swimming at the pool, so he went over there and watched you swim for a while. He was above the pool where there's an observation window or something."

"Yeah. Really? But I never saw him."

"No, he decided maybe you wouldn't want to see him. It was," Dwight hesitated, "well, he thought there was a reason you went off to this little school in the mountains, like maybe you didn't want to see people. So he decided after he saw you it wouldn't be fair to crash your life without asking, and he got in his car and drove back to the city."

"Well, he was right about that, I guess. I did go there to hide."

"I won't judge you for that. Jesus, look at us. We've both been through so many things these past four years."

"What else did Hag say?"

"Quite a bit, actually. He dropped out of NYU during the fall semester of his sophomore year and then he got called up for the draft in February 1970."

"Oh, jeez."

"Yeah, well, they would have drafted him anyway, even if he hadn't dropped out, since the government eliminated the college deferment and replaced it with the draft lottery. His lottery number was really low, 34 or 37, something like that. The news crushed him. Now his story gets even better. Well, not better, but more interesting. He dodged it and went to Canada."

"You're kidding!"

"Nope. That's where he sent the letter from. He had it all planned out because he wasn't about to go to Nam. You remember how he was."

"I remember. He was such an amusing guy until the topic turned to politics or the War."

"Hag said he was working as a bartender in some club and on weekends was doing stand up comedy at the same place. Sounded glad to be there. College didn't mesh well with him. Didn't mesh, that's what he said. Can you believe that? He had a free ride to NYU and just quit in his third semester. This was before the draft lottery, so he didn't know he was going to draw such a low number."

"He was into drugs, too, you know," Ned added.

"Who isn't anymore? I've had my share of that. Weed was practically a staple ration in Nam. But I'm done with that now. Time to rebuild. I've got this carpentry thing going, got my bird, a couple of friends from work. I think I'm on the right track for a better part two. How about you, Ned? What's your plan? You working?"

"I don't know, Dwight. I'm still trying to figure things out. My mother isn't doing well at all, so I need to stay close. I was going to put some feelers out to some builders and construction companies. My degree is in construction management and I had a semester externship in Houston and I've got the degree now, but I don't have any experience other than that. In all honesty, it's difficult for me to picture myself in that role. I like the idea of not sitting at a desk all day and I enjoy organizing a plan and getting all the pieces to fit, but I don't know. I have a hard time staying focused. I suppose I don't actually believe yet that this is what I'm supposed to do."

Dwight nodded toward the baby grand piano. "So, tell me what's going on with that."

Ned walked over to the piano and opened the lid, securing it with the prop. He lifted the fall board to reveal the gleaming ivory and ebony keys that had yet to meet his fingers. Blindly, he played a quick C scale with his right hand, freeing the deep sound within.

"Play me something, Ned."

"I think not, Dwight." He raised his left hand and gave it a shake. "This guy won't cooperate."

"But can't you just play for fun, even if it's not Beethoven or Mozart, for Pete's sake?"

"You'd think, wouldn't you?"

The silence between them took its course before Dwight started, "Well, I guess—"

"Let me ask you something, Dwight. When you were over in Viet Nam, did you ever ask yourself, "What am I doing here?""

"Not at first, I didn't. For a long time, I believed soldiering was my destiny. I went whole hog. It suited me and I saw my future there, in the Army."

"But?"

"Not exactly 'but'. I still loved the Army, serving my country and all. I just started feeling that Nam wasn't the right place for this G.I. Went through some head shit for a long while and then decided it was time to move on. It was weird because I actually was a pretty good soldier. I liked the idea of being a warrior, but I just had to leave it behind me if I was ever gonna have a life."

"I hear you," Ned replied. He swiveled around to face the keys and trilled four bars of an E-flat major scale with his right hand. "I still can't get it through my head that this is over. It's been four years. Pathetic, huh?"

"That's for you to say, not me. One thing I've learned through this therapy, though, is how anger can eat away at your soul. It keeps you down, man, on the ground. And it won't let you up. I saw it happen to lots of guys over there. It had hold of me for most of my childhood, I'll tell you that. I get you can't play like you used to and you can't have the big concert career you planned on, but maybe that's not what's holding you back."

"But, it is, Dwight. I understand that even if I can't stop wallowing in it."

Dwight stood up and readied to leave. "It's been good talking to you, Ned. Let's stay in touch now that you're back in Tribute. And you should find something to do with those hands of yours. Go somewhere and learn how to use all those tools in the garage."

Ned stood and walked Dwight to the door. "Maybe I will. You need to show off your falcon skills to me sometime. What's your bird's name, again? Walt told me, but I forget."

"Cheeky. I named my falcon Cheeky."

"That's it. Where'd that come from?"

"Good question." Dwight looked at his shoes for a bit. "It came to me when he was staring back at me one day. I had him on my glove in front of me and his eyes zeroed in on mine. You know, his expression never changes. You can't tell if he's peeved or chummy, or if he even has feelings. I mean, falcons are smart and all, but just how far developed is that lobe of their brain? I read they're supposed to be some sort of spirit-like animal, signifying freedom and bravery and stuff like that. But the falcons don't know that. It's not like the bird has this lofty ideal—hmph, 'lofty', that's funny—it's not like he has, like, this mission in life, or anything. Maybe he thinks ahead, like when he's hungry and needs to eat, and plans his attack, but he sure as hell has no life plan."

Ned was growing impatient. "So you named him Cheeky because…?"

"Right. So, I decided he could be, like, my conscience. Since he always looks the same way at me, it could be like he's saying, 'So you've done this, or done that, to get better. Well, so what? What about today? What's next, bucko? If you want to achieve great things together with me, you'll need to do your part. I'm not carrying any deadwood. There's no free ride. You gotta do the work.' Ned, it's like he's daring me, being mouthy, you know, lippy. But he doesn't have lips. So I thought: Cheeky. And that's how I think about him. Cheeky's my other therapist, in a way. He's my reminder that there are always possibilities out there. He's loyal to me, but I don't impress him. I have to prove myself every day."

Dwight stepped on the porch, then turned before Ned closed the door. "One last thing, Ned. About your dream? I've been thinking and I've learned from Dr. Broadmore that dreams aren't always about what you think they're about. Maybe your nightmare isn't about me."

"Oh yeah, then what's it about?"

"I'm no shrink, Ned. How should I know? But I do know this. You haven't mentioned your dad all afternoon."

CHAPTER 14

Rose

ROSE EXAMINED HER tired hands as they jittered up and down on her lap. She pretended she was alone in a lushly carpeted parlor in her grandmother's house. The mantel clock hadn't kept time for several years, but the setting sun visible through the picture window told her that Sunday supper would be ready soon.

She closed her eyes and took in a deep breath, relishing the mixture of aromas that drifted into the room from the kitchen: baked bread, onions, coffee, roasted chicken. The air, rich with abundance, completed this oft visited memory as her grandmother hummed her favorite tune, "Twilight Time". At any moment she would hear, "Rose, dear, you should get washed up for supper now. Then I want you to come set the table. The potatoes are done, and all that's left is to mash them. Rose! Did you hear me?"

The memory was subject to change based on the time of year or even the time of day. It could be that her mood played a role, or if she felt drowsy. But in the end, it made no difference. When Rose felt cold, she would imagine herself in bed in her own room at her grandmother's house, snuggling beneath the quilt that her grandmother had lovingly stitched just for her. When she was sad, Rose could lean against her grandmother's shoulder as a story from long ago unfolded. Over the years, Rose had invented an endless number of soothing scenes. She found comfort in these moments, as they allowed her to escape from a situation she couldn't change. Now, these daydreams gave her hope and strengthened her determination to become something better.

Rose opened her eyes and checked her ticket again, even though she knew the number hadn't changed. Based on the dozens of times she had sat here waiting her turn, she calculated it would be another forty minutes before she was called up to the counter to begin the cross-examination.

"Yes, ma'am, I've been working since I was here two weeks ago."

"No, I still cannot earn enough to live in my own place, so I have a room at the old YMCA downtown. Here are my paystubs for the last two weeks."

"Yes, I'll be sure to keep them every week. I understand I have to show them to receive my food stamps."

And then it would be over until next time. Humiliated, Rose wasn't sure how many more next times she could endure the repeated inquisition. She had run away from home three times before she turned fourteen, only to be discovered in a girlfriend's basement, or the back of the cloakroom at the Pentecostal Church, or any number of places that she could no longer recall. It was all so long ago. Once she understood that neither of her divorced parents had the slightest interest in having her return to either of their homes, Rose got serious and spent several months outlining and researching her plan for the final run.

She understood why her mom and dad didn't want her around. She was just a bad kid. Neither of them could figure out why she always had to learn things the hard way. No amount of grounding or smacks to the face seemed to work. Her grades began their steady slide south in eighth grade, when she discovered that marijuana and boys were a lot more fun than algebra. By ninth grade, she'd had enough of that scene. She used the six months leading up to the end of school to amass $205.75. This would take her, along with her boyfriend, Ritchie, by bus to San Francisco, and still leave her with over $100 to start her new life. Ritchie had his own money he had been saving, but he wouldn't tell her how much he had. Richie was in eleventh grade and knew a lot about how to get around in big cities, having grown up in the Bronx until he was twelve when his family moved to Tribute.

They were sure they had it all figured out. It would be summer and they could live on the beach or in the parks, get jobs, and then share an apartment. There would be nobody to hassle them and they could do whatever they wanted. They loved each other and that would get them through any hard times. But they discovered that the hard times rushed in and were more frequent than they had imagined, love getting lost along the way. The details of her three years in San Francisco were so sketchy that she couldn't recall just when Richie left. They had both lowered themselves to petty thievery, or panhandling when they needed something to eat or a place to sleep. She and Richie had been so inseparable for so long that everyone they knew affectionately referred to the duo as Ro and Rich. Rose felt special having a circle of friends that cared about her and her man.

And then one day Richie was gone. Rose spent days wandering Haight Ashbury looking for him, to no avail. In the end, she questioned whether he had been drafted, maybe deciding to go to Canada, or perhaps he grew tired of her. In any event, she never heard from him again.

As time passed, Rose tired of living day to day. The party wasn't fun anymore and many of her friends, as it turned out, were only drug friends. They weren't congenial any longer when she passed the toke on without partaking or waved her hand away at the pill being offered, telling them she had to work in the morning, which was true.

So she decided to go home. To Tribute. Not to any family, but to start over. She stayed off drugs and alcohol, saved up for a bus ticket just like before, and rode the bus east this time, still poor but wiser and with an ambition to succeed that kept her grounded. For even though her hometown had never brought her anything but sorrow, familiarity can be a comfort.

∼

Track 9 of Chicago's Union Station was overrun with passengers, from business executives in three-piece suits to young families with children, from a musician clutching a violin case to a pair of college students with "NORTHWESTERN" displayed proudly on their matching sweatshirts, from a tearful elderly couple saying goodbye to their granddaughter who was dabbing her eyes yet all the while checking her ticket and gently moving away from them, to a father and son, the little boy fidgeting with his bright blue Chicago Cubs baseball cap.

Everywhere Ned looked, he saw glimpses of lives, like snapshots from a family album. He imagined the young man leaning against the wall was embarking upon a great adventure out west, his brand new duffel at his feet as he gazed nervously all around with a peculiarly flat grin, and that curly-haired girl buying a muffin was returning home after an arduous stent in the deserts of New Mexico, her tanned face and bleached blond hair flippantly regarding the crowd with annoyance as she frowned.

Ned self-consciously wondered how he might appear to the strangers around him. Did they see him as a seasoned explorer, accustomed to trains and planes, waiting to embark on a routine leg of his journey? Might they imagine him a college basketball player or even an actor, traveling to Hollywood to film a movie? Fight it as he might, he finally gave up and decided that worldly, he was not. He was 22 now, and it was time for him to be something.

Ned had taken Dwight's advice and found a school near Los Angeles. Apparently, they believed he had the potential to be a fine woodworker because they accepted him into a four-month intensive course that was scheduled to start in just three days. He would immerse himself in the creative process with the other eleven students living in a dorm on the small campus. Ned could finally visit Mitch and catch up. By next year, he would emerge with a skill set and an ability to craft things of worth. His dad would be proud.

And yet, he couldn't explain the lethargy that hung over him. Nearly every morning before getting out of bed, he would lay and stare at the opaque white globe on his bedroom ceiling, imagining the unlit lamp to be a fortune teller's crystal ball. Like a movie reel, he would rewind to his years before the accident. Only now did he appreciate the glory of being fifteen and gifted, of having friends that admired him and his talent. Mostly, he missed the feeling of anticipation, the joy each day in pursuing something that promised an exciting and rewarding life. It had been his path to happiness. Then it vanished in an instant. How do you change your path when the only path you have ever known or wanted disappears? Missing also was the one person Ned always relied upon to support and guide him with common sense. It wasn't fair.

Why was he so ill-equipped to handle this? He wasn't stupid. His brain was lucid and knew well the road to recovery. He had taken measures to move forward after healing physically in the months after the accident. Wasting little time in pursuit of a new trade, he'd gone to college and gained the education and training in the skills which complimented his abilities. He found the work fulfilling and realized that he could establish a successful career with the skills he had gained. And soon he would be on his way to California to learn even more. Why wasn't this enough? When would the mournful sound of his *Concerto* leave him alone?

Ned trudged across the echoing grand hall to the bank of pay phones on the east side of the train station. He entered a booth and pulled out the piece of paper with the phone number on it, dropped four quarters in the slot, and dialed the number. The connection was fast and the phone at the other end rang.

"Good morn… or rather good afternoon, Pacific School of Woodworking, Christine speaking. How may I help you?"

"Hello, Christine. This is Benedict Godwin. I'm enrolled in the four-month course that begins on Monday."

"Oh, hello, Benedict! It's so nice to hear the voice that goes with the name. Yes, I was just working on the course schedule."

"I feel awkward about this. I was wondering, is there a waiting list to get into this program?"

"Well, yes, there always is, but you're already on the roster, so there's no problem for you. What makes you ask?"

"I'm sorry, but I'm afraid I have to withdraw my placement. You see, my mother passed away three weeks ago."

"Oh, Benedict, I'm so sorry. This must be a very hard time for you."

"Well, yes, it has been. You see, her passing wasn't sudden. I had been anticipating it for a while, so I thought I would be okay. I've been looking forward to this ever since I was accepted into the program."

Christine interrupted once again, "But it's too soon, isn't it?"

He let out a sigh. "Yes, I think it must be. I am literally at the train station about to board my train to California and it just hit me. I don't think I can do this just now. Is it possible to fill my slot at this late date?"

"Not a problem. There's a waiting list, as I said. We'll be able to do that easily. Are you sure that's what you want?"

"No. Not sure at all, to be honest. But right now, this seems to be what I have to do. Would it be possible to postpone my attendance to next year's class, or would I need to apply all over again?"

"Hmm, I'm not sure about that, Benedict. I'll need to speak with David, the director, and get back to you. Are you still on Odiorne Drive in Tribute, Illinois?"

"Yes."

"Okay then. I'll get on this. I need to get right to our waiting list and get that all settled. Someone is going to be thrilled. Oh, I'm sorry, that was insensitive of me. I'll get a letter out to you in the next few days about any refund or the possibility of you attending next year. Is there anything else I can do for you today?"

"I guess not. Thank you for being so understanding, Christine. I'm sorry about this."

"Not at all, Benedict. Hopefully, we'll see you next year. You take care, now."

"I will. Thank you. Same to you."

"Okay, goodbye Benedict."

"Goodbye."

Ned hung up and sat still on the little stool, studying the pay phone. Did he actually just do that? What was he doing using his mother's death to get out of that course? Her death had nothing to do with him not wanting to go.

In the days that followed, Ned descended even lower into the grips of depression. He had expected to feel better, less anxious, once the commitment of attending school in California was off the table. Instead, he felt worse. Never had he acted in such a deceitful manner. There was nothing from his childhood that even hinted at the acceptability of lying or cheating. His folks, notably his dad, had set the example. What would they think of their son now?

※

Ned slouched as he headed toward the headstone that, sadly, was now completed with his mother's dates. Two early snows this October had blanketed the fallen leaves in the oak-strewn cemetery, and now that the snow had melted, all that remained were soggy slabs of sandwiched leaves. The disarray of nature surrounding his parents' stone left Ned feeling dismayed. He should have visited more often to combat nature's assault. He dropped to his knees, the left leg angled away at a less acute bend, ignoring the instant wet that seeped into his jeans, and began swiping at the leaves and remnants of flowers Karina had placed before the snowfall. Even old grass clippings thrown against the granite base were composting. By the time Ned had finished, his hands were as soaked and muddy as his pants.

Ignoring the squelchy grass, he shifted his body and faced the tombstone. "Hi Mom. Hi Dad. It's a pretty warm day here. The sun is shining and it's about 55 degrees. I'm sorry I haven't been by in a while. I'll try to come more often. I have a new job. Well, not entirely new. I'm a foreman-in-training for Sabey Builders. I suppose it actually is a new job, my first genuine one since I got out of college after my externship in Houston. I think it will work out. I'm catching on to how everything works up here, a little different from Texas. Do you remember Dwight Kato? Maybe not. We weren't real close in high school. He was kind of a bully, especially to Si, but he's changed and made amends with Si, so he's okay now. Anyway, he helped get me the job. He's been working there as a carpenter's apprentice since he got out of the army and they think pretty highly of him. So, he put in a word for me."

Ned looked away. A car passed by on the access drive, slowing as it neared him. He gave a quick wave to assure the driver he was fine, then watched the car move on. The sound of the engine faded, and all was hushed once more until he heard the geese. Shading his eyes, Ned took a moment to admire their perfect V formation. He recalled the day he had spent with Dwight and Cheeky last month traipsing through the woods. Despite Ned's presence disturbing the duo's synergy, Dwight apologized for Cheeky's poor showing that day. Still, it had been revealing to watch the intensity and focus that Dwight displayed with his avian sidekick. They made quite the pair.

"Mom, Karina has decided to move to Moline and live with her sister. She's missing you intensely and doesn't seem to know what to do with her time, so I can't blame her for wanting some companionship. She's moving out this weekend and keeps apologizing for deserting me even though I've been self-sufficient for quite some time now. You know how she is. She's taking a couple of weeks off before deciding about work, but is pretty sure she can get a job at the nursing home there. So, it will be just me in the house. That's going to be weird, quiet…hard."

Saying the words out loud made Ned choke up. Sputtering, he blurted out in a whisper, "I'm trying, but I'm so lost." He leaned forward and rested his head on top of the cold granite. His nose was dripping now, and he sniffed it back. "I'm sorry. I look around me and see all my friends building their lives, but all I want is what I had when you were here."

Ned's fingers traced the letters: D-E-N-N-I-S, I-S-A-B-E-L-L-E as his voice dropped even further, "Help me, please, I don't know how to do this."

*

Rose smiled as she closed the door behind her. In the months since moving back to Tribute, she had made successful inroads with her new life, even contacting her mother in hopes of repairing their damaged relationship. After a few short weeks living at the YMCA, she struck up a friendship with Gloria, another Y resident. Gloria had been between jobs and landed at the Y just a few weeks before Rose. They had met while paying their meager rent at the front desk one afternoon. Both possessing the gift of gab, they soon became fast friends.

Gloria was an occupational therapist at the Thornwood Rehabilitation Center, where she helped children with disabilities. Rose found Gloria's work fascinating and, with permission from the families and her employer, Gloria had allowed Rose to observe on several occasions. Rose was thinking perhaps she could work in that field as an assistant one day after she got her GED and received some training.

When Gloria finally settled in a new apartment, she invited Rose to share the space with her until she finished her GED and could get a full-time job to better support herself. Rose was grateful, as she was running out of money and didn't know how she was going to afford even the paltry room rent at the Y anymore.

"Really, Rose. I want you to stay with me. I have a futon in my living room and it folds out so you can have your own bed every night. I don't have many clothes yet, so you can use some of my closet space. It'll be great! Roomies!"

"Gloria, that's so generous of you. But what if I get on your nerves or leave wet towels on the bathroom floor?" Rose joked.

"Well, that would be a deal breaker and I'd have to kick you out!" Gloria laughed as she hugged her friend. And so they embarked on their new adventure.

Rose locked the door before descending the single flight of stairs to the ground floor of the garden apartment building. She made her way to the lot where her car was parked. The week before, Rose had asked her mother to have lunch with her, in an effort to continue mending their relationship. Rose impressed her mother by sharing the hard work she was putting in to turn her life around. She explained that Gloria's apartment, although rent-free for Rose, was three miles away from school and five miles away from her part-time job at the grocery store. While she had walked from the Y to school and even to work with ease, a five-mile journey twice daily was too much, even for her. Her mother had surprised her by offering her car to Rose. "I've been looking for a reason to buy a new car. This is perfect timing! I've had mine for eight years, and it's got 115,000 miles on it, Rose, but you can have it if you want it. It's not much, but it can probably get you from here to there for a while."

The weeks ticked by and Christmas approached. The holiday had never been much to celebrate for Rose, not as a child nor when living in San Francisco, but now she and Gloria were enjoying themselves. The previous weekend, they had cut their own tree and Gloria's mother had visited Tribute and taken them Christmas shopping for ornaments and tinsel and lights. They even put a string of miniature Santas around the big mirror in the living room.

Today was Christmas Eve and Rose stumbled into the apartment laden with groceries for their Christmas Eve dinner celebration: steaks and baked potatoes with a bottle of champagne. "I had to drive all the way over to Steigers Meat Market to find these steaks," Rose gushed as she placed the bags of food on the kitchen counter. "Did you hear me, Gloria? Where are you?"

Her housemate walked into the kitchen with a look of dismay on her face.

"What is it?"

"I don't know what to do, Rose." Gloria handed her a sheet of paper that was folded twice, like a letter. "This came in today's mail."

Rose opened the letter and read:

December 20, 1972

To: Gloria Jenkins

Re: Current Lease, Cloverly Garden Apartments, Apt. 245A

From: Cloverly Enterprises

It has come to our attention that two adults are occupying Apt. 245A. This occupancy violates your signed lease, which stipulates the apartment is leased to a single individual.

We require that the lessee immediately remove any additional individuals currently living in Apt. 245A or face eviction. Should you desire to amend your lease to permit two individuals to occupy Apt. 245A, please contact this office before January 1, 1973, to sign a new lease that will reflect the updated rate for two individuals/one bedroom.

Please be advised that all rental rates at Cloverly Garden Apartments will increase by 4% beginning January, 1973, per the notice mailed to all tenants on October 1, 1972.

Sincerely yours,

Richard Vose

Tenant Liaison, Cloverly Enterprises

"Can they do this?" Rose exclaimed.

"I think they can, Rose. I read the lease after I saw the letter and it's right there. The apartment rent is for a single person. I never read the entire lease when I signed it. Who does? But, if two people live here, the rate is more. I called over to the rental office, and they confirmed all this and said the rate for two people is $95 more per month because two people use more water, heat and electricity. Rose, I can't afford that."

"Of course not, Gloria. Come on now, don't fret. It'll be all right. I'm sure I can find some other place to crash. Heck, I've lived on the streets before. I can figure this out."

"But where will you go?"

"I'm not sure just yet, but I'll find something, I'm sure. It's only for a few months until I get my GED and can find a full-time job."

Rose reached out to Gloria and hugged her tight. "Let's forget all this tonight. It's Christmas Eve and I want to enjoy it, don't you?"

"Yes, Rose. I do, too." Gloria glanced at the bottle of champagne. "What do you say we get started on this while we cook?"

"You read my mind. Pop the cork."

◈

Rose had known almost instantly what she was going to do when she moved out of Gloria's apartment on January 1. At this stage of her life, she discovered she could tackle obstacles that came her way with a low level of anxiety. "It's surprising how much one can handle after faltering and rallying," she thought, recalling those years in California. Rose derived satisfaction from managing the affairs of her life and looked forward to the time when she would no longer depend on food stamps and government subsidies. For now, Rose committed to the daily schedule she had meticulously devised. Idle time was her enemy, and the schedule seemed to work. She was back downtown at the old YMCA building, but instead of renting a room, she had received permission to leave her car parked in the lot. She would convert her car into a temporary home.

A trip to the Salvation Army had rewarded her with a gently used sleeping bag and a downy blanket. She kept what few belongings that mattered to her in the trunk, although she soon discovered that the trunk lid seal was defective—rotted, in fact. She borrowed a plastic tarp from BT, who worked at the Y, and the two of them covered the back of the car, tying it all down with fragments of rope from his boat. Inside, Rose removed the back of the rear seat to open up the space and allow her to stretch out flat when she slept in her sleeping bag. She taped thick sections of discarded packing foam on the inside of the trunk to insulate her new home. She also disassembled the front passenger bucket seat, leaving just the seat and discarding the seat back. With this renovation, she had room to maneuver. Black plastic garbage bags cut to size were on hand when needed to cover the side windows for privacy. Snow regularly covered the windshield.

Rose had put in many hours of preparation so that her car would prove habitable, and it was. Even so, she spent little time inside the now permanent fixture at the back of the lot. Each morning, she exited her car and entered the Y for showering and breakfast. The generous staff gave her a locker space and Rose kept non-perishable food there, alongside her toothbrush and other bathroom supplies. When she wasn't working at the IGA or attending GED classes, she spent her time inside the Y reading room. The director took a liking to her after she understood the effort Rose was making to better herself and gave her permission to use all the facilities: gym, swimming pool, and exercise classes. She loved the calming hour of yoga class on Thursday evenings.

Just a few days into January, a green Jeep began appearing in the parking lot almost daily. The driver generally arrived early in the morning before the Y opened its doors, backing into the space two slots to the east of her car and sitting with the engine idling. Rose could peek outside, unobserved, by rolling back a narrow slit of black plastic on the back window, and had observed him reading a newspaper and drinking coffee most days before getting out of the car and entering the building when it opened, well before she was up and about. He had a definite routine.

The man was in his mid-twenties, tallish with long brown hair and a beard. He favored his left leg as he walked to the building, rehabbing a torn ACL, Rose guessed. This particular Monday morning began like any other. There had been the usual inch or two of snow during the previous night, but the plows had not yet arrived to clear the lot. Positioned in the front passenger seat, she started getting dressed, having organized her backpack the night before with her study aids, books, and such. Rose heard the familiar sound of Jeep Man arriving.

❦

The virgin snow squeaked beneath the tires of his Jeep as Ned pulled into the parking lot at the gym. The sun wouldn't rise yet for another hour, and he loved the crackling freshness this time of day. Often he could drive to the YMCA and not see another vehicle on the road. Perhaps a stray fox darting across his headlights or a wild turkey strutting willy nilly in the shadows would catch his eye. He had trained himself to survey the roadside for deer ever since last

December, when he had sent his car into a ditch while avoiding yet another doe.

The scene was familiar. "Why is it we always park in the same spot each time?" he asked himself. Athletic trainer BT's beat-up Chevy truck was backed in near the curb, three spaces from the median. Always three. Maxine, the face of morning cheer who worked the front desk, consistently parked her car, nose in, right next to the front sidewalk.

He maneuvered his Jeep around the median and headed for his usual spot toward the property line. A long time ago, he decided to park a distance from the building and use the opportunity to walk and burn some calories. Ned was like everybody else when it came to picking his parking place. He liked the spot near the security lamp, which gave him some light by which to read as he waited for the building to open. Shifting into reverse, he backed in, stopping when he heard his rear bumper brush the tall weeds. He left the car running and kicked the heat down a bit.

The abandoned sedan sat next to him, also backed in, with the passenger side next to his own driver's side. He had first seen the abandoned car three weeks before after returning from a trip to Chicago. It was quite a sight. The rusted front bumper sagged with just the passenger side still attached. It had a bent radio antennae ("how old would that make it?" he wondered) that would have looked more natural waving a white flag. The car had four doors and a blue tarp where once there had been a rear trunk lid. A ragged length of rope, which twisted in a disorganized web across the back of the car, secured the tarp in place. As winter set in, snow had gradually crept over the vehicle. First, just a dusting, like a sifting of powdered sugar. Then, as the weeks ticked by and more snow fell, the vehicle eventually became entombed. Looking to his left, the abandoned mystery had by now morphed into a child's crayon drawing: just a white outline with soft borders atop a black background of the pre-dawn sky. There was no evidence of its tired, tortured past.

Ned sat behind the steering wheel and gazed outside the Jeep. These hushed hours of morning had become his trusted companion in recent months. Free from the distractions and interferences of daylight and routine, he could finally focus his thoughts and send his mind wherever he chose. He glanced in the rear-view mirror and saw the scar beneath his beard. "Stop it," he thought. He gave his head a quick shake and took a sip from the travel mug he'd brought along. The hot coffee burned the tip of his tongue and he knew it would be sore for a couple of days. The doors to the gym wouldn't open for another fifteen minutes, so Ned settled back in the driver's seat and read the newspaper, starting with the obituaries. He couldn't explain why he always started with death notices. Amidst the tranquility of the deserted parking lot, he glanced upward upon hearing the whispers of the fat snowflakes plopping on the windshield, while the heater defogged the glass. The scene was hypnotizing, and he continued staring at the flakes, losing his depth perception, unable or unwilling to blink his eyes. If only he could capture the serenity of this moment and carry it with him. Then, hearing it before seeing it, the door of the dead car opened.

Ned was so startled when the car door opened he blurted, "Jesus!" Had someone been sleeping in there all these days? How could that be? "She would have frozen to death," he thought, for now he could see that it was a woman. She stole an expressionless look at him through his side window, then shut her car door and walked away.

He eyed the back of her flimsy navy pea coat as she trekked through the snow toward the building. She moved with gusto, shoulders hunched forward, hands gloveless, then disappeared through the front doors. He thought, "This is weird. Is she homeless? Does the Y know she's living out here in her car? They must. But it's odd they permit it." Ned had to know more.

He gathered up his bag and hustled to the front doors and gave a quick hello to Maxine at the front desk before moving on, all the while his eyes darting about for signs of the mystery girl. Peering first into the reading room and the nursery area, he bolted up the steps to the second floor two at a time. Empty. "She must be in the ladies' locker room. Maybe I'll see her in the pool," he thought.

Ned moved on and changed into his swim gear. The pool was busy at this hour with the before-work crowd, and he gave a quick hello to the regulars he knew well, still searching for her, but in vain. He slipped into lane four, secured his goggles to his head, then pushed off to begin his one mile swim of 36 laps. Lap Uno. Ned debated if he should ask Maxine about this person. She'd surely know who the girl is and why she's living out of a car in the parking lot. Maybe BT would know.

Lap 2- twins. But the more he considered it, the more he realized he couldn't do that. At the least, he'd be sticking his nose into someone's private life. At worst, he'd seem like some creepy stalker.

Lap 3- three blind mice. No, he would have to let this go. Ned savored the feeling of his body cutting through the invigorating water, his leg operating like it was normal, his hands propelling him effortlessly with each stroke. With his ears under water and his eyes closed save for half second blinks to avoid swimming off line, or veering into the adjacent swimmer with whom he shared the lane, Ned felt transported to his other world, a place where he imagined everything was different.

Lap 6- six pips on a die. *The Emperor's* captivating melody of the second movement resonated in his head as his fingers glided nimbly across the keys of a Steinway concert grand piano. Telling himself, "No, don't do it," Ned nevertheless surrendered to going there each time he would swim, even though he knew he'd regret it when he climbed out. It didn't matter to him that he'd lose track of his laps, despite Si's hint. The sound of the piano notes were all that mattered, as if he was hypnotized, finally snapping out of the spell only after the final note of the movement played.

Lap 11- goalposts. Phoebe had looked so beguiling when he saw her at Christmas, again by chance, and Ned felt helpless in those moments. More beautiful than ever, could she really still be into him, he wondered? It seemed a possibility when she told him how much she missed being with him, and then reminisced about the time he surprised her by playing her favorite Chopin sonata at the Fall Program, senior year of high school. Or when they had laughed together, recalling one of their high school escapades. Ned revisited how good it had all been back then. But then she had bid a hasty farewell and dashed off. Why had he been such a hard ass when she wanted to make amends after the prom? Why didn't he give her more attention? They were so young back then. Petty grudges, meaningless slights.

Lap 12- a dozen eggs. He should take a lesson from Si about grudges. The tables had turned. He recalled the photo his dad had taken of them, side by side, in his front yard years back. They were raking leaves; it must have been ninth or tenth grade, and they had been making a mess of things but were giddy with how clever each of them was. Fifteen and all knowing. They were wrestling in a pile of leaves when his dad startled them, watching from the porch steps, camera in hand.

"Hey, you two clowns! Stand up and let me get a picture of you."

They hadn't argued with him. Just stood up and faced the lens. As Dennis prepared to snap the picture, it had felt completely natural for Ned to place his arm around Si's shoulder, as if Si was his little brother. When the photos came back, his dad had asked for three copies of that one, one for each of the boys and one for him to keep. It was that good. There they were, Mutt and Jeff, frozen in time.

It always seemed that Si played the role of the little brother and Ned, the older, wiser and taller brother. As he considered those days now, Ned could see how his height advantage and Si's baldness created an unspoken order between them. But now it was clear to Ned that he'd had it backwards. He may have had an enviable talent at the piano, but Si had been stealthily cultivating his life, with no fanfare at all. Even after all the torment Dwight had levied upon him, Si had taken Dwight at his word and forgiven him. How did he do that? What nature of apology must Dwight have offered to garner such an acquittal? And now Si was married and a father of twins, Maria and Edwardo. You could see it all in the way his eyes sparkled in the Christmas photo he and Eva had sent. Si was beaming in a way Ned had never seen him do, his arms around his children with their gorgeous wavy hair.

Lap 13- Friday the thirteenth. Lap 14- two weeks. Ned needed to change the way his life was going. What was the point in continuing to live like this? Everybody else was moving on. The sun shone through the windows, creating a playful display of tiny lights among the melting snowflakes on the branches of the honey locust trees outside. The effect, while beautiful, stabbed at Ned's eyes each time he turned his head to breathe.

Lap 18- the half mile mark- high school graduation, the cap and gown he never wore, his birthday, Father's Day, the concert dress rehearsal, the accident. It was all one jumbled mess of a time, seared in his mind. Jesus, Godwin. Can't you just get on with it?

He flipped the turn and began again.

Uno.

⁂

Ned exited the YMCA building. Scanning the parking lot, he spotted the girl standing between their two cars, bending at the waist as her head disappeared through the passenger door of her car. He stopped. Thinking this might prove awkward, he considered going back inside and waiting for her to…. to what? Walk back toward him, climb inside her car? No, he may just as well walk to his car and get in, as natural as can be, he decided. Of course, he wouldn't be able to open his door unless she moved.

"Oh! I'm sorry, I didn't see you standing there. You probably want to get into your car," the girl said, looking him straight in the eye with a nonplussed smile of apology. She wore big round sunglasses that seemed out of place in January.

"That's okay. I'm not in any hurry."

The girl pulled off her sunglasses, revealing brilliant blue eyes that drew Ned in, leaving him unable to look anywhere else. The contrast with her blonde hair was remarkable; she could have been a model. Her clear eyes fixed on Ned's.

"I see you park here all the time. I take it you like this spot?" she said, smiling.

As she spoke, her engaging manner relaxed Ned. He opened his mouth to say something, a bit too late.

"As you can see, I'm parked here permanently. Well, not permanently, but for now. This car isn't going anywhere, anytime soon, that's for sure. It won't run."

"Oh, sorry. Can I give you a ride somewhere?"

"Thanks, but not necessary. I'm just camped out here for a while. I'm between apartments," she offered in explanation.

"So, you're… you're sleeping here… in the car?"

"Yeah. Don't look so shocked," she chuckled. "It's actually working out pretty well. Would you like the nickel tour?"

The girl showed him the inside of the car and told him how she had set it up, exhibiting a touch of pride at her ingenuity and fortitude in doing so. Ned listened attentively, shaking his head in awe. The sun had melted the snow off their cars, settling in slushy piles after the slow slide off the heated sheet metal.

"Well," Ned remarked, "I'm very impressed, especially with that whole tarp idea there in back."

She grinned. "It turns out sometimes that necessity *is* the mother of invention, after all."

Ned took two steps forward to continue checking out her car, and then he saw it. He stared, trying to reason how this car could be here. "This cannot be a coincidence. It just can't be," he thought.

"What's wrong?" the girl said, moving up shoulder to shoulder next to Ned. With a concerned look on her face, she examined the hood, which was the focus of his attention. "Do you see something?"

Ned looked at the girl. "No, there's nothing wrong. It's just... well, I know this car."

She tilted her head. "What do you mean?"

"I mean I know about this particular car. I recognize this rusting dent on the hood." He reached across the hood and ran his finger along the flaw where the paint had peeled. "This car used to belong to a woman who worked for my parents. She slammed the hood down after checking the oil one day, but she hadn't fully stashed the support hook. Crunch."

At that, the girl gasped, covering her mouth with her palm, her eyes bugging out.

"What?" Ned exclaimed.

She stood with her hand across her mouth, unable to speak, it seemed. Then she began examining Ned, looking him up and down before returning her stare to his face.

"What's the matter?" he demanded.

"Oh... my... God," she said, dropping her hand. "What's your name, if you don't mind me asking?"

"I don't mind. My name is Benedict, Benedict Godwin. What's yours?"

"Did your father used to call you Neddy?"

Ned took a half step backwards. "How could you possibly know that?"

The girl hesitated, then nodded and said, "My name is Rose, Elizabeth Rose Gardeen."

They stared at each other for several seconds, both trying to make sense of the moment. Ned understood now. This was Karina's little girl, Elizabeth, the one that had sometimes hung out at his house when her mother was working there. He hadn't seen or thought about her in years.

"You're little Elizabeth? Oh, wow! This is amazing."

"Yes, it is quite... far out. I don't remember much about you back then, just that I didn't like you. But I remember your dad, Dennis. I loved your dad."

"You didn't like me? Why?"

"Oh, that's a long story, as is yours, no doubt. I heard about that terrible accident a few years back. I'm so sorry you lost your dad. He was always so nice to me."

"Was he? I mean, I'm not surprised he was nice to you. I just don't remember you and him together, you know?" Ned couldn't stop shaking his head in disbelief at this unexpected set of circumstances. How? He tallied the years since he remembered seeing this girl, it had to be twelve years, at least. He couldn't have been over nine or ten years old. Only now did it seem odd to him that Karina hadn't spoken about her all this time. He had completely forgotten she had a daughter.

"Does Karina know you're here in Tribute?"

"Oh, sure, we just had lunch together the other day. What are you doing these days? Still playing the piano, I imagine?"

"Well… I, um…"

"Oh, God, I'm sorry Ned. I'm so stupid. Please forget I said that."

"No, no, you're fine, Rose. It's just that I wasn't sure how to answer the question. It's complicated."

Rose nodded her head in empathy. "I get it." She stopped for a second, then gently placing her hand on his forearm asked, "Do you have time for a cup of coffee and some conversation, Neddy Godwin?"

*

Ned wonders even now how his life might have turned out had he not met the girl in the dead Falcon that day. Had it been the day before or the day after, he might just as readily have minded his own business, pardoned himself, climbed into his car and driven off. Had it been earlier or later in the day, Ned might not have seen the girl, it being pure happenstance that their paths had crossed outside their cars, that day, that time. He never believed in concepts such as fate or destiny, providence or God's will, or even kismet. The world is too full of too many sliding doors for there to be any order or plan. Ever since studying genetics and natural selection in biology class in ninth grade, the randomness of existence had always made sense to him. The way of things beneath the microscope was also the way of things beyond. The disorder of life around him felt logical and ordered to Ned. Yet, during his wanderings after the accident, when he desperately tried to find a path out of his misery, he illogically wished for something or someone to materialize before him, to correct the cosmic mistake that was the surreal accident. The three-dimensional world underwent a temporary short circuit that day, it seemed, and it was only a matter of time before everything returned to normal. But no, there was no going back, Ned finally acknowledged. If there was to be any future for him, he would have to forge it.

Over the next week Rose and Ned had coffee again, then lunch and, on the fifth day, dinner together. Ned was awash with an energy that had been absent for a long time. Talking with someone who had known his dad felt invigorating, and Rose's affectionate words about Dennis warmed his heart as he listened. He felt a deep sadness upon discovering that Karina had been such a harsh mother to Rose. This revelation shed light on the reason behind Rose's intense hostility towards the child whom her mother treated as if he were her own son. After all, she was just a child of four when her mother, a "reluctant parent", as Rose put it, began working for his parents. As for her father, Rose would only say that he was not a nice man. That she had lately reached out to her mother spoke of the forgiving character Rose now possessed. It was after dinner as the two of them sat across from each other finishing their beer, that Ned blurted out, "So, you need to move into my house and get the hell out of that car before someone finds you frozen to death."

"Don't be ridiculous, Ned. I can't do that," she said, stunned by the invitation. "Anyway, I don't feel that way about you. You're too old for me."

"Wait a minute. Hold on. I didn't mean it like that," he said with a grin. "I meant you could, like, rent a room from me, only I wouldn't charge you any rent until you get back on your feet again. You'd be my tenant. To be honest, you'd be doing me a favor. Since your mother moved out, the house is too quiet. We could keep each other company. We could eat together, save money on groceries, you know, like that."

"Ned, I can't afford to pay you rent and I can't accept your charity."

"But, Rose, I'm not thinking of it as charity. I'm just helping a friend. Look, I don't need the rent; there's no mortgage left on the house. I own it free and clear. Do you remember the bedroom with its own bathroom? It's got a sitting area with a couch and it's pretty nice. You can hang out there when you want some privacy or get sick of me. It was my mom's room for many years. Look, if it would make you feel better, you could help do the cleaning and mopping—do some cooking, if you want. I'd really like you to do this. Please."

Rose locked on to Ned's eyes, trying to assess his sincerity. It seemed as if he was being truthful, but how well did she truly know this guy? Not well at all. You can flatter yourself that you have a sixth sense about others, that you can tell if someone is honest, moral. But what Rose found is that anyone can get bamboozled. You can be so sure a person is a straight shooter only to discover too late you were wrong. Still, the thought of having a warm bed and a home to live in was so very tempting, and she knew she could pull her own weight. But it was more than that. In the last few days, as they shared their lives, Rose gleaned from his stories a picture of a loyal, caring friend who had surrounded himself with classmates of equal stature. She might be mistaken about him, but could they all be so wrong?

"Okay, Ned. Let's give it a go. And let's agree right now that either of us can end this, for any reason, okay?"

"It's a deal." Ned reached across the table and they shook hands to cement their new relationship. "Let's go get your things out of your car and set you up at the house."

The two stood up and donned their coats. As Ned led the way he felt Rose's hand on his shoulder, stopping him. He pivoted and saw a tear in her eye.

"Thank you for this, Ned."

※

By Easter the housemates were like an old married couple. Ned was now in command of a building project on East Main Street where a new Pizza Barn was going up next to McDonald's. As a newly appointed project manager, he felt considerable stress from the responsibility, but appreciated that his boss kept tabs on him, mentoring with morning huddles.

Now that the weather had warmed, Rose bought herself a used bicycle and began riding it to work and to classes. She had just six weeks remaining before she would finish the last of her classes and, hopefully, pass her final exams for her GED. Ned seldom had to shop for food as she had attached a basket to her bike and brought home groceries after work. He continued to cover most costs, but Rose contributed what she could, depositing money in a fruit bowl in the kitchen. Ned tossed in dollars that mingled with Rose's contributions.

Disagreements were few, each being open to compromise. Rose didn't make a fuss when Ned left his shoes on the rug in front of the sofa and Ned didn't care that Rose didn't rinse her dirty dishes. The house was big enough that they didn't trip over one another. Rose relied on her bedroom sofa for studying and Ned spent his free time cleaning and re-organizing the wood shop or tending to the yard. They pitched in and planted pansies along the sidewalk leading to the front door. They cleaned the remaining fallen leaves from the foundation shrubs and Rose took cuttings from the lilac bush. Isabelle's tall cut-glass vase found life again supporting the tall stems. The scent perfumed the air all the way up the stairs.

They were sitting on the front porch one Saturday morning, gazing across the pond, sipping coffee and enjoying the banana bread they had proudly baked the night before, though neither one of them was particularly skilled in the kitchen. Rose asked, "Why hasn't anyone built houses on those vacant lots? They seem so out of place and lonely. What happened, do you know?"

"Dad told me the developer died before he could finish the rest of the homes that were planned. Then World War I came along and afterward nobody was interested, I guess. Dad always hoped somebody would finish the neighborhood, get more families here, get the pond and park back in order so the neighborhood would look settled. My parents purchased this house expecting it would come to pass, and it was disheartening for them that it never materialized."

"This could be so lovely if someone would finish it. It needs love and children. Why didn't your parents have more kids after you?"

"My mom got sick right after I was born. Well, not sick, sick. She got depressed pretty bad and was never the same after. Postpartum depression, they called it. Dad told me they had wanted lots of kids when they got married, but it just didn't turn out that way."

Rose mused, "Maybe that's why he took me under his wing. You weren't around much, but he was so fatherly to me, Ned. Mother was always annoyed with me, yelling at me not to bother Mr. Godwin, that he didn't have time to fool with me. But your dad was so even-tempered. He'd just answer back, 'That's okay, Karina. Elizabeth is no problem at all.' Then, he'd let me help plant flowers, or tell me how rabbits eat his garden."

Rose pointed to the edge of the property. "I found a dead bird once, right over there. I didn't know it was dead, though. I thought it was just hurt. I remember being pretty upset at the sight of the poor thing, crying and all that, but your dad quieted me down, and we buried it in the backyard. I don't know what made me think of that just now."

Ned paused. "When did this happen?"

"What? Oh, I don't know. Before I was in school, must have been."

"That's really strange. I must have heard Dad tell someone about that, probably your mom. I used to have this recurring dream and there was a part in it where Dad was consoling a little girl about a dead bird. It was a falcon, I think. My friend Dwight was in the dream, too. It was very unsettling, a nightmare actually."

Rose responded, "Aren't dreams something else? It's so fascinating how we take moments in our life, then, while we sleep, toss them around in our brain and rewrite them into bizarre little stories, like yours. I've had my share of bad dreams, but I can't remember any of them as recurring. Did you ever tell your dad about it?"

"I must have, I told him everything."

Rose waited a bit, then said, "Can I ask you a question about your father?"

"Of course."

"Why do you keep his bedroom door locked?"

Ned blew out a sigh. "I don't know. Wait. That's not true. Of course I know. It's because I'm afraid to go in there. Sounds ridiculous, I know, but I've just been afraid to face what might happen if I see his things or smell his clothes. I know I'm being foolish about it. I tell myself that if I don't go in there, I can think of him as still here. It's a twisted thing, I know, a fairy tale. It's just been, well, comforting, I guess is the word."

"I can understand that," Rose said.

"I've been tempted many times. I'll turn the doorknob back and forth, all the time knowing it won't open. Sometimes I'll stand there and talk to him through the door." Neither one of them said anything for several minutes. Rose stretched her legs out in front of her and took a sip of coffee. Ned carried on. "I miss him so much. It's supposed to get easier with time. But it doesn't, not for me."

Rose laid a hand on his forearm. "This is just a thought, Ned, but maybe if you sorted out his room, you might find some relief. You might find a shirt or something that you could wear that could make you feel close to him."

Ned said nothing, just looked skyward, as though searching for a response. Then he turned his head and gazed vacantly in Rose's direction as she spoke.

"I could help you."

⁂

Rose and Ned climbed the stairs together, with Ned in the lead and holding the skeleton key he had retrieved from the kitchen drawer. Upon reaching his father's bedroom door, Ned stopped short of inserting the key as he looked at Rose with a questioning pause.

"It'll be alright. We can stop anytime you want," she reassured him.

Ned looked back at the keyhole and pushed the key in, turned it 360 degrees, and heard the click as the lock moved. He pulled out the key and rotated the knob. Despite giving the door a push, it didn't budge. He pushed harder, but still nothing happened.

"I bet the paint has stuck the door to the frame," Rose offered. "Put your shoulder to it and give it a big shove."

Ned did as Rose suggested and as he shoved his weight against the door, it gave way unexpectedly, carrying Ned's weight with it and sending him stumbling to the floor of the bedroom.

"Oh, boy! Are you alright?" Rose said, offering her hand.

"Yeah, I'm fine," Ned muttered as he stood up and brushed himself off, embarrassed more than hurt.

He surveyed the room for the first time in nearly five years. But it wasn't what he saw that struck him first. It was the musty, stale smell with no distinguishing scent of his dad. He thought there would be something of his father in the air, but he now realized that wouldn't be the case after such a long time. It smelled just like a room that had been closed for five years.

"Let's open the shades and get some light in here," Rose said, stepping forward to raise the blind on the east window. Immediately, the midday sun poured through the glass panes, highlighting the microscopic smog of dust in the air. Rose moved beyond the bed and did the same thing with the other window. Now Ned could see every detail of the room. It was just as he remembered. The dust layer was fine and thinner than he would have guessed, but the room was tidy and the double bed was made. Atop the tallboy dresser there was a sparse collection of items: coins in an old ashtray, a ball-point pen, a pocket ruler, a hairbrush and comb, a corroded metal tube of lip balm, and a partially filled bottle of English Leather. Ned grabbed the cologne bottle and sat on the edge of the bed with it in his lap. From this vantage point he could see the closet door ajar, and a head shot mirror on the wall above the threadbare cushioned bench. Below the bench rested his father's shop boots, the laces flung aside as though he had just put on slippers and would wear the boots again tomorrow.

Ned had forgotten about the wall map of the United States mounted beside the bed. "Dad brought this map downstairs when I was in seventh grade. I had to memorize all fifty states and their capitals for social studies class that year. He quizzed me every night before bed."

Rose smiled. "How did you do on the test?"

Ned looked her way with a toothy grin. "I got a 100."

Rose sat down on the bench. At the same time, Ned set the bottle on the bedside table and lay back on the bed, resting his head on the pillow.

"Did your folks always sleep in separate bedrooms?"

"No, I think that started after Mom got much worse with her mental illness. I was pretty young and wouldn't have paid much attention to that. Dad always read the bedtime stories to me in my room. I can't even recall a time when my mother did that. He used to spend so much time with her in the other bedroom. She liked her door left open, and I would hear him speaking to her in hushed tones. Couldn't much hear the conversations, he did most of the talking. But I remember hearing the whisper of his voice. Do you remember how rich his voice sounded? Probably not, you were so little. I can still hear him singing along to the radio in his shop and how on pitch he always was, like he could have been a real vocalist if he wanted. Oh! I just remembered. He used to sing this one song to her, from the forties, I think. Something about rainbows."

"'Somewhere Over the Rainbow', maybe, from *Wizard of Oz*?" Rose asked.

"No, it wasn't that. Rainbows and clouds, maybe…"

"Oh!" Rose sang, "I'm always chasing rainbows, watching clouds drifting by…"

"Yeah! That's the one," Ned said, nodding his head. "I can't believe I forgot that. He'd sing that to her while he sat on the edge of her bed, brushing her hair before she went to sleep. I think it must have been devotion, you know? Rose, I can't remember ever hearing a cross word between them."

"That would have given you a real sense of security. I mean, I know what I had as a kid and it was nothing like what you describe. Of course, my parents weren't together like yours. Probably for the best, they would have fought all the time."

Ned stood and opened the closet door. Peering inside the cramped, dark space, the naked light bulb on the ceiling lit up when he pulled the string. Rose watched him disappear inside, then heard him say "Oh".

She got up and pulled the door back further. "What is it? What's wrong?"

"Nothing."

Ned was standing among the hanging clothes and had pulled the sleeve of a brown flannel shirt to his face, smelling it. He removed the shirt from the hangar and used both hands to bring the neckline to his face. "Can you smell this, Rose?"

She brought a sleeve to her nose. "Not the way you mean, I can't."

Ned took deliberate breaths in and out several times, all the while looking at Rose. "It's him, Rose. It's my dad." Ned slipped the shirt on over his tee shirt and buttoned it. He couldn't hold back the tears. "He's here, Rose."

"It looks great on you, Ned. You can probably wear all these clothes." Rose brushed her hand across the sleeves of all colors of shirts and sweaters. Jeans and other work pants were stacked on a makeshift wooden stool. A pair of polished black dress shoes was tucked neatly below the suspended clothing.

"Here's the suit he bought for my senior prom. He was a chaperone." Ned fingered the sleeve. "That was the night Phoebe and I fought…"

Ned's voice drifted off, so Rose stepped back into the bedroom. She picked up the bottle of English Leather, examined the label, then opened the lone drawer of the bedside table. Inside was an eight by ten black-and-white photo of what Rose supposed were Isabelle, Dennis and baby Ned. "Come look at this," she said.

Ned stepped out of the closet as Rose handed him the photograph. "Yeah, this used to be on top of the dresser. I guess he liked to look at it up close sometimes." He ran his fingers over their beaming faces. "That must have been a happy day." Ned moved over to the dresser and pulled open the top drawer. He let out a chuckle when he saw it looked like his own. "These top dresser drawers never hold any clothing, Rose. It's a throw all drawer. Just about anything can wind up here. And once here, it never leaves. May as well start here. Pull that trash can over and help me sort this junk."

Rose picked up a set of cufflinks shaped like owls. "I've never seen those before in my life," Ned said. He walked back to the closet and handed her an old Thom McCann shoe box. "Here, put them in here."

Together they sorted out the obvious trash: a rock hard pack of

Beaman's chewing gum, some equally hard Clorets, another comb, this one with two tines missing, a combination lock—closed with no combination, and scads of little papers with chicken scratch that may have been to-do lists at one time. In a small, felt pouch with a tiny drawstring, Rose discovered a polished, flat, gray oval stone. It measured about one inch by one and one-half inches and had an unusual streak of pink slicing through it. The stone had a small hole in the narrow end, suggesting it had been worn as a pendant on a necklace or chain.

"What's this?" Rose asked.

"I don't know." Then it dawned on him. "Wait a minute." He moved over to the bedside table and picked up the photo. "Here it is," he said, tapping his finger on the glass.

Rose looked over his shoulder. They could see just the very top of the stone hanging on a chain around Isabelle's neck, the remainder of it disappearing beneath her blouse.

"Your dad must have given it to her as a present. It was obviously very dear to her, and to your dad," Rose said, pointing out the felt bag.

"I guess so." Ned rubbed the polished surface between his fingers once or twice before securing the stone back into the felt bag. He put it in his pants pocket.

Rose picked up the last two remaining items and handed one to Ned. "This looks like some sort of receipt," she said.

Ned squinted at the paper, flipping it over in his hands. "Oh. This is the receipt for the piano Dad bought me for my eighteenth birthday." He studied both sides more closely now. "Look at this, Rose. It's more than just a receipt. These must be each of the payments he made on it. Holy cow! He paid on this for ten years!" He passed the receipt to Rose. "I had no idea, you know. It was a complete surprise. The store delivered it to the house after the accident, but I was still in the hospital. Karina knew it was coming, though. That day, when I came home from the hospital, I was only stopping in to get some of my things because Portia had insisted I stay with her and Edward so she could take care of me, and Si had already left for college. I was still lightheaded, but remember walking into the house and seeing the baby grand. It just stopped me in my tracks. I couldn't speak."

Ned hesitated for a moment, recalling the day. "I stared at it for the longest time. Didn't even sit down on the piano bench, never struck a key. I think it was awkward for Karina and Portia, too. Then I hobbled upstairs, it took me forever, and grabbed some stuff and made a slow retreat out to the car."

"I can't imagine what that was like for you. It's a gorgeous instrument, Ned. I hope I'll get to hear you play it some day."

Rose handed Ned the last item. "This looks like a card, maybe. It's still sealed up."

Ned tentatively tore at the flap and pulled out the card. On the front it read: *It's Your Birthday!* Then, inside, there was a cartoon monkey wearing a party hat jumping up and down on a piano. The caption read: *Let the Shenanigans Begin!* Dennis had written: *Happy 18th birthday, Neddy! We're so proud of you. You deserve this! Love, Mom & Dad.*

Ned stared at the card for the longest time. Rose finally said, "You never got to see this, did you?"

"No."

Ned tucked the card back into the envelope and put it in his pocket. "Okay, I guess that's all for this drawer. What's in the next one?"

Rose ran her hand along the side of the chest. "This is a beautiful piece of furniture. Did Dennis build it?"

"Hmm, I don't know, I never asked. It's just always been here."

Rose started to close the top drawer, but hesitated. With a puzzled look, she twisted her head to examine the underside of the drawer. Then straightened up and studied the inside once again.

"That's odd. There's something funny about this, Ned. Look

how shallow the drawer is. But the bottom of the drawer is way down here."

Now Ned was studying the underside with her. "That *is* odd."

Rose pulled the drawer all the way out of the dresser and set it on the bed. "Look, Ned! There's a catch at the back, on both sides!"

Ned exclaimed, "Dad must have built the dresser and put a false bottom in the drawer."

Rose asked, "Should we take a look underneath?"

Ned could see the eagerness in her eyes as Rose placed her fingers on the catches.

"Sure. Why not?" Ned replied.

At the last second, Rose stopped and backed away from the drawer. "No, Ned, you should open it."

Ned leaned forward and released the catches, raising the false bottom hinges hidden beneath the front of the drawer. He pivoted the bottom toward him as Rose peered at the true drawer bottom.

"It's another card, Ned, just a single card, nothing else." Rose lifted the envelope and studied the fine, pale blue stationery. The flap was unsealed.

"What's it say?" Ned asked.

Rose pulled out a sheet of matching paper, opened the single fold, and read it to herself.

Ned looked her way again. "Well, who's it to… or from?"

Rose's hand shook and her voice trembled when she answered, "It's to your father." She passed it to Ned. "You should read this."

Ned read the brief note aloud:

Dearest Dennis,

I'll have to keep this one short, as Clark has asked me to travel today with him to New York for a conference. I just wanted you to know that you are in my thoughts, always.

I'm so pleased you've decided to tell Neddy the truth. You're doing the right thing.

I pray for the day when we can be together again. You are so dear to me.

Love and kisses,

Lucy

"Who is Lucy?" Rose asked.

Ned looked up, stunned. "I have no idea."

PART III

Rondo: Allegro ma non troppo

CHAPTER 15

Two weeks passed. Then three. Ned felt a needling agitation mixed with confusion, but mostly he was scared. Unfounded, growing resentment toward Rose was threatening their amicable relationship. He tried to own the present situation, but in his weakest moments blamed it on her. If Rose hadn't been there, he might never have stumbled across the disturbing letter.

His life had been turning around, finally, and work was good. The Pizza Barn project was proceeding well, and Ned felt as if he was on the right path to something better than his life had been since the accident. Meeting Rose had genuinely been a positive turning point for him, but now the letter was an obsession that he could not quit. How could the father that he loved and admired have been the same man that what, had an affair? A long-time girlfriend? A lover? The thought made him sick to his stomach. Is this what he did on those trips out of town for his wood business? Or did his father simply sneak away for day trips to Springfield when Ned was in school and Karina was minding the house and his mom? It was all too sordid to even imagine.

He poured himself a cup of coffee, took the envelope out of the drawer and flipped it over. Having inspected it over a dozen times, he knew there was nothing on the back. The face revealed little beyond the lilting, feminine script, just a post office box number and the Springfield post mark. There was no last name of the sender.

The deception was so puzzling. Or maybe it wasn't a secret, at least not to everyone. What if Karina knew about it? What if—? No, his mother couldn't have possibly known. She could never have accepted something like that. Or could she? Ned asked himself how much he really knew about his mom and dad and their relationship. For the better part of his life, he had never had a reason to think their marriage was anything but normal. But it wasn't normal. His mother wasn't normal. His parents slept in separate rooms. His mother was… unavailable, he presumed. Actually, though, what did he know? He was just a self-centered kid back then. The knock at the door woke him from his thoughts as he put down his cup of coffee and shoved the letter back in the drawer. Dwight had let himself in before Ned got to the door.

"Morning!" he chimed at Ned. "Got one of those for me?"

"Sure. I'll let you sugar and cream it. How do you stand all that stuff in it, Dwight? I mean, can you even taste the coffee?"

"You drink it your way and I'll drink it the right way, buster. Don't lecture me, or I'll turn around and you can finish up that gazebo by yourself."

Ever since Ned had returned from Texas, he had been eyeing the gazebo when he would sit on the front porch. He remembered how it had looked when he was little. His father had faithfully kept it cleaned up and painted for a while, but eventually stopped maintaining it. That hadn't stopped Si and Ned from playing on it. The pair had gotten yelled at frequently for shimmying up onto the roof. They had mastered the technique when Si brought over a thick climbing rope like they used in gym class. With knots placed just so, even Si could zip up to the top with little effort. With no other kids in the neighborhood, the two of them claimed the gazebo as their exclusive domain. Sometimes a friend or two from grade school joined them, but otherwise they had it to themselves. In the beginning, it served them as a pirate ship, a train, an army tank, a skyscraper, a hideout and once, even as a cloud. As they got older, and the fantasies tapered off, it became just their cool place to hang out and talk about the things teenagers talk about.

Now Ned had received permission from the city to refurbish the gazebo after presenting his cogent job plan that spelled out the current defects along with the methods and materials he proposed to bring it back to life, at no expense to the city. He had cajoled Dwight into helping him with the promise of talking him up to Rose, on whom he was sweet. Ned orchestrated the sneaky deal since Rose was already interested in Dwight, but Dwight didn't know that. They would all have a good laugh about it one day if the relationship jelled. If not, there was no harm done and the neighborhood would once again have a gazebo of which it could be proud.

Ned laughed and said, "Is Cheeky with you?"

"Of course. He's out in the truck. I'm thinking we'll load up your tools and stuff and then we can back the truck up to the gazebo. It's been dry the past few days, so I don't think the truck will damage the grass there."

"I agree. Not much of a lawn left out there, anyway. That'll have to be a Phase II job."

Dwight sipped his coffee. "Uh, is Rose here?" he asked, trying to sound casual.

Ned had been waiting for this. "No, Dwight. Why do you ask?" he replied innocently.

"Oh, I just thought maybe she'd want to hang out with us, maybe help?"

Ned started toward the garage with Dwight on his heels. "She's got an appointment in town this morning, but she'll be back before lunch and join us then with her work boots on."

Ned looked over his shoulder to see Dwight's ear to ear grin.

"Solid!"

The traditional fanfare accompanying high school graduation—proms, presents and parties—was not a part of Rose's GED celebration. Although eighteen, Rose felt much older and had been firm with Ned and Dwight that there should be no surprise parties or ridiculous accolades. After all, attaining a high school diploma, of sorts, wasn't much of an achievement. Ned could still hear her deadpan delivery when she had told them, "Don't be dim, you guys. I mean, what else was I supposed to do?"

The recurring presence of Dwight during those bright days that spring of 1973 lifted Ned's spirits. He and Dwight and Rose were a trio now, usually fixing things about the house, or playing board games, learning how to cook by trial and error. Ned's fondness for his housemate grew, and he let go of the ambivalent feelings he had experienced for Rose when they found the letter. She was a kind and reliable person who genuinely cared about him and he felt lucky to have her in his life.

As they ate spaghetti in the kitchen after bowling, Ned watched with amusement the unsubtle body language going on across the table between Rose and Dwight. She was twirling her hair with her fingers, laughing at everything Dwight said, and Dwight couldn't take his eyes off of her. Ned could almost see little hearts floating above their heads, their feelings were so apparent. It made him chuckle inside to wonder if his own friends had observed the same thing between Phoebe and him back in high school. Earlier that day, Dwight had declined joining Rose and Ned in a round of pool at the bowling alley, preferring to drink beer and heckle Ned as Rose gave him a run for his money at eight ball. Though his left leg hampered his bowling abilities, Ned remained a commanding presence with a cue stick, even while subtly dampening his shots to keep the game even. A lovelorn Dwight had used the opportunity to cheer Rose whenever she made a shot.

Rose began working as an aide at Tribute Physical Therapy on July 1. The pay was just minimum wage to start, but the job would give her health insurance benefits once she had worked there for six months. If she proved herself in that time, she would get a pay raise and could pay a bit of rent money to Ned. She was pleased with how her life was going, the future seemed bright. Living at Ned's had been a lifesaver for her, providing both spiritual and financial relief, for Ned had renewed her faith in people through his kindness and support. Never the religious sort, Rose surprised herself by saying yes when Dwight asked her to attend church with him one Sunday. The pair aligned in their quest for a more purposeful life, further strengthening the bond between them. Dwight continued his search for something to have faith in, a belief system that was distinct from God. He found himself unable to connect with the notions of hellfire and damnation, yearning for something that he could embrace without hesitation. Long into the night, when he talked with Rose about his pursuit, she listened intently, absorbing the tenor of his troubles, understanding him. The Unitarian Church became a refuge, of sorts, for the couple. They welcomed the fellowship that came with sharing companionship with folks who accepted people from all backgrounds and persuasions, even if the idea of God remained a question mark. Together, Dwight and Rose felt centered. The church continued to be the vehicle for them, but their deepening trust and devotion to one another shone through as the personal bible by which they flourished.

One evening in September, Rose and Ned were washing and drying supper dishes at the sink when Rose said, "I've been singing in the choir at church."

Ned looked at her with bright eyes. "Really? I didn't know you sang."

"Neither did I. Well, that's not true. When I was in San Francisco, I often sang with friends. You know, someone has a guitar and we're all smoking pot and so we would all just sing: Peter, Paul and Mary;

Joni Mitchell; Crosby, Stills and Nash, that sort of thing. I found out that I have an okay voice."

"That's great, Rose."

"The reason I bring it up is that I'll be singing a solo in church two Sundays from now and I need to practice."

Ned dried the last glass and reached up to put it away. "Oh, that's fine. I don't mind. It'll be nice listening to you."

"Well, thanks. But that's not what I'm asking."

"Huh?"

"I know this is a big ask, but do you think you could play the piano accompaniment for me as I sing?"

"What, you mean in church, at the service? Oh, no. I couldn't—"

"Not in church, Ned," Rose interrupted. "I mean here at the house, while I practice. The organist will play the accompaniment at the church service."

"Oh, right, of course."

The grim look on Ned's face told Rose what she needed to know. "It's all right, Ned. I understand if you're not up to it."

Ned thought about what to say. He wanted to tell Rose that he would be happy to help her, but he couldn't say he truly felt that way. His eyes drifted through the kitchen into the living room where the untouched baby grand stood. He felt a sweat beginning under his arms. "Hmm, ... What's the song?"

"'Jesus Is Calling'. Do you know it?"

"I think so. It starts out, 'Softly and tenderly, Jesus is calling….' Is that the one?"

"Yes!" Rose exclaimed. She went into the living room and grabbed the sheet music she had borrowed from the organist. "Here. Does this look like something you could play for me?"

Rose watched as Ned scanned the score, absorbing it rapidly, flipping to the second and third pages. "This isn't hard. I mean, technically it isn't hard. It's just that I haven't…" Ned stopped. He was being ridiculous. There was no reason he couldn't stumble through this in his own living room with no audience other than Rose. She wouldn't be listening to him anyway, she'd focus on her voice. "All right, Rose. I can play this for you. I'm just not sure about hitting these left hand chords very well."

"Oh, that's okay, Ned. I'm sure whatever you can do will be just fine. This is so great. Do you want to run through it by yourself first?"

"Yes. Let me do that. Maybe you could leave me alone with it for a bit?"

"Sure. I'll go upstairs and take my shower. I won't hear a thing!"

Ned waited until he heard the bathroom door close, and the shower was running. With the sheet music in hand, he stepped over to the piano, lifted the fall board, and sat down. The bench was slippery, and the untouched keys sparkled. Their mirrored reflection on the polished black enamel transported him back to a time when there was no other place he would rather be. He'd forgotten how white the ivory was, how black the ebony.

Ned stood and cautiously lifted the lid, raising the prop to engage in the lid's underside. Staring in awe, as though for the first time, he took in the elegant splendor before him: the gleaming gold of the iron plate, the scent of the fir soundboard, the precisely aligned rows of strings and dampers. Reflecting on his father's years of hard work, Ned imagined the immense pride his father must have felt when he could finally present this incredible instrument to his son, only to have the moment denied in the end. His knees weakening, Ned dropped to the bench, and as he did, he heard his father's voice enjoin, "Play, Neddy."

Ned took his time studying the time signature, touching the keys, assessing finger positions for the bass chords. Then he turned his attention to the treble clef, fingering the notes, again without striking them, just as Gretchen had taught him when he first began sight reading when he was five. He went through the entire song like that, without playing a note, gently mouthing the poetic words.

Straightening his back, he took in a breath, then began the two bar introduction. His beautiful piano enlivened the dormant room with a breadth of sound worthy of the angelic melody.

> *Softly and tenderly, Jesus is calling,*
> *Calling for you and for me;*
> *See, on the portals, He's waiting and watching*
> *Watching for you and for me.*

※

The languorous days of summer dwindled as burgeoning signs of fall replaced picnics, swims and shorts with frosts, rakes and jackets. Rose kept silent about the letter, and Ned had not mentioned it since the day they discovered it, months before. She could understand, on some level, Ned's apparent decision to let it be, but her heart told her that in the long run he would regret not knowing what it was all about. He could be keeping a door closed that should be opened. Rose decided to share her thoughts regarding the letter. It was also time to inform Ned about her decision to move out. She opened the door to the shop where Ned was puttering away the morning, constructing replacement steps for the basement stairway.

"Got a moment, Ned?"

"Yeah. What's up?"

Rose sat on the step and motioned for Ned to sit on his work stool. "There's a couple of things. First, I'm moving in with Dwight next month. He's been wanting this for a while now and I've been putting him off because I wasn't sure about it, about him and me, that is. I hope you're not upset."

"No, Rose, I've been expecting this. You were never going to stay here for the long term, even if Dwight hadn't come along. You two seem peculiarly well suited to one another."

Rose chuckled, "I don't know about the peculiar part, but, yes, I think you're right. Dwight and I are… in tune with one another. It feels like we've each been looking for the other all along. Doors, and hearts, apparently, open and close in our paths. I love him, Ned, and he loves me."

"Yes, he does. I'm happy for you both. Maybe you can make Dwight's place more comfortable, you know, more homelike. I've seen it and it suits Dwight just fine, but it may be a bit too, what's the word for it? Unadorned?" They laughed together, discharging any awkwardness that hung in the air.

"I promise you'll be our first guest for dinner after we get the place arranged for two. I'm glad you like spaghetti."

"But now I'll have to cook for myself, deserter."

"You'll be fine. You and I both know that."

Changing the topic, Ned asked, "What's the second thing?"

Rose hesitated before charging forward. "It's about the letter. Just let me speak before you say anything, okay? Please?" Rose took it as a positive sign when Ned nodded with no hesitation.

"I know you've been thinking about it because I've been thinking about it, like all the time, every day. I'm eager to hear what you have to say after all this time, but not just yet. I think you should try to find out about this Lucy person. Maybe she's what the letter seems to indicate, but you need to know for sure. Personally, if I was in your position, I couldn't sleep 'til I knew the truth. I would need to know, even at the risk of it changing my feelings about your dad.

"There's a back story to everything," Rose continued. "Hell, look at me. I grew up thinking my mother hated me because she didn't love me the way I thought a mother should. I know she's not gonna turn into June Cleaver. And we're never gonna be *that* mother and daughter, but I think in time we could become friends. Look, life is messy. People and relationships are messy. All I'm saying is give yourself a chance to understand your father more completely. Really,

Ned." To lighten the mood, Rose playfully slapped him on the back and proclaimed, "It's unlikely he was a serial killer."

Ned snickered, grateful to Rose for this nudge but at the same time annoyed to be chided for his inertia. "I guess I've been thinking the same, but only in the past few days. I've spent years avoiding a lot of things since the accident. To tell the truth, I've been lazy about it because it's just been easier to ruminate than work on rebuilding." Ned caught himself, suddenly realizing the truth in the words he'd so casually tossed out. "That's it: I've been lazy because it's easier than being strong."

They stared at one another until Ned finally confessed, "I know how to work hard for something, Rose. But I'm afraid of what I'll discover about him. He's my hero, you understand. My hero."

"I know."

"What will I do if it turns out…"

"Give yourself some credit, Ned. You're 22 now. You're not a boy anymore. Think of it like this: Which would make your dad proud? Stagnating with weakness and fear, or braving the path of truth?"

Ned let out a deep breath. "Don't be afraid to spell it out, now," he said sarcastically. "Okay. Any ideas how we find this woman?"

"We?"

"Yes we. You can't desert me just yet, Rose. Help me find her and I'll take it from there."

"Deal," Rose replied. "I actually do have an idea: we hire a private investigator."

"A private eye, like in the movies, you mean?"

"Exactly like in the movies," Rose chimed. "Get me your phone book and let's look them up."

Ned went into the house and Rose followed him to the kitchen, where he pulled the phone book out of a drawer. "What do I even look under?" Ned asked, even as he began thumbing through the yellow pages.

"I don't know. Try "Investigators" or "Private investigators" for starters."

He flipped to the "I". The term "Invest" was listed in relation to stock brokers. Then there was "Investigation". Under the heading it said, "see Private Investigators". "Aha!" Ned shouted. "Found it." Rose looked over his shoulder as they together perused the only two listings. The first was for one Robert Dowling, PI. His one inch ad provided minimal details, stating that he possessed a license, was bonded, and specialized in divorces and background checks.

Rose said, "Sounds like a lawyer that couldn't make it or something. Or maybe he works mainly with lawyers, for lawyers."

"That's probably it," Ned replied. "Also, he's here in Tribute. Would he even take a case that's in Springfield?"

Their eyes tracked down to the other listing that made them smile. Silver Spur Investigations operating out of Springfield.

"Well, this looks more encouraging," Ned remarked. He read, "Private and confidential investigations throughout central Illinois. Twenty-two years' experience in fraud, blackmail, theft, missing persons, divorce. No job too small. Licensed and bonded. Telephone Roger Vinely at 547-225-0001. Discretion guaranteed."

Rose blurted out, "Missing persons, Ned! It's his specialty! And he's in Springfield, to boot. I bet he can find her."

"You're probably right on that account. What do you think the silver spur business is about?"

"Maybe he's a cowboy?" Rose mused, grinning. "Let's call him right now."

⁓

Roger Vinely was, indeed, a cowboy. He wore his meticulously combed curly hair to his shoulders beneath a lustrous, golden palomino Stetson, perfectly cocked just so, pristine as the day he'd bought it in Dripping Springs, Texas. The pure silver spurs on the heels of his rattlesnake boots cost more than the boots and always announced his approach. Roger was untrammeled by convention and cared not a whit what others said about him.

Roger was born in Chicago, Illinois, on July 23, 1914, to Oscar and Faith Abbons Vinely. Faith's father, Chesterfield Abbons, had made a modest fortune in banking in New York. Chesterfield had fallen in love with Cornelia Mains, eldest daughter of his banking partner, Walter Mains, though she was nineteen years Chesterfield's junior. In spite of its May-December complexion, Cornelia's and Chester's marriage was a fine one. They had three children together: twin boys, John and Frederick, in 1881, followed ten years later by a daughter, Faith, named such in reverence to their almighty Lord and Savior, Jesus Christ, for answering Cornelia's barren ten years of faithful prayer for a baby girl.

When Chester succumbed to a heart attack in 1901, a wealthy Cornelia and her ten year old daughter were induced to move to Springfield, Illinois, by Cornelia's younger brother, Rocky, also a banker, so he could look after them. The twins, now twenty, remained at Columbia University, enjoying football games, girls and their trust allowance, at the expense of their business studies.

Mother and daughter settled into a fine home in a fashionable neighborhood and lived a contented, privileged lifestyle. Rocky made sure Cornelia met all the right people, and Faith charmed friends with the facility that accompanies childhood beauty on the brink of adolescence. Eventually, however, Cornelia tired of her growing daughter's teen-age antics, Faith being spirited and not inclined to follow rules, even after stern lectures from Uncle Rocky.

Faith was enrolled in private boarding school in Oak Park, where she continued her high jinks and rebellious nature until being expelled months before graduation. Her mother begged her to reform, to come home to Springfield, but she refused. Instead, much to her mother's and uncle's humiliation, she took an assembly line job at Western Electric's Hawthorne Works in Cicero, leaving her nights free to gallivant the dance halls and night clubs of Chicago, where she met and fell for the handsome and worldly Oscar Vinely, a dashing twenty-three year old reporter for the Chicago Tribune.

Marriage and pregnancy ensued, though not in that order. Nine months later Roger Vinely entered the world. On the morning after gaily celebrating Roger's first birthday, July 24, 1915, Faith and Oscar boarded the Eastland passenger steamer on the south bank of the Chicago River. They had left Roger with their trusted neighbor, Milly Perkins, so that they could enjoy the holiday provided by GE for its thousands of Hawthorne Works employees. The Eastland and four other passenger ships would carry the enormous numbers of employees and their families to Michigan City, Indiana, for a picnic.

The pair, along with over 2,500 additional passengers, had filled the Eastland to capacity. With a track record of minor listing incidents caused by its top heaviness, the ship had undergone modifications to improve its stability. Tragically, despite the improvements, after the passengers had boarded, the ship listed away from the wharf and quickly rolled completely onto her port side where the vessel ended up on the river bottom, twenty feet down. Hundreds of passengers, including Faith and Oscar Vinely, were trapped beneath the surface and drowned as the river water poured in.

And so it was that Roger was taken in by his wealthy grandmother, Cornelia, and raised by her in Springfield. Roger was a smart boy, skipping first grade and then, again, third grade. He grew impatient with the plodding pace of his education, so Cornelia sent her charge off to boarding school, hoping to challenge the boy and regiment his recalcitrant energy.

Young Roger flourished away from the confines of Springfield and eventually earned acceptance at Phillips Exeter Academy in New Hampshire, which pleased Cornelia. She could see a bright future for Roger in finance or medicine or law. However, Roger shattered Cornelia's hopes when he explained to her he would not attend college back east, or anywhere, for that matter. He had fallen in love with the west after spending the previous summer working at the Utah ranch belonging to his Exeter roommate's family. "Nana," he had exclaimed after graduation ceremonies, "I'm going to be a cowboy! I've got a job on a big cattle ranch in Texas and I'm going to ride the range, drive cattle, and learn how to rodeo! It's going to be amazing!"

For the next ten years, Roger lived his dream, leaving behind a conventional life for the excitement of riding horses and roping cattle. The self-centered exuberance of living his youthful dream left little room in his heart to consider the sadness with which he left his beloved grandmother. Letters to her grandson often went unanswered. To compound her grief, she had received word from her son John, a revered journalist with the New York Times, that his twin brother, Frederick, was divorcing. John did not tell his mother that Frederick had fathered an illegitimate daughter with a young woman named Estelle, whom Frederick refused to marry, offering only to pay for an abortion. Estelle implored Frederick to help her, so she could raise their daughter, Lucille, but Frederick, always reckless and prone to mixing fiction with truth to suit his needs, denied he was the father and turned down her plea, sending Estelle and the baby on their way, penniless. John, forever the Abel to his brother's Cain, hired a private investigator to find Estelle and Lucille, but the investigation came to a halt after determining that Estelle had died from tuberculosis in 1927. The investigator could not find any information about Lucille's fate. John continued keeping this drama a secret from Cornelia, as her health was declining, but maintained hope that one day he would find out what happened to the little girl.

Roger's dream life as a cowboy ended in 1940, at age 26, when a bucking bronco threw him at the Calgary Stampede, destining him to a future of back surgeries. He returned to Springfield to live with Cornelia, now 82. This time it was Roger who was the guardian. Cornelia passed away less than a year after his return, leaving Roger the house and an abundance of money. She also left Roger devastated by grief and remorse for his thoughtless indifference to his grandmother's unwavering love. Cornelia had been the only mother he had ever known.

With his selective service classification of 4F, Roger sat out World War II in Springfield, earning a private investigator's license and forming his own business. Financially secure, he didn't need to work, but enjoyed being an investigator, and flourished in that capacity. As the years passed, Roger's back condition worsened. Still, he kept at his craft and saw a steady number of cases come his way. By the time the call came in from Benedict Godwin in 1973, Roger was semi-retired and semi-crippled. Still, the case seemed pretty straightforward, and he accepted it.

Roger glanced at the envelope the client had given him the day before. He was parked across the street from the Springfield Post Office. He shut the car engine off and got out. At seven in the morning, the doors to the building were unlocked for mail drop offs, even though the post office didn't officially open for service until eight. Those same open doors allowed access to the rented boxes. Roger was interested in just one of them: # 79. The cowboy sauntered up the steps, checking his surroundings as he went. A young woman passed him on her way out as he held the door for her. "Thank you, Roger," she said politely. Everybody in town knew the cowboy private eye even if he didn't recognize them in return.

"You're most welcome, ma'am," Roger replied with a tip of his hat. "Have a fine day, now."

He walked along the corridor of boxes. Fortunately, they faced the street windows of the building, which ran floor to ceiling. Without turning his head, he spotted #79 and kept walking, as if it held no interest for him. It sat low, in the second to last row of boxes, making it impossible to view from his parked car. Still, he'd be able to see if anyone stopped at that area and stooped to open a box. It might be a long shot, but could just as easily pay off quickly.

Roger continued his walk to the end of the corridor and pretended to read the service desk hours on the interior doors. Then he did an about face and walked back out to his car the way he had come in. He settled in the driver's seat, positioned binoculars in his lap, and started the engine. Pushing the radio pre-set to WSPR, Roger heard the familiar voice of his pal, Donny, delivering the morning weather report: rain. It could be a long day.

CHAPTER 16

WHEN NED HEARD the telephone ring that Thursday evening, he had an inkling who it was and wasn't looking forward to a fourth call from Mr. Vinely, informing him there had still been no breakthrough in his case.

"Hello?"

"Ah, hi Ned. Roger here."

"Hello, Roger. How did things go today?" Ned sighed.

"Well, buckaroo, I finally have something for you."

Ned was stunned. He had thought Roger's plan to stake out the post office was weak. For three days, Roger had watched the post office box from his car and had seen no activity at box #79. For all Ned knew, the lady wasn't even using the box anymore. If it had been a secret, then she had likely stopped using it after his dad died.

"What did you find out, Roger? Who is she?" Ned exclaimed.

"Just hold yer horses, now. Gimme a second and I'll explain everything."

After Roger finished telling the story, Ned fought to contain himself as he waited for Rose to return from choir practice. When she finally strolled in at 9:30, Ned jumped up from the sofa and met her at the door. "You won't believe this, Rose! Her name is Lucy

Holcomb. She lives at 224 Brandywine Avenue in Springfield, a posh neighborhood. He found her!"

Rose couldn't stop smiling. "That's terrific. When are you going to see her?"

"*We* are going to see her Saturday morning, that is if you'll come with me. I can't do this alone, Rose."

She looked at Ned and said, "Of course you can do this alone. But, I get it. I'll go with you. I'm as curious as you about this mystery woman." She plopped down on the sofa and patted the seat next to her. "Now then, tell me everything Roger said, word for word."

✤

Trepidation had set in for Ned as the pair drove in silence to Springfield on Saturday morning. The exhilaration of finally locating the woman had faded and now he wasn't so sure this was a good idea.

As Roger told it, he had watched the post office each morning from seven a.m. to one p.m., then took a thirty-minute break each of the three days to grab a sandwich and use the bathroom a few blocks away. He continued watching in the afternoon until six p.m. in case the woman worked. Nothing. Then, on the third day, he changed his break time, worried that he might be missing her. He had gone inside to look more closely at box #79. Each box featured a small pane of glass, which easily allowed one to check for mail. Sure enough, there were three envelopes in #79 that third afternoon. There was still hope.

Then, on Thursday afternoon around 2:45, he watched as a gray Cadillac Sedan de Ville pulled up to the curb of the post office parking lot on its west side. A woman who looked to be in her late forties or early fifties got out and walked into the building. Determining her age proved challenging, as she was stunningly attractive and donned a stylish red wool jacket, gray slacks, and a felt beret that shielded her eyes. She was about five feet four with styled blond hair, stud earrings, and an expensive-looking watch on her left wrist. The red leather shoes matched the leather handbag in her right hand. Roger had tracked her every step with the binoculars and sat up straight when he saw her stop near #79 and bend slightly. This had to be her!

She was there only a moment. He had watched her stand back up and glance at the mail before placing it in her purse and walking to her car. Roger had put down the binoculars and shoved his car into gear, readying himself to tail her home. Roger was used to this aspect of investigation, having tailed countless individuals over the years. But this one was even easier than it should have been. To his surprise, the woman had driven straight to Brandywine Street, just three blocks away from Cornelia's house, now his house, on Grant Avenue.

He had parked a few houses short and watched as the woman pulled the Caddy into a double garage that housed a second sedan. He couldn't identify the make or model, but it had a sporty appearance. The automobiles and the mystery woman disappeared as the automatic garage door closed. Roger had eased his car forward, needing to get a look at the house and find a last name. The properties on Brandywine were spacious and, even though within the city limits of Springfield, the street had the air of a country road. The mailboxes were mounted to posts on the street, not attached to the houses. And there it stood, precisely what he had tirelessly sought: HOLCOMB engraved on the side of the mailbox. Now he had a full name: Lucy Holcomb.

Ned was perspiring now as he and Rose walked up to the front porch of 224 Brandywine Street. They tentatively stepped up to the door, then looked at one another.

"Are you ready for this Ned?"

"Yeah, I can't go back now. I have to know."

He reached forward and pressed the doorbell button. From inside the house, a muffled tone carried the classic "ding dong" ring as they stood at attention and waited, hands folded in front. Ned heard steps growing louder, then the door opened. A short, soft faced woman with white hair and a pleasant smile looked up to them and said, "May I help you?"

Ned said, "I hope so. I apologize for being here unannounced. I was hoping we might speak with Mrs. Holcomb? Lucy Holcomb?" His heart was beating a mile a minute.

The woman smiled back in response. " I'm the Holcomb's housekeeper. May I tell Mrs. Holcomb what this is regarding?"

Rose took over. " We would like to speak to Mrs. Holcomb about something of a personal nature. It would take only a few moments and we'd be happy to remain here on the porch. Do you think she'd be willing to speak with us?"

"Let me ask her. She's quite busy today, but I'll see what I can do. Please have a seat here on the porch. I'll be right back."

Rose sat next to Ned on an upholstered glider. "Are you all right?" she asked.

"Yeah. Now that we've reached the point of no return, I actually feel okay." Ned looked around the porch and across the street at the neighboring homes. "Quite the neighborhood, huh?"

Rose replied, "Well, at least she wasn't after your Da-" She cut herself off when she heard the housekeeper open the door.

"Won't you both come in?" She held the door for them as they thanked her and stepped inside to a resplendent foyer, fragrant with cut flowers, a rich marble floor and matching federal chairs on either side of a mirrored back setae. "Please follow me. The living room is more comfortable."

The living room was beautifully appointed. A custom made wool carpet covered the entire room except for a perimeter of polished oak flooring. The fireplace crackled with a modest fire, and two matching sofas faced each other. With original oils on the walls, a second seating area at the far end, and a triplet of casement windows adorned with stained glass figures that Ned couldn't quite identify, the room was remarkable. Transom windows above the three interior doors extended all the way to the ten-foot ceiling. However, the most amazing piece was the ebony Steinway grand piano glistening at the front.

"Oh, gosh," Ned stuttered. "This room is really beautiful."

Seconds later, Mrs. Holcomb walked in and said, "Thank you, Jane." Turning to her guests, she held out her hand. "Hello, I'm Lucy Holcomb. How can I help you?"

She was smiling, but somewhat reserved. Understandably, she did not know who they were. Ned was about to speak when the woman's demeanor changed, her face turning pale. "Oh!" she blurted out, taking a half step back.

Puzzled, Ned hesitated before saying, "I'm sorry. Are you alright?"

A strained sigh escaped from Lucy Holcomb's lips as she entwined her hands, gathering herself. "Oh, mercy, where are my manners? I'm so sorry. I've been rushing around this morning, readying for a trip. But—oh never mind, it's not important. Please, sit down, won't you?" Taking a seat opposite Rose and Ned, she said, "Now then. I'm sorry. Who are you again?"

Now her face seemed flushed. "Is she nervous? This is all getting peculiar," Ned thought. He needed to get down to business. "Mrs. Holcomb," Ned had his wits about him now and plowed on, "This is Rose Gardeen and my name is Benedict Godwin. My father was Dennis Godwin. He passed away five years ago, and I recently found this letter in his bureau." Ned removed the envelope from his pocket and handed it to her. Without looking at it, she accepted it and started to speak, but Ned cut her off.

"Please, if you'll let me finish?"

The woman nodded and opened the envelope, briefly eyeing the letter.

"Is that from you?" Ned asked. He sat transfixed by the woman across from him even as she reverently folded the letter and slid it back into its envelope. She was beautiful, he couldn't deny that. Ned supposed his father could have been tempted...

With an air of integrity, she said, "Yes. It's from me."

Neither of them said a word, and Rose had the sense to keep quiet, this was not her show. Finally, Ned asked, "How long had you and my father been having an affair?"

The woman's mouth dropped open. She stuttered, "H...how long? An affair?"

"Yes. How long? When did your relationship begin?"

"Relationship? Oh, goodness, no. No, no, no. My dear boy, I was never your father's girlfriend. I wasn't his lover. There was never any affair."

Ned pointed to the letter. "I don't understand. Then what would you call it?"

The woman inched toward the edge of her seat, so close to Ned that their knees touched.

"I am Dennis's sister." She paused only for a moment as tears clouded her eyes, then reached for his hand. "Neddy, I'm your aunt."

∽

"His sister?" Ned drew back, his head pounding. "Now I know you're lying. My father didn't have any siblings. Do you think I'm stupid?" He struggled to contain himself.

"No, Neddy, I know you're not-"

"Don't call me Neddy! Only my dad called me that."

"Of course. I'm sorry, uh, Benedict."

Lucy Holcomb's eyes searched the familiar room as she tried to formulate what she wanted to say to him. Having pictured the boy's face so often over the years, she had always known, even hoped, this day would come. But now, coming face to face with him in her home, just a few feet away, she felt ill-equipped to begin. Bits and pieces of the story were now all a jumble in her brain and she couldn't think straight. "Benedict, I understand how confusing and upsetting this must be for you. I'm sorry." She paused a moment, staring at Ned, with a brief acknowledgement of Rose. "I can hardly believe you're here. Please listen to what I have to say before you judge the veracity of who I am. Give me ten minutes, can you do that?"

Rose at last spoke. "Ned, I think we can give Mrs. Holcomb ten minutes, don't you? After all, it's why we came here, yes?"

Ned looked at Rose with muddled eyes. "What did you say?" His expression was flat and Rose could see he was trying to process what was happening.

Lucy Holcomb jumped in, "Why don't I give you two a moment. I'll ask Jane to bring us some tea."

Once she had left the room, Rose grabbed Ned by the shoulders and whispered, "Listen, Ned. This is why we came here, right? To find out who she is, what she is. If she's lying, you'll be able to tell pretty quickly; she can't possibly know the endless details you know about your dad and his life, can she?"

"I guess not."

"Of course not. And, if she really is your aunt, then, well, the same thing goes, she'll know lots of things. Maybe she even has some proof. At the very least, she'll be able to tell you why your dad kept her a secret."

Ned had settled down now and nodded at Rose in agreement. "Okay. I'll listen to what she has to say."

Rose patted his arm. "Good plan."

Mrs. Holcomb returned, with Jane following behind carrying a tea service. Silence filled the air as the uncomfortable trio settled in, sipping their tea. Finally, Mrs. Holcomb smiled and spoke.

"First, I hope you'll both call me Lucy. My given name is Lucille, of course, but only my parents called me that. But that's another story. Benedict, before I begin, would it be all right if I ask you some questions? I just want to get an idea of what blanks I need to fill in for you, about your dad and me, I mean."

"Go ahead," Ned replied, trying to keep the belligerence out of his voice.

"All right. Did your dad tell you much about his childhood?"

"As a matter of fact, no, he didn't. Only that he grew up on a farm during the Depression."

"Yes, that's right. Did he tell you any stories about the farm, his parents, school life, things like that?"

"He told me he had to work on the farm, all the time, after school, weekends, like the work was never done. So he didn't have much time for friends and goofing off."

Lucy nodded once more in agreement. "All true enough. And what did he tell you about his, our, parents?"

"Just that they're both passed. They died while he was in the army."

Lucy sat back on the sofa, seeming to ponder what Ned said. "Did he tell you about his desk job in the army during the War?" Lucy continued.

She knows about that, Ned considered. Nothing secret about that, though. Lots of people know that. "Yes, he told me. He said it was boring, and he never got overseas or did any fighting."

"I see," Lucy replied in a measured tone. In short order she stood and walked over to the piano bench. Lifting the seat she removed a large book, an album of some sort and brought it back, tenderly cradling it in her lap. "Benedict, I'm going to need more time with you to explain the reasons why you don't know about me. I know it sounds like I'm putting you off, being secretive, or such, but that isn't what I'm trying to do. I've actually longed for this opportunity to share my story with you. You see, my story is also your father's story. And I want to tell it right so you'll need to be patient with me. Are you willing to do that?"

Ned scrutinized her, bewildered. "I don't know what to believe just now. You seem sincere, but you have to understand how questionable this all sounds to me. I mean, what reason could there be for my dad to hide the fact he has a sister?"

"What reason, indeed. You're very bright, Ned. I know that about you, and I know about your early piano accomplishments, too. And I know about *The Emperor*." She observed Ned's startled expression. "Yes, I know all about that. And, you've asked the right question: Why didn't Dennis tell you about me? The answer to that simple question is not so simple. It's long and puzzling, but I'll tell you the complete answer in time." Lucy lifted the cover of the album. "These are family pictures, Benedict. I'm not going to show you the entire album just now, but there are two photographs I want you to see today that, I hope, will help you believe me, that your dad and I are brother and sister."

Rose scooted forward to the edge of the sofa to look at the album. Lucy delicately removed a square, black-and-white photo from a page, being cautious not to bend the corners as she slid it from the four corner mounts before passing it to Ned.

"This was taken at the farm in 1930. It's the only photo I have from that time, so it's very precious to me. As you can see, it's Dennis and me. It might be hard for you to tell that it's me since I'm just six in the picture, but I imagine you can recognize your dad. He would have been—"

"Twelve," Ned finished the sentence. "Dad was born in 1918, so he would have been twelve."

"That's right," Lucy said.

Ned studied the photo. The boy in the picture was definitely his father. He wore overalls, the kind with the denim straps that came up and over the shoulders. The boy's face displayed all the facial features Ned knew so well. His hair was buzzed cut, accentuating his large ears. It was unmistakably him, and a wave of emotion suddenly washed over Ned. The girl could be Lucy. She had what looked like blonde hair, carelessly cut to shoulder length, with bangs. Both children were thin, even bony. The girl wore a gingham dress with a floral print, a strand of hair carelessly crossing her face. They were barefoot, standing beneath a large tree and squinting into the sun. Their stance seemed awkward, forced. Two things stood out to Ned. First, the girl was leaning her head against Dennis' side as he protectively held his arm around her shoulder. Second, neither one of them was smiling.

Rose said, "1930. So this would have been during the Great Depression?"

"Yes, Rose, that's correct." Lucy flipped several pages forward and removed another photograph. "Here's one from 1950. See if you can guess who's in it."

This one was sharper. There were four adults and a baby. Clearly, it was Ned's mother holding him in her lap next to his dad as they perched on a picnic table bench. Lucy and a man were standing next to his parents with drinks in their hands. It looked like they were all at a park for a picnic. A swing set stood in the background.

Ned pointed out each person. "Well, these are my folks holding me. This one is you, but I don't know who this man is."

Lucy laughed. "Oh, you couldn't know. That's Clark, my husband."

Ned was starting to believe Lucy as far as it went. Still, the whole thing made little sense to him. He heard a door in the rear of the house open, releasing the sound of Sarah Vaughn singing "He's Only Wonderful" as footsteps approached the living room.

Lucy hollered, "Clark, is that you? Come in here, please."

Clark Holcomb walked in, taking in the scene. He glanced at his wife, expecting her to say something to him, but she simply smiled and drank her tea. Clark spotted the photo album on the coffee table next to the tea service, then studied the blank faces of the unknown visitors.

"Hello, I'm Clark Holcomb," he said, moving further into the room as he introduced himself, still puzzled about what was going on. In just a few seconds, however, recognition set in and a huge smile appeared on his face.

"Oh, my God. Neddy!" He wasted no time and tossed formality out the door as he stepped straight up to Ned and wrapped his arms around him. The only thing Ned could do was awkwardly return the greeting. Clark pulled back to see Ned's face, but still held his shoulders tight. "Oh, I'm sorry," he said, letting go. "Bad form. It's just that, well...." And by that point, words failed him as he wiped his eyes.

"Rose, Benedict, this is Clark, my husband," Lucy said.

Ned gave a hesitant hello and Rose said, "Hello, Mr. Holcomb. It's nice to meet you."

Clark looked about at the group, then said, "Luce, I hate to be the bearer of bad news at this very special moment, really, but, honey, we need to move along or we'll miss our plane."

Lucy glanced at her watch. "Oh, gosh, you're right, Clark. Benedict, Rose, Clark and I are leaving for New York this afternoon. Look, you'll just have to come back again. We can spend the day together next time, maybe?"

Ned looked at Rose, who nodded her agreement. "All right."

"Here, take this photo of you as a baby. You can keep it. Eventually, I can show you the others. Oh, my gosh." She scrutinized him. "I can't believe it's you. You look just like him, you know." Lucy was crying again. "I can't stand it for another moment. Please, can I give you a hug?"

She didn't wait for an answer.

⁂

"Okay, Ned, talk to me," Rose said after the two had closed the car doors. "Do you believe what she's telling you?"

Ned turned toward Rose and replied, "First, I want you to tell me, objectively, how all that sounded to you."

"Okay. Objectively, I have to say, Lucy was pretty convincing in her sincerity. She came across to me as telling the truth. Her body language and her sentiment—Ned, that didn't seem staged. She seemed thoughtful about what she said, you know, genuine. And then there's the picture."

Ned handed it to Rose.

"I mean. This sort of backs up her story, doesn't it? Unless she and Clark are running some sort of make believe, for what reason I can't imagine. I think it's pretty clear that she and your father were never lovers or anything like that. So, it's a matter of does the brother and sister story ring true."

There was a chill in the air, so Ned switched on the heater after starting the engine. "I hear what you're saying and I agree they weren't having an affair, which is a big relief. But, I just don't understand the brother and sister story. It doesn't make any sense."

"I know. You're right, it doesn't. Could you argue they were just friends? Like friends when they were kids? They stayed in touch, got married, are still friends? That can explain even this picture. Nothing says these people are anything more than friends."

Ned countered, "But if they're just friends, then why the secret all these years? And why lie about the friendship now, today? Claiming kinship seems like a bigger lie, in that case. Why dig a deeper hole?"

Rose nodded. "Yeah."

"I wish she had more time today. Maybe this trip to New York on business is just a story to stall for time. Maybe Clark was listening the whole time to the conversation we were having and came to her rescue. I mean, we don't really know anything about these people. Maybe we could hire Roger to do some research on them. To see if their backgrounds are, you know, normal. Like, what does Clark do for a living? And Lucy. Maybe Roger can find out something."

Rose reflected on Ned's suggestion. "Hmm. I'm not so sure about that. I think it might be a decent plan to have Roger check out any character issues, you know, arrests or trouble with the neighbors, that kind of thing. If he can get a clean report on that, then I think it would be smart to stop there. If they're good people, then I for one am on board with Lucy being your aunt. Once you accept that, then wait to hear the story firsthand from the horse's mouth."

"You're right, Rose, that's a better plan. Let's stop over at Roger's house now before we drive back to Tribute. I can write him a check for his services and see if he'll do a little digging for us. Besides, I'd like to see what a cowboy's house looks like in this neighborhood."

※

It took the duo less than three minutes to get to Roger Vinely's home on Grant Avenue. They dismissed any thoughts they had conjured up about discovering a big log cabin with a horse or two saddled up in front when they pulled up to the property. Roger's home was more imposing than the Holcomb house. While the Holcomb house looked very arts and crafts like, Roger Vinely's home was older with more classical architectural details. It was a three story structure of stone and stucco with a covered side portico entrance where the driveway passed through to a separate three-car garage. The narrow garage doors spoke of an era when horses and buggies may have occupied the spaces. Despite the conservative design, Ned knew it was Roger's house when he saw the mailbox. It was totally out of place for the neighborhood, and he suspected Roger had gotten some grief from his neighbors about it. The mailbox had unmistakably been custom made. It appeared to be cast in metal, then painted. It was a cowboy hat! To be precise, someone had affixed a meticulously shaped cowboy hat on top of a plain black box. The hat mirrored the one Roger had been wearing the first time they met. His house number was on the side of the black box, the letters in a continuous script lasso: *one thirty-eight.*

"I guess this must be the place," Rose chuckled.

Roger must have seen them from a window because he had the front door open before they reached the porch.

"Howdy do, strangers!" he yawped. "Git on in here. I've got a fire on in the library. We can talk there. Y'all had any lunch today?"

Rose answered, "Hi Roger. No, we haven't eaten lunch. We just stopped by to—"

"Alrighty, then. I've got Kathleen in the kitchen rustling up some chili and cornbread. You two like chili?" he asked, even while he was whisking them forward and around the bend in the enormous front hall.

"Uh, sure, Roger." Ned looked at Rose and she nodded, grinning. "We like chili."

"That's fine, then. Sit yourselves down anywhere, I'll be right back. Feel free to check out any books that look interesting. Just steer clear of that crossword table over there. I'm designing a new puzzle for the Chicago Tribune."

And he was gone, to the kitchen, presumably. "He designs crossword puzzles?" Ned whispered.

The afternoon flew by as Roger entertained Rose and Ned with his endless stories about the West. At first Ned was worried it would be a long afternoon of mournful lamentations when Roger began his narrative about the death of his parents in the boating disaster. Ned felt as though it saddened him more than it did Roger. Perhaps Roger found it easier to talk about them since he never knew his parents, not really. But he certainly knew his grandmother, Cornelia. Roger was in his glory animating the stories of his childhood in this house, all the while admiring her enormous portrait above the fireplace. Near the end, he revealed to his guests the shame he still suffers from his detachment towards her love while he was living as a cowboy out west.

"I'm sorry for going on and on about Cornelia, like I have. To be honest, I don't have many visitors and I just don't get to talk to anyone about how special she was."

Rose said, "Oh, Roger, no. Your stories are wonderful! Thank you so much for sharing them with us."

Ned took just a few moments to describe the sort of information he wanted about the Holcombs. "Don't go crazy with this, Roger. I don't want to invade their privacy anymore than necessary to verify that they are who they say they are. Even as I'm standing here asking you to do this, I'm not sure. I feel like a stalker or something."

"Not to worry, Ned. I get what you're after. It won't take me long and I won't dive too deep."

Rose glanced at her watch. "Do you mind if I use your phone to call Tribute? Our little outing today has taken longer than I expected and I'd like to let my boyfriend know I'll be back soon."

"Sure thing, missy. You can use this phone right here. I'll meet you two at the front door when you're set to go."

Roger closed the library door behind him as Rose picked up the phone to call Dwight. She dialed the number, then plopped down in the leather chair. Dwight's quick "Hello?" after a single ring surprised her.

"Hi Dwight. It's me. This took a lot longer than Ned and I thought—"

Dwight interrupted her. "I've been waiting for you to call all day!"

"I'm sorry, babe."

"Never mind about that. Is Ned there with you?"

"Yes, you want to talk to him? He's right here."

"Yeah, put him on, please."

Rose covered the mouthpiece with her palm, extending the phone to Ned. "He wants to talk to you. He sounds funny, hyped up or something."

Ned grabbed the handset. "Hey Dwight. What's going on?"

"Ned. I… I…."

"Dwight! What is it, what's the matter?"

"It's Hag."

"Hag? What about Hag? Dwight!"

"Do you remember his girlfriend, Josy? Josy Steib?"

"Of course."

"She called me this morning from Toronto. Oh, man, I don't know how to tell you this. Hag is dead."

CHAPTER 17

Rain was falling as Ned drove his Jeep to the Springfield airport to pick up Mitch. He could see to the south that the rain was going to get much worse, and soon. Mitch had taken the redeye flight to Chicago from Los Angeles, but he would be on a commuter plane from Chicago to Springfield. A delay was inevitable thanks to the tropical storm in the Gulf of Mexico.

He hadn't seen or spoken to Mitch since the night of the dress rehearsal for his *Emperor Concerto* five years ago. Ned could still recall waving to his friends in the darkened mezzanine at the end of his performance. Mitch had visited him during the long hospital stay after the accident, but Ned had no memory of him being there. And now Mitch was an actor. Ned couldn't get his head around it. It would be amazing to see him again, to see everyone again. The weekend was going to be filled with equal measures of sadness and nostalgia as Si, Phoebe, and Mitch all returned to Tribute to honor their lost classmate.

Ned flicked the wiper setting to high as the rain pelted down in torrents. He slowed to a crawl, but his sightline to the road ahead was still poor, so he pulled over to the side of the highway and turned on his flashers. All around the sky was dark, itching to explode with lightning. Ned hoped Mitch's flight was not battling this storm.

He closed his eyes and lay his head back on the headrest. The FM station seemed unaffected by the storm as Simon and Garfunkel sang "The Sound of Silence", which triggered his recollection of seeing "The Graduate" with Phoebe on Valentine's Day in 1968, the year they all graduated. The song faded into the background, replaced by the calming white noise of rainfall as he fingered his class ring and nodded off, half asleep. Ned hated that he'd been cheated out of high school graduation and imagined the lighthearted moments his friends would have experienced with their families and with each other after the ceremony that June. He missed those times from high school when so much seemed possible, when he was so focused, even admired, the guy that had his life all figured out. He remembered the summer after tenth grade when he'd performed Aaron Copeland's "Hoedown" from his *Rodeo Ballet* at the Tribute Farm Days, receiving his first standing ovation. He'd been so confident, so proud of what he could do at the piano. "Now look at me," he thought, "the one left behind."

Ned jolted awake as a tractor-trailer truck roared past him, horn blaring, at what, he couldn't tell. Annoyed with his self pity, he took a sip of coffee and shook his head to wake up. The rain was letting up, and the sky had brightened.

※

Ned stood at Gate 3 and watched the passengers from Chicago file into the terminal, a full seventy minutes late. Even though he had seen Mitch on television last year, grainy and from the waist up, Ned wondered if he would look the same as he had five years ago. But it wasn't his appearance that registered with Ned as Mitch made his way toward him, so much as the way he walked—upright, relaxed, confident. Handsome as ever, people noticed him. Their eyes met, followed by smiles, as Mitch quickened his pace to meet up with

Ned. Mitch dropped his bag and grabbed Ned in a bear hug, just like old times. Only, this time, he didn't let go right away.

"Ned, it is *so* good to see you again." Mitch released his grip and looked at him intensely.

"It's great to see you, too, Mitch. You haven't changed. California agrees with you?"

"It does, Ned. I love it. You have to come visit me soon."

Ned reached for Mitch's suitcase and said, "Here, give me your bag and we'll head out to the car. Did you fly through the storm we just had here?"

"As a matter of fact, they delayed the departure out of Chicago to try to avoid the storm. But we ran into some terrible turbulence for about two minutes near the end of the flight. Everybody was gripping the seat arms, me included."

"Well, the weather has cleared now, so the drive to Tribute should be fine. I'm glad you're staying with me at the house, Mitch."

"Me too, thanks. I can't stay with my parents. You mind if we grab a coffee here at the airport? I'd like to chat with you a bit before everybody's around."

"Sure thing."

The two ordered and paid for their coffees, then sat at a table near the giant windows that offered a view of the planes. There was a constant hum of Muzak mixed with announcements of plane arrivals and departures.

Mitch didn't hesitate before jumping right in.

"So, old friend, you need to know that I didn't actually make it in the Navy. I enlisted and went to basic training back in '68, but, well, do you know any of this?"

"No, Mitch, I don't. So, you didn't stay in the Navy?"

"No, I didn't. Ned, I'm a homosexual. The Navy doesn't want me."

"What? Gee, Mitch, I had no idea. You didn't seem the type."

Mitch chuckled. "Type? You mean like limp-wristed and all that?

Of course not. That's a ridiculous myth, Ned. Most of us do not have that affectation."

Mitch acquainted Ned with his story, about his struggles at home in high school, his father, his exit from the Navy, everything.

"I didn't know you were dealing with this back in high school," Ned sighed, "So, your folks don't approve, is that it?"

Mitch frowned. "My father doesn't. Not too hard to understand, there. You remember him, right?"

"Yeah, I do. What about your mom and your brother?"

"You know what? That's a tough question. Maybe another time, okay?"

"Sorry."

Mitch waved the comment aside and took a long sip of his coffee, turning to the windows to watch a new plane taxi in. Noting Mitch's profile, Ned viewed his friend in a new light. The guy was brighter now, that was it. Like he finally discovered who he is, and was comfortable with it. Ned thought back to Mitch's puzzling uneasiness in high school and felt he understood things more clearly now.

"So, did you know you were, uh, like this all along?"

"Not when I was a kid, of course. It was when the hormones kicked in around sixth grade when I started feeling different." Mitch stole a glance at Ned. " I had a crush on you all through junior high and high school, you know."

"No, you didn't. Be serious," Ned joshed.

"Oh, I'm dead serious, man. I thought you were the neatest guy. Didn't you see how I was always trying to be next to you, wanting to do things with you? Why do you think I was always hugging you?"

"Huh. I never… I never saw it like that."

"Of course not. You only had eyes for Si."

"That's not right, Mitch. Si and I have always been just friends. There's nothing else there."

"I know that. It's just that he was your best friend and I wanted it to be me."

Ned shook his head. Despite the agreeable look on Mitch's face, Ned could hear a sadness in his voice. "I don't know what to say, Mitch. You've had some hard times. It's sad knowing you carried all this inside you, that there was nobody you felt you could confide in."

"Yeah, well, everybody has hard stuff, don't you think? Hell, you're exhibit A on that count, Ned. We all just deal and try to move forward, right?"

"Yup. In theory, anyway. No, you're right, Mitch. That's precisely what we do. It's not always easy, though."

"No, Ned, it isn't."

The two men were stumbling over their words now, as an awkwardness fell between them, the kind that happens when you haven't seen a friend in a long time. Mitch kept his eyes focused on Ned. "Tell me."

"Tell you what?"

Mitch furrowed his brow. "Tell me, Ned."

"Mitch, I don't think I can. I'm still pretty messed up. Up here, I mean," Ned said, tapping his temple. "You don't want to hear about it."

"Yes, I do, actually. C'mon." Mitch gave Ned his best Hollywood smile and said with a wink, "Give me three paragraphs." Ned laughed, recalling Mr. Logan's eighth grade English class.

He stared across the table at his old friend and tried to appreciate what the guy had been through, the struggles he must have endured for years, how he'd pretended to be what his family and friends expected him to be, all the while feeling like someone else. Ned tried to imagine the persistent fear and loneliness Mitch must have felt for so long, and considered Mitch's ultimate bravery in refusing to deny his truth. "Maybe this is a man who can understand what I'm going through," Ned thought.

"All right," Ned surrendered, "three paragraphs. But you have to promise not to get all sorry for me. I just can't take that."

"Of course."

Ned took a deep breath, exhaling steadily. "It's like this. There's a bunch of guilt for causing my father's death. I know the facts of the accident and I know my part. I lost Dad, my best friend. So, there's that.

"Second, I lost my dream, my life plan, the thing I lived for and the part of me that was me. I had this talent, Mitch, that was special to me. It brought me so much joy and meaning, and, I confess, admiration, especially from my dad. I lost my future.

"Third, and I think this is the hardest part just now, I don't know who I am anymore. I have nothing special to offer up. Without my talent, I'm just an ordinary man," Ned proclaimed, raising his left arm, "with a bum hand."

A moment passed before Mitch said anything. "That's a plateful, buddy, no doubt about it." He stopped, searching the room before going on. "Look, I don't pretend to be a therapist, but here's how I see it. Your dad was a special man. You lost him and that's a big deal, I understand. But blame is something that should have no place for you now. I remember your dad and I know he'd be upset with you for blaming yourself all this time. Remember, the trucker was blinded by the sun that afternoon, not your fault. As for your talent, it never disappeared. Ned, it's still inside you, right here," Mitch implored, thumping his heart with his fist. "Never forget that. Now, about that third part? I'm going to tell you something I bet you've never heard in all your self talk. Yeah, I know all about self talk. Listen up. You don't seem to understand that who you are has *nothing* to do with any piano talent you may possess." Mitch stopped speaking so his words would sink in.

"Think back to grade school and junior high. Consider all the dozens of kids who called you friend. Think of me! What did I just tell you? I was crushing on you way back when, man. I didn't even know 'til high school you played the piano, never heard you play until that amazing dress rehearsal night. So, your friends, Ned, weren't your friends because you were some kind of piano prodigy. We weren't groupies attaching ourselves to some famous pianist. We were just your friends because of who you were, as a person. You carried a kind of energy with you that just drew people in, like a magnet. It was charisma, Ned, and you had it in spades." Mitch leaned back in his chair, apparently finished speaking his mind. Then, as an afterthought, he grinned and added, "And you're still a very charming guy."

❧

It had been hard that night for Josy to explain to the group what had happened to Hag. He had been living in Toronto ever since leaving NYU during his sophomore year. He had found an apartment that three other people were sharing and they were looking for a fourth after the roommate moved to California. The first year there, Hag was pretty happy. He earned enough from bartending to get by and he was doing his stand-up act everywhere he got the opportunity. He imagined himself being discovered and winning a slot on Johnny Carson's Tonight Show.

Josy shared that she had heard from Hag only a month ago. "I don't know where he got my Columbus address from. I hadn't shared it with many people, certainly not with anyone who knew Bert. Hardly anyone knew I'd finished my bachelor's degree at Washington University in St. Louis in three years. I was only a month into medical school at Ohio State at the time. Anyway, we'd exchanged a few letters when he was at NYU his first year, I was still at Tribute High, but when he left for Toronto, he didn't tell me or anyone, except Dwight, I guess."

"It was my sophomore year at WU when I finally asked his mother, and she gave me his address. I wrote so many times I lost count, but he never answered back. Mrs. Glasby was protective of him and shied away from giving me much information for some reason. Still, I'd write him brief notes now and again because I wanted him to know I still cared about him."

Josy was in shambles now and couldn't go on. Rose comforted her the best she could, but there are moments when words fall short. A glass of water and shoulder pats eventually brought Josy back around enough that she could continue. "Even though Bert didn't answer my letters, I believed he had received them since none of them came back. So I drove up to Toronto on spring break last year to find him.

"The apartment he shared was dreadful. It was in a run-down neighborhood with abandoned buildings and cheap bars. I felt scared just being there. One of his roommates, Felicity, was at home when I knocked. I explained who I was, and she told me Hag was out but that I should hang out and wait for him. So I did, even after Felicity left for work. She was so trusting. The place was creepy, I'm sorry to say. Messy, of course, littered with cigarette butts, dirty glasses, discarded newspapers, clothes everywhere, dust. The air was thick with marijuana smoke and alcohol. I wanted to wash my hands but the bathroom was too disgusting. I sat on a threadbare sofa and cried thinking about Bert living like that. I waited all afternoon for him, but nobody came back to the apartment, so I finally gave up and wrote him a brief note asking him to write to me. I said that I loved him and was worried about him, then placed it on top of the TV and left. I was so upset.

"I didn't hear from Bert after that. Nothing, until last month. I was shocked, but so relieved when out of the blue he sent me a letter, long and detailed. He was apologetic, about so many things. It was uplifting, actually. He said he had stopped using drugs, including alcohol and marijuana. I was so happy to hear that." Josy gazed out the window, perhaps reliving the feeling.

Phoebe interjected, "But what happened then?" Phoebe, who had always been unflinchingly reserved, found herself touched by the story. "How did he die, Josy?"

"It was his heart," she answered flatly.

Hag's roommates had discovered him in bed on a Sunday

morning. He hadn't responded when one of them called out to him, which was uncommon considering his restless sleeping habits and the late hour. Don, the guy who had recruited Hag to the apartment, found him. Hag looked as though he was just sleeping, but his body was cold. Don frantically summoned an ambulance, but it proved futile. The EMTs pronounced Hag dead at the apartment.

"How could it be his heart?" Si interjected. "You mean he had a heart attack? He was only 23!"

Dwight waved a hand at Si and chided, "Just be quiet and let her finish!"

They were all sitting around Ned's kitchen table, stunned. Rose placed her hands on top of Dwight's fist to calm him down. Turning back toward Josy, who was clenching a tissue in her hand, she said, "Go ahead, Josy. Tell us the rest, please."

There had been little more to tell. His had been an unwitnessed death, so an autopsy had been required. The report revealed Hag did, indeed, die from a heart attack. The coroner believed alcohol abuse had worsened an apparent congenital defect in the left ventricle. She had found microscopic tears and scars in the valve that had been deteriorating for years. She believed that an earlier diagnosis would have allowed Hag to have the valve replaced. Because of his condition, he would have been classified 4F by the draft board.

"Oh, God. I can't believe it. After everything he went through to avoid being drafted," Ned blurted out.

Josy went on to say Hag told her in the letter that he wanted to come back to the United States, that he was going to face whatever he had to face as a draft dodger. He missed his mother, and he missed his friends.

"Did he say anything about his dad? They didn't get along, as I recall," Phoebe said.

"Only that he hadn't communicated with him at all since he graduated high school. I know from talking with his mother that Rev. Glasby was still unforgiving, and this weighed heavily on Bert.

He was so conflicted, you see. He couldn't understand how his father could be so callous to his own flesh and blood while professing dutiful love to God."

"Is that why Hag was cremated? Is that why Hag's father wouldn't allow him to be buried in the church cemetery?" Si asked.

"Partly. Mrs. Glasby went to Toronto to claim her son and ordered the cremation. She felt certain that's what Hag would have wanted. He just didn't believe in any religion, nor did he like the idea of bodies decomposing in the ground." Josy's eyes were puffy and red as she wiped at her nose once again. She looked exhausted. "I have to go now." She paused. "I loved Bert, I still do, but I imagine you all knew him better than me." Josy looked around the room. "I'll see you all tomorrow."

∽

Josie's departure left the group grappling with a set of disquieting mixed emotions. Exhaustion from grieving their friend kept them all together in the living room for a spell, some in chairs, others on the floor, unable to gather enough energy to get up and go to bed. One comment after another would put them all in tears while the next one turned the tears to laughter, as they would retell some of Hag's comedic antics from school.

It was after midnight before the group dispersed, with Si and Ned toting their beers outside for some fresh air. They meandered over to the gazebo, Ned's arm slung over Si's shoulder, friends forever, drinking beer and chatting while the others cleaned up in the kitchen. The muffled sound of Mitch's voice drifted out from the kitchen window and across the pond as he told of his acting life in California. Dwight and Rose and Phoebe would occasionally interject with a "what?" or "when was that?" or "really?", captured as they were by his spell.

Ned said, "So, tell me everything, Si. Show me pictures of your kids."

"Well, I've got this one of all four of us," Si said, retrieving a photo from his wallet. It was a classic Olan Mills portrait like they take at JCPenney's. "This was taken in May." He handed it over to Ned with pride.

"Oh, man, Si. You've got a beautiful family. How old are… I forget their names?"

"Maria and Eduardo. They'll be two next week. Of course you know Eva."

"Did you ever think this is where you'd be now, married with kids and all?"

"Of course not," he chuckled. "That's the beauty of it all. It's icing on my cake—or maybe it's the cake. Whatever it is, it's fantastic."

"When will you finish with your degree?"

"I'll be done in December, a whole semester early!"

"What will you do after you finish up?"

"We're moving back here, actually, to Tribute. I'm going to work with my dad until I get a footing."

"Back here? You're moving back here? That's super!"

"Yeah, I think so, too."

"What does Eva think of this? Won't she miss being with her mother?"

"Not at all. It was Eva's idea, actually. Her mom's coming back with us. Pamela has totally bonded with my mom, and Texas is so hot. We all like the idea of the twins growing up in a small town, and I get an instant start with my career."

"Where are you going to live? Is Pamela going to live with you?"

"Yeah. I'm not sure where we'll live yet. Probably rent a house to start. Eventually, I'd like to design and build a house. I've even talked with Dwight about that. He's thinking of starting his own construction business, you know."

"Well, sounds like you've got it all figured out."

"Oh, I don't know. Things always change. And that's not such a bad thing, keeps life interesting, don't you think?"

Ned replied, "I guess it can," but thought to himself, "I think that's what you think, Si. It's easy when everything seems to go your way."

"All right, your turn. Tell me stuff, Ned."

Ned reluctantly began with a summary of the past year since returning to Tribute. He filled Si in on his job, how he changed his mind about wood school, meeting Rose and re-connecting with Dwight, and finished up with finding the letter and meeting his presumed aunt for the first time just a few weeks ago.

"That's incredible! And you never knew about her?"

"Never had an inkling."

"So why didn't your dad tell you about her? I mean, she was just up the road your whole life. Isn't that a bit weird?"

"Totally weird, yes. I don't know. Lucy says she'll explain it all to me next time I see her. I'm going to Springfield next weekend."

Out of the blue Si reached over and took Ned's left hand, studying it. "What about this? Doesn't look like you've had any surgery on it lately."

Ned jerked his hand back and said, "Cut it out. No. I haven't had any surgery."

"Why the hell not?"

"Si, let's not get into this again, all right?"

"Actually, no. It's not all right. Five years, Ned. It's been five years and you need to bloody well get on with it. Have you at least seen Dr. Elwood? Have you spoken with Gretchen like I told you to?"

"Si! You don't get to tell me what to do. It's my life."

"That's right. It's your life. And I expect you to do something with it. Don't you remember how we used to talk about our futures? How we would pump up each other? How we just knew that each of us would do amazing things? Don't you remember that, Ned?"

"Yeah. I remember. Remembering is all I do anymore.

"So what are you doing to live up to my expectations?"

"Your expectations? That's funny. Why should I live up to your expectations? What about my own expectations?"

"Okay. What about them? Tell me what they are, because I'm not hearing any."

Ned grew silent. He turned away and grimaced at the night sky.

Si kept his eyes on his best friend. "I'm waiting."

Neither one of them said anything for the next few minutes. They drank their beers and looked around the neighborhood. At one point, Ned said, "I...", but then just faded out. The dead air between them wasn't awkward, even now. In a sense, the two had always been more than brothers, but they didn't have any of the sibling rivalry that so often can needlessly damage those relationships. Grudges had been short-lived in the rare instances they even existed, and now, kicking back under the gazebo, it was as if nothing had changed.

"Phoebe is still amazing, don't you think?" Si finally broke the silence.

Ned cocked his head with a smirk at Si. "Where did that come from?"

"Oh, come on. Are you the only one who doesn't see it?"

"See what?"

"Krickey, you stupid little man. Don't make me explain it to you, lest I think you really are dimwitted."

"Si, she's not interested in me anymore. I've talked to her. She's all focused on school and going into business with her dad and her roommate, Regina. Phoebe says her year in Africa opened her eyes to the problems in the world so she and Regina want to do something together with their lives, something that can make a difference."

"All true. So what? Phoebe still wants marriage and a family. She told me so."

"That may be, but it's not with me, Si. Phoebe's changed. She doesn't have room for me. Her life is getting big and I'm just an old boyfriend. Whatever we once had is gone, I'm afraid."

In a startling maneuver, Si seized Ned by the shoulders and spun him around, bringing them face to face, eyes a mere foot apart.

"Listen to me, you dope. Snap out of this… whatever it is. Remember me? Remember us? I can't stand it anymore. There's a life ahead of you, Ned, a wonderful life, if you'll just open your eyes and grab it. It's all right in front of you. Can't you see that?"

Si dropped his hands, abruptly realizing what he was doing. Grinning at his friend, now, while examining his face as though for the first time, he tweaked Ned's left earlobe and chuckled, "These ears, man."

Defenseless against his best friend's heartfelt outburst, Ned smiled. "Do you think Phoebe genuinely cares about me?"

*

It had been an uncommonly warm day for November, and the setting sun cast the long shadow of the gazebo onto the pond as the mourners congregated the following afternoon. Rose and Dwight had stepped up, cleaning Ned's house, stringing mini-lights around the gazebo roof, setting up a music stand for Phoebe and were now serving up cheese and crackers, beer and wine.

With so little time left before they would be returning to their individual lives, the friends were talking all at once. Phoebe would return to Urbana on Monday to continue her fall semester and Si was flying back to Houston in the morning; he had Eva and the twins to get back to. Mitch needed to be on set on Monday, so he would also leave the next day. They all seemed to be racing to get everything said.

Dwight, profoundly shaken by the news of Hag's death, had sprung into action, organizing the memorial for his old friend. Unwilling to sit for even a moment, he seemed to be everywhere, all at once, issuing orders to the others, as if he would fall apart if he sat still. Dwight had asked Phoebe to play the violin to accompany Rose when she sang at the memorial. However, Phoebe vetoed Dwight's idea of using "Jesus is Calling", affirming that Hag would never have wanted such a song. Instead, she suggested a song she remembered Hag often whistling.

"I think we can begin now if everyone can take a seat," Dwight announced, indicating the seating around the gazebo. At the center sat a bouquet of roses and lilies that Bonnie Glasby had brought by earlier to honor her son. Ned had asked her to join them, but she had declined, saying this was a time for her son's friends to be together. She had kissed his cheek and told him how often Hag had reminisced with her about how much he had loved high school and being with his friends.

Dwight began, "I think we are all still shocked about the passing of our friend, and it will be a long time before we recover. Right now, however, I'd like everyone to close your eyes and listen to Rose and Phoebe as they perform a song that was a favorite of Hag's. As we listen, see if you can step back in time a few years and picture a moment or two that you recall about Hag. If you're like me, it may bring a smile to your face, and that's okay. He would have liked that, I think."

Dwight nodded to Phoebe and Rose. Phoebe picked up her violin and began playing "Both Sides Now", by Joni Mitchell, as Rose's lovely soprano filled the neighborhood. The haunting words were fitting, yet Hag's grinning face sprang to mind as Phoebe held the last note, her vibrato carrying across the pond in the otherwise tranquil neighborhood. It was a lovely moment that touched the emotions of everyone present, and Ned silently wished he had insisted that Bonnie stay.

Rose and Phoebe sat down as Dwight slipped his heavy glove over his right hand. Cheeky had been content and at ease in his cage during the music, but was now alert, cueing on Dwight.

"Cheeky is an important part of this ceremony in which we honor Hag. If you can all remain still and avoid any sudden distractions,

Cheeky's going to hang out on my arm for a bit." Dwight opened the cage and offered his arm to the bird. Cheeky hopped onto the glove, then Dwight withdrew his arm from the cage and began reading his prepared eulogy.

"Hag and I became brothers, of sorts, during senior year of high school when we both joined the falconry club. At the time, each of us just wanted an activity that got us away from school and our lives at home. However, through this club, I found something I hadn't realized I'd been searching for, and more importantly, so did Hag. What I found foremost was a friend when I didn't have one. Hag didn't care that I was a bully. He didn't judge me for my crappy behavior, both in school and out." Here, Dwight gave Si a knowing glance.

"But Hag, being much wiser than me, found something more valuable than friendship, something that took me a long time to track down. He found solace—solace in connecting with his bird. None of us at the time were aware of his struggles at home. Hag shared with me the frustrations and sadness concerning his personal life and how he tried to look beyond his situation to claim the truths about who he was and what he stood for. Unfortunately, his personal feelings about religion kept him at odds with his father. Perhaps things might have turned out differently if he had taken his falcon to college with him."

Looking up from his notes, Dwight went on, "In just a minute, I will release Cheeky. I've attached a jess with a swivel to his leg." He indicated a short leather strap fastened around Cheeky's left leg above the talon. A metal swivel hung from the jess, permitting a small cloth sack to dangle from it. "Inside this perforated sack are some of Hag's ashes that Mrs. Glasby has been kind enough to relinquish to us. As Hag understood, falcons, his falcon and this falcon, are more than just birds of prey."

Dwight read from his notes once again. "This noble kestrel falcon will help us now by paying tribute to our lost friend. As he soars to the highest heights, behold the grace and speed with which Cheeky celebrates a life returning to a new world of possibilities. In transporting these sacred ashes of a tormented soul from the chains of mortality, this falcon sets free the spirit of Hag into the sky. Let him now climb to the clouds above, carrying with him the beauty of the man we all loved, who lost his way for a time, but now returns to shine another day."

With that, Dwight raised his arm, and the raptor took off. Spreading his resplendent feathers, Cheeky climbed high above them as ashes flitted from the bag, then floated and disappeared before their eyes. Circling twice, the falcon glided to Dwight's raised arm that signaled for the bird's return. Cheeky's wings fluttered, controlling the landing as Ned glanced down at the table on which the cage sat. Only now did he realize the table was an old high school desk. There, in the pencil tray, were the words:

HAG WAS HERE

―⁂―

"Where is Rose?" Lucy asked Ned as she closed her front door behind him.

"She thought it was best for me to do this on my own and I sort of agree. I might never have discovered you if it hadn't been for Rose, but, clearly, this is my journey now."

Lucy sized up her nephew for a moment. He was standing taller and looked more at ease than last time.

"Yes, I suppose it is," Lucy acknowledged. "Come on in."

Ned followed his aunt into the living room where a tea set was once again laid out on the coffee table.

"Are you hungry, Ned? Oh, I'm sorry, is it okay if I call you 'Ned'?"

"Yes, Lucy, that's fine."

She gave Ned a warm smile. "Would you like something different to drink? I have soda or beer if you'd like."

"Tea is fine. I ate before I left Tribute."

Lucy poured as she spoke. "I'm so sorry about the passing of your friend, Hag. This must be a difficult time for you and your friends. How are you holding up?"

"I'm all right. The service we had for Hag helped all of us, I think. But it's still hard to believe he's gone. I feel like we failed him somehow."

Lucy handed Ned his cup of tea. "Yes, I know what you mean. I think it's quite common to feel that way when you lose a loved one. But Ned, I'm sure you understand, at your core that it's not true. He had a medical condition, yes?"

"Yes. His heart."

"I see."

They busied themselves with their cups, adding cream and sugar, stirring, blowing, as if waiting for a third person to join them. In due course, Ned asked, "Are you going to tell me about my father today? I have lots of questions."

Lucy delicately placed her teacup on the matching saucer.

"Yes, Ned, I am, if you'd like me to. Where shall we start?"

"Where was the farm that the two of you grew up on?"

Lucy smiled and sat forward on the sofa. "Our farm was in Le Claire, Iowa. It's a small town on the Mississippi River, just north of Davenport."

"Was it a big farm? Did you have cows and pigs and chickens? Did my dad drive a tractor and bale hay and stuff? He never shared with me any details about his youth. Whenever I asked, he would always dismiss things as trivial or uninteresting."

"Yes, I know, he told me. Ned, your questions weren't trivial. I think it was painful for him to talk about his early days."

Ned nodded. "Yeah, I guess the Depression was really hard on a lot of people. Was your family poor?"

"Let's see, how shall I put it? We weren't rich, but many families were worse off than we were. I would have to say that our life was meager. Don't get me wrong, there was always food on the table, but there were few extras for us. But it wasn't always like that, not at first. It was after the stock market collapsed in 1929 that things got bad."

"Dad would have been eleven and you were how old?"

"I was born in 1924. I was five."

"Did you and my dad get along? Did he have to take care of you, or did he do farm work all the time?"

Lucy didn't answer right away. She picked up her cup and held it to her lips, not drinking, just looking at Ned, contemplating. Ned stared back at her, waiting for her reply that was not forthcoming. Lucy finally set the cup down, and dabbed her mouth with a napkin. "How about I tell you the story of your dad, the best I can, from the beginning? Then, you can ask me questions after. Would that be all right?"

"Of course. I'm sorry. It's just that there's so much I want to know, so much I don't understand."

"I know. Let's both sit back and get comfortable."

Lucy refilled their cups, kicked off her shoes, and curled her legs up on the sofa. "Go ahead, Ned, slip off your shoes and stretch out if you like." Ned felt awkward removing his shoes, but was relieved that his socks were presentable. Lucy deliberated as she spoke, measuring her words while keeping her eyes directed at Ned. "Your father's story, and mine, really begins in New York City in 1928. You see, Ned, Dennis and I were orphans."

CHAPTER 18

Murky steam from the train engine sent billowy clouds of vapor across Track 9 of New York's Grand Central Station. The air was laden with dust and pungent with greasy odors from vendors nearby. Seven trains could be seen from the doors to the terminal, their cars aligned in perfect, straight rows, like dominos.

Seventeen children stood solemnly straight along the red brick wall near the walkways to the tracks, some clutching small suitcases, others holding paper bags or satchels. None of the valises appeared to hold very much, yet each child's knuckles were white as he held tight to his meager possessions.

That morning, before boarding the bus that transported them away from the orphanage on 51st Street, in the shadows of St. Patrick's cathedral, they had scrubbed their faces and hands clean, but it wasn't the cleanliness that made their small faces remarkable. Uniformly, it was the wide eyes of fear and the down-turned mouths of dread that betrayed their bearing. Passersby couldn't help but stare at the bewildered assembly of children dressed in strikingly similar outfits, the girls in plain gingham dresses covered with an apron, and the boys in charcoal colored knickers and white shirts. It was an all too familiar scene, a train laden with homeless children, embarking on a journey to an uncertain future.

The New York Children's Aid Society (CAS) had been in operation since 1854, overseeing the operation of dozens of orphanages in the New York area. For over seven decades, the Society had helped to find homes for orphaned children. Not all the children were genuine orphans, some had parents who visited their child in the orphanage. Typically, a single parent, often a mother who could not or would not provide for the child, left the child in the Society's care. The Great War caused a significant number of children to be left without fathers by the 1920s, which led to mothers lacking sufficient means to support them.

The nine boys and eight girls preparing to board the train on Track 9 ranged in age from two to fifteen. Nurse Margaret Stephans, a matron from the orphanage, along with Nathan Sills, an administrator from the CAS, would accompany them on the five-day journey. As the orphan train traveled west, nurse Stephans would see to the daily care and monitoring of the children while Mr. Sills would handle logistics and procedures in the placements of the children with their prospective foster families.

"Now then, children, please pay attention. In a moment, you will walk in a line down this sidewalk until you get to the sign that reads 'Track 9'." Nurse Stephans motioned with her hand and all the children turned their heads in unison. "Can you see it?"

Most of them responded by nodding.

"Mr. Sills will lead you to the sign. There you will wait for further instructions. Be sure to remain next to your partner. It is particularly important that the older ones hold the hands of the little ones. Is that clear?"

Margaret Stephan's voice wasn't harsh, but it may have sounded so to strangers nearby. She had a pleasant face, smelled nice and could muster a smile under the right circumstances. The children knew she was fair, if not always kind. Behind her back, the older children called 44 year-old Nurse Stephans an old maid and thought that accounted for her stern demeanor. They suspected she had eyes for handsome 29 year-old Mr. Sills.

Nathan Sills had led the group to their train and climbed aboard first to direct each of his charges to an assigned seat. One by one, they climbed the steps, the shorter ones receiving a helping hand from him. "Here you go, Janey, I've got you. Becky, you watch out for her, now. Can I count on you?"

"Yes, Mr. Sills. I'll watch her. Keep walking, Janey, we're back a little further, row seven."

Mr. Sills checked his roster and looked down at the next passenger. "Hello, Dennis. You look ready and willing, young man. Nice to see you again."

"Hello, Mr. Sills. I guess I'm as ready as I'll ever be. I figure this will be an adventure, you know. I just hope somebody wants me—and they're not mean."

"I'm sure things will work out, Dennis. Remember, I'll be right there with all of you. I'll watch out for you and little Lucy, too."

Mr. Sills shifted his eyeglasses down onto his nose and looked over them past ten-year-old Dennis. Lucy, just four-years-old, was still standing on the walkway.

"Hello Lucy! Is Dennis taking good care of you, little one?"

Lucy didn't answer. Her face was red as she looked up at Dennis, reaching for his hand as he helped her climb the steps.

"Aw, Lucy. You'll be okay, dear. You two are in row four, on the right. Go ahead now and get settled. I've got to get everybody on board." He looked at his watch. "Goodness. This train leaves in less than twenty minutes."

⁂

Dennis' earliest memory was when he was four years old. The afternoon sun had wakened him from a nap. He rarely took naps on any regular basis at this age, but remembered how sleepy he had been this particular afternoon, as though he hadn't slept the night before. He was damp all over with sweat. Dennis continued lying still with his head on the blankets beneath his body, his thoughts still fuzzy, only half awake. He slept on the floor in the corner of his mother's bedroom. He couldn't recall ever seeing his father and as time went on, he understood from remarks his mother made that his father would not be returning from wherever he had gone.

Dennis and his mother lived in a small, two room apartment. Mother and son occupied the basement of a row house on a busy city street, but Dennis could not remember the name of the street. This first memory must have been in the summer, because he remembered the room was always cold in the winter. His mother frequently voiced her complaints to the landlord, questioning how people could live in a place with frozen water pipes.

When Dennis was little, before he started school, his mother would give him the radio to listen to when she entertained a visitor. On these occasions, Dennis would help his mother fabricate a tent by moving her bedside table to his corner and draping it with the vinyl dining room tablecloth with the orange poppies. The soft glow of the tubes from the back of the radio gave him enough light to look at comic books while he listened to cops and robbers stories. Most of the time, his mother and her visitor were soft spoken, but sometimes the man would be rowdy. That's when Dennis would switch to a music station and turn up the volume. Sometimes his mother would suggest he do so even when it wasn't noisy.

Dennis couldn't be certain, but he felt that his mother's health declined around the same time he started attending first grade at Public School 34. After walking home from school, he would often find his mother sleeping, with nothing in the apartment disturbed from when he had left that morning, as if she hadn't gotten out of bed at all. Dennis learned how to brew tea and toast bread. Anna would say, "I'm not very hungry just now. Perhaps some buttered toast and Earl Grey?" More times than not, he would find her asleep once again when he returned to her bedside with the tray.

But other days, she seemed better. The two would take short walks in the park around the corner. Dennis would make sandwiches to bring along, since by now he had become more of a mother to Anna than Anna was to him. Dennis told himself he didn't mind, that he enjoyed being useful and his mother needed him.

One day, after school, Dennis returned home to find a stranger wearing a suit standing next to Anna. It was a change to see her seated at the table instead of propped up in bed. The man was checking his watch, which was attached to a chain on his belt. Dennis had never seen such a thing. Then he saw a black bag on the table, and Dennis thought to himself, "This must be the doctor, and he's made mother all better. She's sitting up and smiling!"

But, no, he had misread the situation. Anna had motioned for Dennis to come sit next to her. "Dennis, this is Doctor Jines. He's been taking care of me."

Dennis, grinning, had reached out to shake hands with the doctor. "Hello, Doctor Jines. Is Mother all better now?"

The doctor had taken hold of Dennis' hand to shake it but stumbled in his effort, seeming uncertain of what to say as he stood above the boy, his giant hand obscuring the slight appendage he held in his palm. Dennis had stared at the bushy eyebrows on the gray-haired man as the doctor fell silent. Anna had broken the spell by coaxing Dennis's hand loose and cuddling it in her lap.

"Dr. Jines is going to help me get better soon, Dennis. There is a special hospital for people like me who are sick. Dr. Jines works there, and he says they have room for me to come and stay there until I get better. Isn't that wonderful?"

Dennis had looked at Dr. Jines to see his reaction. The doctor's demeanor didn't change as he turned and began closing up his bag.

"How long will it take for you to get better, Mother?"

Finally, the doctor spoke. "It's hard to say, son. Tuberculosis is a very serious illness and it can take many months before we'll know how your mother responds."

Dennis had stared back at the doctor, confused. "Many months? Am I going, too? I can take care of Mother at the hospital, then she won't need a nurse. I'm very good at making tea."

Anna had lost her smile now but tried to be upbeat when she closed her arms around her boy. "Yes, you are, Dennis, you make excellent tea. But, no, dear, you can't come with me to the hospital. It's against the rules."

Dennis had wondered how he could get by in their apartment all alone, but if it had to be this way, then he would just have to figure it all out. The important thing was that his mother was going to get better. He had faced her with a burst of enthusiasm in his smile.

"I can make toast and sandwiches, too. Will you give me some money to buy my food, Mother? I don't eat much, so I don't need a lot. I can come visit you every day after school and you can tell me how you're feeling, and I'll read to you those digest stories you like. And you'll get better and better every day and then you can come home and I'll keep everything clean and the bed will be all ready for you and we'll get back to just the way it used to be."

Anna, wiping at her eyes, had brought the boy to her bosom, enfolding him with her whole being as she kissed his head. "Oh, Dennis. You're not such a little boy anymore, are you?" Dennis had caught the quiver in her voice when she said, "Yes, it will be lovely once more."

Collecting her thoughts, Anna had then glanced at Dr. Jines, who stood idle at the door, pointing to his watch. Anna continued in a gentle tone, "Now then, Dennis. You're not going to stay here by yourself. I know you're a big boy and you're very strong and capable, but there are rules about this, too. You're not allowed to live alone until you're much older, so, until I get better, there is room for you with lots of other girls and boys on 51st Street. You know that big building next to St. Patrick's that we pass by on our way to the grocery store?"

Dennis knew the building. It was an orphanage. Billy Monger's stepfather had sent him there in second grade when he didn't want him anymore. Billy didn't much care for the place, but he'd said it wasn't as bad as living with his stepfather, who was mean and hit his mother.

"I know the building," he had mumbled without lifting his head.

"Good. Let's get your things together. Dr. Jines will drive us there and we'll get you squared away."

After settling in at the orphanage that evening, and kissing Anna goodbye, eight-year-old Dennis never saw his mother again.

⁕

Nurse Stephans peered down at Lucy and Dennis, clutching the back of the train seat to maintain her balance. The night sky loomed overhead as the train took a severe bend in the tracks. Lucy was sound asleep, but the subtle bump of Margaret Stephans' hand on the seat back had stirred Dennis and he opened his eyes.

Feeling groggy, he glanced first at Nurse Stephans, then turned to look through the window. All he could see was a lifeless black sky. "The stars must be hidden by clouds," he thought. Suddenly, he remembered hearing thunder before drifting off to sleep earlier in the evening. Lucy had been frightened and had cuddled up to him, burying her face at his side.

This all felt like a dream to him. Here he was, ten years old and on his way to what, or where, he didn't know. He hoisted himself from the seat and glanced behind and then in front of him, all the other kids were fast asleep. It seemed odd to him that the train had been chugging along now for close to two days, stopping momentarily on two occasions, but none of the children had gotten off and the adults hadn't told them anything. Dennis wondered if the reason for the stops was to load more coal or switch engineers.

The steady rhythm of the wheels on the track and the chugga

chugga sounds of the steam engine were old friends to him by now. He enjoyed watching the towns and farms and people come into view, then vanish. But right now, he was uneasy. He nestled his body in the bench seat, the warmth of Lucy's head against his ribs pleasantly reassuring. Outside the train, he could see nothing pass by them, couldn't sense anything near or far, just a black unpopulated, dimensionless void. Dennis wondered if there was a cornfield next to the tracks, or perhaps a bunch of grain silos. Were there houses and people nearby, sheltered down in their sleep? Dennis didn't need to close his eyes to take the eerie strangeness a step further. He recalled the Christmas card his mother had always taped to the wall as a decoration every holiday season. It pictured Santa and his reindeer climbing into the sparkling night sky that twinkled with stars. The card had glitter on it, and Santa's beard felt as soft as down, with a real feather on it that Dennis would rub between his fingers each time he passed by. Now, as his eyes lost their focus, gazing into the night, he imagined the train gliding from the tracks and, just like Santa's sleigh, sweeping into the sky to carry all the children on board to places of wonder and joy. Dennis turned his head to check on Lucy, who was still sleeping peacefully. Nurse Stephans was also peering into the night sky. Maybe she had dreams of her own. He whispered to her, "I'm not really sleepy, Nurse Stephans. Can I come sit with you in your cabin and talk?"

Margaret Stephans and Dennis had become close during the year and a half that Dennis had lived at the orphanage. Upon their meeting, she had developed an immediate fondness for the boy, who showed a sensibility and maturity beyond his eight years. She knew of his background and how he had single-handedly sustained his mother's life for months before her hospitalization, even enduring his own deprivation to ensure she remained nourished. Dr. Jines had told her about how the boy, despite knowing he wasn't allowed to see her because of her contagious disease, visited the hospital every day after school to check on her condition with the nurses. On the day of her passing, Dennis pleaded fervently for one last chance to see his mother, but his request was turned down.

Margaret found it easy to be kind to such a boy when so many of her charges tested her patience each day. She put her finger to her lips. "Shhh. Don't wake Lucy. Follow me." With special care, Dennis gently separated himself from Lucy, folding the blanket he had been given in a way that supported her head. He followed Nurse Stephans to the back of the car and into the next one, where she and Mr. Sills kept their separate cabins.

"I have tea, Dennis. Would you like a cup?" Nurse Stephans asked.

"Yes, thank you, ma'am."

Nurse Stephans' cabin had a real bed, at least as real as you could get on a train. She sat back and put her feet up while Dennis sat next to her on the floor. Margaret handed Dennis a pillow for him to use even as he fumbled with something in his pocket. "What's that in your pocket, there, Dennis?"

"What? Oh, nothin', just a sock."

"I see." Margaret let his answer hang there. She pulled out her knitting and started in on another row. She knew the boy well and understood he had something on his mind and would get to it eventually, so she had no reason to rush him.

Dennis was an unusual boy in that he could see things from other people's perspective. His empathy was most unusual for a child of ten. At first, Margaret Stephans thought he had developed this talent from being a caregiver to his mother for so long. But, as she got to know the boy better, she suspected he had been born with the gift. She had seen him intervene several times to calm a disturbance at the orphanage. The boy seemed to always know what to say to dampen some troublemaker's fury. He was strong and tall for his age, but he didn't use his might to intimidate others, at least not intentionally. The other boys just knew that Dennis' power could stop a fight anytime he chose and so they respected him rather than feared him.

"Ma'am, I was thinking. Lucy had to leave her doll behind at the orphanage, like all the other girls. It doesn't make sense to me, but I know the rule that she's not allowed to bring things with her from her old life, that we all have to break with that as we start a new life. But she's awfully shy and scared."

"Yes, Dennis, I know. This is scary for all the little ones. Probably even you, if I may be so bold."

"Oh, I'm all right, ma'am. But, I was thinking I could maybe, with your help, turn this sock of mine into a sort of doll for her. I mean, it won't look anything like what her dolly looked like, but it could be something soft for her to hold and take care of. It would be hers, if you know what I mean."

Margaret looked at the white sock the boy had presented. "Where is the sock's mate, Dennis?"

Dennis had expected this question. The orphanage had issued him the pair of socks just before the train departed from New York. They were part of his set of new clothes, to be worn only when he arrived at the destination. He pulled up his pajama leg so she could see the socks he was wearing. He had practiced this in his head.

"Nurse Stephans, ma'am, as you can see, the socks I'm wearing are in fine condition." Dennis lifted both of his feet and rested them on the side of the bed. "There aren't any holes in either of them. And! These socks are black, which will look much more handsome with my new pants than the white socks would."

Margaret tried to hold back her smile, but they both knew Dennis was going to get his way.

"I can sew pretty good. Mother taught me and I used to mend things when she wasn't feeling very good. I was thinking if you could let me have a thread and needle and maybe some old rags, I could cut them up and stuff them inside the sock and sew a head. Then

I could use some red thread, if you have some, and make a mouth. What do you think?"

"What about the rest of the doll's face?"

Dennis knew he had her now and explained his plan to Nurse Stephans, barely stopping to take a breath.

The pair had stayed up through the night, Dennis working tirelessly to get the face just right. He had to rip it all apart once because the face just didn't look happy. But, the second time, he felt satisfied that the doll would make Lucy smile. It had nothing more than a doll's face and a body below, where Dennis had cinched the white sock, but the doll's smile was warm. Dennis couldn't make any hair, so he just drew some short hair on top with a loose piece of graphite that Nurse Stephans had borrowed from the train engineer and sharpened into a pencil for him. The two of them were pretty messy after that, but they neatened up with soap and water. By the time Lucy woke up, Dennis was sitting next to her and the doll was in her lap.

"Is this for me?" Lucy was holding the sock doll with both hands just inches from her face. She was beaming.

"Yup. It's yours, Lucy. All yours."

Lucy examined the doll, touching the buttons that made up the eyes and nose, petting the side of the doll's face and rubbing the body of the sock against her cheek. She looked overjoyed.

Dennis said, "I'm sorry I couldn't make it a girl doll. Nurse Stephans only had green yarn, and I didn't think you'd want your doll to have green hair."

"Oh that's okay. I like it just like this. I've never had a boy doll before."

"Well, you'll have to think of a nice name for him. You can't call him 'Boy'."

They both laughed, then Lucy said, "I know just what to call him. His name is Denny Boy."

※

Le Claire, Iowa, sits on the banks of the upper Mississippi River, fifteen miles east of Davenport and 160 miles west of Chicago. The children were informed on the morning of the fourth day that the town was their first destination. Mr. Sills explained to them they would need to dress in their good clothes and to be sure and wash up after breakfast before changing.

"Nurse Stephans will inspect each of you before you dress, so be sure to clean behind your ears. Today is very special because for some of you, Le Claire will become your new home. At the train station, you will see dozens of grown ups that have come just to see you, so you'll want to look your best! They're all eager to welcome a child or two into their homes, so when they ask you a question, be sure to stand up straight and smile when you answer. They won't want a grumpy child now, will they?"

Mr. Sills surveyed up and down the train car, smiling at each child, meeting their eyes with his own, doing his best to reassure them. He saw a wide display of emotions: excitement, fear, even scowls and tears. It always looked this way. He concluded the best way to handle the situation was by ensuring the children stayed focused on getting ready, minimizing their worry and restlessness. By the time the train pulled into the station, Mr. Sills and Nurse Stephans were leading the children in a chorus of "Jesus Loves Me."

In the years that followed, Lucy would often look back and remember the sweet sound of the little voices singing the refrain and the seemingly never-ending walk from the train to the station. Dennis had told her he didn't remember the song at all, but recalled vividly how responsible he had felt for Lucy. She had trembled with fear, gripping Dennis's hand and clutching Denny Boy to her chest.

Over a hundred people waited to see the orphans. Not all of them were looking to take a child home with them. Many turned out just to see the spectacle of it all. The younger children didn't quite grasp what was going on, except for Lucy. Dennis had explained to her what was happening, but all she cared about was remaining by Dennis' side. Some adults came forward and began looking more closely at the children, some migrating toward older boys, many zeroing in on the youngest girls. Lucy refused to stand on her own even after Mr. Sills squatted down in front of her and tried to coax her with a sucker.

Dennis had decided that no matter what, he must hang onto Lucy. The night that he had sat with Nurse Stephans, she had shared with him that he and Lucy have the same birthday, six years apart. Dennis thought that must be some kind of sign that they should remain together, like brother and sister. Nurse Stephans had warned Dennis it would be unlikely for them to be placed in the same home and advised him to remain strong for Lucy if she was chosen without him. This was likely because she was a pretty little girl and he was older. He didn't know what he was going to do if that moment came.

Dennis had observed a couple earlier when Mr. Sills had been briefing the people about the process. The young woman and older man were engrossed in deep conversation as they glanced repeatedly in Dennis' and Lucy's direction. The man sported a beard, stood tall, and exhibited a powerful physique in his overalls and long sleeve blue shirt. He kept a lit pipe in his mouth and seemed to scowl at everything the young woman, presumably his wife, said. Her attire consisted of a pale blue dress and a wide-brimmed hat with white lace trim. Both of them wore obligatory name tags. Dennis couldn't make out what was being said, but it made him nervous to see them staring his way.

Other people looked at the boy and girl as Mr. Sills continued on. When he had finished distributing forms, he announced folks could step forward to see the children more closely. There was a sudden rush of people coming at the children, all of them, from all directions. It startled the youngsters, and many stepped back, cowering. Lucy tried to climb into Dennis's arms.

"Ladies and gents! Easy now, please! You're scaring the children. They've been on the train for four days. They're tired and frightened," Mr. Mills scolded.

Ignoring the reprimand, the couple that had been watching Dennis and Lucy made their way forward, determinedly aspiring to be the first ones to reach them. The man spoke first.

"What's your name, boy?"

Mr. Sills had instructed all the children to use only their first names.

"My name is Dennis, sir."

"How old are you, Dennis?"

"I'm ten years old, sir, tall for my age."

"Yes, I guess you are. And strong, it would appear, for a ten-year-old."

Dennis said nothing. The woman stepped forward and crouched in front of Lucy. "And what is your name, sweetheart?"

Lucy frowned and squeezed Dennis's hand tighter. She looked up at him without answering.

Dennis took a half step toward the woman as he pulled Lucy back his way. He puffed out his chest and in the deepest voice he could muster declared, "Her name is Lucy. She's four years old. And she's my sister! We have to stay together."

Mr. Sills had watched the scene from several yards away and idled over when he observed an apparent standoff between the two pairs. "Oh, hello, Mr. and Mrs...." He leaned across to get a better view of their name tags, "Hart. So glad to see you today. Welcome. I see you've met Lucy and Dennis. These are two of the most delightful children here!"

Mr. Hart kept sizing up Dennis as Mrs. Hart responded. "Yes, Dennis was just telling Mr. Hart and me that he and Lucy are brother and sister."

"Brother—and sister," Mr. Sills stuttered. "Well, they are very close, as you can see. Certainly they could be brother and sister."

This time Mr. Hart spoke up. "What are you saying? That they aren't brother and sister?"

"Well, technically, no. I think Dennis meant that the two of them, well, they feel like they are brother and sister. You see, they were born on the same day, March second, six years apart."

"My word! Isn't that something?" Mrs. Hart exclaimed. She bent forward so that she and Lucy were eye to eye. "Tell me, Lucy, would you like to live on a farm with your brother?"

Mr. Hart grabbed Mrs. Hart by the elbow and raised her up, pulling her away from Lucy. The couple looked toward Mr. Sills, and Mr. Hart motioned for him to join them. "Look, I'm only here for the boy. I think this Dennis kid could be just right for us, but the girl… well, we just don't need her."

"But, Albert, can't you see? They belong together, the two of them. Just look at how protective of her the boy is. He'll be a good brother to her and she can help me in the house, in the kitchen, and I'll teach her how to stitch. And you know how hard it is for me to keep up with all those rooms. You're out in the fields all day and I'm so lonely. Please, Albert. We could be a proper family, like we've always wanted."

Mr. Sills spoke up. "I feel strongly that keeping these two children together is advisable. They've bonded so closely. Won't you reconsider?"

Dennis and Lucy spent the next hour huddled together on a bench while the Harts and Nathan Sills consulted, signing and exchanging papers. Nearby, Margaret Stephans watched the negotiations. In the past several months she had developed a fondness for Lucy, and even more so for Dennis, and with a heavy heart said to herself, "Bought and paid for".

∽

"Did the Harts really pay money to Mr. Sills? Like you were slaves?" Ned interrupted.

"No. It wasn't like that at all. In fact, the Harts received $100 for each of us. It was the way they did it," said Lucy.

"So, did they adopt you?"

"No. Not right away. It was actually much, much later." Lucy waved her hand, discarding the topic. "That's another story. It was a challenging time, those early years, for Dennis, especially. I was so young that I wasn't aware of the tensions between Father and him. Mother, I started calling her Mother almost immediately, was clearly in charge of me and Father was in charge of Dennis, as simple as that. Father rarely spoke to me at all, and if he did, it was always through Mother. Even if we were next to each other, at the dinner table or what not, Father might say to Mother something like, 'Esther, tell Lucille that Janet Huskers has a parcel of fabric scraps for her.'"

"Fabric scraps?" Ned asked.

"Oh, that's just an example. I started making shirts and things for Denny Boy. Then when I got an actual doll, clothes and dresses for her. I was always on the lookout for discarded fabric or ribbon to use. Your dad would bring me things, too, like buttons and pieces of leather; sometimes he'd find a bracelet or ring or such, along a road or abandoned on a street. By the time Dennis left home, I was twelve and I could sew just about anything. Eventually, I sewed my own clothes, made some for my friends, even their mothers. It was all hand stitching because we didn't have a sewing machine."

"What was the tension about, between my dad and Mr. Hart?" Ned asked.

Lucy sighed and leaned back. "That's a big question. I look back on those years and ask myself why I didn't see it. I guess it's because I was a child. You see what you expect to see, not what you don't expect. Mother always treated me well, Dennis too, truth be told, but I understood that Father's and Dennis's relationship was different. I mean, they were men, and men were different. So, I didn't question it. And your father never let on to me that anything was other than fine." Lucy paused, perhaps reliving a past moment. "Dennis was always my rock, my protector, too, you know. That was his nature. But you know that, you grew up knowing how he was, the way he took care of your mother and you. Dennis was special like that."

Ned nodded in affirmation.

"I think Dennis was always meant to be a father," she added, surveying the room as if measuring what to say next. The grandfather clock in the foyer disturbed the stillness of the room with Westminster's chimes as Ned freshened their cups. He savored the sight of the Steinway across the room, gleaming in the afternoon sun that cast a glow of gold across the polished ebony finish.

Lucy said, "When Dennis was in junior high, I don't remember which year this would have been, he had a friend named Scott. I never knew him. It's not like we had friends come to the house, especially after the Depression hit. Dennis would mention Scott's name more than any other of his schoolmates, so I surmised they were good friends. One day after school, three bullies cornered the poor boy outside, behind the school. Scott was Jewish, you see. Bullies—I guess things like that never change. The prejudice preached by their parents had influenced these boys, no doubt. Back then, after the run on the banks, there was a great deal of anti-Semitic attitude in the United States. So many small minds wanted to blame the Jews for ruining the banks.

"Well, these bullies were having their way with poor Scott, beating him and saying awful things to him, when Dennis happened upon the scene. Your father tried to talk these boys down, but they wouldn't have it. So they went after him instead. Your father was a reserved kid who never got into fights. With three against one, they probably believed he'd be an easy target. Those boys were mistaken. They got a couple of licks in before Dennis fought back, but once he did, the fight was all but over. With his powerful height advantage, your father laid into them. He was very strong, even then. Dennis took care of the business at hand and sent the boys cowering away. There was a crowd of students that had gathered to watch the show. They had actually booed when the fight was over. I don't think it mattered to them who was right or wrong, they just wanted to see some excitement. Your dad helped Scott get cleaned up, and that was it."

"I didn't see Dennis that afternoon at home because he was working in the fields with Father. When Dennis finally came in for dinner, I was shocked to see that one of his eyes was swollen, his lip was bleeding, and there were cuts on his cheek. He looked just awful. I was so upset to see him like that. Mother already seemed to know about the fight. Neither Father nor Dennis were saying a word about it and Mother made it clear to me I wasn't to broach the subject. The four of us just sat in silence throughout dinner. The three of them all had their eyes glued to their plates, but I was looking back and forth at Dennis and then at Father. It was all very confusing to me.

"Several weeks later, I learned the truth. Mother sent me to the barn to gather eggs and when I walked inside, I found Dennis sitting on a bale of hay using a dirty rag to wipe his face. I thought he was just sweaty from working, but as I got closer, I noticed his face was bloodied and bruised. I thought, 'Oh, no. He's been in another fight.' But that wasn't it at all.

"You see, Father had been beating him. Dennis told me how it happened the first time. When Dennis had gotten home from school after rescuing Scott, Father had summoned him to the barn. Apparently, word had gotten around town about how Dennis had stuck his nose in a business that didn't concern him and how he had defended the 'Jew boy'. Father shouted at Dennis, cursed him out, beat the daylights out of him. He warned Dennis that if he ever heard of him doing anything like that again to defend a Jew, he could pack his bag and get out, that he could no longer stay."

Ned asked, "Why did your father beat him up that day?"

"I asked Dennis that very question. He just said it didn't matter, that Albert was always looking for a reason to kick him or slap him around. Either he hadn't hoed the potatoes right, or didn't set the barn right, or he hadn't kept the hay mow neat enough. Father looked for things to criticize."

"Why was he like that? So mean to my dad?"

Lucy rubbed her hands as she thought. Again, Ned could see she was laboring hard about what to say and wondered if she was telling him everything. Still, he waited.

"Father was not a pleasant man. He was stern. I think he must have had a rough childhood, maybe a hard father. He believed in hard work and little play. And he was miserly, didn't trust the banks because he was convinced the Jews controlled them, an anti-Semitic product of his heritage. His family moved here from Austria when he was a boy and Albert grew up speaking German at home, even here in the United States. Father never quite gave it up, even with us. As for why he was so disagreeable, I asked Mother once. She never would give me an answer. She'd said, 'That's just the way he is, Lucille. That's just the way he is.'

"What happened to all of you after the stock market crash?" Ned asked.

Lucy didn't hesitate. "Surprisingly, it had a negligible effect on us. You see, Father didn't keep his money in the bank. And he didn't own stocks. He only believed in cash and gold. Oh, he had a handful of money he kept in the Savings and Loan, enough so that folks would know he goes there. But the fact was, he kept his money hidden in the house. Dennis and I didn't know any of this, of course, Mother told me later. Father had secreted his money away in a hidden compartment in the attic under the floorboards. By going to the bank periodically, he could look like every other person in town and nobody would guess that he had money stashed at home. Then, once the banks began foreclosing on other farms because the owners couldn't pay their mortgages, Father was there to step in and grab the properties for cents on the dollar. I wouldn't say he got rich doing that, but he did very well, acquiring many hundreds of acres of prime farming land. Of course he kept it all hush, hush. Father was always careful to maintain an air of meager middle class. He didn't want others to know about his business. That's why he didn't allow Mother to buy us decent clothes, even though he could have readily afforded to do so. Dennis and I didn't mind, though. We didn't know any better, it was all a secret to us, too. We thought we were just like all the other families, then. Doing our best to get through hard times."

❧

"I've been watching you eye that piano," Lucy said with a grin.

"It's beautiful, Aunt Lucy."

The sound of her nephew calling her "aunt" for the first time brought a lump to her throat, and she felt a glimmer of hope in her mending heart. Dennis's death had devastated Lucy, sending her into a depression from which Clark worried she might never emerge. Lucy had clung to the belief that Dennis would eventually alter his thinking and realize that denying her the chance to be with Ned caused more harm to his son than it offered protection. However, she hadn't been able to convince him until it was too late. And so she had remained loyal to her brother's desires, always her hero, even from the grave. She closed her eyes now and spoke to him, something she did every day, to keep him alive in her heart. "Dennis, he's here with me now."

Lucy reached across the coffee table to take Ned's hands in hers. She took her time studying his left hand and the scarred evidence it displayed. "Tell me about this, Ned. What exactly is happening with your hand?"

He resisted the urge to pull his hands back. For some reason, he felt safe with Lucy, understanding now that she was on his side.

Ned explained to her how the hand could no longer play the soft, lilting arpeggios.

"But you can still play, other than that, yes?"

"Well, yes, I suppose that's true. But…"

"Well then, I want you to play something for me. Play something that makes you feel wonderful, that lifts you up. Look over there at that gorgeous Steinway Grand. It's been waiting for you, you know."

"It's what?"

"I have it because of you, Ned. I don't play, of course, and Charles plays only rudimentarily. No, this piano isn't for Charles or me, it's here for you. It belonged to Edgar Kaufmann, my boss, but he's dead now. Have you heard of Kaufmann's Department Store?"

"Well, yeah, there's one right here in Springfield."

"That's the one. The flagship store is in Pittsburgh and I'm the buyer for women's clothing for the entire chain. Edgar bought the piano for his house at Fallingwater, the one that Frank Lloyd Wright designed. Do you know about that? Frank Lloyd Wright and Fallingwater?"

Ned nodded hesitantly. "I've seen a picture at Si's house. I think his dad used to work for Wright a long time ago."

"That's right, he did. Did you know Edward Sissel designed this house?" She took a sip of tea. "He's told me stories about Simon and you. Through Edward, I've been able to keep abreast of your childhood, even when Dennis wouldn't share information with me. Of course, I had to be careful not to divulge my relationship to Dennis, but I'm not sorry for being tight-lipped about that. If the ends ever justify the means, it did in that respect. I wanted so much to be a part of my brother's life and to know you, Ned. But I'm sidetracking here. Edgar Kaufmann left the Steinway to me in his will. He knew I admired it. I had this irrational idea that it would bring Dennis, and you, back to me somehow. Sounds silly, I know, and yet here you are. So, what will you play for me?"

Ned didn't answer right away. He took his time getting up and strolled to the piano. Hovering above the keys, he took everything in. The instrument was truly splendid. The piano's pristine condition was apparent from the shimmering white and deep black keys to the mirror-like reflection on the fallboard.

"Has someone tuned it lately?" Ned asked.

"Yes, I called the tuner right after you and Rose left last time. I thought I might get lucky." Lucy winked at him and he smiled back.

Ned sat down, softly brushing the keys with his fingertips, adjusting the bench position and shifting it again. Was he stalling? No, he was relishing. This is the thing he loved most in the world, and these keys had been waiting for him. He closed his eyes and fingered them. There was no question about what he would play.

"I think you know this one," Ned said to Lucy casually.

Once he began the Adagio, his beloved second movement from the *Emperor Concerto*, his fingers and brain melded, transporting him. The haunting melody that had become the soundtrack of his life for the past five years poured out of the Steinway. His body shuddered with awe at the sound as goosebumps formed on his arms and he could scarcely believe the beauty, the fullness, the solid perfection of tone that was at his command. Unable to play the left-hand reductions as scored, he blocked many of the chords, but still the Adagio lent itself so well to the right hand that he didn't dwell on what he couldn't do. Instead, Ned played, trancelike, diving into Beethoven's emotive notes, as if he was the master's voice. The feeling was euphoric. Approaching the final agonizing notes of the eight-minute movement, his eyes found Lucy's across from him. Ned hadn't noticed Charles enter the room, but there he stood, at her side, Lucy on the very edge of the sofa, transfixed, tears streaming down her cheeks and Charles' mouth agape.

Ned didn't stop. He charged into *The Emporer*'s third movement as the concert grand thundered before him. The sound reverberated through the room as he continued on, playing the piece that had defined him for so long. Unwilling to stop, he ignored the deficits in his left hand. Ignored them! This had never happened. All he wanted to do was continue playing it through, reveling in every note, every inversion, filling the home with the most beautiful music ever written.

He kept playing. By now Jane had stepped in and was standing at the archway between the living room and the hall, wringing her hands. Ned glanced up for only a fraction of a second, for by now the audience was unimportant to him. The music was in his head, in his heart, and he played it for himself. Minutes flew by and still he couldn't stop. Another 90 seconds remained before he would reach the climactic finish, the impossible final cadenza that he would execute for the first time since the accident. His hands had taken on a life of their own, as if he was watching them, detached. Up and down the keyboard they raced, building and rebuilding the trilled scales, recapping the theme, then slowing to nothing before he delivered to his impromptu audience the astonishing final ten seconds. Ned leaned back from the keyboard, panting in the deafening silence that seemed like an eternity, but was only a few seconds.

"Bravo! Outstanding, Ned!" cried out Charles. Jane couldn't stop applauding.

"My God!" Lucy blurted out. "I'm speechless. How have you done this? It's been, what, five years? How?"

"It's all I hear, Aunt Lucy. It's the only thing I play. I've never stopped."

"You've got to perform this, Ned! For a real audience. You can't let this kind of talent just fade away. It demands to be heard!"

Charles chimed in, "She's right, Ned. You have to follow through with this. You must."

Ned shook his head. "But you see the issue here, don't you? I mean, you must hear it. It's one thing to play here for you, blocking chords. It's another thing to perform the concerto with an orchestra. I can't do that."

Lucy jumped up from the sofa and marched over to him. Squaring his shoulders to her own, she locked her eyes with his. "Then figure out what you have to do and fix it, Neddy."

CHAPTER 19

Aunt Lucy's words had reverberated in Ned's head over and over in the weeks after she had uttered them. Why did he care so much about what she thought?

As 1973 drew to a close, Ned grew weary of the person he was. The notion that sullenness had become his normal state hit him out of the blue one afternoon while he was in his father's shop. The oldies station on the radio was playing the songs his father had listened to so many times. He heard Lloyd Price shout out "Stagger Lee", mouthed the words when Cliff Richard was "Travelin' Light" and found himself misting up when Brenda Lee lamented about "The End of the World". How did she know? These songs always took him back to the days of his childhood. So many of them had become part of his core because his father had listened to them, and their echos over and over, muffled by the power saw or sander, were like coming home.

Ned pictured his father's face as he closed his eyes and absorbed Timi Yuro lamenting about how "Hurt" she is. He traipsed over to the hook where his dad's favorite flannel shirt still hung and snatched it up to his face. He knew his father's scent was long gone, but the feel of the threadbare cotton still brought him comfort.

Why had he taken so much for granted? Everything had been possible when he was eight. Phoebe and Si and Ned, the grade school triumvirate, were always so good together. Everyone changes, but after the reunion at Hag's funeral, Ned couldn't deny the endurable connection the three of them still felt after all these years. He didn't want to lose that. He didn't want to lose Phoebe.

And then "Wonderland By Night", of all songs, came across the airwaves. He didn't even know he knew it, yet hummed along with the trumpet's melody, somehow conjuring up what came next. Without words muddling the sound, the melody captivated Ned as he listened and this forgotten, uplifting melody from 1959 brought him back to 1973 with a newfound resolve. He heard his father's voice quoting FDR, "Do something. If it works, do more of it. If it doesn't, do something else," and Ned resolved to make a change.

After a couple of sleepless nights, with his to-do list in hand, he put his plan into action. He reached out to the Pacific School of Woodworking and they readmitted him for the spring 1974 term. Ned telephoned Mitch and arranged to live in his guest house during the four-month woodworking course. Then, just before Christmas, Ned wrapped up the Pizza Barn project and resigned.

He offered his house to Rose and Dwight. They could live there for free while he was gone. His friends were grateful for the opportunity to accelerate their savings to buy a house, and Ned knew they would leave the house in better condition than they found it.

Ned had debated about seeing Lucy before he left. He knew they still had unfinished business, and there were things Lucy hadn't yet told him. There had to be, for she hadn't shared with him anything that would justify his father keeping her a secret. But Ned was afraid. He wasn't sure he wanted to know. Now that he was ready to move his life forward, he didn't want to risk it with any additional emotional baggage. It would have to wait.

Ned called on Si at the offices of Sissell & Sissell Architects, in downtown Tribute, and explained his plan to his friend. Si was enthused and told Ned that he and Dwight could use a guy like Ned with supervisory skills in their new business venture. If Ned could design furniture and build interiors as well, that would just be icing on the cake. Neither of them made any promises, but they left the door open.

Before departing, Ned lifted out his wallet and showed his friend Dr. Elwood's tattered appointment card Si had given him in Houston two years before. The letters had faded and the corners were ragged from the countless number of times Ned had handled it. "I have an appointment next week. We'll see what—". Si hadn't given Ned time to finish before grabbing his shoulders and embracing him, just like Mitch used to do. "Good for you, chum."

Finally, he telephoned Phoebe and had a heart to heart with her. He poured out his soul, holding nothing back, and begged her to give him a second chance when he returned from California. She replied, "Let's see how things go when you get back, Ned." Phoebe was eager to finish her degree, and she and Regina had business plans with Mr. Reid, but she didn't go into any specifics. The three of them were still working out a myriad of details. Ned had one last thing to take care of before he packed up the Jeep and headed to Houston.

§

"Hello, Gretchen."

Ned had been hesitant to call on his former piano teacher. It had been a long time since they had talked, and that was his fault. She and William had sent Ned Christmas cards, birthday wishes, even sympathy cards on the anniversary of his father's death, but he had ignored their kind words and loving invitations to visit. Ned was as ashamed of his behavior toward them as he was toward any of his friends. Yet, when he had finally mustered the nerve to call, William had answered, exclaiming for Gretchen to come to the phone, "It's Benedict, Gretch! Come here!"

And now he was at the door to the studio, face to face with the woman who had been as much a mother to him as his own, more in some ways. Gretchen looked older, with more wrinkles and a stooped posture. When Ned clasped her hands, they felt slight, cool. But when Ned looked into her bright eyes, he could see the same woman he had loved and admired for so many years in this very room.

"Come, come in, Benedict!" she exclaimed. "Oh, but you're a man now, aren't you? Give me a hug."

The embrace was mutual as they each stepped forward and refused to let go for the next several seconds. As Ned stood there with his arms around Gretchen, he perused the room. Little had changed. The two pianos sat in the same spots they had always occupied, but the two chairs were more worn. And had William painted the room? There was a unique aura, almost a radiance to the space that Ned didn't recall from before. Books, busts, and sheet music still filled the bookcase. He recalled the day Gretchen had extracted the orchestral reductions for *The Emperor Concerto* and when they had begun work on the piece so long ago. The same old photographs were in the same places on the walls and atop the piano. So much of the room still felt the same. But the most memorable aspect was the air in the room. He remembered now, and it drew him back to those days when he was just a boy learning how to play, a scent unique to Gretchen and this studio. It was the redolence of old woolen textures and aging sheet music that settled on his skin, reminding him he had belonged to this room, and it had belonged to him.

"It's so wonderful to see you again. I have missed you! William will join us soon, but he wanted to give me some time alone with you, the dear."

And just like that, the intervening years melted away, and they were back together again, teacher and pupil, now friends. Despite Ned's prowess having long ago surpassed Gretchen's, he would always consider himself her pupil. He owed this teacher everything. They spent the next half hour exchanging information, an endless stream of questions and answers, anecdotes and laughter. Ned attempted to tell her everything about his life. Gretchen tried to not interrupt, yet her questions were boundless. William entered with tea and cakes, always the European even now, then left discreetly, not wanting to disturb their reunion. He hadn't changed, such a kind man.

"You've been through so much, Benedict. I'm happy that you found your aunt. You've been alone for too long," Gretchen said.

Ned didn't know how to respond to her comment, so let it hang in the air as he looked around the familiar space. Crossing the room to the old photographs displayed on the upright piano, Ned eyed the one of Gretchen, William, and the boy. He had scanned it a million times without actually seeing it. His eyes moved to the wall and landed on the photograph with the bird's-eye view of an orchestra. "I can't believe I never asked you about these pictures." Pointing to the orchestra, he said, "Tell me about this one."

Gretchen smiled as she stood. "Well, you already know someone in that picture." She moved in closer and Ned followed her. "There," she said, pointing to a head in the woodwind section. Ned leaned forward until his nose almost touched the glass.

"Oh! Is that William?"

"Yes. I knew you'd get it. That was taken in 1936. He was with the Berlin Philharmonic, second chair oboe back then."

"He looks so young," Ned chuckled. "I guess everybody was young once upon a time. Were you involved with the piano back then?"

"Oh, sure. I had students every day. William and I were like a pair of half notes back then—together we made a whole."

The two smiled at each other over her little joke. Ned motioned toward the piano with the other photos. "Who is that?" he asked, pointing to the trio sitting on the steps. It was the boy he was asking about, of course.

"That's our son, Conrad."

"Your son? You never told me you have a son."

"Well, you never asked, not that you'd have reason to, of course."

"Does he live in the U.S.?"

"Conrad was killed in World War II. He was a soldier."

"Oh Gretchen, I'm sorry. I-"

"Tsk. That's all right. It was a long time ago."

"Still, you miss him. What was he like?"

"What was he like? Conrad was…well, he was our son, and we loved him."

"How old was he when he…?"

"Conrad was sixteen when he died."

Ned was taken aback. "Sixteen? But how is that even possible? Don't you have to be eighteen to be in the army?"

Rubbing her hands together, Gretchen answered, "Not then, not in Germany in 1945. Things were very different back then."

Ned studied the photo, wanting to understand it better. There was something wistful in each of their eyes. "Will you tell me about it, Gretchen? I don't want to pry, but I'd like to hear about your son if you'd care to tell me."

Gretchen said, "It was so horrendous, the War, for so many people. I remember your father looked at these photos, but he didn't ask about them. Dennis fought in the War, so he knew. Survivors from that time rarely want to relive it."

Ned interrupted. "No, he didn't, actually."

"He didn't what?"

"My father didn't fight in the War. He had a desk job stateside."

"Really? I didn't know that."

Gretchen peered out the window. It was a bright day, and the accumulated snow was melting in the sunlight. She didn't want Benedict to leave. "Let's bundle up and go for a walk. It's a beautiful afternoon. You'll give me your arm, yes? I'll tell you a story as we walk."

❧

Gretchen and Ned strolled along the sidewalk of the neighborhood, reminiscing about their sessions working on *The Emperor*. It wasn't a melancholy conversation, as Ned might have imagined. Perhaps the fresh air and having Gretchen close to him allowed them both to enjoy the anecdotes from back then without relating them to the tragedy that ended it all. Gretchen was the only person he could talk with about those months. It was their story alone. Ned felt an unexpected warmth reliving those sessions together at the pianos.

They walked on, leisurely making their way across the street and into the next block. Gretchen's slight frame linked to his reminded him of the rare walks he had taken with his mother on the nursing home grounds in the months before she passed away. The silence that always accompanied them had made Ned nervous with his own mother. Isabelle didn't seem to mind, but for Ned those times felt like an awkward intimacy with a stranger, such was their life together, so different from what he felt just now with Gretchen.

"The short story, Benedict, is simple," Gretchen began. "Conrad was a soldier in Hitler's army and the American army killed him in battle. But those are just facts and Conrad's life and death were about much more than facts. I should begin, I suppose, with William and me. We were both born in 1902, me in Munich, Germany, he in Cambridge, England. My family in Germany was well off. My father ran a factory that built shoes, of all things. Not fancy dress shoes, more like utility shoes, a workingman's boot, I guess you'd call them. He was not an educated man, but he was wise. When he and my mother married, they had very little, but they did all right. My father apprenticed with a cobbler and he learned how to make and repair shoes. Father built his reputation and by the time he was 32, was able to buy his mentor's store. Then he and my mother worked hard, building the business. She managed the books while he made the shoes. Eventually, he expanded into a warehouse and invested in the latest industrial innovations of the time, which permitted him to manufacture more shoes than he could by hand. With the increased production came bigger contracts and with bigger contracts came more money. He was making boots for the army by the time World War I broke out.

"But, getting back to the story, my parents saw the storm coming and sent me to England to live with my grandmother. She'd been married to an English gentleman but was widowed by the time I arrived. I must have been twelve, I think. She put me in music classes after she saw me banging out melodies on her old parlor piano. And that's what I did for the next ten years. I went to school, studied the piano and learned the Queen's English. That's when I met William, while I was studying at Cambridge. He was a dashing, high cheekboned oboist in the orchestra and I was captivated by him. Those times were wonderful. We flirted around, it seemed, for months, before he proposed and soon after, we had the magistrate marry us. Of course, the Depression was everywhere, and we lived on beans and toast, but we were in love. We didn't care that we had so little.

"I missed my parents, and I missed Munich, so after a time I begged William to take me home so we could live there. Well, he loved me, so of course he said yes." She paused before adding, " I live with that regret to this day." A breeze had picked up as a light flurry of snow began to fall. Gretchen fluffed her scarf about her neck, slowing her gait and tightening her grip on Ned's arm.

"William began taking German classes soon after we relocated to Munich. After a couple of years he applied for citizenship, believing it would improve his chances for a more lucrative, professional position as a musician. As a German citizen, he gained acceptance into the Munich orchestra and I taught piano students. Then we had Conrad. He was so beautiful, all blond hair and rosy cheeks. He was born with an eye condition: heterochromia. It wasn't serious and he could see just fine, but one eye was brown and the other one was blue. William and I thought it just made him unique, but as he grew up, the kids teased him. You know how that is."

Ned nodded, recalling Si's bald head and the torment he had endured.

"After eight months in Munich, William did a blind audition for the Berlin Philharmonic Orchestra and they accepted him, so I closed my Munich studio and off the three of us went to Berlin. This was 1931. We didn't regard Hitler as a major threat then. He was some sort of trashy renegade, but he methodically built his political army and parlayed it into a populace of disenchanted Germans who were ready for retribution after being treated so unfairly at the Treaty of Versailles after World War I.

"He and his thugs seized power in 1933 and he got himself elected. Over the remaining years of the decade, his stronghold over the country increased, and, as of course you are aware, his persecution of the Jews escalated violently. Benedict, it was truly terrifying. We had Jewish friends, you see. Witnessing their situation was devastating. The smart ones left early on, while they still could. But, well…"

Gretchen stumbled on a crack in the sidewalk and Ned grabbed her other arm to keep her from pitching forward. He turned to face her, steadying her against his chest. It was only then he noticed she was crying. "Gretchen, we don't have to talk about this anymore. I can see that you're upset." He patted her back as she dabbed at her eyes with a pink monogrammed handkerchief. He recognized it as the one he had given her for Christmas when he was nine or ten.

"Just give me a moment, Benedict. I don't want to stop. Now that I've started, I want to finish. It's been so long since I've told this to anyone."

Ned looked around. "Why don't we go over to that bench and sit for a bit? You can finish telling me while we rest awhile."

She looked up and studied the bench. "Okay."

Ned brushed the snow from the bench with his handkerchief and Gretchen started back in after they sat down. "So, where was I? Ah, the Jews. The Nazis were fundamentally strong arm terrorists.

They'd arrive at homes in the night, and the next day, people you had known for years would mysteriously have vanished, never to be seen or heard from again. We all lived with fright that we might be next. You can't imagine how crushing constant fear can be. Then there were the threats about joining the Nazi Party and the recruitment of the children into the National Youth Movement. Hah! It was pure indoctrination, the uniforms and the brainwashing of these young minds. It was all too much.

"William and I tried our best to keep Conrad safe from all that, but his friends were joining and he aspired to belong. We were afraid that keeping him away from his peers would bring trouble upon us— William and I were not members of the Nazi Party and that was already problematic—so we agreed. By the time Hitler invaded Poland on September 1, 1939, Conrad had converted. He'd have terrible fights with William, declaring his patriotism and love for the Fatherland while mocking his father for not being a real German. Well, William was evidently a real enough German for Hitler's army and he was drafted in 1940. They sent his group over to Africa to fight with General Rommel's Afrika Korps in 1942. He came home on leave for two weeks in the summer of '43. That's when our neighbor took the photo you saw. I'll never forget that moment. The night before, I had asked our neighbor, Hildy, if she would come over in the morning and take a picture of the three of us since William had to return to his unit that afternoon. Little did I know that he and Conrad would get into an argument at breakfast. It was awful, and such an awkward situation for Hildy, too. She, of course, didn't understand what was going on. So, we posed reluctantly for the photo, none of us able to smile, and Hildy left. That's what drew you to ask about it, isn't it, that we weren't smiling?"

"Yes, you can tell something is going on. It's in your eyes, all three of you. You're staring beyond the camera, not at the photographer. It's like you all know something dreadful and you're searching the clouds, hoping to avoid whatever it is."

"Yes. Conrad was fourteen and he no longer respected his father. Even though William was born in Britain, mind you, and English through and through, here he was fighting against his own country! Conrad couldn't appreciate that. Can you imagine what this poor man was dealing with? Of course, Conrad bore the wisdom of youth and had it all figured out at that age. You remember what it's like, Benedict, to be fourteen? When you realize how stupid your parents are? Then, of course, Conrad felt he had something to prove. The other boys ridiculed him, jeered at him. They said he wasn't a true German, that he didn't have the fortitude to be a real soldier. It was his eyes, you see. They were all of them children, playing at being soldiers, none of them understanding what it all meant, not one of them with an independent thought in his brain. Conrad was no different. Honestly? Conrad may have been the worst among them, it breaks my heart to say. He would memorize the drivel of his teachers' preachings, then time and again spout it back at William and me, as if we were too brainless to understand."

Gretchen choked again, and the tears flowed into her handkerchief. "Benedict, they ruined my boy, but Conrad couldn't see it. His young mind had been so completely brainwashed with evil that William couldn't get through to him anymore. With crushing sadness, William returned to the desert war that afternoon."

"When did William come home again?" Ned asked.

"It wasn't until after the War. While fighting in Africa, he got captured and taken prisoner, along with hundreds of his fellow soldiers. But William was fortunate. He wasn't a Nazi, and he was alive. Now here is the part that I know will surprise you. He spent the remainder of the War in a POW camp in Oklahoma."

"Oklahoma?"

"Yes. There were dozens of German POW camps in the United States. This one, Camp Tonkawa, housed several thousand prisoners, many of them from William's Afrika Korps."

"I didn't know that. I bet none of my friends know, either. We didn't study World War II in school. POW camps here, in the US? That's incredible."

"It wasn't so bad for him, you know. In the German army, all the soldiers knew that being captured by the Americans was the best-case scenario. The Russians were as brutal as the Germans, maybe more so. Thousands of German prisoners in Russia just disappeared, worked and starved to death."

Ned interjected, "What was POW camp like for William?"

"He wrote letters, but only a few made it to me. And when they got through, I could see he was censoring his thoughts. I didn't understand until after the War what it had been like for him at Camp Tonkawa. The barracks were adequately equipped with sufficient food and clothing. Despite having no issues with the Americans, he refrained from behaving too at ease because of fanatical Nazis in the prison camp. William just tried to keep his head down, follow rules, and get by each day. Of course, he missed Conrad and me, and he worried about what was happening in Germany, in Berlin. I would write and remind him we were safe, but I exaggerated a bit. I didn't want him to fret, and I didn't want my letter to get stopped by the censors. Complaining posed a danger.

"By 1945, everyone except Hitler knew that the War was lost. Maybe he knew it, too, but he wasn't ready to give up. Hitler began conscripting old men and younger boys. I was frantic because Conrad wanted to go; he was so eager to serve his country and prove his courage. Benedict, you can't imagine the terror I felt, but I was powerless. Conrad didn't need my permission to join up, and so he just did. The day he left, I packed some of his favorite foods, and waved goodbye when I left him on the train. Conrad *saluted* back to me, Benedict. It broke my heart." Gretchen was sobbing again. "Conrad wouldn't even let me give him a goodbye kiss. He said it was undignified and unbecoming for a soldier. Can you believe that? I was his mother!

"I never saw my boy alive again. They sent me his dog tags. We keep them in that porcelain dish in the studio. An army Oberst that came to the house that day told me Conrad had died instantly, performing his duty, and I should be proud that he had fought bravely for the Fatherland. They brought him back to Berlin, and I forced myself to look at my son. Reflecting on it now, I deeply regret that decision because I still picture his pitiful, exquisite face, and his shattered body. My only consolation is that he didn't suffer in the end."

Ned was speechless. All he could do was put his arm around Gretchen's shoulder to comfort her. All these years, she and William had carried this crushing loss with them.

"Did William know Conrad had passed? I mean, while he was a prisoner?"

"Yes, he got word. He was the boy's father, after all."

"Gretchen, how did you go on after that?"

"You have no choice. What else can you do but endure what you cannot change?" Gretchen studied Ned's eyes, carefully framing her message. "Benedict, time doesn't always heal all wounds."

Ned felt drained. What could he say to this woman now? If she still mourned for Conrad thirty years after he died, if she found no peace after all this time, what did that say about his own chances? Was he, too, doomed to a life of remorse and guilt?

Sensing Ned's anguish, Gretchen turned toward her pupil and faced him with clear eyes, finally. She clasped his hands in hers. "Benedict, the unembroidered truth is that closure does not exist. But, and this is more important, let me explain what does. Life, Benedict. And sun. And memories of his smile and stories of his boyhood, all of them, treasures. I honor my son each day by keeping him in my heart. I believe Conrad hears me when I speak to him, when I tell him how much I love him. Little by little, you climb out of the hole in which you buried yourself. You find love again when you think it's deserted you forever. And you build a new dream. After we reunited, William and I did that.

"When he was in prison, William played oboe in the camp band.

He met some American musicians in the process and when the war ended, we left Germany forever and came to the United States and to Tribute. One of the Americans at Camp Tonkawa had put William in touch with the Springfield Orchestra. We both took on students and started over."

After hearing about his dad's early life, Ned believed he had the ability to cope with sad stories, but the casual manner in which Gretchen concluded her horrific story about Conrad left him feeling despondent. He wasn't at all sure he knew how to recover from his loss the way Gretchen had hers. Ned stared at his teacher, red eyed, fighting back tears. "Gretchen, do you think that can happen for me?"

"Benedict, don't you see that it already has?"

CHAPTER 20

Ned's hand felt good. Doctor Elwood had done a remarkable job, but months of therapy had been required after the surgery in Houston before Ned could move his fingers naturally. The doctor had warned Ned that the results were unpredictable due to how long it had been since the original surgery. So much scar tissue had remained, and the tendons had shrunk from disuse, therefore he could make no promises. But, in the end, the second surgery was a success, the result better than Ned had dared hope. His recovery was swift once the bandages were removed two weeks after the surgery, and he could play almost immediately, however it took weeks to build up his stamina and even longer for the stiffness to lessen. He kicked himself for waiting so long.

Mitch had taken him in like a lost puppy, loaning Ned his back-up car, a blue 1967 Mustang, after Ned's Jeep went kaput from a failed transmission. Mitch's acting career had taken off when he landed a minor role in a major motion picture, *Lenny*, the Lenny Bruce story. He had taken Ned to the premier, gently nudging his friend each time one of his three scenes as the bartender approached. At the after party, the old friends raised their glasses in a toast to

Hag, reminiscing about their deceased buddy and his senior year obsession with the dead comedian.

Mitch's place on La Castana Drive in Laurel Canyon was a modest affair with just two bedrooms, but still had amenities one might expect when living among the famous. Nestled among groves of fruit trees and lush succulents, sliding glass doors opened onto a stone terrace with a small swimming pool and guest bungalow, where Ned had his own space. Each morning Ned would drive to wood school, often working into the night on assignments.

Mitch had a bevy of friends from the television studio who welcomed Ned into their impromptu get-togethers. Seldom alone, Ned found he thoroughly enjoyed California life. He had met Carly Simon while taking an early morning walk and they had exchanged a few words about her mutt, Rocky. Mitch and his beau, Anthony, had taken Ned to Linda Ronstadt's place, where Ned played piano for hours as folks drifted in and out. Here he was with these pop music icons, and all they wanted to hear were Gershwin and Cole Porter. Ned teemed with delight. Mitch spread the word that Ned was a classically trained pianist and convinced him to perform Beethoven and Mozart now and then. Ned felt like a star.

The Pacific School of Woodworking had proven to be a successful fit, although a challenge at first. He had difficulty with the dexterity required with the hand tools, but was in his element when it came to design concepts and prototypes. Encouraged by his instructors to further develop his natural talents in this area, Ned reaped newfound confidence in himself along the way. As the weeks passed, the stiffness in his hands diminished, his proficiency with hand tools improved, and he discovered the freedom in creating new takes on traditional designs. By the time his four months of school ended, he had decided he would build out his father's shop into a business.

On June 29, 1974, his twenty-fourth birthday, Ned sat alone in his compact compartment on the train as it rambled eastward to Chicago. The day was blazing hot and seemed to get worse with each mile. The primitive air conditioning system on board struggled to keep too many people cool. Ned cocked open the door to his compartment, hoping to let in some air, but found the hallway even more stifling. The porter breezed by, announcing that lunch would be served in the dining car between noon and 1:30. He further declared that table reservations were not being offered. It was a first come, first served arrangement, unlike dinner, when one had to commit to a specific seating time.

Ned didn't mind dining with strangers, for the most part. The previous evening at dinner, he had met a British professor of theology returning to Chicago with his daughter after two weeks of hiking in the Grand Canyon. The girl, Linda, looked to be about fifteen, tanned and freckled, with dark brown hair to her shoulders, and an engaging smile. Both of them were eager to share their exploits with Ned, and he prodded them with questions. He had finished his dinner, but they had scarcely touched theirs, having been so engaged in talking of Black-Tailed Rattlesnakes and Beavertail cacti.

On another evening, there had been a family of five traveling on a train for the first time. The mother had apologized to Ned for being seated with him across the aisle from the rest of her family. "This must be so intrusive for you. I'm so sorry, but only four of us can fit into these booths at once. Our kids have gotten so big! My name is Sylvia, and this is my husband, John." With a wave of her hand, she pointed across the aisle. "And these are Betsy, Bonnie and Bill." Ned found amusement in the "B" names and reassured Sylvia that he was fine with the seating arrangement.

"Hi, John. I'm Ned," he offered, then gave the youngsters a wave.

During this meal, it had been Ned who hadn't finished dinner. Betsy played the flute and Bill played piano, so there was no end to the back and forth between the three of them. Ned didn't know why he opened up about his past, sharing his story with this family he didn't know. Perhaps that is precisely why he rambled on about his career being cut short. By this time tomorrow, they would return to their separate lives in Chicago, and Ned's story would be but a minor footnote to their train adventure. Still, as he sat in his compartment, watching the Kansas landscape, he felt a certain gusto in knowing he had shared a part of himself with John and Sylvia and the kids. All three of the teenagers had been engaging, perhaps relishing the opportunity to talk with someone other than their parents. Ned smiled at the idea of having children one day.

He gazed out the window after dinner, recollecting his last conversation with Phoebe, just a few days before. How ironic that it had taken a 2,000 mile divide for them to become closer. In the beginning, their weekly phone calls felt like installments in a serial magazine tale, as each relayed the latest digest of encounters and decisions. But as Ned's time in California came to a close, their topic of conversation changed to sharing their hopes and dreams for the future. Phoebe spoke to him now with a rekindled warmth in her voice and Ned asked her to call him Neddy. California's calming influence gave Ned a fresh perspective on how poorly he had managed his relationships back home. He was interested in everything Phoebe told him and tried to let his guard down when Phoebe asked him something that made him uncomfortable. Her questions pushed him to be brutally honest with himself and to clarify his life goals. Their voices had taken on a fresh enthusiasm for one another and he felt revived. In short, Ned hoped he had won Phoebe over again. Back in January, she had asked him, "When are you coming back?" Ned had understood, even then, she hadn't meant specifically returning to Tribute. Phoebe wanted to know when she would once again see the man he used to be, the man she wanted, the man she loved. Might he be that man now?

The path of the train paralleled a river now, the shoreline stretching out, broad and parched. Nearing a bend up ahead, Ned could make out a group of campers on the far side. There must have been fifteen or twenty young people, men and women, dancing about and waving at the passing train. Tents and debris lay scattered behind them, while smoke billowed from the dying embers of a campfire. Ned could see as the train approached that all of them were stark naked. He chuckled and heard shouts and hoots from other passengers as they spotted the unclad group. The engineer gave them two loud toots which inspired them to jump up and down, linking elbows and carrying on without restraint.

A year ago, Ned could not have cheered them on, possessing no inclination towards such misguided happiness, being so self-absorbed in his inertia. Ned had wallowed in sorrow for five years, living without living, harboring feelings of loss that he was certain nobody could understand. Now, like his father almost 50 years before, Ned was an orphan on a train. But he was on a mission now. "What a difference four months can make," he thought.

✥

Ned wriggled his left hand as he drove west on I-88 behind the wheel of his new Jeep. His train had arrived in Chicago on Tuesday afternoon and he had wasted no time in enacting his plan. On Wednesday, after checking into the Sheraton Hotel two blocks west of Grant Park, he had located a Jeep dealership and purchased a 1974 white Wrangler. He liked the pristine glow of the white paint, like a blank canvas on which he could paint his future. By dawn on Thursday, he could see the Chicago skyline in his rear-view mirror.

Ned exited off I-88 shortly before noon and pulled into a McDonald's for lunch, reviewing the map as he ate his Big Mac. It should only take another thirty minutes for him to reach Le Claire, Iowa. Once there, he'd ask for directions to North 26th Street, which didn't appear on his map.

When he had spoken to Lucy and told her he wanted to find the farm where she and Dennis had lived, Lucy was thrilled. "I think that's a wonderful idea, Ned. I haven't been there in years.

Of course, Mother sold off so much of the land after father passed in 1958, I think much of it's been in the hands of developers. My photos of the farm were taken decades ago, so it may not look like what you expect."

"Oh, I can't say I have any expectations. I just want to be there, maybe see the old train depot, see the house, get a feel for how he lived, where he slept, the barn, if it's still there. I just want to feel a connection, if possible," Ned had clarified.

He put down the map and studied the pictures Lucy had given him before he had left for Houston. The three black and white photos were grainy with cracks through their glossy finish. One of them showed the house with the barn out back. Another captured the dining room with the table set for Thanksgiving dinner. But neither of these had any people in them. The third one, however, showed his father standing in a tire swing that hung from a tree limb with Lucy nearby, a doll in one hand and a stick in the other. Just two kids passing the day outdoors. Ned wondered if this was before or after Dennis's father had started beating him.

He dumped his trash and returned to the Jeep. He was hot, and the Jeep wasn't air-conditioned, but the discomfort didn't dull his excitement because he was going to see a piece of his father's past, his father's old homestead. Maybe.

※

Ned crawled through dense traffic in downtown Le Claire, heading west. When he spotted a service station without a line of cars waiting to gas up, he pulled in. The pump listed gas at 55.9 cents per gallon, pretty high for the Midwest but much cheaper than what he had been paying in Los Angeles. Since OPEC had ended the oil embargo with the United States back in March, the supply chain had opened up, but the price of gasoline was still high. He remembered the hassle in L.A. of timing his gas-ups. Like everywhere, when the gas shortage was at its worst, his odd numbered license plate dictated he could only buy gas on odd-numbered days. Often, consumers could only buy $5 or $10 worth at a time. That didn't get him very far. He remembered sitting in line to buy gas for 70 minutes one time.

"Pardon me. Could you tell me where North 26th Street is?" Ned asked a lady who had pulled up to the adjacent pump. "My map doesn't show the street names here."

Shielding her eyes from the bright sun with her hand, the woman turned towards the voice. "North 26th?" she questioned.

"Yes. I'm looking for a farm," Ned explained.

"Oh, I don't think there are any farms on North 26th. That area is pretty much built up with houses now, hundreds of them. It used to be farmland a long time ago, though. Of course, North 26th runs a good long way…". The woman gestured westward. "It's not really a city street, even though it sounds like it is. I suppose there could still be a farm out that way if you kept going far enough west."

Ned said, "Well, if you could just steer me in the right direction, I'll see if I can figure out the rest."

"Oh, sure. Just keep heading up Jenkins Avenue here. You'll go through, um…" she stopped herself and looked down at her feet, concentrating, "two, no, three lights. At the third traffic light, turn left, then go about a mile. You'll see a shopping center with a Goldblatt's Department Store on your right. That's North 26th. Turn left. That'll take you out of town. It's probably going to be two or three miles before you see any open land where a farm would be. I don't know…"

Ned gave her a big smile. "That's fine, ma'am. Thanks very much."

With a wave goodbye, the lady wished him luck.

Ten minutes later, Ned turned left at the Goldblatt's Shopping Center and began driving west on North 26th Street. The woman had been right. Houses were everywhere. There seemed to be three basic models: the classic three-bedroom ranch, the larger bi-levels and then some with attached garages that were built out at a right angle from the house, making the houses seem larger. Each home had a neat little lawn. The streets followed gentle curves, instead of right angles, and they had inviting names like Huckleberry Lane, Crimson Drive, and Lilac Street. Ned passed an elementary school and a junior high school.

The tidy developments with names like Crescent Fields and Mayfair came to an abrupt end after a few miles and the road deteriorated to a tarred gravel. Ned slowed down to minimize stones kicking up and chipping the paint on his new car. The flat plains reminded him of Tribute, and a gnawing homesickness washed over him. Left and right, the view was the same, soybeans and corn and an occasional dormant field, rejuvenating for next season's planting. Ned smelled hay being harvested as he spotted a black and white mixed breed spaniel approaching him. The dog kept to the shoulder as it neared the car, its floppy ears bouncing up and down with each determined stride. Ned smiled. The dog was just trotting along, head focused forward, tongue hanging out as though he had some place to be. The mutt disregarded Ned's vehicle, didn't even give it a sideways glance, just meandered on, minding his own business. "Where is he going?" Ned wondered with a chuckle.

The road curved north, and as he rounded the bend, Ned saw it. About two hundred yards ahead sat an old house with some outbuildings nearby. He decelerated even more and took his time in his approach, feeling a sudden wave of nervousness. This had to be the farm. Ned came to a stop in front of the house and stared at it from across the road. He picked up the photo that had the farmhouse and the barn in it. Yes, this was it. He had found it.

It was an eerie feeling seeing the structure before him, then looking down at the photograph of this same house from 50 years ago. Before him was a transitional Greek revival house, so popular in its time, standing proud and in worthy condition. The siding looked well-maintained, with a recent coat of fresh white paint. The front porch spanned the entire length of the house, creating a welcoming picture. A wicker table sat between two chairs to the left of the front door, completing the scene. Crowning the entrance above the wooden door was a four-paned transom window. The absence of a screen or storm door, as well as the lack of a walkway to the porch, suggested the door's disuse. Ned considered that folks would have used the back door, the kitchen door, to come and go from the barn and the fields, donning and shedding work boots on the back porch, keeping the front parlor protected for when company came.

Despite having plenty of room to make them taller, the second-story windows were short, consistent with the Greek revival style. At the end of the house, just below the roof peak, there was a slight square window in what was most likely the attic. An old utility building, listing slightly northward, stood nearby. Perhaps they kept their car in it, although Ned did not see any vehicles on the property.

Opening his car door, tarry stones stuck to Ned's shoes as he stepped out to survey the scene further. If there was someone at home, he didn't want to seem creepy. He leaned his back against the Jeep, then spied some movement away from the house. It was a cow, appearing from behind the edge of the barn, also recently painted, red. The cow swatted flies with its tail and all the while chewed grass, ignoring the stranger at the road. Shortly, a boy in overalls came into view. His skin was dark, and he sported a tremendous Afro haircut beneath his baseball cap. The languorous duo didn't seem to be heading anywhere in particular, and the boy did not look Ned's way.

A crow perching on the electrical wires above Ned let out a loud "Caw, caw!" which captured the boy's attention. He saw Ned and stopped in his tracks. They stared at each other for a moment before the boy's high-pitched voice yelled, "Hello! You broke down or somethin'?"

The boy's self-assurance surprised Ned. He couldn't be more than eleven or twelve, yet seemed unconcerned by a strange man. He sported a cast on his left arm. Ned hollered, "No, I'm fine.

Sorry to bother you. Is your mom or dad at home?" The boy didn't answer, but started walking toward Ned with purpose. Not wishing to frighten the kid, Ned thought it best that he stay where he was.

When he got nearer, Ned introduced himself, and the boy replied, "My name is George. This is my aunt's place. She's gettin' groceries, but she'll be back soon. Are you lost?"

"Uh, no, I'm not lost. At least not now. I've been looking for this place, this farm. My father grew up here."

At that, the boy's face beamed. His smile grew from ear to ear, revealing his beautiful teeth. Ned walked over to the boy and reaching out, shook his hand. "Nice to meet you, George."

"Wow, isn't this somethin'? So your daddy was born here, huh?"

"Well, not exactly. He and my Aunt Lucy moved here when they were little. I only recently found out about it and I wanted to see the place for myself."

Just then, George dropped to his knees and looked down the road past Ned. It was the dog Ned had seen earlier, running at full tilt. The dog came to an abrupt halt in front of George.

"Slow down, Jody! Whoa there!" Jody whirled to smell Ned's shoes and pants, her nose dancing every which way. "It's okay, girl. This is Ned."

Ned stooped and rested on his haunches as he offered his hand to Jody, who began slobbering all over it as Ned laughed. Looking up at George, he said, "You've got a real friendly dog here."

"Oh yeah, Jody's a terrible watchdog, but I love her."

"How did you break your arm?"

George displayed the cast with an air of chagrin and motioned with it toward an enormous oak tree. "Oh, I was messin' around up there and stepped on a limb that turned out to be rotten inside. Down I went, hard. But, it's all right now. I get the cast off in five days. Can't wait."

Ned said, "I saw Jody back along the road earlier. She was going the other way, like she had someplace to be."

George turned his body to gesture over to the pasture where the cow stood. "That Holstein is mine, too," he said proudly. "I'm gonna show her at the State Fair in Des Moines."

"Well, I imagine you work pretty hard taking care of such a big animal. Do you milk her, too?"

"Oh yeah, twice a day, by hand." George held up his arms with his fingers widespread. "See? I've got really powerful hands now."

Ned smiled and admired the youth's exuberance. It brought back memories of the fun days when he was twelve.

"Hey, I just thought of somethin'." George looked at Ned and asked, "Was your daddy's name Dennis, by any chance?"

Ned's eyes perked up. "Why, yes. Yes, it was. How did you know that?"

"Follow me." George did an about face, waving Ned to follow as he marched to the front yard. He followed the boy to the gigantic maple tree that Ned recognized from its position in the photo with the tire swing.

"Come around over here," George said. He had dropped to his knees at the far side of the tree and was pointing to a spot on the bark.

"Here. See?"

Ned squatted down next to George and saw it right away, carved into the bark:

DENNIS + LUCY

"Oh, my gosh," Ned said, stunned. He reached forward, gently touching the letters even as his eyes welled up. Through the blur, he continued to trace each of the letters. "I can't believe this is still here."

George volunteered, "I wondered who they were. I figured it was a boyfriend-girlfriend thing. But this is a much better story, I think, don't you? Lucy is your aunt, right?"

"Yes, George, I agree. This is a much better story." An immense feeling of loss and love came over Ned. Turning to George, he asked, "Would you take a picture of me next to the carving?"

"I don't have a camera," George said apologetically.

"Oh, that's okay. I have one in my car."

After George had taken the picture, Ned took a close-up of just the carving. "Well, George, it was nice meeting you. Thanks for everything. I should get along now—"

"No! Wait a minute, don't leave yet. Aunt Gwen will be — Oh, here she is."

The two of them looked to see a faded blue truck approaching, driven by a gray-haired woman who could barely see over the steering wheel. Her dark, piercing eyes studied Ned suspiciously as she turned into the driveway.

∽

An hour later the three new friends were on their second glasses of lemonade and Gwen was puttering around the kitchen looking for baking powder. She had convinced Ned to stay for lunch and was making biscuits to have with a ham and cheese scramble. George was in the barn gathering fresh eggs for the feast.

Ned said, "I'm kind of blown away at how hospitable you and George are being to me. I don't think most people would be so welcoming to a stranger."

"Aha! Found it. How did it get behind the flour?" Gwen had found the baking powder. "I don't know if that's true, young Ned. It's been my experience that folks in general like to make connections with other folks—at least that's the way things have always been where I come from, in St. Louis. I confess, though, that I worry about George starting school out here. He's at a tough age to be thrown in among kids he doesn't know, black and white, that have grown up together in this rural area. Junior high can be rough and kids can be so cliquey. I just hope he can find one friend, that's really all you need."

Gwen was adding milk a little at a time, working the dough and talking non-stop, as if she'd been waiting for Ned to arrive and needed to get it all out. It occurred to Ned she must not get visitors very often.

"I know sure as tootin' he's not leaving behind anyone worth crying about back in Chicago. No, sir. That neighborhood was a decent place when my sister, Willa, and her new husband bought their townhouse back in 1960. But, well, in 1968, when Martin Luther King, God rest his soul, got murdered, all hell broke loose. Willa told me things that I never would have guessed people could do to one another. And then the gangs started. It seems everyone is so hateful, anymore.

"I told Willa and Robert, I said, 'You got to get out of there before your boy George gets himself in trouble, or something worse. Come out to Le Claire and live with me,' I said. 'Y'all can help me with the farm and Robert can find another nurse's job at the hospital. They always need more.' So that's the way it's going to be as soon as they sell their house."

Ned interjected, "That sounds great for all of you." He opened his mouth to say something else but stopped, mesmerized at the speed with which Gwen rolled and cut the biscuits. "She's done this hundreds of times," he thought.

"I wish I had known my mother's and father's families. There's a lot of stuff I'm just finding out," Ned offered. When Gwen popped the biscuits into the oven, checked the clock, and looked at him, he took it as a sign to go on. For the next twenty minutes, he sat and shared his story with Gwen. She didn't move a muscle as he spoke, just listened attentively. He felt so comfortable sitting with her.

When he'd finished, Gwen said, "My, but you've been carrying a heavy load. It's good you're headed home. It'll do you good to get back with your friends and family. I bet they've been missing you as much as you have them."

George burst through the door just then, exclaiming, "Lookie here, fourteen eggs today, Aunt Gwen! My hens are the best!"

The three of them chattered away as they ate. Ned couldn't get enough of Gwen's biscuits, piling seconds, then thirds, onto his plate. "I swear, Gwen, I didn't think it was possible for biscuits to taste better than the ones Karina makes, but I was mistaken. These are out of this world."

After they finished eating and pushed their chairs back from the table, Gwen suggested to George, "Why don't you show Ned the attic? He says his granddad used to hide all his money up there in a secret place. Maybe you can find it. Here, take this flashlight up with you, and while you're up there I'll get that tar off your boots, Ned."

"No, you don't need to do that, Gwen."

"It'll take me just a minute. I've got the exact tool for it."

"You've got a tool to take tar off of boots?"

She chuckled, "Yes, I do. I'm a single woman living on a farm in the middle of nowhere. I have to be prepared. And like I've always said, if I don't have it, you don't need it."

Ned burst out laughing, "Aren't you something, Gwen."

Heading for the back porch, she added, "Now you two get on upstairs."

As George led the way, Ned's heart was brimming with emotion as he thought about his dad climbing these same steps to the second floor. Lucy had sketched the layout of the house when Ned told her he wanted to visit the farm, so he knew which had been his dad's bedroom. It belonged to George now, but standing there gave him goosebumps. Ned wanted to linger there for a bit, and yearned to examine the other rooms, sensing an eerie familiarity with the space, but George's excitement about the mystery that awaited them in the attic compelled Ned to follow his guide up a narrow stairway to the third floor. As they reached the top of the steps, George turned on the lonesome, bare lightbulb, revealing scattered remains of open boxes with old clothes, a dresser with no drawer fronts, a big, cast iron dutch oven that was rusting away, boxes of Christmas decorations, and containers of empty canning jars tucked back among the eaves.

"Lucy said his hiding place was near the back on the east side, just under the window," Ned said, pointing the way. They inched over the dusty boards, ducking their heads and pulling cobwebs away from their faces as they got further away from the center.

"I don't come up here much. It's too dark and creepy, spiders and stuff," George confessed.

Ned replied, "We can go back downstairs if you want, George. No need to do this."

"Heck no! This will be so cool if we find a secret hiding place." George impishly put a finger to his lips and whispered, "I can put stuff in it. And Aunt Gwen won't know where it is."

They reached the area Lucy had described and George shined the flashlight on the floor as he shoved a couple of boxes away from where the roof met the floor, exposing a four foot by seven-foot area that was indistinguishable from the other areas of the attic floor. The sections of wood planking, possibly a hundred years old, had irregular hand-sawn ends and were butted against one another. Buckwheat flies droned in the window as George reached forward, down on his knees, and brushed away dust to inspect the boards beneath the window more thoroughly.

"George! Be careful with your broken arm. Gwen will kill me if you hurt yourself any more," Ned chided.

"I am being careful, Ned," George said dismissively. Then, turning his head, "I don't see anything here, do you?"

Ned was also surveying the cleared area. "No, I don't. Try pushing down on those boards to see if they move. Or bang on them to see if anything sounds different."

George followed Ned's suggestions. None of the boards seemed to move or otherwise seem unstable, but when George started tapping, they both cried out, "Wait!" George clawed at the area, and it became clear there was a group of boards that were joined. It hadn't been obvious when they had examined them earlier because they had been expecting a cutout to be a straight line. Now, as George began prying with his fingers, Ned could see that his grandfather had cleverly disguised the trap door. Using the fingers of his left hand, George tipped up a single loose board about fourteen inches long. In doing so, he gained a purchase with his right hand beneath the edge of the irregular lid to the compartment below. The lid was three boards wide, but the ends were of different lengths. This way, the lid did not stand out as anything unnatural if someone unknowingly stumbled upon it.

"This is so cool!" George exclaimed.

Ned kneeled, then fumbled as he crawled next to his partner in crime. They both stared into an empty cavity.

"Aw, shucks! There's nothin' here," George grumbled.

Ned was disappointed, too. "Yeah, but at least we found the spot," Ned said, attempting to boost their spirits. "Now it'll be up to you to bury some treasure in it. Are you going to tell anyone where it is?"

George was running his hand over the floor of the chamber. "Heck no. This is my secret place now." He turned to face Ned. "You won't tell nobody—"

Ned thought he heard a board slide.

George shouted, "Wait a minute! This joist board is loose back under here." His right hand was out of sight, beyond the top edge of the compartment. The boy was straining to reach even further into the void, his arm disappearing up to his shoulder. "Hey! I think I found something. I think it's a box! The sides look just like the floor joists. You'd never know this was here unless you poked around way back." George deftly tugged the primitive coffer to the center of the space and sat cross-legged at the edge, holding a rudimentary box about eight by ten inches in size. The lid was missing, and when Ned directed the flashlight towards it, he detected something inside.

"What's that, George?"

George pulled out a piece of paper, a newspaper clipping, and handed it to Ned. It contained neither a date nor a photograph, the single column just two inches in length. The paper was undeniably old, fragile but not crumpled or folded. Ned lifted it and read it out loud:

> Cpl. Dennis Godwin, 1447 26th Street, Le Claire, Iowa, has been awarded the Purple Heart for wounds received and meritorious performance of duty on the field of battle in Germany, March 9, 1945.

Ned sat wide-eyed and silently read the sparse lines once more, then a third time. "What?" he said.

"That's your dad, right?" George queried.

"Yes, it is. But I don't understand. My dad worked at an Army desk during World War II. That's when this article must have appeared." Questions raced through his mind as Ned read the clipping again, "Wounds? Meritorious performance of duty? Germany? What did this mean?" Ned asked himself, shaking his head as he tried to regain his senses. "George, I'm going to keep this, okay?"

"Well, sure, Ned. Of course. It kinda belongs to you, wouldn't you say?"

Ned didn't answer. Instead, he replied, "I need to get going, George. Let's go downstairs and tell Gwen you found the hiding place. But, George?"

"Yeah?"

"Can we keep this newspaper clipping just between you and me, for now, until I can figure out what it all means?"

George was feeling like he was part of something important and it felt exciting. "Sure. I won't say a word. I understand. It's private, right?"

"Yeah, George, thanks. It is private." Ned and George extended their right hands and shook on it.

CHAPTER 21

Ned sped back to town. The Jeep was kicking up gravel as he pulled away after farewell hugs with Gwen and George. It had been such a remarkable visit, but now he was troubled. Everything Lucy had shared with him about her adoptive father, Albert Hart, was the antithesis of a man that would treasure a newspaper account of Dennis's Purple Heart Award. The man had treated his father abhorrently. He beat him, demeaned him, and chastised him as though he was unworthy to be cared for, let alone loved. And yet the man must have felt something for the boy. Perhaps Hart had felt remorse later on in life for mistreating Dennis. Maybe Albert only regretted his actions after Dennis left the farm. Ned hoped Lucy could provide insight into what had happened there. Did she have any knowledge about the clipping? That seemed unlikely. Albert Hart appeared to be the enigmatic type who kept others at an emotional distance, even those closest to him.

Ned was impatient and catching every red light on his way back to the hotel. As he sat at yet another stoplight, Ned concluded that Albert Hart's narrative, regardless of whether Lucy could expound upon it, was just that, his story, filled with woes and triumphs that helped shape him, for sure. Had Albert suffered a tragedy that transformed him into someone less than what he might have been?

Ned would visit Lucy and find out the actual story behind his father and the War. He would learn why his father had kept it all a secret. Albert Hart's history might always remain a mystery, but Ned felt it crucial to know his father's in order to understand who the man was. He deserved to know the entire story, all of it, whether laudable or shameful. Only by knowing the inexorable truth could Ned unravel his own life. At this moment, though, he needed to hear Phoebe's voice. After arriving at the hotel, he went straight to his room and called the Reid residence, where Phoebe was living.

"Hello, Frank Reid speaking."

"Oh, hello, Mr. Reid. This is Ned, Ned Godwin."

"Ned! Is it really you? Of course it is, what am I saying? Where are you? Are you here, in Tribute?"

"Not yet. I'm in Le Claire, Iowa, but I'm heading out in just a few minutes. I'll be in Tribute later on this afternoon. May I speak with Phoebe?"

"What? Oh, sure. Of course. Here, talk to Si a minute while I find that daughter of mine. Hey, Si, guess who's on the phone?"

Si's voice came on the line. "Hello?"

"Simon. It's Ned. What are you doing at Phoebe's?"

Ignoring Ned's question, Si replied, "Well, it's about time we heard from you. We've all been making guesses about what day you'd pull in. Where are you?"

"I'm in Le Claire, but I'll be getting into Tribute in a few hours. What's all that noise in the background?"

"Well, just about everyone you know is here. Rose and Dwight, Eva, my parents. Phoebe's throwing a pool party. Is it hot in Le Claire? It's 94 here today. Yeah, we're all covered in suntan lotion. You should see the twins. Eva's got them so slathered up they look like Kabuki dolls. Hold on, Ned."

Ned heard a muffled sound as Si tried to cover his phone.

"Eduardo! *Desacelerar!*" *Stop running!* "Te resbalaras y te romperas la cabeza!" *You're going to slip and crack your head open!* "Sorry about that, Ned. Wait 'til you see the kids. They're amazing! Oh, here comes Phoebe. By the way, Dwight and I need to talk to you. Will I see you tomorrow?"

"I hope so, yeah. I'll call you in the morning."

"Okay. Here's Phoebe. It's so good to have you back, Ned. Old times, righto?" Then Si was gone.

"Ned, is that you?" Phoebe burst in.

"Phoebe. It's so good to hear your voice."

"What did you say? I can't hear you. Wait a minute. I'll go into Dad's office."

Ned heard the background noise fade, and then, as the door closed, quiet.

"There. You were saying…?"

"I couldn't wait to talk to you, Phoebe. I need to tell you something." Ned paused. "Phoebe, can you hear me?"

"Yes, Ned. I can hear you."

"I'm coming home today." He waited a moment more. "Do you understand what I'm saying?"

Ned's question was met with an extended silence on the other end of the phone. He relaxed his shoulders and tried to calm his voice. "Phoebe. I said I'm coming home." Ned cocked his head, then heard Phoebe crying. "Oh, Sweetie! Are you all right? What's wrong?" Ned pleaded.

Ned heard her sniffle as she said, "Nothing is wrong, Ned. I think everything is pretty all right, actually. When will you get here?"

"I'll be there around five. But, Phoebe?"

"What is it?" she answered nervously.

"I have to see Aunt Lucy first, I just have to. I need her to tell me the rest."

She sighed, and Ned heard the disappointment in her voice when she said, "I understand. Tomorrow, then?"

"Yes, tomorrow. I'll come over early. We can make bacon and eggs together and splatter grease all over your mother's stove."

"Sounds perfect," Phoebe replied.

"And Phoebe? I think I've figured out some things while I've been gone." Ned paused before declaring what he truly called to say. "I love you, Phoebe."

"I know, Ned. I've always known, even if you didn't. You go take care of what you need to do. I'll be here in the morning. And one more thing?"

"What's that?"

"I love you, too."

⁂

Ned approached the steps of the stately home on Brandywine Avenue. It never failed to impress, with its stained glass and leaded inlay that graced the bank of windows above the portico's slate roof. Si's father had done a remarkable job balancing the proportions in his design for Ned's aunt's and uncle's house. He rang the doorbell, expecting a greeting from Jane, but his aunt ambushed him by flinging open the door. Without so much as a "Hello", Lucy enveloped Ned in her arms. "Finally! I've been looking forward to this day for months, Ned!"

Ned returned the hugs and said, "It's good to be back, Aunt Lucy. I've missed you, too."

Lucy released her grasp and held Ned at arm's length, cocking her head. "Hmm. There's something different about you. Maybe the California tan?"

"Could be. But I think what you're noticing is that I shaved off my beard."

"Ah, yes. That's it. You look very handsome this way! Well, come inside. Have you eaten? Clark won't be home until late tonight; he has an evening seminar to lead. So it's just you and me, Ned. We can talk all night if you wish."

"Aunt Lucy, it's okay if you call me Neddy. And yes, I would like to talk. I want to know everything."

"I imagine you do. And it's time." Lucy linked her arm with Ned's, resting her head on his shoulder as they stepped into the living room.

After sandwiches and coffee, over which Ned detailed his months in California, the two retired to the living room. Ned ran his hand along the piano keys as he passed by.

"Maybe you'll play something for me later?" Lucy begged with a smile.

"Love to, if it's not too late. Cole Porter and I are old friends, like I said."

Before sitting down, Lucy opened the bottom drawer of a secretary and removed a stack of papers tied together with a blue ribbon. "Before I begin, Neddy, I want to give these to you. There are 47 letters here, from Dennis to me." Letting out a sigh, she passed him the bundle. "They've been mine for a long time, and I cherish them, as I know you will, too. You must keep them safe. I know you will, so that your children can one day know their grandfather. Dennis mailed these to me after he left Le Claire. In them, you'll hear your dad describe his ambitions, his trials, his hopes and dreams, even his shenanigans and regrets. I want you to discover for yourself your father's years from 1938 to 1942. That's when he wrote them. If you're like me, you'll hear his voice when you read them, and I think you'll feel a closeness and a love beyond what you have known in your life until now."

Ned's eyes watered as his aunt spoke. Tenderly, he slid his finger across her name on the topmost letter. Not the graceful penmanship that had decorated the envelope Rose had discovered in his father's bedroom so long ago, his father's handwriting was more jagged, sharper, yet every bit as legible. He instantly recalled the grocery lists his father would post on the refrigerator. Ned flipped the stack over and read the return address on the bottom letter. His father had sent it from Fort Sill, Oklahoma.

"That's the last letter I received from Dennis before he joined the Army. It's postmarked October 13, 1942. I won't get into the details of your dad's life during these years because you'll find out for yourself as you read the letters. Suffice it to say that Dennis spoke of his adventures during this time with the exhilaration of a young man finally experiencing life on his own. He had challenging times, for sure. I mean, he stoked coal on a train for months, for example. But his spirit never faded. Eventually he found his calling with Roy Hubberman, a fine wood artisan in Philadelphia. Roy taught your father woodworking, simple as that. You'll especially enjoy reading about that now that you're following in his footsteps, which, by the way, just delights me so, Neddy. Anyway, you take these with you and keep them. They're yours now."

"Why did he stop writing to you?"

Lucy nodded her head. "Well, that's why we're here. I'm going to tell you." She sipped her coffee one last time before continuing. "Okay, like I said, the last letter I received from Dennis was in 1942, when he reported for basic training at Fort Sill. He enlisted just after Pearl Harbor. When I stopped getting letters from him, after Fort Sill, I kept writing to him in care of the Army. My letters never came back, so I assumed, as I later confirmed, that Dennis received them.

"Regularly, every couple of weeks, I would send him a letter, in which I described in great detail, everything I was doing. Oh, Neddy, how I loved writing those letters. After finishing high school, in June of '42, I ventured off to Chicago for design school, where I specialized in fashion design and textiles, but that's a story for another time. Not hearing anything back from him, I was worried sick, as you can imagine. The War was so long; I thought I'd never see Dennis again. Then Mother sent me a clipping from the Le Claire Herald about him winning the Purple Heart."

Ned interrupted, "I know about that, Lucy." He shared his story of meeting George and Gwen, discovering his grandfather's secret spot and finding the newspaper article.

"What do you know?" Lucy responded. "I don't think even Mother understood him. I suppose he loved Dennis, after all, in his own way. There were times, this was long after Dennis had left, when Father seemed softer, not so resolute in his bearing, as if, maybe, he'd found some peace from his demons. I know he was driven by some hard core beliefs, tenets of life that he picked up from his father and mother."

Lucy took a brief pause, as though revisiting times from long ago. With a mournful look in her eyes, she said, "My poor brother. Father was so hard on him. When Dennis left after high school graduation, I was happy for him, but, honestly, Neddy, I cried myself to sleep every night for weeks afterward. I missed him terribly. Dennis had been so concerned about leaving me he told me he would stay if I wanted him to. Can you imagine that? I've never met anyone as selfless as your father. So, the Purple Heart. When I read that, I jumped for joy. Of course, I wasn't happy knowing he'd been injured, but it meant that he was alive."

Ned felt exasperated as he stammered, "But why did he always say that he worked at a desk, stateside?"

"I'm sorry, Neddy. I'm off track. Let me go on. When your father returned from the War, this was just before the German surrender in May of '45, he came to see me. I was still in Chicago at the time. We were so happy being together again. He wanted to know everything about what I'd been doing, what my plans were after I finished school, if I had any boyfriends. I tried several times to ask him about his experience in the Army, but he would wave his hand and ask me about the latest movie stars or which restaurant we should go to for dinner. I finally stopped pressing him. That first night together again, I took him to my favorite restaurant, Del Vechios. It was a wonderful evening. We drank chianti, we laughed and danced. Everybody knew that the end of the War was imminent, so folks were just giddy with anticipation.

"When we got back to my apartment after dinner, we sat around, talking about, gosh, I don't even remember what. Both of us were pretty tipsy from the wine and your father had gone quiet, so I figured he was sleepy, but I was mistaken. We must have been sitting there for ten or fifteen minutes, not saying a word. I was just basking in the joy of being with my brother again and then your father started talking, out of the blue. I think he'd been sitting there, deciding if he wanted to tell me about it. He said, 'Luce, I know you want to know about the War and my part and all, and I'll tell you now. But understand this: I'll never speak of it again, to anyone, and I want you to promise me you won't, either.'

"I did, Ned. I promised him. Dennis was my hero and always had been, and I would have given my life for him if necessary. So he told me this story I'm about to tell you. I feel certain now he would want you to know, to understand why he hid this from you. Your father was an amazing man, the most noble and decent person I've ever known, but he was human. You'll have to forgive me if some details are sketchy. It's been thirty years, and true to his word, he never spoke of this a second time.

"During basic training, at Fort Sill, his drill sergeant pulled aside seven recruits from his regiment that could speak German. Of course, Dennis and I had picked up the language at home since that's about all Father spoke. Anyway, the men were given an exam. I guess it would have been like an SAT type of test, but the directions were all in German, and it focused on mathematics. Dennis performed well enough that when he finished his basic combat training, they pulled him and two others out. Instead of heading to combat in the European theater, they sent Dennis to Camp Tonkawa, just a couple of hundred miles north of Fort Sill, to work in the records office of the POW camp.

Ned interrupted, "Wait! Camp Tonkawa? For German POWs?"

"Yes, that's it."

"Are you sure?"

"Yes, Ned, I'm sure. What are you driving at?"

Ned was too startled to respond to his aunt's question. "It's just... never mind. I'm sorry. Go on."

"If you're sure." Lucy studied her nephew for another moment before she continued. "Dennis served there for two years. This was the desk job he told you about; so your dad wasn't lying when he told you that. He genuinely enjoyed his work at Camp Tonkawa. A good number of the German POWs at Camp Tonkawa had been captured by General Montgomery's British Eighth Army in Africa after defeating Rommel's Afrika Korps. Most of them were actually relieved to be in a US prison, since the alternative would have been a Russian POW camp, which could be as deadly as a Nazi concentration camp. Your father was responsible for tracking new inmates, assigning them to barracks, and keeping tabs on all the prisoners' movements. The camp remained pretty calm and organized, except for one uprising when fellow POWs murdered a German informant. Apparently, one POW was feeding information to the Americans about subterfuge among the prisoners. The German officers caught wind of it and had the soldier killed. The POWs were offered English classes and cooking classes, and they granted permission to some prisoners to work outside the camp. The POWs even had an orchestra and performed musicals."

Ned nodded, remembering his conversation with Gretchen about William's experience at Tonkawa.

"After his two years there, Dennis had the option to be discharged, but he felt he hadn't truly served his country. He wanted to go to war and fight the enemy, so the Army sent Dennis to Fort Bragg, North Carolina, for infantry training. This is where your father met your Uncle Dean, Isabelle's brother." Lucy let this sink in.

"Dean. That was my mom's brother?"

"Yes. I suspect you didn't know about him?"

"Well, yes, and no. My mom had said his name a few random times. But I didn't know who she was talking about. Dad said he didn't know either."

"Well … I'll go on. The Army liked to team up soldiers in pairs, so they assigned Dean and your father to be buddies together. It was good for morale and it was necessary for strategic purposes when deployed in combat. Dean became a valued friend to your dad. He was gregarious and boisterous, sort of the yin to your dad's quieter yang. The two of them were always together, even when on leave. They were a team on and off the court, each watching out for the other. Your dad told Dean every detail about his life and about me. In turn, Dean bragged about his sister, your mother, Isabelle, and what a catch she would be for some lucky fellow. Dean asked your father to promise that if he didn't come back from the war, Dennis would look out for her. Around his neck, alongside his dog tags, Dean wore a chain with a quartz stone that Isabelle had given him for luck."

Ned reached beneath his shirt and revealed the necklace that held the stone he and Rose had discovered in his father's dresser. "This one?" Ned asked.

"Oh, my goodness! Where did you find that?" Lucy exclaimed.

"Rose and I found it while sorting through my dad's bedroom dresser. We saw the stone on a necklace my mother was wearing in a photograph, too."

Lucy eyed the chain Ned held in his hand. "That's so wonderful that you have that. And now you know the story behind it. Oh, that reminds me." Lucy walked over to a highboy dresser and pulled something from the top drawer. "I meant to show this to you last time." She was smiling.

Ned examined the threadbare cloth, recognizing right away he was holding Denny Boy. The doll had to be nearly fifty years old. It was evident to him that the red thread lips had been repaired and the button eyes had undoubtedly been replaced over the years. "My dad made this for you when he was ten years old."

"He did. Denny Boy is my most cherished possession. I should keep him locked up, but I can't. There isn't a month goes by that I don't take him out and reminisce. I know every time I do, I'll cry, but I don't care." Ned handed the doll back to Lucy and she placed it on her lap.

"This next part is sketchy, because your dad just breezed over it. The evening was getting late when he told me all of this. I think he was deliberating over the rest of the story and didn't want to linger much on unimportant details leading up to what followed.

"The Army shipped Dennis and Dean over to Europe on an enormous transport alongside thousands of soldiers. It was to be the last major deployment of recruits from the United States. This was in the early spring of 1945. Just days after the ship docked, the officers informed the men of their assignments and transported them to the battlefields. They were replacements, you see, for the soldiers who were going home, who had completed their tours.

"One late afternoon, the commanding officer assigned your father's platoon the task of holding a town near the German border. Dennis didn't tell me just where. The platoon spread out in teams throughout the bombed-out village, in case the Germans tried to re-take the town. Because Dennis was skilled with a rifle, they stationed him and Dean in an abandoned bakery at the edge of the main street. Their job was to serve as sentries, protecting the rest of the town, and ambushing the Germans who might try to enter. Dean used binoculars to keep watch and communicated with their lieutenant using hand signals, following orders to remain silent. Out of nowhere, artillery shells bombarded the village from some point east, and the sound of approaching Panzer tanks echoed in the distance. Dennis secured his rifle on the ledge of the window that faced east and watched as the onslaught of Germans approached the town.

"The lieutenant gave the order to fire at will and so the platoon began its counter-attack on the Germans, firing away with hundreds of rounds. All the while, Dean was spotting targets and shouting out positions to Dennis, alerting him to look out for this one and that one. Your father was a very accurate rifleman, Ned. Dennis was zoned in with his eye glued to the rifle's sight and never turned his head until the last moment. He heard a thunk and automatically knew that someone had tossed a grenade into the bakery. It lay just a couple of feet behind him. Dean shouted to him, 'Look out!', but there was no time for Dennis to react before Dean jumped toward your dad, grabbed the grenade, and leaped to the back of the room, cradling the grenade to his chest. The explosion occurred just as Dennis screamed, 'Dean! No!' But it was hopeless. Dennis was frantic, covered in debris, blood, and pieces of his best friend. He ran to him and turned him over, couldn't stop himself, even though he knew there was nothing he could do. It seemed like minutes, but in fact was just seconds later when he came to his senses. He dove back to the window and peering out, saw a German soldier running for cover across the street. When the soldier turned his head to look back at the bakery window, Dennis knew he'd identified the grenade launcher. He took aim and fired two shots to his head. The soldier collapsed instantly, dead."

◈

"Dean saved my dad's life, then. He sacrificed himself."

Lucy affirmed, "Yes, he did."

"And the Purple Heart?"

"That came later," Lucy explained. "Dennis actually felt embarrassed by it. Dean's death crushed your father. Oh, Neddy, I'll never forget how difficult it was that night for Dennis to tell me this. His voice got so quiet, I could barely hear him, and he wouldn't look at me, just spoke into his lap in starts and stops. It was as though he was reliving things in his head. It's no wonder he wouldn't speak of it again. His lieutenant put him on leave for a psychiatric evaluation several days later because your dad wasn't himself. He remained in a stupor, a daze, and spent a week in the hospital because there were some minor cuts that needed stitches. The Army chaplain talked to him quite a bit, and eventually they sent Dennis back to his unit, where he completed his tour, but not before he was grazed in the shoulder. The wound was minor, but your father told me it was a wonder he didn't get himself killed since he'd stopped caring about whether he lived or died.

"Lying awake at night, he'd wish it had been him and not Dean, who had been killed. Your dad felt an overwhelming amount of guilt, you see. He kept Isabelle's quartz pendant around his neck after that. Holding it between his fingers as he lay there, rubbing it back and forth, he renewed his promise to Dean that he would watch over Isabelle. Dennis felt by taking care of her, maybe Dean would forgive him. I don't know about that, but I know your father found it hard to forgive himself."

"But it was a war. Surely he understood men die, that it wasn't his fault. He didn't do anything wrong."

"You would think, wouldn't you? Of course your father did nothing wrong. But in his head, I think, he convinced himself that he must have, since it had been his responsibility to look out for his buddy."

Ned considered the story he had just heard, grappling with how to interpret it. He ventured to imagine what actions he might have taken had he been a soldier facing similar circumstances. The idea of facing life and death during combat was difficult to conceptualize. How would he have dealt with the constant fear of being killed? Could he have been as brave as Dean had been? Or was it bravery? Perhaps selfless love compelled Dean to do what he did.

"When did Dad meet Mom?"

"They met within days of your father returning stateside after his discharge. Dennis knew where Isabelle was living and took a taxi to her apartment in Chicago. She knew who your dad was the instant she opened the door," Lucy explained.

"But wasn't my mom resentful of him? I mean, she had lost her brother because of him."

"I know I would have expected her to be. But, it wasn't like that, surprisingly. Isabelle was … you'll have to pardon me, Ned, this may be difficult for you to hear. Isabelle was a fragile young lady. She had always relied upon Dean for emotional support, and now that he was gone, she saw in your father a way to keep the memory of her brother close. I think Isabelle needed Dennis in order to carry on. I know for a fact that your father came to love your mother; he didn't marry Isabelle out of some sort of obligation he felt to Dean's memory. I also believe that each of your parents found relief in having each other. They had both lost someone they loved and their shared grief was a mournful glue that bound them together."

Ned interrupted, "That doesn't sound like much of a foundation to build a marriage."

"Many marriages have been built on far less, Ned. Relationships can be complicated. We don't always know what draws two people together. Still, your folks moved forward. They moved to Tribute, your dad got work with a cabinetmaker, and your mom became a docent at the Lincoln House here in Springfield. They saved their money, and then they had you! Those were such joyful times. They both seemed just tickled to have you. They were going to have lots of kids, a 'whole brood' is how they put it. But things changed. Your poor mother, it all happened so quickly. She just—I don't know how to put it."

"Faded away?" Ned submitted.

Lucy looked into Ned's eyes and put her arms around her nephew, "Oh, Neddy, yes. That's exactly how it was. I'm so sorry." Lucy dabbed her eyes, and now it was Ned who consoled her with his embrace.

Disconcerted, he freshened their coffee, then gazed around the room. Ned still wasn't sure he understood why his father had kept all of this a secret. He didn't want to stress his aunt any further, but he didn't want to leave feeling so shaken. "Lucy, I'm still not sure I understand why Dad hid all of this from me. Surely this war story is not unique. Why couldn't he tell me? I mean, knowing now about his medal, and his experiences, and my uncle, why couldn't he tell his son, his only child? Why didn't he care enough to share his war story with me?"

Lucy instantly answered, "Never think your father didn't care, Neddy. In fact, it may have been the opposite." Lucy swallowed hard and thought for a moment. Finally, she faced her nephew. "I'll tell you what I believe. Beyond that, you'll have to decide for yourself. I believe Dennis suffered from a kind of battle fatigue. I think your dad felt he and your mother could be happy if only he could lay aside the trauma, leave it in the past. And it was more than just the War. Right or wrong, Dennis decided he had to erase his traumatic childhood, too, because once he opened that story to you, the never-ending questions would follow and he would have to tell you everything. I think he wanted to protect you. Dennis envisioned a perfect life for you, Neddy. Again, right or wrong, I think that's why he kept it all a secret from you. Even including not telling you about me. He couldn't bear to think about his past. You see, the life your father had always wanted, Ned, the life of which he could be proud, began when you were born."

Ned continued pressing his aunt. "But he always seemed so alive, so content. How could he be like that when he was holding so much guilt and sadness inside?" Ned's eyes glistened as he sat at the edge of the sofa, grieving that he'd never told his dad how much he meant to him.

Lucy patted him on the knee. "It's all right. Wait here. I have something else I want to show you."

As Ned dried his eyes, he heard Lucy climb the stairs. After just a few minutes, she returned, holding more letters in her hand.

"Here. I want you to take these. I want them back, but I think you'll feel better after you've read them. These are letters your father sent me during your lifetime. They're almost all of them about you. The truth is that you helped Dennis more than anyone else. Read them, you'll see things from the perspective of an adult now. You'll find out that even though your parents worked hard to raise you, and teach you and nurture in you the values and ideals that they believed in, you gave them back so much more in return.

"As the years went on, I kept praying Dennis would come around and share his story with you. I asked him once, when you must have been fourteen or fifteen, if maybe the time had finally arrived. He told me he considered telling you, but in the end couldn't. His nightmare about that day in Germany when Dean died wouldn't stop, and it remained unchanged. Except in the dream, everything unfolded like a fast-paced movie: the Germans arriving, the sound of the tanks, Dean shouting to him, the explosion, Dennis shooting the soldier. All of that would flash by in an instant. Then, what followed would happen in slow motion, when he approached the dead soldier that had tossed the grenade. The soldier was lying face down on the edge of the street, with blood congealing on the back of his head where the bullets had exited his skull. Dennis rolled him over, and what he saw made him vomit. The soldier was a kid, Neddy, just a boy. No more than fifteen, with peach fuzz and soft cheeks. It haunted Dennis."

CHAPTER 22

Ned's lungs were ready to burst, but he'd be damned if he'd let Si's lead get any bigger. As he approached the wall of the swim lane they were sharing, he kept his head down, only surfacing for quick breaths. Despite his all out effort on this last 200 yard race, he knew Si had reached the wall several seconds ago because the wake in front of him was minimal now.

Ned slapped the wall with his lead hand and stood up, gasping for air and staring at his longtime friend who looked back with such an air of nonchalance you'd have thought he'd been meditating and chanting a mantra, not swimming a 200 yard medley. Ned grinned, panting, "I think I was faster on that one. What did it look like to you, Mr. Spitz?" referring to the five-time Olympic medalist.

"You were faster by about two lengths on this one. Well done, chap."

"Well, I'm never going to beat you, that's a given."

Si retorted, "And I'm never going to play the piano."

They had regained their breath by now. Si pulled off his swim cap and said, "Check it out", as he pointed to his scalp with his finger. Ned squinted toward the bright sun coming through the windows, backlighting Simon's head. He pulled on Si's shoulder to bring him closer and saw it—hair. Ned reached forward and rubbed Si's scalp, feeling the first vestiges that were emerging.

"When did this start?"

"I started noticing a hint of stubble about two weeks ago. I called my dermatologist, and she said it's unusual but not unheard of in alopecia ariata. Pretty amazing, huh?"

Ned gave his friend a nuggie and laughed. "What did Eva say?"

"Oh, she thinks I'm totally hot. She says I am her *semental sexy*," Si intoned in his best Spanish accent.

"What's that mean?"

"It means 'sexy stud'."

Ned splashed water on Si's face as his reply.

"Hey," Si went on, "You remember Sue Ford from Mr. Chu's Comparative Lit class?"

"Uh, yeah, short, brown hair, cheerleader?"

"Yeah, that's her. She called me yesterday. We've stayed in touch. She's in charge of the Saturday dance night on August 10, for our ten-year class reunion and wanted to know if I wanted to buy a table. So I told her yes and got a table for eight. I figure the four of us plus Dwight and Rose and Mitch. And there's a place for Anthony, if he comes. You haven't heard from Mitch, have you?

"No, not since he said he hoped to come," Ned replied.

"Well, tell Phoebe about it, so she knows."

"Okay. Oh! Guess what? Rose is pregnant. She told Phoebe yesterday, but don't let on. Nobody's supposed to know yet. She wants to wait 'til the first trimester is over, to be sure."

Si popped his eyes wide. "Ah, *maravilloso*. Dwight's got to be thrilled."

Si checked the wall clock and said, "All right. I gotta go pick up the twins. Pamela and Eva want to get their hair and nails done for tomorrow. You staying?"

"Yeah, I think I'll just do some easy laps for a while. The water feels good today."

They bumped fists and Si boosted himself out of the water. He gave Ned a nod and a thumbs up. Ned pushed off the wall and started the count: Uno.

His breathing was easy and steady now. A sense of lighthearted strength surged through his hands and legs as ribbons of sunlight shimmered on the floor of the pool. Thinking about the upcoming reunion reminded Ned how much had changed over the last ten years.

It had taken six years to get his head straight after his father's death. He recalled the incredible events leading to his discovery of his parents' history. Without that first chance encounter in the parking lot with Rose, in her dead Falcon, he might never have learned about Lucy. Without George finding the newspaper clipping about his dad in the secret attic space, Lucy might never have discovered a part of Albert Hart she never knew.

And now Simon, Dwight and he were building their business: Falcon, Incorporated. Joining forces had been Dwight's idea. He had enlisted Rose to design the business logo, a triangle with the words DESIGN, BUILD, FURNISH on each of the sides, and Cheeky's head in the center. They worked with Phoebe's and Regina's real estate development company that Frank Reid supported financially—Reid Acquisitions and Development. RAD acquired property and contracted with designers and builders, including Falcon, Inc. Phoebe and Regina developed cost-effective housing for the marginalized and disadvantaged. Committed to developing family neighborhoods with green spaces, they scorned the tall, stone, low income fortresses that were rising in cities across the country. Simon, as architect, created the designs. Dwight and Ned met with the city planning board to present site plans and environmental impact statements and negotiate the permits. Ned, as general contractor, oversaw the construction process, and Dwight was foreman of the construction crews. Falcon, Inc. also produced single-family homes. Even now, construction had begun on two of the vacant lots on Ned's own Odiorne Street. Additionally, Ned designed custom interiors and built commissioned furniture. With the financial support of Phoebe's dad, they expanded the business.

It had been a shock to Ned when Joe Mains told him about the trust fund that he inherited when he turned 25. Esther Hart's attorney in Le Claire had set it up for her when Albert died, in 1958, crushed under a combine in a farming accident. As she sold off the extensive farm acreage her husband had amassed over the years, she placed the proceeds into investments for Lucy and Dennis. When Dennis passed, the assets passed to Ned's trust fund. Though not a fortune, it was a considerable sum.

Ned grappled with conflicting emotions in the weeks after Lucy shared the details about his father and mother. Lurking somewhere in those events was a truth that he could never know with any certainty. Ned's aunt insisted he was obliged to form his own conclusions. What Ned knew, for certain, was that he would forever cherish his memory of this remarkable man, his father, who had overcome countless tests of courage in his life, who had touched so many lives and who, even in death, had instilled in Ned the value of honor and the treasure that is family. Never wanting to burden his son, Dennis Godwin had carried the weight of his past inside him until the day he died. Ned would not dishonor this man now, his hero still, by disparaging his decisions that arose from the heart. No, he concluded, the story was as complete as he needed it to be.

❧

Ned regarded the piano before him. Spreading his hands wide, he delicately fingered the E-flat major chord. Holding his hands still and shutting his eyes, he concentrated on the familiar sensation of the pads of his fingertips on the piano keys. He raised, then lowered them again, replicating the initial feeling. Home. Opening his eyes, Ned announced to the empty room, "These are my hands."

There was a tentative knock at the door, muffled by the surround of acoustic tiles that framed the soundproof space. He knew that knock.

"Come in, Izzy," he said in his kindest, fatherly voice. He watched as the doorknob turned and the door burst wide open.

"Daddy! How did you know it was me?" the tiny three-year-old voice chortled.

"It had to be you. You told me this morning you'd come by to wish me luck."

Ned reached forward, lifting the little girl onto his lap. Phoebe stood in the doorway observing the tender moment between father and daughter. As she rested her hands on the bump in front of her, she felt a kick.

"The next one is restless," she said to her husband. "I guess he heard you playing."

Phoebe and Ned exchanged smiles of unspoken devotion.

Ned said, "Izzy! You're wearing a new dress!"

Izzy slid off her father's lap and twirled. Phoebe had tied their daughter's lovely auburn hair back with a pink ribbon to match the pink ribbons in the little girl's white patent leather Mary Janes. Izzy lifted the petticoat up and fluffed it back and forth.

"Do you like it, Daddy? Mommy said I could wear it here, but I would have to change into my play clothes when I get to Pamela's."

"I think the dress looks beautiful on you. Come, give me a good luck kiss."

Izzy grinned and planted her lips on Ned's. "Are you going to play the dagio, Daddy?"

"The A-dagio," Ned corrected. "Yes, sweetheart, I'm going to play the Adagio. After all, it's our favorite part, right?"

"Yes!" the little girl exclaimed. "Are you going to play the hard parts, too?"

"Yes, Izzy. I'm going to play all of it tonight, just like you heard me do at home yesterday."

The little girl beamed. As their eyes locked, she said, "I love you, Daddy."

"I love you, too, munchkin. I'll see you tomorrow morning. You and me and mommy will go out for pancakes at LouAnne's."

Izzy patted Phoebe's tummy and cried out, "and baby Dennis! Don't forget baby Dennis, Daddy!"

"Of course! I musn't forget little Dennis."

Phoebe sidled past Izzy, embracing Ned for a last kiss. She nuzzled his neck and straightened his hair with her fingers. Examining him from head to toe, she nodded, satisfied.

"I'm very proud of you, Benedict Godwin."

Phoebe took her daughter's hand. "Okay, little one, let's go find Pamela and the twins."

⁕

From his vantage point in the shadows to the side of the orchestra, Ned could view the house without being seen. He observed the audience as they wiggled in their seats, coughed and whispered last remarks to their neighbors. Ned turned his head and waited for William Polk to play the A that would begin the brief tuning process, but to his surprise, he saw that William's chair was empty. The second oboist was performing William's duties, tuning the orchestra. Turning his head, Ned noticed William descending the side steps of the stage, then making his way to the front row of the audience to assist Gretchen as she struggled to stand. He escorted his wife to the stairs, and together they ascended the four steps to the stage and approached the podium. After making sure Gretchen was settled, William took his seat in the orchestra, and the audience fell silent, focusing their attention on Gretchen. She faced the side of the stage and waited as Jonathan Rimble, the conductor, approached the podium to renewed applause. He bowed twice, then stepped back, relinquishing the floor to Gretchen.

"Welcome, everyone, to this final special concert of the spring season of the Springfield Auditorium Classical Series. My name is Gretchen Polk. To many of you, I am the wife of William Polk, that man back there who plays the oboe." Gretchen shifted her focus and waved to her husband, who returned the audience's gaze with a reserved smile. "And I am privileged to say that I was Benedict Godwin's piano teacher. In 1955—" Gretchen halted as the audience broke out in applause. A few affirmative hoots echoed from the audience.

Gretchen continued, "Thank you. In 1955, Benedict's father, Dennis, came to me and asked if I would give his son piano lessons. He'd brought the boy with him that day and told me that Neddy had been playing tunes on the piano for over a year. I told Dennis that I would be happy to teach his son how to play. When I asked Benedict if he would like to play something for me, he said yes, he would. He sat down on the piano bench, taking his time to settle himself just so. Then, sitting up straight and tall, his five-year-old legs dangling off the edge, he proceeded to play the Schubert Minuet in A major."

Once again, Gretchen paused and waited for the laughter to subside. "I knew then, of course, that I had an extraordinarily gifted new student.

"Ladies and gentlemen, I asked the maestro if I could say a few words to you tonight, and Mr. Rimble has graciously consented. Today is Father's Day, so happy Father's Day to all the fathers in the audience. Ten years ago tonight, Benedict, days shy of his eighteenth birthday, was scheduled to perform Beethoven's *Piano Concerto No. 5* in E-flat major, Opus 73, *The Emperor Concerto*, right here, in this very auditorium. But tragedy struck, and young Benedict was unable to perform the musical masterpiece to which he had devoted himself for so many months. In fact, it looked as though he might never play the piano again, for the automobile accident that took his father's life also crippled Benedict's left hand. I know Benedict would tell you he is here tonight because of friends and family who encouraged and supported him in his recovery, and he would be right. But we must also credit Benedict with reclaiming his instrument. It is he who journeyed forward. It is he who found his way despite a multitude of obstacles. It is he, Benedict Godwin, who, when all that was dear to him seemed lost, made a new dream, a dream buoyed by love and his parents' newly discovered legacy. This is the man we celebrate tonight after his long anticipated return to the stage. Ladies and gentlemen, Benedict Godwin."

Thunderous applause filled the air as Gretchen turned to welcome Ned to the stage. The two embraced without attempting to exchange words above the uproar. As Gretchen made her exit, the audience stood, applauding with gusto, and with no regard for decorum, whistled and stomped the floor.

Ned peered out at the staggering display of affection. That thousands of people should honor him in such a manner seemed surreal. His eyes traveled up to the mezzanine, so seemingly void of life that night of the dress rehearsal, now teeming with faces awaiting his performance. The sheer enormity of the moment threatened to paralyze Ned as he felt the sound of the audience disappear in his ears even as the standing ovation continued, as though a silent movie pantomime was unfolding before him. And in his mind, the sound of Beethoven supplanted that of the crowd, calming him. The back of his neck prickled as the lilting melody of the second movement returned, as if he was channeling the composer's spirit. In the imaginary silence of the auditorium, the same Adagio that had first compelled Ned to choose *The Emperor Concerto* played in his ears, just as Beethoven must have experienced, even as his hearing was deserting him. This melody that had been the soundtrack of Ned's life for ten years, these notes he had ceaselessly relied upon to escape his distressing reality, he heard anew. What had been his song of refuge now felt like one of salvation, resounding with joy, like a re-birth, much as Beethoven claimed he had finally experienced despite his deafening isolation.

As his senses returned to normal, Ned located Phoebe in the front row, her eyes twinkling with emotion. Next to her were the three empty seats upon which Rose had scripted on framed parchment: *Isabelle, Dean,* and *Dennis.* Ned touched the chain around his neck that held the quartz stone so dear to him as he continued scanning the audience. He was astonished, for it seemed every important person in his life was there. Gretchen, of course, had returned to her seat. Simon, Eva, Mitch, and Anthony were all there. It warmed his heart to see Karina with Rose and Dwight. He saw Mr. Chu and Donna Bowman, the high school English teachers, the Reids and Joe Mains. To Lucy's left was Clark, to her right, Roger Vinely, Lucy's long-lost cousin, the two finally united. Ned's eyes locked on his beloved aunt as she blew him a kiss. The audience was still on its feet, in a fit of elation. Ned spotted Si's parents, Portia and Edward. Even Hag's Josy was clapping her hands. George and Gwen, his dear friends now, waved to Ned, which took him aback.

"I was never actually alone," he murmured to himself.

It came time to take his seat and Ned moved to the piano bench as the crowd quieted and sat down. In a matter of seconds, the cacophony had ended, supplanted by a sweet serenity that seemed impossible in such a cavernous space. Jonathan and the orchestra members remained relaxed and motionless, waiting for their cue as Ned repeated the ritual of laying his hands atop the keys. Taking his time, embracing this noteworthy moment, he closed his eyes and listened to his father's voice before answering him. "I hear you, Dad. This is for you."

He lifted his head and gave a slight nod to Jonathan. The conductor turned to face the orchestra and raised his baton. With a flick of his wrist, the opening E-flat major chord of *The Emperor Concerto* resounded throughout the auditorium, signaling Ned, who couldn't help but grin as his hands flew across the keys.

Coda

The man walked deliberately, eyeing the houses and yards with glancing familiarity, more a distraction than a curiosity on this crisp November morning. He paused for just a moment to enjoy a cascade of falling maple leaves before sidestepping the crack in the heaved sidewalk where a pin oak tree had spread its roots. He forced himself to keep moving forward as he neared the turn into the neighborhood he knew so well.

In July, when he had first approached Odiorne Street and the parallel world of Benedict Godwin, it had not been his intention to add it to his weekly route. It had been a novelty, nothing more. But with each passing week, as he became more comfortable with the neighborhood, he asked himself if perhaps now was the right time, after all. Yet, here he was again on a Sunday afternoon, the good intentions still too scant to free himself enough to follow through on his pledge. The man reminded himself to straighten his back, head up straight, and keep his eyes in front of him, not on the laces of his scuffed oxfords. Still, he couldn't help stealing a quick glance at them, recalling the day he bought them for just this purpose, that he might literally put a best foot forward when the moment arrived.

He had reached the gazebo now, the heart of this charming community of families. A place where mothers and fathers play ball in the yards with their kids, where neighbors chat about birthday parties and recitals, where children catch frogs in the duck pond and bring them home, begging to keep the amphibians in the bathtub.

Keeping to the opposite side of the street, he approached number eight. He slowed his step when Mr. Godwin appeared from behind the house, rake in hand. The man had not expected to see the homeowner outside, and it upset his self-effacing calm. This had never happened on any of his previous excursions. Realizing that he couldn't just stand there, he turned and began walking back the way he had come.

As he trudged off, the pathetic shuffle of his stride returned, and he cursed himself. Was this not the opportunity for which he had hoped? Isn't that why he kept returning to the gazebo, hoping to treat the meeting as happenstance, just a casual encounter on an afternoon walk? His head throbbed. "Don't be foolish!" he chided himself. Convinced that seeing Godwin was a sign, the man shook his head, resolving to turn back. Pivoting, he resumed his journey toward number eight, crossing the street before he reached the pond.

Ned had promised Izzy she could play in the leaves today and began raking the red and yellow and brown menagerie into a pile. As he turned to attack another scattering of leaves, he spotted a man walking toward him from the other side of the street. Ned recognized him as a regular in the neighborhood, one of many walkers who made Odiorne Street part of their route. Now that the empty lots were filling out with homes, the duck pond had become a destination. Ned leaned on the rake handle and waited for the man to come closer. "Beautiful morning for a walk," Ned remarked when the man stopped in front of him. He could see now that he was in his early thirties, about six feet tall and wore heavy framed sunglasses that masked his eyes.

Ned's words momentarily startled the man, causing him to stammer, "Uh, yeah, it is. The sun is so bright today."

"Do you live nearby? I often see you walking here."

Again, the man hesitated before tripping on his answer. "I live about, oh, about a mile from here, on Riverton Avenue, in the Oak Grove Apartments."

Ned knew the place well. Oak Grove Apartments was the first joint project that Falcon and RAD had completed. "Do you like living there?"

"Oh, I like it fine. It's a lot nicer than the place I used to live. That place was kind of a dump, but, well …" Averting his eyes, the man let the rest of his thoughts trail off.

Ned extended his right hand and introduced himself. "My name is Ned, Ned Godwin. Pleased to meet you." The man tentatively shook Ned's hand, then removed his hat and clutched it at his waist with both hands. When he failed to answer back, Ned asked, "And yours?"

At this, the man removed his sunglasses. To Ned, the man's dark brown eyes almost looked panicky, his breathing strained. In a subdued manner, he replied, "My name is Sonny, Mr. Godwin. Sonny Gordon."

There was dead silence, and the breeze that had been sending leaves adrift abruptly stopped. It took Ned only a second to process the name. Instinctively, he drew back with his left foot, stumbling on the tines of the rake as he distanced himself from the man who had crashed his truck into him ten years before. Ned set his jaw, scowling as he raised his voice and blurted out, "What do you want? My God, have you been stalking me?"

Sonny retreated a step with an apologetic bow of his head. "No, Mr. Godwin, sir, that's not what I've been doing. I'm very sorry to interrupt your morning. No, I haven't been stalking you. I've been trying to work up the courage to talk to you."

Ned continued eyeing the man with suspicion. "Courage? What are you talking about?" he responded harshly.

Sonny retreated, back-stepping to the sidewalk. "I apologize, Mr. Godwin. This was a mistake. It was presumptuous of me to expect…" He turned and began walking away. "Please excuse me."

"Wait!" Ned blurted out. Then, more calmly, "Come back."

Sonny looked over his shoulder at Ned, deciding what to do.

He took just a moment before stepping back and facing Ned once again, this time with his shoulders slouched and eyes to the ground. Ned was curious to know what the guy wanted, yet he couldn't help himself. Years of resentment boiling inside came bounding out of his mouth. "I hope you've enjoyed your life the past ten years, walking around scot-free after leaving a dead man and a crippled son behind, the way you did." It was a cheap shot, and Ned instantly regretted the remark. Nevertheless, he felt justification and a measure of relief.

"I suppose I deserve that," Sonny replied.

Ned tried to settle his nerves as he debated what to say. Relenting, he conceded, "Never mind. In the end, I suppose it was an accident, the setting sun blinding you and all."

Sonny seemed to find his voice. Lifting his head, he announced, "That's what the police report said."

Ned frowned. "End of story, then. No repercussions for you."

Sonny seemed to ponder what Ned had said, and after a few seconds, he replied, "Mr. Godwin, it wasn't the sun."

"What do you mean, it wasn't the sun?"

"I mean the sun didn't blind me. That's not the reason I hit your car."

"But, the police report—"

Sonny swallowed and cleared his throat. "The truth, Mr. Godwin, is that I fell asleep."

"You fell—you fell asleep? At the wheel?"

"Yes."

Ned couldn't process what he was hearing. What did this mean? He fell asleep? So, the accident didn't have to happen? If this man had—. Ned's face sagged, his skin ashen. "Oh, God."

"I'm so sorry. I've wanted to confess to you for such a long time, but I couldn't persuade myself that it was something you'd want to hear. Or by confessing to you, would I just be trying to ease my conscience? Did I have any right to invade your life after all the pain I caused?"

"Why now?" Ned asked.

"I saw you. I mean, I was there, at your concert on Father's Day. You see, I needed to hear you play. After the accident, the newspapers reported your piano career was over and you'd gone off to college somewhere. The situation became unbearable for me, and, as a result, my life unraveled, but that's another story. When I heard you play, it sort of inspired me, your concerto was so moving. But it was more than that. The way you play, my God… sorry, I don't have the words. I know this sounds peculiar, but it felt like you were telling your story through the music. And I thought to myself, knowing you'd been able to come back after those injuries and losing your mom and dad and all, well, I thought maybe I could, you know, sort of come back, too. It wasn't fair that only I knew what really happened. You deserved to know, too."

Ned dropped the rake and stepped over to the porch. "Come over here and sit down." When Sonny had settled on the steps, Ned said, "Tell me the other story. I want to know."

"Oh, Mr. Godwin. I don't know about that. It's not your burden, you know? I didn't come here for that. I don't think it will help you."

"Why don't you let me decide that?"

The breeze had returned as Sonny picked up a leaf and absentmindedly began shredding it into strips, watching the pieces fly away. It took him a minute to decide. Finally, keeping his eyes focused on his shoes, he told Ned his tale.

"Me and Susie had been married for six years in 1968. We have two little girls, Robin and Marcy. Susie had come down with a stomach bug the day before the crash and she was all messed up, so she stayed in bed all day. I was off work. I drove long haul back then, so I was four days on and four days off.

"Anyway, it was my last day off. After supper, Robin came down with the bug, too. She was just five, and I hardly knew what to do for her. Kept giving her water, some children's aspirin. I tell you, it was coming out both ends, poor thing. Between changing her pajamas and sheets, I covered her forehead with a cold washcloth and sat by her bed reading her stories, trying to keep her mind off being so sick. Well, by morning Susie was feeling well enough to tend to Robin. I hadn't slept at all, but we needed the money and I figured I would drink coffee and keep the truck window down, listen to some rock and roll. Unfortunately, that didn't work." Sonny stopped himself and looked up at Ned. "Are you sure you want to hear this?"

"Go on."

"What you said earlier, about me getting off scot-free and walking away and all? That's partly true, for sure. I didn't get hurt like you and your dad, but it's not the whole truth. I couldn't come to terms with what I had done to you and your dad. Every day for weeks, the paper seemed to follow each step of your recovery and report about the accident. I started having the recurring nightmare, then. I couldn't drive anymore because I'd get panic attacks just climbing in behind the wheel. Each night I'd wake up in a cold sweat, reliving that awful moment over and over. I was consumed with guilt, desperate, you might say. I couldn't think of anything else.

"I started drinking a lot after I quit my job, wallowed in self pity. Poor Susie, I was so unkind to her. After a couple of months, she kicked me out, told me the girls weren't safe around a drunk and that I needed to get some help if she was ever going to let me come back. Course, it was a whole lot easier for me to stay drunk than to face the world. And every time I'd think about what I did to your family, well, I'd just drink some more.

"I was homeless for the next six years, Mr. Godwin. Hitchhiked to Florida in search of warmer weather and ended up living on the streets in Jacksonville for a number of years, resorted to begging for money and food, and drinking, always drinking like some sort of low-life criminal. I suppose that's what I was. I finally met a counselor at the homeless shelter they opened. Tommy Grey was his name, and he helped me a whole lot. Got me off the drink and found me a job at Burger King. Every night, I had a clean cot to sleep on.

"So, I came back to Tribute this past April even though Susie divorced me a long time ago and moved away to Colorado with her new husband. I have a good job now over at Kroger in the meat department. I hope one day I'll get to see my girls again."

As Sonny narrated the story of his fractured life, Ned revisited that fateful day and place. Might he have missed something all these years? Had he refused for himself the same thing for which his father had felt unworthy? As he had done a thousand times before, he replayed the word 'forgive' that his father had muttered before trailing off, moments before the crash. And with a clarity that had eluded him until now, Ned grasped the sweeping message. He went there now, to their car in the intersection on that afternoon, the sun illuminating his father's face as he turns to Ned, their eyes meeting for an instant before Dennis envelopes his son in his arms, and Ned once again feels the strength in his embrace, breathes the scent of his shirt and hears his father's voice as he whispers, "Oh, Neddy."

The storm door creaked as Phoebe came out of the house and looked down at the two men on the steps. "Oh, there you are. Who's your friend?"

The men stood up, and Ned smiled at his wife.

"Babe, I'd like you to meet Sonny."

THE END

Thomas Shields is a retired dentist and lives in Ithaca, New York, with his wife of fifty years. He is the father of two remarkable daughters and five delightful grandchildren. *A Noteworthy Man* is his first novel.